A Date in Your Diary

Jules Stanbridge

First published in 2009 by
LITTLE BLACK DRESS
An imprint of HEADLINE PUBLISHING GROUP

A LITTLE BLACK DRESS paperback

1

Cataloguing in Publication Data is available from the British Library

ISBN 978 0 7553 4713 1

Typeset in Transit511BT by Avon DataSet Ltd,
Bidford-on-Avon, Warwickshire

Printed and bound in Great Britain by
Clays Ltd, St Ives plc

HEADLINE PUBLISHING GROUP
An Hachette UK Company
338 Euston Road
London NW1 3BH

www.littleblackdressbooks.com
www.headline.co.uk
www.hachette.co.uk

For my mum, my dad, my brother and my sister.
This is also for Blair – the date in my diary x

Acknowledgements

I have been blessed with the amazing team from Little Black Dress, who have held my hand through the dark and scary alleyways of grammar and timelines. Without Claire Baldwin, Sara Porter, the copy-editors, proof-readers . . . the list goes on, this book wouldn't have made any sense at all. Their patience is incredible and I for one would have given myself a big boot up the backside and told me to try harder. So thank you to them and the team at Gregory and Co. for their continued support.

'We should get married,' Jason said, and kissed me on the tip of my nose. Normally I would hate this. Not the getting married part, because I quite liked that particular idea, but the kissing on the nose thing. Tonight was different, though. Tonight I offered my nose freely. Tonight the stars were shining brightly just for me. Tonight I finally got it; I got the whole 'finding the one' thing.

'Tomorrow! Let's get married tomorrow,' he suggested. 'No, even better, let's wait a week and fly out to Las Vegas. We could have Elvis take the ceremony . . .'

'I love it.' I laughed at the deliciously ludicrous nature of our conversation.

'That's sorted, then.'

The image in my head was almost perfect. Almost. Then the panic set in. 'But what should I wear?'

Jason laughed and squeezed my hand. 'We'll buy you something.'

'Vintage Chanel?'

'Whatever you want.'

'Hurray!'

Hurray indeed. It was our second date. Well, technically it was our first, because the one before wasn't really a date; it was more of an accidental realisation.

Forty-eight hours earlier we were wandering around

Hyde Park, dodging the rollerbladers and eating ice cream. That's when we discovered a mutual love of all things Italian, Angelina Jolie as Lara Croft (but for different reasons), picnic blankets, vodka, Washington Red Apples, salted popcorn instead of sweet and outside swimming pools. He said I was different, that I reminded him of a foal; all legs and cheekbones. He said it like it was a good thing. He made me feel beautiful and funny and lucky.

Those lost hours in between were a blur of romantic daydreams. Some of them were dirty, but the majority of them were romantic. When I wasn't daydreaming I was phoning everyone I knew, worrying about what to wear and counting the hours until I saw him again.

Tonight we laughed that I didn't particularly like him when we first met, and at what our mutual friends would say when they found out. Tonight we kissed for the first time and it was perfect. There was no overenthusiastic tongue action, excess saliva or one of us keeping our eyes open. Tonight the air was balmy and seductive. Tonight I was feeling dizzy with lust.

We stopped walking and he turned me towards him. I held my breath as he took my face in his hands and kissed me softly on the lips. He lingered there for a second and I closed my eyes. His lips felt soft and dry, his hands were warm. He smelled of lime, tuberose and sandalwood. When he released me, I opened my eyes and looked into his. They were liquid brown and framed by the longest eyelashes I had ever seen on a man. He smiled at me like someone who knew something. I wanted to ask what. WHAT?

'Do you fancy an Indian?' he asked.

'I'd love an Indian,' I replied, and floated on my own little pocket of air towards the Bengal Palace.

Two years later . . .

Chloe removes her hair clip and pops the end into her mouth. Long hair, the colour of buttermilk, falls gently down over her shoulders and back. She is advert-pretty.

'What do you think of each guest holding a balloon? It would look great in the photos.'

'They could have messages attached to them,' I suggest. 'Romantic messages.'

'And at the end of the photos everyone could let them go.' Chloe claps her hands excitedly.

'Can't do it. Air pollution,' Josie adds dryly.

Our shoulders slump with disappointment. Chloe opens this month's edition of *Wedding* magazine and the three of us peer into its romantic, tastefully arranged pages. A handsome couple reveal perfect white teeth as guests throw biodegradable rose petals at them.

'They asked their guests to plant a tree instead of giving gifts,' Chloe informs us.

'No presents?' Josie says, unimpressed.

'No presents,' Chloe confirms.

We all shake our heads no and agree their wedding must have been rubbish. I hide the bride and groom with a plate of biscuits strategically placed over the magazine. These happy do-gooders have no place in our Harvey Nichols wedding-list world.

This is what we talk about now. Wedding lists, dresses, menus, and whether anyone can really tell if it's cava and not champagne. Six months ago we talked about other things, but for the life of me I can't remember what they were. We take a moment to contemplate the big day and eat another biscuit. I check the calorie content and then wish I hadn't. How many minutes is that on the Stairmaster? Ten? Twenty? Who cares? I do.

'Jason has confirmed.'

I hold my breath and mask my internal trauma with a smile. I realise this makes me look slightly manic but the alternative is crying out loud in a strangled, slightly disturbed way.

'And he's bringing Sophie.'

I am still holding. In fact, I am not sure if I can stop holding. I may need those paddles they use on *ER*.

'Are you okay with that?' Chloe asks. There is a moment, probably no more than a nanosecond, when I consider telling the truth. It's my default. Josie looks to the ceiling.

'Of course I am.'

'I knew you would be. You're brilliant, Harry.'

I nod, but all I can think of is Jason and Sophie in the hotel room. My hotel room. The one I booked when Chloe and Tad announced they were going to get married.

It was going to be perfect. Mr & Mrs Smith recommended the hotel in their *Hip Hotels* guide, the cost was reassuringly expensive (Jason was of the opinion it was a bloody rip-off and suggested a Travelodge), and they had coloured mood lights under the bathroom sink. The breakfast and pillow menus were amazing and I had already decided on the haddock with poached egg, and a Russian goose with a four-hundred-thread count. I was going to be half a stone lighter and, after what I hoped would be a naughty afternoon sex session under the sink, he was going to tell me that I was right to book the room. I was also pretty sure he was going to look at me (probably at the reception, during a ballad – Ray wotshisname, or Leona Lewis) and confirm those sentiments uttered on our second date, but without Las Vegas, Elvis and probably the Chanel. He was going to tell me he wanted to spend the rest of his life with me, that it was time we made the final commitment.

And it was time. After nearly two years together we were happy and in love. We had moved fast; but it seemed right. When Josie moved out, Jason moved in. It was only a matter of time before we announced our engagement. Everyone said so. Then Tad proposed and so did Ben, and I waited. Then Jason went to Manchester. Be good, I said. He kissed me and laughed. We both laughed because it was ridiculous to think he wouldn't be. Well, that's what I thought.

'Are you sure you're okay about Jason coming?' Chloe asks. She looks worried.

'Of course,' I lie. My head is full of Sophie kissing Jason, Sophie raiding the minibar, Sophie lying naked on crisp, white cotton; Jason producing a diamond ring.

'It's just that he is Tad's friend and I don't feel as if I can say no. They've known each other for years.'

'Chloe, I understand, and it will be fine,' I reply, and hug her close. She feels tiny in my arms, as if she might break. I wonder what it must be like to be petite and doll-like. Would I have had more boyfriends if I wasn't built like a giraffe? When I asked Josie this, she said yes. I told her to feel free to lie to me at any point in our friendship but she refuses to. She says tall is good – that I just need to stop fancying men smaller than me.

'Thanks,' Chloe mumbles into my jumper. 'I want it to be perfect.'

'It will be,' I reassure her, because even with a Sophie-sized blip in the love landscape, their wedding will be amazing and beautiful.

Chloe and Tad are the perfect couple: pretty, successful, impossibly trendy and in love. She is pixie-like with a tiny waist and her own business making handbags from vintage fabrics. Tad is tall, dark and skinny. He wears his jeans low with studded belts and directs independent films destined for greatness. They live in a flat full of art installation pieces and talk of drunken nights with BAFTA award winners in the same way I talk of going round my sister's for a cup of tea. I have known Chloe since school. Two became three when I met Josie.

We were both working for Bath's favourite monthly regional magazine, *Life to Live*, and she took me under her wing. With her wide smile, untidy mind, and can-do attitude, Josie has always been the bossy one. She is our alpha female; the one who says we should and we could. A curvy and voluptuous size sixteen, with a short glossy dark bob and a sexy confidence that takes no notice of her body's refusal to be a size ten, she is striking in looks and personality. Josie is the dark and strong to Chloe's light and delicate. Chloe is one of the happy people: sunny, light, and always smiling. Sometimes her eyes will reveal a slightly manic edge to her smile and we have to tell her to turn it down a bit but, on the whole, she is one of the most easygoing people I know. She will agree to anything Josie suggests, even if it smacks of insanity, whereas I am a little different; more cautious, maybe. I don't say yes straight away. I have to dither for at least twelve hours and then consult my horoscope. This is probably why I am still working at *Life to Live* instead of climbing up the media ladder of success with Josie.

When she left to work in London, I felt a certain amount of pressure to follow. I applied for similar jobs because I thought I should, but then couldn't ignore the sense of relief when I didn't get the interview. I like living and working in Bath, where it takes me half an hour to get to my parents' house, where I know I can walk around at night without feeling nervous, where the honey-coloured stone and sense of history inspire me every day, where I can sit by the canal with the best ice cream known to man, and where I don't have to take the tube to go shopping. So while Josie gets to schmooze with the likes of Justin Timberlake (well, his PR), I interview St Saviour's Church about their tea and buns afternoon with all the enthusiasm of a TV weather girl. I am a modern-day Jane Austen: keeping it real, writing about the people who live in my favourite city.

Well, I was. At the moment, I am finding it hard to write about anything. The space left by Jason has coloured my whole world a rather dull shade of grey. My previous enthusiasm has disappeared and in its place is a reluctance to do anything. I rarely go out; I have phoned in sick for the first time in five years and I can't remember the last time I went for a pre-work swim. Stories that once might have captured my imagination now seem lacklustre and not worth the effort. I wake up in the morning and the girl who looks back at me in the mirror bears little resemblance to the one Jason professed to love, even when she had an allergic reaction to rubber and had to go to Accident and Emergency with lips that looked like Cumberland sausages. Everyone tells me this feeling will pass. I wish it would, sooner rather than later. It's been three months since Jason left, but sometimes it feels like yesterday.

Chloe leaves for late-night sushi with Tad and an Arctic Monkey, Josie makes cinnamon toast and hot chocolate, and I get emotional about a song on the radio. Someone is singing about leaving a cake out in the rain, which is a bloody ridiculous sentiment, but it's breaking my heart.

'Are you crying?' Josie asks. She has a stocking on her head. Someone told her it was great for keeping short bobs glossy and perfect. Personally, I think they were having her on. She looks like a bank robber. I shake my head.

'Oh, Harry, you are, you're crying.'

She turns the radio off, puts her arm round me, and leads me away from the fridge. That's where the wedding invitation is; stuck to the door.

Designed by an award-winning artist, known by the bride-to-be since university, it taunts me with its heavyweight quality and the gorgeous colours selected to reflect the bride's and groom's personalities. In ornate gold lettering it invites Harriet Peel and Jason Mortimer to the wedding of Chloe Miller and Tad Declan.

'I can't go to the wedding on my own. Not now Jason and Sophie are going,' I say with absolute conviction.

Weddings are a celebration of love and finding the One. Going to one on your own is like turning up to a barbecue without food and drink when everyone else has brought both. I have been to two weddings on my own. The first was to cousin Tracey's and the second was to my friend Vicky's. On both occasions I was the one who made the wedding photos look uneven and was assigned to the odds and sods table making polite conversation with the relatives whom nobody knew what to do with. I seem to remember getting horribly drunk at both.

'You'll have met someone else by then,' Josie reassures me. 'Look at Chloe five years ago. Who would have thought she would end up getting married to Tad?'

'I don't want anyone else.'

'Of course you do.'

I ignore Josie's comment and consult the calendar. 'I have eleven months – eleven months to find a man who will make Jason jealous enough to realise what a dreadful mistake he's made.'

'Harry, you don't want Jason. You're better off without

him.' Josie shakes her head at me as if I'm a naughty child.

'And that's where you're wrong. I'm not better off without him. I'm rubbish without him – the dirty, rotten, two-timing bastard.'

Josie sighs.

'Okay, what about work? Is there anyone at *Life to Live* you can take?' Josie asks.

'Only Ed, but Jason knows him.'

'But he might be a good emergency option. I'll put him on the list,' Josie says, getting a notepad from the kitchen.

I sigh heavily. 'Eleven months . . .'

Josie rubs my arm reassuringly. 'Don't worry. Anything could happen in eleven months.' She sounds confident and I believe her like a child waiting for Christmas.

'Anything?'

'Anything. Within reason.'

'What's outside reason?' I ask, feeling a little indignant at the limits imposed on what I might achieve in eleven months.

'Let's just stick with getting you a date for the wedding, shall we? What about Frankie? He'd go with you.'

'Frankie with the weird laugh? I thought he had a girlfriend?'

'He does, but I'm sure she wouldn't mind.'

I shake my head. In my fantasy world, I would be with someone sexy, successful and gorgeous; someone who would look good in a suit and possess excellent conversational skills and a killer sense of humour. After dancing all night I would lean in to him in stockinged feet (he would be holding my heels for me and planting gentle kisses on my lips with the promise of something more) and I would barely notice Jason snapping at Sophie in a jealous rage.

'Jon Jo?'

'No, I want someone believable, someone Jason doesn't know.'

'Okay, let me think . . .' Josie crosses out Jon Jo's name from the list of two.

As she flicks through her phone list, I do the same with a magazine.

'My horoscope says I will meet someone musical and mysterious this week, but to watch their ascent into Pluto,' I read out. This is hopeful.

Josie scoffs. She doesn't believe in horoscopes.

'I know, I've got it!' Josie throws her pen down. 'Why didn't we think about this before? What about Internet dating?'

'No.' I am adamant.

'Why not?'

'Because.'

Go on, do the bungee jump, buy those heels that will make you taller than ninety per cent of men, eat that dessert, go for that job. Yep, there's always someone who is keen for you to fulfil your potential as a human being, someone who is quite happy to throw caution to the wind. Josie is that person; the one who pushes me from behind and tells me it is a fabulous idea. I should know better, but sometimes, usually against my better judgement, I allow myself to be persuaded. Today is not going to be one of those occasions. There is no way I am going to do Internet dating.

'No!' I shake my head emphatically.

Josie shakes hers in despair and switches the TV on. We open a box of liqueur chocolates left over from Christmas and go through our favourites. Josie throws her head back and sucks the filling from the ends.

Despite having officially moved out over a year ago, she continues to divide her time between my flat in Bath and her boyfriend Ben's in London. This makes her feel secure, because ever since the big romantic proposal on a flight to New York, she is suddenly asking herself if Ben is the One. He doesn't know this, and her excuse for the odd night back and forth is that she feels sorry for me. The fact that he readily accepts this is slightly disappointing.

'I think you're being a little hasty. Lots of people do Internet dating nowadays. Carrie at work said some of her friends go out with a different man each week.'

'No!' I snap back.

'Think about it.'

'No.'

'Tia Maria or Jack Daniel's?' Josie asks.

'Tia Maria.'

She throws me a chocolate foil miniature. I unwrap it and knock back the contents.

'Can you get drunk on chocolate liqueurs?' I ask.

'I don't know, but we can find out.'

Josie flicks through the TV channels. Normally it would get on my nerves, but tonight I feel satiated with chocolate and alcohol and too lazy to protest. Foil wrappers litter the floor. The only light in the room is from the TV.

'I hate weddings,' I announce to the living room.

'Me too.'

'I feel sick.'

'Me too.'

Josie switches the TV off.

'What would I say about myself?' I ask.

'On what?'

'Internet dating.'

*

Girl Without a Date in Her Diary – Blog entry – January 15th

Apparently Brad has proposed. Will Angelina say yes? What dress will she wear? I'm thinking slinky, but tasteful. I aspire to be the Jolie. It's the whole luscious lips, kick-ass thing. That girl is superior and she knows it. The thing is – it's all on the inside. On the outside she gives that enigmatic smile and leaves us all wondering about the whats, hows, whys and whens. I practise this smile in the mirror but I look as if I have constipation.

What a wedding that would be. The air would be heavy with the scent of lemons and nougat. The sun would shine (Brangelina don't do rain) and there would be laughter and dancing on cobbled streets with jugglers and a violinist . . . or something like that.

My friend Chloe is talking about having a three-foot meringue stack as a wedding cake and arriving on the back of a Hell's Angel motorbike. Tad wanted to buy the Batmobile on eBay but somebody got to it first.

Good things about weddings

- It's the best justification to buy an expensive outfit.
- You have the perfect excuse to buy new shoes and a handbag.
- There's always a free meal.
- You can justify a night in a hotel room you can't really afford.
- You get to cry.
- There are men in top hats. This is good for those film-moment fantasies you drift into whilst the photos are being taken. My particular favourite is

the one when man in top hat (the devastatingly handsome one, not the lecherous uncle) removes slice of wedding cake from my hand, cups my face in his strong hands, kisses the sugar from my lips, then lifts me off my feet (because he is very tall and strong, and I am as light as a feather), pops top hat on my head and carries me off to a four-poster bed where unspeakable but rather lovely things will happen. Normally I wouldn't sleep with someone on a first date, but in this particular instance I would make an exception because, technically, it wouldn't be a first date. Where was I? Other good things about weddings . . .

- There is cake and dancing.
- And champagne.

Bad things about weddings

- It's another lie on your credit card.
- You end up with another pair of shoes that don't go with anything.
- The meal is always somebody else's choice.
- You feel the pressure to stay in an overpriced room when you just want to go home and cry about being single.
- Crying is good. Unless you can't stop.
- In my experience, the men in top hats rarely look like Jude Law. They are also usually brothers and cousins and I have this thing about it not being a good idea getting into relationships with the relatives of close friends. It usually ends in tears. Nobody wants to hear that their brother is no good on the foreplay front. Josie lost a very good friend this way.
- There is nothing bad about cake or dancing.

- Or champagne.
- And thinking about it, another pair of shoes that don't go with anything is hardly a bad thing. When you are old and sitting in a plastic-covered chair, they will serve as a reminder of a time when you were young and carefree; when four inches meant you were closer to the stars. In my case it would be more Saturn or Jupiter, which are a little darker and lonelier.

Eleven months . . . God, I hate weddings.

My horoscope:

Neptune is moving forwards and that means an unexpected surge in your love life, especially from the eighteenth to the twenty-eighth. Opportunities could be in the most unexpected of places. Don't discount your local bank, tax office, or local supermarket. Your career also goes from strength to strength this month. Hold on tight for success and romance. You shall be belle of the ball!

I love weddings. Love 'em!

It has been raining for three days and my umbrella is now a hazard to health and safety. One of the spokes has broken and is now exposed, ready to poke eyes out or pick at ear wax. I give up, throw it in the bin and come to terms with the fact that I am wet and will be soaked by the time I get home. I have been on a preview of the Laugh, I Should Georgian Hope So Tour. Laugh? I Georgian didn't. Following a man with a joke bow tie and a balloon around Bath in the rain is not something I would normally sign up for, but as the editor for the What's On page for *Life to Live*, I had no choice. After an hour of not laughing I dropped out behind the abbey. The trouble with being tall is that it isn't easy slipping away. The key is to crouch down in stages until I'm the same height as everyone else; then I make my exit. This is quite hard on the knees and I open myself up to questioning looks from passers-by.

Pools of light from street lamps shimmer like tiny moons on the wet, slippery pavement. People rush by, heads down, jostling umbrellas. I step into an invisible puddle and it soaks my shoe. I feel miserable, grey and wet. My mobile rings and my heart misses a beat, because it always does. *Hello, Jason . . . no, I'm not going to take you back . . . you do? Oh okay, then.*

'Well?'

'Well what?' I ask.

'Have you done it?' Josie asks.

'What?'

'Internet dating.'

'No.'

'Why not?'

'Because it doesn't feel right. You should like me because of the following five reasons. You should have sex with me because—'

Josie laughs. She laughs a lot and it's one of the reasons why I love her.

'Sex?'

'You know what I mean. I'm just not sure. It feels so false,' I whine.

'And you have a better suggestion?'

Josie knows I haven't got one. We have been down this route at least twenty-five times in the past two weeks and the outcome is always the same.

'But you said yourself that anything could happen in eleven months.'

'That was over a fortnight ago and I forgot you don't go out.'

'I still have ten months and five days.'

'Ten months and two days, actually.'

I open the door of the flat and take off my now drenched coat. Droplets of water roll down my back and I shiver.

'Harry, you need a date and the Internet is our last resort. Now, I've been researching this and it looks like DateMate is the best one.'

'You seem to be taking quite an interest in this.'

'See me as a manager/coordinator of sorts.'

'I'm not sure, Jose. What if it's full of weirdos?'

'It will be full of people just like you: lonely, desperate

and with hermit-like tendencies. That doesn't make you a weirdo; it just makes you a little bit sad.'

'Thanks.'

I gratefully slump on the sofa. My legs are killing me, my feet are cold and my tights are leaving a line round my waist.

'Come on, if nothing else, it will be fun, and who knows, you may find your dream man.'

'Yeah, right,' I reply and sigh. My shoulders hunch inwards and I rest my head on my knees. 'There is nothing that will make me want to do Internet dating,' I mumble.

'What did you say?'

I sit up and say it again.

Josie takes a deep breath. 'Chloe mentioned that she couldn't move Jason from our table. It would screw up the whole table plan. She's too scared to tell you.'

Josie has produced the red rag, and predictably I go running towards it.

'Okay, okay – I'll do it.'

'Good. Let me know how it goes. Wow, I'm so excited.'

So says the person who is secure in the knowledge that she will never have to resort to this.

'I just want a date for the wedding! That's it,' I protest.

'Yes, yes! Okay, I've drafted something you might want to use. Listen to this—'

'I don't speak three languages, nor do I belly dance. I also don't go sailing or know the girls from Girls Aloud.'

Josie sighs. 'Okay, forget the sailing part.'

Ten months and two days? I have lost three days. I register for WeightWatchers, make a note to join a gym, run a bath, and pour myself a glass of wine.

I stick my toe into the tap and with the phone lodged

under my chin, begin shaving my legs. If I don't make good of the time I am here, the water will be cold by the time my mother has finished. I contemplate putting my head under the water to see if she notices.

'I thought we could have a barbecue. Emma is making the trifle.'

My attention is brought back with a snap, and my hand jerks. Blood leaks into the water.

'Bugger.'

'Did you just swear?'

'No,' I reply, and realise this is the second time I have lied today in as many months, but then decide this one doesn't count. Sometimes people know the truth, but they just need the confession. My mother knows I said bugger.

'Emma is making the trifle?' I ask.

'Yes.' My mother sighs.

'I thought I made the trifles?'

'You can make it next time, dear.'

'What? The next time Dad is sixty, you mean?'

'Your sister said she wanted to make the trifle, and I said yes. I didn't think it would be a problem.'

'But she always makes the salads, Katie makes the cheese straws and I make the trifle.'

'Well, talk to your sister. She said she was going to make a Black Forest one.'

'A Black Forest trifle? Dad will hate it.'

'I invited your Aunt Barbara.' Mum always changes the subject when she has no answer. You can repeat what you just said, but she will continue to ignore you. 'But she can't come.'

'Well, that's a relief.'

I'm not a great fan of my Auntie Barbara. She scares me with her penetrating gaze and attitudes about capital punishment.

'Harriet!' my mother reprimands. 'Sarcasm is the lowest form of wit.'

'It wasn't sarcasm.'

I take a sip of my now lukewarm wine.

'Are you drinking?'

'No.'

My mother thinks that because I have the odd glass of wine on my own, I am on the rocky road to alcoholism.

'She said it was her leg again . . .'

I zone out and manage to dry myself off with one hand, put on a dressing gown, and paint my toenails while she talks. I don't know why I paint my toenails, or shave my legs, because there is no one to appreciate my efforts, but it is a matter of principle; like using jelly in a trifle so that my father gets the much sought-after glooop sound when he takes the first spoonful. I bet you don't get that with a Black Forest trifle.

What is it about Emma? She is the eldest with nothing and everything to prove. Why couldn't she just leave me to my one and only triumph? When I was young I dreamed of being a ballet dancer, but I was too tall. Then I dreamed of being a show jumper, but I discovered a fear of horses. I was desperate to be like the heroines of the books I read, but showed little aptitude for anything active. Emma, on the other hand, did. She was already striving to live up to her own expectations, and while I daydreamed my days away, she would be doing her Duke of Edinburgh Award, or playing hockey. My mother was so proud.

I can't remember my younger sister, Katie, demonstrating a particular aptitude or love for anything, but she always added something pretty and really rather lovely to any occasion. For that reason she was adored by my mother, family relations, and boys. She never noticed how the opposite sex stared at her. Emma and I did. Emma scoffed at the good-looking airheads who threw their hearts into the driveway with the morning paper, but I suspect, like me, she secretly longed for something of the same.

Emma had a fair number of boyfriends, but they were strange, serious types, with lanky hair and bad skin. She would keep them at a distance, reprimanding and issuing instructions with a voice more suited to a forty year old than a sixteen year old. They would nod, forlornly, shuffling behind, avoiding my mother's questions and any form of eye contact. Her husband Alan was just an extension of all those boring, serious boys, but with less hair and a car. Jason had suggested that behind those big white knickers and industrial-strength bra was a woman with a dirty mind. I couldn't see it myself. I have never seen Alan and Emma display any form of emotional attachment. If the twins were biologically theirs, then at least we could be sure they had sex. Katie is convinced that Emma is still a virgin and only allows Alan to touch her breasts when he is very good and does his chores.

Despite the attention of many, Katie has only had two boyfriends. Troy, who rode a moped and broke her heart, and the wannabe surf bum and music promoter, Lawrence, who is now her fiancé and father to baby Alfie.

As the middle child I am used to blending into the background and getting on with it. With a bossy, dominant older sister and a fairy princess baby in the family, I could easily be forgotten. I have on occasion been waiting at the school gates while my mother has been halfway home with her two other children. My love life has had a similar thread running through it. It has been littered with too many occasions where I have been infatuated from a distance with either my teachers or boys older than me; all of which were unrequited. Before Jason, I went out with Tim, Dan and Franz. Tim thought he might be gay and went to the US to become a professional swimmer, Dan fancied Chloe and Franz said he was worried about the world and went off to Nepal to find himself. I still don't know if he did. They were boys, whereas Jason was grown-up and gorgeous. He had no issues that diverted his attention away from me. He knew what he wanted and I had a major starring role in his world; well, for most of the time anyway.

'And Harriet.'

'Yes, Mum?'

'Try and arrive on time.'

My timekeeping, so admired in the workplace, doesn't transfer to family occasions. I have no idea why. I think it's something to do with being too early and then finding something else to do to pass the time. The something else always makes me late.

'Love you, Mum.'

'Yes, dear.'

I try and summon up some enthusiasm for my pasta. It tastes bland. I used to cook a lot when Jason was around. He had a hearty appetite and I loved to impress him and his friends with my culinary skills. He said I was feeding him up so that no one else would find him attractive; looking back I should have tried harder. Now, I can't be bothered with the whole cooking thing. It's easier to microwave something someone else has prepared. The phone rings and gives me an excuse to leave what's left.

'Ben wants to buy a sofa,' Josie declares.

'And?'

'A sofa with nothing to pay for three years.'

'I'm not with you.'

'It just seems a bit permanent.'

'Not if you've nothing to pay.'

'But what if we're not together in three years?'

'You will be. You'll probably be married with a baby by then.'

'Exactly. That's just what he's thinking.'

'That's good, isn't it?' I ask, but she ignores my question.

'Have you registered with DateMate yet?'

'I've made a start,' I reply cautiously.

'In what way?'

'In that I've been thinking about it.'

'Harry!'

'I'll do it tonight.'

'Do you want Jason to think you are still pining for him, or do you want to be the girl he shouldn't have let go?'

'I said I'll do it.'

This is tough. I scroll through other profiles on DateMate. There are no shrinking violets on here. Vivacious, funny, dynamic, successful, creative, exotic . . . God, what the hell do I say? I start typing.

I am a fun-loving girl. Tall, with brown hair and brown eyes.

Fun-loving? That sounds weak and if I was a man I wouldn't believe me. What does it mean anyway? That I like fun? And there's too much brown? Brunette hair? Am I brunette? Maybe chestnut. Should I replace tall with statuesque? No, that sounds scary; like Xena Warrior Princess. I delete five foot nine and replace it with five foot eight, because if I do meet someone, they are not going to have a tape measure in their back pocket.

Am I attractive, averagely attractive, above average or average? Above average?

I rush to the bathroom and look in the mirror. I smile with teeth showing and then without. I flick my shoulder-length hair in a seductive way and attempt sexy. Well, I'm okay, but I'm guessing that's not going to win me any admirers. I pucker up to my reflection and put some lip gloss on. I'm not ugly like the woman in the chemist's, or plain to the point of nondescript like Caroline from next door. She has skin the colour of skimmed milk, as if she hasn't seen natural light since birth, and has no discernible lips or eyelashes. I have passable lips and eyelashes (not full and luscious like Josie, but okay) and there are moments when I'm dressed up ready to go out and I have been known to nod my head and think, *I would*. When did I last think that? Pre-break up!

I peer into the mirror and try to see myself as others see me. Someone once said that I reminded them of one of those antelopes that bounce on the nature programmes before being devoured by a lion. I was upset at the time, but Josie said it was a compliment. I didn't believe her. Men don't go for antelopes, they go for pretty butterflies like Chloe. My height is challenging for any man less than five foot eight. Jason said that I turned heads; that I was striking. He only said it the once, when we first met, but it was enough for me to believe that it was okay. Now I am left with the thought that it probably wasn't.

Oh God, this is hard. I return to my computer and scroll through the website for clues. Attractive seems to be the way to go, but I have been brought up not to lie and there is no point in pre-empting a fall. I tick averagely attractive, but then question if there is such a thing.

Okay, next. What do you like to do? The 'About You' box taunts me with its empty white space. I resume my typing.

I like December days and snuggling up to watch old films with a pot of tea, some toast and strawberry conserve. That makes me sound old and boring. I should have skydiving in there somewhere.

After a day of charity skydiving, I like to snuggle up and watch old films with some toast and jam. I should change that to granary toast. That makes me sound healthy. *Good with old people and children*. This is a lie. Old people frighten me. So do babies. This is not going very well. I press delete.

I am intelligent. No, you can't just put intelligent. Somebody will want to quantify it with qualifications and a certain level of general knowledge. There is the expectation that I will be a female Stephen Fry, casually casting my brilliance around with witty observations and facts. If not intelligent, what about creative? *I am currently writing a children's book*. That makes me sound creative. It also says fun and caring – another lie.

I keep fit and would like to run a marathon. This is nearly true. Well, if I am going for an exaggeration of the truth, what about scuba diving? That makes me sound like I'm sucking the marrow from life. Maybe a bit of volunteer charity work with a remote tribe in the rainforest – so remote that nobody has ever heard of them. Yes, I like that.

I delete *I love food* and replace it with *I love cooking*. This says I like food in a healthy way, and I am also a whiz in the kitchen. This is not really a lie. I can make a range of pasta dishes and Delia Smith said on TV the other day that it's okay to use potato wedges. Okay, so I am fit and healthy with a creative streak and a heart of gold. What else? I stare at the screen. Come on, what else . . . there must be more to me than this? I take a break and cut my toenails. My feet aren't too bad.

I have nice feet and a good sense of humour?

I like going to the theatre, museums and galleries. This makes me sound cultured, and it is true, in a sense, because I do go to these places. For work, I have to.

I retype. *I am looking for someone to accompany me to museums, restaurants, theatres and galleries*.

I upload a photo. I am smiling and look like a girl happy with life. I was when it was taken. I have photoshopped Jason's head from the image. Hey, nobody will know he was ever there – in Barcelona, with me, when we were happy and in love. Well, I was; now I'm not entirely sure if *he* was, or when he stopped being – happy and in love – with me. I never asked. Now it consumes me. When did the death knell toll? Was it when I wore tights instead of stockings, or when water went up my nose on the water slide? Was it when I admitted to his mother that I might be in love with her beloved son, who was destined for greater things, that I could see us together for ever, with kids and a holiday home in Italy, or because I talked over the rugby world cup and refused to dress up as a schoolgirl? Or was it none of the above but simply because somebody who looked like a WAG, with round breasts and champagne breath, whispered in his shell-like ear that he might be better off sleeping with her? Josie wasn't surprised, nor was Chloe. It was Chloe and Tad who'd introduced me to Jason.

He had been to university with Tad and just returned from working in Hong Kong for the diplomatic service. He had made quite a name for himself, with his ambition, quick smile and dreams to conquer the world. That's what Tad said as he introduced us. Jason just smiled knowingly, basking in the glow of admiration. I took it for smug. Our conversation didn't get past the 'nice to finally meet you' from me. A girl with a short red dress took him by the arm and swept him away. I remember thinking that he was good looking but not my type. I decided he was arrogant and not to like him very much.

The second time we met was at a private screening of one of Tad's films. It was a scorching July day and the roads and my skin were sticky with heat. I had got lost and by the time I arrived at the trendy East End address, I was flushed and agitated. As I walked into the completely white gallery space, everyone turned and looked; their eyes like supermarket scanners. I nervously waved to Chloe and everyone resumed their conversations, leaving me to sweat a little more. Chloe and Tad were engrossed in conversation with a man sporting a large curly moustache and I was reluctant to interrupt. Instead, I located a waitress and sought sanctuary in a drink decorated with a slice of cucumber. Looking around the room, Jason was the only other face I recognised. He was wearing a white shirt and jeans. The girl with the red dress was nowhere to be seen.

I attempted to mingle, but the groups of beautiful creatives were closed. I thought of waiting it out in the ladies' toilets, emerging just before the film started, but like my guardian angel, Chloe came rushing over and rescued me before I had to.

'Thanks for coming, Harry. You're a star.'

'No problem. I'm really looking forward to it.' I tried to sound enthusiastic. Tad's films tended to veer towards the obscure and depressing.

'Isn't it great? Oooh, have you tried the apple martini yet? There's Grayson from the *Independent* over there,' Chloe gushed.

'It's amazing. Great venue, and a fantastic turnout, although I don't think I know a soul.'

'You know Jason a little. I'll call him over, he'll look after you.'

'No, no.' I reassured her. The last thing I wanted was Mr Smug Smarty Pants looking after me.

Someone looking like Sienna Miller hugged Chloe from behind.

'Martha wants to speak to you about singing at Tad's birthday party.'

'This is Harry, one of my oldest friends,' Chloe said proudly, beaming at me.

The girl looked at me as if she was waiting for me to do a trick. I racked my brain for something to do. Going cross-eyed seemed a bit churlish.

'Hi,' the girl said sullenly, before turning back to Chloe.

'I'm going outside for a smoke.' She turned and left and I wondered how she didn't topple backwards. She walked as if someone was pulling her hip bones forward.

'I'd better go and talk to Martha.'

Chloe disappeared, and I stood like a beacon of hope. I'm not great at mingling with people I don't know and my height doesn't help. It means that I can't fade into the background and hope nobody notices that I am Bobby-no-mates. I looked around in panic and an elderly usherette dressed in authentic fifties style smiled sympathetically. I smiled back and grabbed a carton of popcorn from her tray.

'Can't let you in. The film hasn't started yet,' she said as I moved the rope cordon to one side.

'I know, but I just need to escape.'

She nodded. 'Don't blame you, love. This lot have no manners,' she replied and moved to allow me through. I looked around the empty cinema and chose a seat at the back on the end of a row. The popcorn was good and the seats were like big red armchairs. I made myself comfortable and imagined being a movie star waiting for a private screening of my latest film. 'Darling, I simply can't have normal people in here with me. I have to be alone with my art and my popcorn.' I was beginning to enjoy myself when the door opened a fraction and Jason peered through. I smiled in a 'I'm quite happy on my own, thank you very much, so off you go and leave me be'-type way. He pushed the door open and walked in.

'Hi,' he said and his voice filled the empty room.

'Hi,' I replied and went back to my popcorn.

'Can I sit next to you?' he asked. I frowned. The cinema was empty and he had sixty other seats to choose from, but he just smiled as if no was never an option, and shuffled past my legs. He settled himself down with a lot of fuss about where his drink, jacket and popcorn should go and I attempted to ignore him, but when the lights eventually went down, I became aware of him in my personal space. I could feel his elbow next to mine and I was conscious of his every move. The air-conditioning made the hairs on my arms prickle and I shivered. He looked at me but I stared resolutely ahead pretending to be engrossed in the film. I wasn't; my attention kept wandering and I found myself enjoying his laughter at the funny bits and wondering what other things made him laugh.

Afterwards, as the gathered film buffs and critics discussed what they had seen in a mumbo-jumbo of superlatives, I made my apologies and left. Just as my taxi was about to pull away, the door opened and in climbed Jason.

'You can drop me off. I don't live that far from the station,' he announced. I was shocked at his audacity but pretended to be nonchalant.

'No problem, hop in.'

We made small talk as the traffic got worse. Forty minutes of sitting motionless exhausted our politeness and we sat in silence, watching as people in shorts wandered by. My mouth felt dry and I was aware of him turning towards me and looking at my legs. I pulled my dress down.

'We'll take it from here, mate,' Jason suddenly called out to the taxi driver. He grabbed my hand. 'Come on. Let's get outside. I'll buy you an ice cream. I'm guessing you're a rum-and-raisin type of girl.'

'More of a chocolate person, really.'

'It's close enough.'

He never let go of my hand for the rest of that hot afternoon.

I thought Chloe would be pleased when we got together, but she wasn't. Instead, she dropped little hints that his past was littered with casualties. I convinced myself that I was different. She said that for my sake she hoped I was.

Thinking about it all has made the hole in my stomach bigger. It's a cavernous black space that is gradually eating away at me, taking me over. It hurts. I miss him so much. I thought we were happy? Weren't we happy? Okay, so his mum clearly thought her son could do better and he had started going out a bit more with the people from work, but I thought it was good to have a bit of independence after our loved-up first few months. As for his mum, he said I was imagining it, that she had always been like that with his girlfriends. He didn't seem to grasp the fact that I wanted to be the one she gave the thumbs-up to. He said it didn't matter what his mum thought, but it did. She had pushed him to be exceptional since the age of six with after-school lessons, getting his teeth cosmetically enhanced, laser surgery for his eyes, and employing language and music tutors. Jason was always going to excel at something, and I got the impression she thought I was holding him back from his plan to conquer the world. Did he think the same too? Was I the underachiever who should have done something with her life? The thought makes me feel angry. I won awards! Well, one, for best global story for my article on the travelling Polish dance troupe.

That was two years ago.

I make myself a cup of herbal tea and attempt to clear

my body of toxins; including Jason. A mini Mars bar helps. Refreshed, I return to the computer and DateMate. Describe your ideal mate? I would like someone with blue eyes, brown hair (more light than dark, I think), tall – six foot and over would be nice – with a sharp sense of humour, intelligent, kind, generous . . . someone I can trust. Someone who is into me, even when I am not the prettiest girl in the room. I want someone who can cook and will scrape the ice from my car windscreen; someone I can look up to, literally, and who will laugh when I am trying to be funny. I want someone who will tell me I have a sexy arse when it's more soft white bap than peach. Above all, I want a hero! Is that too much to ask? It appears my DateMate word limit thinks it is.

I read through my entry. Well, I don't sound too bad. Not great, but not bad. I do some editing until I sound better. Now I need a name to protect my anonymity from the weirdos who lurk behind their screens, ready to steal my identity or fulfil their destiny as a stalker. I scroll through other entries: Minxie, Diamond Eyes, Delicious Dumpling, Gorgeous Gal, Hot Lips, Mandy Maybe . . . Oh God – I begin a list of possible names. These include Culture Vulture, Hot and Harry, and Girl to Go, as in coffee to go . . . no, it doesn't work, I know it doesn't. I decide on Belle of the Ball as in wedding belle, but without the scary wedding bit.

Belle of the Ball
Girl seeks boy to save the last dance for her
I am a twenty-nine-year-old girl with nice feet and a sense of humour. When I am not scuba diving and volunteering in the rainforests I like keeping fit, cooking and watching movies. I am also interested in the arts and spend quite a lot of my time at the theatre or exploring galleries. All of these things are

much more fun with someone, and that's where you come in. I would like to meet someone who is tall, confident, intelligent, slightly quirky, funny, kind and generous. In short – I need a hero. (Who sang this?)

I cross out the last sentence and hover over the download button. Go on, do it . . . do it . . . DO IT!

I do, and then feel sick. I am now out there in DateMate land for all to see. I have been picked up from the dusty bottom shelf of life and placed on the top shelf where every pervert, murderer and mentally unhinged person can see me.

I lie in bed and worry. I worry about work, about the people of Zimbabwe and being on DateMate. The light from my mobile phone flickers green. It's a text from Josie: Stop worrying! Your moon is in Saturn. X

I log on to DateMate. Belle of the Ball has been out there for twenty-four hours and two mates have viewed me. I go into my message inbox. Nothing! Does this mean that I am not pretty or clever enough; that Hot Lips from Guildford is a much more attractive option because she calls herself naughty but nice? Humph! So, out of seven thousand members, not one of them is interested in me. I need to be proactive, so says Josie, Miss DateMate Expert. The thing is to find the ones I fancy and make them my favourites. This apparently will encourage them to get in touch. I click on this week's gallery of male mates in my area.

Synergy Seeker
I am a mathematician seeking new adventures.
Looking for intelligence and beauty. Too much to ask?
Read my statistics and come to your own conclusions.

First-class Post
Postie by day, singer by night.
Good looking, cuddly, funny and looking for Mrs Perfect.
No second-class post accepted in this postbox.

Slimshady
Get your coat.
Looking for a girl to share a chicken korma on a Saturday night.
Must like pigs and cornflakes.

See, I knew it would be like this. Weirdos, the lot of them. I shut my computer down. That's it. I'm going on my own! I don't care. Didn't my horoscope say that romance was to be found closer to home? I don't need to do this. My wedding date is probably waiting in Sainsbury's . . . but preferably not behind a till. Does this make me a snob? It's the sort of thing my sister Emma would say. I make a note to have an open mind.

I slump on the sofa, decide I need to replace it, and flick through a copy of *Hello!* magazine. Nothing, boring, nothing, boring, oh, what does she look like, boring, nothing, WHAT? In the bottom left-hand corner is a photo of Sophie and Jason with an England rugby player. Sophie has very white teeth and a big mouth. Jason is beaming like a child who has been given his first bike for Christmas. I examine Sophie for flaws. Her right breast looks slightly bigger than the left. Her make-up is perfect, though, and she has a fantastic figure. She curves in all the right places. She is slightly smaller than Jason in high heels.

I feel a lump in my throat. Staring at them doesn't make their smiling faces disappear. Did he joke with her about getting married on their first date? Did he tell her she was different, different enough to be special? Has she met his mum and his sister? Did they like her? Did she tell his mum that she couldn't get enough of her home-made strawberry jam? Do they watch *24* together? Can she boil the perfect egg?

I feel sick; as if I am mourning the loss of something precious. No, that's wrong, I didn't lose it – someone stole it from me.

I throw the magazine in the bin and log back on to DateMate. When Jason sees me with my hot date at the wedding he will hopefully realise what a fool he's been. I scroll through the profiles. There must be someone out there who isn't a freak.

It's two o'clock in the morning and I am going blind. There must be someone. Ooh, hang on.

EcoWarrior
My job as a marine biologist means I have spent the last few years travelling the world, but now I want to settle down with the right girl. I love cooking Indian food, wind surfing, reading, cuddling up with a good film. I am looking for a girl who will love my dog Donald and my tiny niece Maisie as much as I do.

Oh yeah, baby. This is more like it. I add him to my favourites and dream of being dragged from the sea in a skimpy bikini and having the salt licked off my skin.

The next day, I get a message from EcoWarrior asking me what my favourite films are. I tell him and wait. I never hear from him again. It seems I fell at the first question. It's a bit like being on *Who Wants To Be a Millionaire*.

Girl Without a Date in Her Diary – Blog entry – February 22nd

My horoscope says that now is the time to be

positive and look to new horizons. This is a little different from last month's when it told me to look closer to home, but I suspect the powers that be up there had a look around my immediate geographical love zone and could see there wasn't anything of note. I've also had a look and can confirm that there is nothing out there and, frankly, I'm bored with wearing lipstick every time I go to the supermarket or bank. So, despite my initial misgivings, I am determined to be positive about Internet dating. Maybe I am wrong and meeting someone over the Internet is the way to go. In ten months' time there is a chance I could be holding hands with the man of my dreams, or at least someone who looks great in a suit and loves a good wedding. Maybe I need to look for a gay man? No, I need someone I can fancy.

The thing is, if I did meet someone, I wouldn't admit to it. How did we meet? Oh, it was a friend of a friend. He wore blue, I wore red. He told a joke and I laughed. Why the snobbery? Because there is still the opinion out there that it smacks of desperate? Well, I am desperate! I need someone to take me to a wedding and if it means talking rubbish and saying I love macaroni cheese and camping, I will.

I see it as a social experiment on behalf of all single women out there who don't look like Angelina.

If, like me, you are heading towards Internet dating, here is my list of things to do to ensure you are in tip-top condition and in with a fighting chance against the likes of Mandy Maybe and her expressive tongue:

- Watch *QI* and *Mastermind* to update general and obscure knowledge.
- Watch *Masterchef* to learn how to cook new dishes to impress.

- Read reviews of books and films.
- Watch the news. Good for conversation.
- Pretend you're someone else. (I have, and she's called Luscious Linda.)

March 1st

What the hell is going on? I hate this! I mean, what happened to good old-fashioned eyeing someone up in a nightclub or pub, disappearing off to the toilets to redo your make-up and getting your friend to say 'My mate likes you'? There was no 'name your favourite colour/film/food/music/historical figure' or 'list your aspirations for the next five years'. It was all a bit sweaty and largely dependent on Jack Daniel's, subdued lighting and that old thing called chemistry. It was basic and exhilarating and made the weekends something to look forward to. This Internet dating thing is devoid of anything that is exciting or romantic. It is bland and logical and there is no way of knowing if the guy you are chatting up is really five foot two with body odour issues. I have nothing against men who are five foot two . . . actually, I do. I look stupid with anyone under five foot six and in my experience, small men are like small dogs: lots of noise and macho behaviour – two things I hate. I want to be somebody's favourite. God, it's like being back at school.

March 8th

Luscious Linda has twenty-five favourites and counting. She looks a bit like a Sindy Doll. In fact, if anyone had taken a closer look . . .

I settle in front of the TV and prepare my day's viewing list. This is my second day off sick in as many months. I'm not sick; just tired. Life without Jason saps my energy and my job takes any that is left. I used to love it, with its quirky characters and no two days the same, but now it's become like everything else: representative of everything that is now wrong. Today it all seemed a whole lot worse. I have no idea why. I think it might have been my hair.

The alarm went off as normal and I woke up, as I always do, on the third ring. It wasn't raining and the boiler was working – all good so far. I got up, put my dog slippers on and padded into the bathroom. Then I caught sight of my reflection in the mirror and came to the conclusion that it was because of my hair. Jason, my job . . . everything. I tousled and clipped, scraped back and brushed. Whatever I did, it still looked like shit. I looked like shit. I was shit. I began to cry. Today, it seemed, I couldn't face the world.

When I met Jason I was moderately successful. I had just won the award for my article and was producing work I could be proud of. I was in a good place and felt confident that my decision not to move to London had been the right one. The glamorous job opportunities editing *Marie Claire* and *Elle* that had fallen by the wayside didn't seem to matter any more. I was doing okay. Jason said I could do better. Maybe now was the time, he suggested. With him spurring me on, I applied for a job as an assistant editor for *Vie Magazine*. He said I could do it in my sleep; that it would be good for me to get out of *Life to Live* and think further afield. He inspired me to be more and I started to see myself as the can-do-more girl he saw.

I began to feel dissatisfied with *Life to Live* and started imagining the alternative in my head. When I didn't get the job at *Vie* I was devastated. If Jason was as disappointed as I thought he was, he didn't show it. Instead, he urged me to apply for more jobs, and I did. When I looked at him, always striving for better, I wanted to do the same. I redecorated the flat, enrolled in an evening course making jewellery (one of my ideas was to become a Jade Jagger type) and perfected every pasta dish known to Jamie Oliver. I told myself it was only a matter of time before something came up, and in the meantime, we filled our time with romantic weekends away and hosting evenings where I impressed his friends with my home-made beetroot tagliatelle.

Now it seems a world away.

A now coffee-and-soup-stained copy of *Hello!* lies on the table. I have taken it out of the bin at least four times. I can't help myself. I open the page and Jason is still smiling. I am sinking into that black hole of self-pity again and he is smiling with his arm proprietorially round the waist of a woman with perfectly round but wonky tits. I stare into the abyss that is Sophie's mouth. She is eating my boyfriend – sorry, my ex-boyfriend – whole and laughing at me. I sink into my hands. It's dark in here. The blood rushes to my head. I feel lost and it hurts. Perhaps

I'll go to sleep. Then I remember what happens when I sleep: I have nightmares. Last night's was horrible. Jason and his mum were shaking their heads in disappointment as I juggled six Washington Red Apples and two hit the ground. The one in my mouth was making me gag. I woke up drenched in sweat.

Something snaps. It's a bit like when I went to a chiropractor and told him he was a bastard. He should have warned me. I screamed. This is more of a mental snap. I remove my head from my hands. What am I doing? I've wasted too long drowning in this, hurting, unable to make a decision, waiting for him to make it okay again, make me okay again. I feel angry. Not with him; but with me. I'm better than this. He may have taken my coffee-maker, sofa, bath towel, cacti and heart, but he didn't take the little bit inside that waves its fist in the air and shouts, I'll show you!

My breasts are real and straight and I am tall enough to wear Zara trousers. I am going to get into that shower, wash my hair, get dressed and go to work. I'm going to show him that I can be fabulous and successful. At Chloe's wedding he is going to weep with the knowledge that he made a mistake letting me go.

'Afternoon,' Ed says sarcastically, and I stick my tongue out at him.

I switch on my computer and watch his tall, almost lanky frame walk across the office. Ed is a freelance photographer and provides the majority of the images we use for the magazine. He is also the only man I know who is taller than me and can wear a cardigan and a tweed cap without being gay or looking like a prat. Ed is relatively new here. New being two years. Not long after he started we found a mutual interest in the comings and goings of the man in the office next door. Every morning, at precisely eleven o'clock, he runs up and down five flights of stairs. We haven't been able to ascertain if he is doing it to keep fit or suffering from some sort of Obsessive Compulsive Disorder. It makes us laugh. So do repeats of *Will and Grace* and the *A-Team*.

I think every girl should have a good-looking friend, one who in a different life would probably be your boyfriend – a friend who is less intense than your girlfriends, will make you laugh, and can do wonders for your ego when you need it most, without having the emotional baggage that comes with relationships. Ed is mine.

Apart from Georgina, our editor, and Derek, the accountant, I have been here the longest. Eight years next week. This is nothing short of shocking for someone who thought she would stay for six months max. Some things have changed over the years, such as the installation of a photocopier that's bigger than my flat, and fresh filtered coffee. Sadly, though, our collective creativity hasn't. We are still using the same format and pulling in the same advertisers. This didn't seem to overtly bother anyone and we spent more time discussing the *X Factor* results in our Monday morning meetings than brainstorming our plans for groundbreaking journalism. Three months ago all that changed when a young contender hit the region's letterboxes. *Bath at Large* is glossier, smarter and trendier. If I thought I was any of those things, I would have applied for a job there. Now, the panic is palpable. It is evident at the editorial meetings, around the photocopier and when the stationery is being ordered. Georgina hasn't smiled for the last three months. Rare sightings of a curvature to her mouth are emailed throughout the office so that we can all speculate on the cause. The pressure to come up with something new and exciting is a real one, and I am struggling.

The What's On page for *Life to Live* is my responsibility, but it is a formula that doesn't require much creativity. It's a list! Now and then I can squeeze in a little editorial freedom, or an interview depending on space, but mostly I just add a few lines – must see, fascinating insight, blah, blah, blah. Sometimes, if I am feeling a little reckless, I add one of my own suggestions – gerbil wrestling or cheese catapulting. Nobody seems to notice. I am also one of the feature writers, but over the past six months my stories have been few and far between. Any talent I seem to have possessed appears to have dried up like the nasty coffee substitute Judith drinks. It smells of cat pee.

I scan my email inbox and it is full of the usual suspects. Bell ringing, a concert by a Canadian folk singer, a poetry reading and a crazy new cocktail from a pub going up-market. There is nothing sexy in there. *Bath at Large* is sexy and Georgina has become obsessed with the word.

Despite it being nearly mid-March, I am now planning my summer placements. God, soon it will be Christmas. I look through my diary. Chloe's wedding is written in big red letters. Just under nine months left. I check that Judith is doing whatever it is she should be doing, and log on to DateMate. Oooh, I am someone's favourite. *Half-Man-Half-Biscuit*. Well, it sounds like he has a sense of humour. *If I was a dog I would be a labrador. I need a woman to feed me treats*. I check out his photo. He looks like a basset hound. I read on. He also doesn't have a sense of humour. I log out, and leave for an interview with a woman who takes photographs of doors. I am well aware this is not sexy or particularly interesting, but it is filling a space and my plans of becoming more fabulous than Sophie need a little more thought.

When I walk through the front door, my neighbour, Mrs Gennings (call me Martha), appears like something from *Exorcist 3* and almost pins me to the shared post table in the lobby.

'Have you seen my copy of the *Guardian*?'

'No,' I reply a tad too quickly.

She looks at my fingers. She is searching for evidence of newsprint, but she won't find it, because I haven't started flicking through it yet. Martha Gennings's copy of the *Guardian* is in my 'being kind to the environment' cotton bag.

Her eyes narrow and she leans forward, revealing yellow teeth and eyes that have lost any hope of love. Is she going to frisk me, take me by surprise with a drop kick? I lean back, and shuffle crab-like towards my flat door.

'I have to go, things to do,' I stammer, feeling like a criminal. I only wanted to borrow it, to look through the job section.

Martha's eyes follow me and bore their way through my door, setting fire to my footsteps as I walk away. Martha Gestapo Gennings is our rubbish and post watch woman. Put your bags out before eight p.m. on a Sunday night and she will swoop down with all the vengeance of a woman widowed by lightning. One night I heard her in the shared corridor, and made the mistake of looking out of my peephole, only to find her peering right back at me. She scares me, and now that I have pinched, no, borrowed her newspaper, the dark lord will be called upon in a midnight ceremony and horrid things will start happening to me.

I read a magazine, flick through the TV channels and wonder if I should, as the nice lady on *West Today* suggests, make some chutney and sell it at my local Farmers' Market. When I am at work I think of being at home. When I am at home, I am bored. I should get a cat. It would stop me talking to myself and the TV. We had one when I was little but it died. Dibby was old and had fits. We would be having our tea and there would be a thump as he fell off a chair. Minutes later he would get up, shake his head and act as if nothing had happened. One day he didn't get up. I was the one who found him, stiff as a board. I screamed and Emma came in and slapped me round the face. She told my father she had seen people do it on TV.

My flat isn't trendy or full of designer items but rather a mishmash of hand-me-downs and throws. It reflects the side of me I want to be and for that reason I have resisted making it a carefully constructed space of items that fit together. There are odd pieces of IKEA furniture, a coffee table made by my dad and an old, slightly worn dark green two-seater sofa given to me by Josie's mum after Jason took the brown leather one. None of the cushions that cover it match, but I like it. Like a hot chocolate on a winter's day, it's reassuring and comfortable. I decide that this is exactly the sort of man I should be looking for.

I phone Josie. 'I've decided I'm going to look for a comfortable man.'

'What, fat?'

'No, not fat – I was thinking more in terms of a duvet.'

'Have you been drinking?'

'No. I just think that good looking and dynamic are a bit last year.'

'How is the dating thing going?'

'It isn't really.'

'What about EcoWarrior? He sounded perfect.'

'Yes, I thought so too, but I haven't heard back from him. It seems my film choices weren't up to scratch.'

'Well, stick with it. It's early days yet. If you see anyone else you like, let me know and I'll take a look.'

'Okay. What are you up to tonight?'

'We're going into Chinatown for dim sum with Ben's brother and his girlfriend, what about you?'

'Updating my CV. I need to be fabulous, and changing my job is first on the list.'

'What else is on the list?'

'Losing a stone in weight, getting a gorgeous man to take me to Chloe's wedding, and with the money from what will be a huge and frankly obscene salary from my new job, buying a pair of Christian Louboutin shoes and not giving a damn about being taller than my boyfriend.'

'I like it! And remember, Belle of the Ball, as we speak, your prince is probably perusing your profile to see if that slipper fits. Go, Cinderella, go and pucker those lips.'

I look at my own dog-faced slippers and wonder what kind of man will find me enchanting. I log on to DateMate and look for a comfortable man who has the potential to be good in bed; like the chef on *Saturday Kitchen*.

Every morning I am the first one in. The office is still and quiet, waiting for the day to begin. I make myself a cup of coffee and get more done in those first forty minutes than I do the rest of the morning. Sometimes it feels weird; as if the whole world has been turned off, but then at eight forty-five, somebody switches it back on again and the fluorescents flicker, the phones begin to ring and the chatter of people fills the open-plan office with its tired blue carpet and now grubby, felt-covered partitions.

This morning, the appearance of Judith shocks me. Is

that the time? My coffee has been untouched in favour of a new addiction. I have been perusing the DateMate website and picking favourites like un-bruised apples in the supermarket. I hurriedly get my notes together for our editorial meeting. What I should have been doing instead of reading about someone called Skydiver, was making bullet points of all the sexy things I have planned for my page. I look down at my notebook: 1. Ask famous people what their favourite thing to do when in Bath is, 2. There is no number two.

We gather around the circular table and chatter amongst ourselves. Judith is talking about Jesus whilst Jeremy is talking about his satin sheets. When Georgina appears, the room falls silent. There is no sign of a smile and we make ours disappear accordingly.

'So what have we got?' she launches in immediately, looking towards Judith. Georgina is a Jewish fifty-something, with a frighteningly low tolerance level, and a large crimson mouth. I imagine she drinks whisky or bourbon – neat. Georgina is a relic of the eighties, with backcombed, plum-coloured hair and shoulder pads. She is always immaculate in long jackets (to hide her rather large bottom), with a coordinating scarf (to hide the jowls) and huge ceramic disc earrings (to disguise rather large earlobes). Georgina shoots from the hip and never takes prisoners. I like her. There is no pretence about wanting to be your best friend.

Judith coughs nervously and looks at her notebook. 'We were thinking of models dressed in floaty summer dresses, standing in the fountain.'

'Who is we?'

Judith shuffles uncomfortably in her chair and the colour creeps up her beautiful white swan-like neck. I almost feel sorry for her. Whilst the confident and *über*-cool Kiki is away in South America doing good somewhere, Judith is looking after the fashion features. She is out of her depth.

'I meant me,' she says quietly.

'Go on,' Georgina instructs.

Judith seems to have lost her thread and coughs again.

'Fountain,' Georgina says, clearly bored.

'Oh yes. I was thinking *Atonement* – you know, when Keira Knightley dives into the fountain.'

'And when she gets out you can see through her dress,' Jeremy from advertising remarks. He grins and raises his eyebrows. It makes me shudder a little. Judith frowns.

'We could have Keira-like models – you know, that whole ethereal English beauty thing,' she continues.

'I like the idea of see-through,' Georgina comments, writing something in her leather-bound notebook. I am betting it's the word sexy.

Judith looks horrified. She coughs again. It's starting to irritate me, and I pass her a glass of water.

'I was thinking more Edwardian glamour.'

'But Jeremy is right. The see-through element was the key thing.'

'And the way she parted her lips . . . just slightly . . .' Jeremy is having his own wet dream in the corner. Georgina looks at him and he shuts up.

'I like the idea of the fountain, but let's get those girls wet and' – we all wait for that word – 'sexy.'

'We could make it a double fashion feature – the dresses and the underwear? I could follow it up with a list of stately homes and gardens to visit this summer,' I venture.

Georgina looks at me with surprise. I look back, equally surprised. Was that me who just came up with a brilliant idea? Judith shoots me a look that says she is less than impressed at me stealing her thunder. I smile an apology. Georgina begins barking instructions to make it happen.

'Jeremy, let's get some phone calls to the companies featured, and Phoebe, can you help Judith – let's get some wellington boots in there somewhere.'

Judith smiles and I suspect she is praying for my punishment. Judith is a Christian, which always surprises me, because everything else about her points the other way. A blonde, vacant waste of space, I never had her down for spiritual leanings. It just goes to show, you can never be too sure who is lurking in your office.

'So, Harry. What have you got?' Georgina fixes me with one of her 'impress me in two minutes or less' looks. I avert my gaze and make a big thing of looking down my list of one.

'Well, the one idea that really stood out for me was asking celebrities to tell us what they like to do when they are in town.'

'Mmmm.' Georgina nods her head and sucks on the end of the glasses she never wears.

'We could intersperse them with suggestions from the general public. A photo gallery of sorts.' I am on fire now.

'Who cares what the man on the street says? We don't want to know where Sharon from the post office goes at the weekend,' Georgina barks. 'But you're right about celebrities. Did you have someone in mind?' Georgina demands.

'Johnny Depp,' I offer excitedly, imagining our interview over coffee and blueberry muffins. Someone told me he always likes to have fresh blueberries on location. These kinds of facts, though not immediately fascinating, can prove their worth when you least expect them to. He would like it that I cared about his well-being. We would become friends and go shopping down

Walcott Street. He would like the cheese shop.

'Johnny Depp doesn't live here!' Jeremy scoffs.

'He does,' Judith and I reply in high-pitched unison.

'Well, if he does, I'd like to know where.'

So would I. The rumours are not specific enough, and nobody I know has actually seen him.

'What about Nicolas Cage?' I suggest. Now I know he has been here. A friend of a friend of a friend passed him going into a jeweller's shop.

'So do you think you can get him to talk to you?'

I hadn't thought this far ahead, but I can't back out now. I do an impression of my mother and pretend not to hear. 'There's that guy who used to be in that sitcom. What was it called?'

'No, you're thinking of that guy in the bank advert,' Jeremy interrupts.

'I'm not. I mean the guy that always used to wear the deerstalker hat,' I counter, although I am not sure which one I mean.

'We were talking about Nicolas Cage?' Georgina barks.

'Yes, Nicolas Cage – I'll get my people to talk to his people,' I joke, but nobody thinks it's as funny as I do, and my second career as a comedian is cut short. Clarissa gives us all a rundown of the interviews she has planned, but I lose interest after somebody from *Britain's Got Talent*.

Ed walks over to my desk and I quickly click out of the recruitment company website.

'So how did it go with the Johnny Depp suggestion?'

'How did you know about my Johnny Depp thing?'

'I saw the word celebrity on the Post-it note stuck to your computer, and figured out the rest.'

'Am I always that predictable?' I ask, trying hard to hide my disappointment. I don't want to be predictable. I want to be living on the edge, pushing the envelope, thinking outside the box, way out there, sucking that marrow – and all those other things that are not predictable and like me.

'Yes,' Ed replies, picking up his camera.

'Thanks, thanks a lot,' I reply, clicking into my emails to indicate that I am too busy for such nonsense.

'You make it sound like it's an insult,' Ed says, shaking his head at me. 'See you later.'

I wave without conviction. My attention has been taken by a message on DateMate. I click on to his photo first – not that I'm swayed by looks over substance, of course.

So, Belle of the Ball. Do you fancy a drink?

He's a bit forward. Aren't we meant to be asking questions like, what's your favourite colour, name your favourite CDs of all time, if you were an animal what would you be? Have you any criminal convictions? Space Cowboy obviously thinks not. I like it, though. It seems more normal, and normal is a good word in this crazy Internet world I am currently tiptoeing through. I look at his profile.

I have good teeth, nice shoes and great lips. I like wild, intellectual girls who drink pints and ride motorbikes. Failing that, I would like to meet someone sexy and crazy in a good way.

Space Cowboy . . . mmmm. He strides over with purpose and grabs me by the waist as if I'm a rag doll. His stubble grazes my chin. His lips are full and they are rough with mine. I feel bruised. His eyes are dark and he is smouldering underneath his battered leather jacket. He plays the guitar and strums me in the same way, with a natural talent and an intoxicating disregard for my protests. He unzips—

'Harry?' Judith interrupts. 'Reginald Dixon from the Allotment Society is on the phone for you. He says they have an odd-shaped carrot competition next week.'

God, what was I thinking? Space Cowboy is probably a complete nutcase who spits when he talks and has a moustache. My horoscope said I should be looking towards new horizons, not hovering in the ether, talking to psycho strangers. I delete my reply email. No to Space Cowboy! No to this whole Internet dating thing.

After an hour's walk around Hampstead Heath in our bid to lose weight for the wedding, Josie is making poached eggs. We wanted fried egg sandwiches but Chloe was strict with us and said a categorical no.

With coffee and reading matter we fill the tiny living room. Despite Josie's protests that she is not putting down roots, that no decisions have been made, that the future is uncertain, etc. etc., Ben's flat is full of her touches. There is a square mirror in the bathroom, and if you look closely enough, you can just about read the words engraved in the middle. *You are gorgeous. Now wash your hands and go live it*. She has also replaced the oak kitchen units with red lacquer, installed a coloured-glass chandelier in the bedroom and replaced the safe and sensible beige rug with a Union Jack design. Ben is being remarkably good about having his clean lines and understated accessories ripped out from beneath his feet.

'I think it helps if you have an idea of what you want to do,' Chloe suggests.

'I want to be successful and dynamic,' I say, flicking through the recruitment pages of the newspaper.

'You are,' Chloe replies. She has her head in a copy of *Vogue*. Josie is singing 'Sweet Home Alabama' in the kitchen.

'No. I mean in the way that you and Josie are. *Life to Live* is a sinking ship and if I'm not careful, I'm going down with it.'

'It would be a shame if it did. There's huge potential there.'

'Like what?'

'I don't know. I sew buttons on handbags. You're the writer.'

Potential? Mmmm, I know I should have loads of it tucked away in my bottom drawer, but . . . maybe I should try something completely different; something inspiring and impressive. Yes, Jason. I'm a teacher now. I've been in Uganda teaching the orphans. Hi, Jason. I've just got back from the launch of Gucci's new fragrance. Did I tell you I've started my own PR company? This is my boyfriend. He rides a motorbike. Lives life on the edge . . .

'I was thinking of having something really cheesy like karaoke at the reception. Each guest has to sing their favourite love song. What do you think?' Chloe asks.

'You don't want to know what I think.'

'I do.'

'It stinks!'

'Oh Harry, come on, it will be funny.'

'For whom?'

'You're being grumpy.'

'I'm not being grumpy.'

Josie walks in doing bicep curls with two tins of baked beans.

'Harry is being grumpy,' Chloe says.

'It's because she's slowly turning back into a virgin.

Look at nuns. They always look grumpy,' Josie replies.

'Actually, my sex life could be taking a turn for the better,' I retort smugly. I am also exaggerating.

'You've met someone?' Josie asks incredulously. Her eyes are wide in surprise.

'Don't make it sound like the Holy Grail. No, I haven't actually met someone face to face, but, I might be going on a date with someone from DateMate.'

I wasn't, but now I am. Space Cowboy has just got lucky.

Georgina ushers me into her office with impatience.

'Harry, sit down,' she says.

I do, and within seconds feel a headache coming on from the heady perfume of white lilies. Georgina always has fresh flowers in her office. They are always extravagant, like her. There are photographs of minor celebrities and Georgina smiling at various award ceremonies on her wall, but none of her family. I am not even sure she has one.

'It occurred to me this morning that we haven't had a chance to talk, really talk, lately.'

She's going to sack me. No, she isn't. My horoscope said I was going to go from strength to strength. She's going to give me my own double-page spread. Harry's page.

'Happy?'

I nod. She saw the *Guardian* job section on my desk.

'You've been doing the What's On section a while now, haven't you?'

'Nearly six years.'

'I've been thinking about how we can make *Life to Live* a bit more glamorous, more go-getter and sexy.'

'Me too—' I begin hopefully, but Georgina interrupts me.

'I have a friend who has a daughter living in London, and it strikes me we don't feature enough from the city. Many of our residents commute or have moved here. They are cosmopolitan people and expect us to be the same.'

I nod, but I am lost. What has this got to do with me? Is she saying I am not cosmopolitan? I wear shoes from Office and use Mac eyeshadow.

'Poppy would be a breath of fresh air – a vibrant twenty-one year old talking about her life in the city. Lots of cocktail bars, etc. The youngsters would love it.'

'Poppy?' I ask.

'My friend's daughter; a beautiful, funny thing with lots of hilarious little anecdotes.'

I nod. I hate Poppy.

'What do you think?' Georgina asks.

That I am not a breath of fresh air, funny or beautiful, that my anecdotes are not of the hilarious variety? I think of Sophie, then I think of Jason, and then I go hurtling towards my damp, dark, black hole of insecurity all over again. Somebody give me a ladder!

'I'm not sure,' I reply, because the ladder is not forthcoming and it's dark down here.

Georgina looks at me as if I haven't surprised her. I long to surprise, but today is not the day. I look at my fingers and wish they were not quite so long. When I was at school I fancied a boy called Troy. We kissed with tongues and he said with all certainty that we would get married. He held up our hands and we both saw that his were smaller than mine. He finished with me the next day. His friend Lee told me that it was the hands thing.

'We need to do something to attract those readers under sixty – the young are our future.' Georgina gets up and stares out of her window. Is she looking for the young and bright who will suddenly pick up *Life to Live* because of a girl called Poppy?

'I agree, but—'

'But what?'

'I just think there must be other ways of doing it than getting an It girl to write about spending her father's money.'

'Do you have another suggestion?' Georgina snaps back at me.

See, I was beginning to sound as if I knew what I was talking about, and now I'm going to blow it.

'I can't think of anything right now, but if you leave it with me, I could get something to you in the next couple of days,' I bluff.

Georgina walks back to her chair. She looks at her own inflated hands.

'The Poppy idea is just one of many I am discussing with Donald.'

Donald is the owner of the magazine. A mythical tanned figure who spends most of his time in Tuscany, I can't imagine Donald having any more idea of capturing a younger readership than Georgina has.

'It's a time of great change, Harry, and we all have to adapt,' she says, picking up her phone. It is the sign that I can leave.

'Oh, before you go. What's happening about Nicolas Cage?'

'His people are getting back to me.'

'Are they?' Georgina asks, looking surprised. 'Aaah, hello, sweetie,' she says into the phone and I shuffle back to my desk, feeling shorter than I did fifteen minutes ago. It seems it's only a matter of time before the ever-popular Poppy Darling replaces the ever-predictable Harriet Peel.

I check my horoscope for miracles and make a note to come up with something amazing.

Girl Without a Date in Her Diary – Blog entry – March 15th

Life is funny. You say you don't want something and you're absolutely adamant. No, I don't want it, I need something else; something bigger and better. Then they tell you that actually it's okay, because you can't have it anyway – someone else wants it. It's like the boy-next-door scenario. He has fancied you for years. You're sweet, but not my type, you say with the confidence of the loved, then the girl next door but one takes an interest and suddenly he's the hottest boy on the block. Why is it always a surprise when it happens? I have realised today that I don't want to do anything else. I want to do what I have always done, but better. I want to be Angelina Jolie, taking no prisoners, smiling enigmatically with a successful career and a gorgeous, equally successful husband.

What makes someone gorgeous and successful? What makes someone beautiful and funny? Surely it's all in the eye of the beholder. Another person's gorgeous and funny is someone else's nightmare. I guess that's what makes the world go round.

Saying all that, there are exceptions to the rule. Brangelina are a case in point. They are a template to which we all aspire. When I say all, I mean me, most of my friends and the readership of *Heat* magazine. We rarely know if we are the someone beautiful and funny unless, of course, your betrothed tells everyone at the wedding. We hope, but it's the first few moments that define whether you are that person to someone else. If you're not, then there is nothing you can do about it. This is the heartbreak that accompanies those times when you fancy someone rotten and they just don't fancy you back. I am an expert on this and have spent hours wondering what it was about me that wasn't right. I even took up juggling once because I thought that would be the thing that would ultimately swing things in my favour. When I met the boy in question years later, he said it wasn't me or the lack of me; it was just that he fancied someone else.

When you look at Brad and Angie, you can see what they saw in each other. I mean, come on; if one of them was remotely boring, not funny, or had an irritating habit of clicking their teeth or picking their nose, I am pretty sure they pretended not to notice. Brad is clearly in love with everything Angie. You can see it in the way he looks at her. Does he thank his lucky stars every single day that he sees that perfect arse every morning? I want that. I want what she has with a cherry on top. Please don't let me be the Jennifer Aniston one for the rest of my life – dumped and forever going for the wrong ones who don't thank their lucky stars.

P.S. I have high hopes for Space Cowboy. My horoscope says there is a lot of promise in Neptune. Thank God! My local convenience store, bank, garage, post office and swimming baths (I've checked them all) are lacking in anything that could remotely be called promise. It's depressing out there. Neptune is my only hope.

I have ten minutes before I have to leave. It is my father's sixtieth birthday and I cannot be late. I look out of the window. It's definitely not barbecue weather, but this will not stop my mother. She saw a sun symbol on the weather chart. I said it was over London but she said it was near enough. I find my 'exploring polar ice caps' fleece jacket, the one I bought for my trip to Scotland with Jason. It is green and taupe and makes me look like a pistachio nut. I have ten minutes. I log on to DateMate. Just a quick little look.

Oh, shit. I'm going to be late. Shit, shit, shit!

When I arrive at my parents' 1930s semi in the village of Boxley, my mother is arranging some 'tapas'. It sounds exotic, but they actually have very little Spanish influence other than a tub of olives from the local supermarket. No matter what the weather or time of year, if you visit my parents at approximately six thirty, the chime will ring out, 'Tapas, dear?' to which my father will arrange the cushions for the outside chairs and put on some Neil Diamond. If it's cold, he will collect a couple of blankets. Even in minus temperatures he has his pre-dinner bottle of beer whilst Mum treats herself to a gin and tonic. She treats herself on a daily basis. Apparently drinking with someone else is okay.

This afternoon, the tapas consist of taramasalata, peanuts, crisps and a rather sad-looking bowl of olives with tiny cubes of oil-drenched feta cheese.

'Everyone is in the garden,' Mum says, and I know this is her way of saying everyone but you. I lean down and kiss her soft, powdery cheek. She is a tiny woman, although her late fifties have seen an expansion in the waistline. Unfortunately, she is reluctant to acknowledge the extra pounds and refuses to go up a size in clothes. This means flesh is pushed up and out by waistlines, seams and bras. She likes to wear slacks and tight-fitting jumpers in pastel colours. She says they complement her complexion and the baby-blond hair she wears in the same style she wore when she was twenty. Katie has taken after her, but Emma and I have missed out on the tiny delicate genes. We are both tall, like my father, although Emma seems to be broader in shoulder and shoe fit.

'You look nice,' I say.

She visibly softens. 'You look a bit peaky.'

'Do I? Oh, work is a bit stressful at the moment.'

'That's a shame.'

Mum thinks I am just playing at jobs, like we did when we played post offices as kids. With her plastic date stamp and tiny envelopes, my older sister Emma was always the postmistress, whilst I was the postman. I never got to touch the date stamp. Mum assumes that when I stop playing I will do what every woman is supposed to do – marry and have babies. She thinks there is something wrong with me. There must be. Why else does every man I have been out with leave? Too much sarcasm, is one of the suggestions.

'No Josie?' She slices into a radish. There are little radish flowers lined up on her chopping board. It's a new board, bought to go with the new, recently fitted kitchen.

It's a bit of a mystery to me why they bothered. Everything is exactly the same as before; just cleaner. The one new addition to the model is the inclusion of drawers that silently glide in and out. Mum isn't sure about them. She prefers to slam.

'No, she said thank you for the offer, but she had to get back to London.'

Not only has Josie adopted my flat as her own, but she has also adopted my family. It's not that she hasn't got one, but she prefers mine.

'Has she thought about setting the date yet?'

'No, not yet.'

'Who would have thought Josie would get engaged. It just goes to prove, there's someone for everyone.' She stops slicing and stares out of the window. 'My word, how time flies. What with Katie and Lawrence next year . . . well, that will be it.'

'You never know, Mum,' I say indignantly. 'I might surprise you with an announcement one day.'

My mother turns and looks at me as if I'm a puppy about to be put down. I can see that she wants to say something, but for once in her life she's holding back. I pick up a bowl of crisps.

'You know you could have brought another friend, don't you?' she says.

'Like who?'

'You know, a friend, friend.' She nods to the floor as if this will tell me all I need to know.

'I don't know what you mean,' I say, because I don't. Why does she think I need a friend to keep me company?

'Your father and I are very open-minded. Louise Donovan brought her friend home the other day and Carol said she was quite nice. She said she was really quite pretty, and not what she expected at all. She had long, curly hair. I thought they were all skinheads.'

I look at my mother and wonder what exactly goes on behind those blue eyes.

'Mum, I am not a lesbian.'

'Well . . .'

'I'm not!'

She doesn't believe me. I can see she doesn't. I make my way to the patio before the conversation goes any further.

Everyone is sitting around the white plastic patio table, braving the chilly spring weather. They are all dressed in sweaters and jackets, their eyes bright and noses red. Dad is proudly flipping things on his new birthday gas barbecue. He is not part of the conversation and seems quite happy in his own little world, which is the one he mostly inhabits, much to my mother's consternation. Everyone sings hi and resumes their conversations. Emma is poker-faced and reprimanding her twin six-year-old daughters, Bethany and Victoria, for picking the heads off Grandma's flowers. Despite their very English-sounding names, they are Chinese. After years of fertility problems, Emma and Alan were lucky enough to adopt them at birth. They are cute, very cute, with their shiny black hair and round faces, but appearances are deceptive. Bethany and Victoria are horrid children and we are all hoping it's just a phase. They look at their mother in the way that only devil children can, their pretty, matching dresses hiding the evil that lies inside. I am joking – a little.

Katie, the youngest and prettiest of my parents' daughters, is cooing over her three-month-old little boy Alfie, whilst her partner Lawrence talks football with Alan. Lawrence doesn't like football but he is making the effort because he knows it makes Katie happy. I feel for him because I also try hard with Alan. Talking to him is a necessity rather than a pleasure. His voice never strays from the one monotonous tone and his conversation topics are chosen for the quality of their ability to bore one rigid. He talks of miles to the gallon, the price of petrol, and everything you need to know about Bob Dylan.

I walk over to my father and hug him from behind.

'Hello, munchkin,' he says, and hugs me back.

'Happy birthday. I bought you something you are going to love,' I say excitedly.

'You always do.' He hugs me close again. This is the man I want. Someone who thinks I am near perfect despite missing his last birthday. I went away with Jason. I clearly made the wrong decision.

'What do you think of my shiny new barbecue?' He flips a burger on to the waiting rack to demonstrate its versatility.

'But does it have the smoky, unpredictable appeal of a real barbecue?' I ask. This is an ongoing discussion. Dad knows my opinion on gas versus real barbecues. As far as I'm concerned, he has sold out and I don't hide my disgust.

'I thought you might say that, but your argument is outdated, my dear. See these little wooden chips? They can give me hickory, smoky, thyme, burnt – all those aromas of your old barbecue at a moment's notice.'

'That's like saying you can have all the qualities of Heinz tomato soup without the Heinz,' I reply, removing the metal spatula from his hand and attempting a few flips for myself.

'My darling old-fashioned girl.'

'Is that like sensible and predictable?'

'You make them sound like swear words.'

'Wouldn't you rather be daring and exciting, rather than sensible and predictable – old fashioned, even?' I mutter, poking savagely at a sausage. Dad removes the spatula from my hand.

'Harriet, daring and exciting are good in short bursts, and they have their place, but in the same way a tequila slammer is good for a couple of minutes, you wouldn't want them all the time.'

'What do you know about tequila slammers?' I ask, surprised. Is my father leading a secret life, baring his belly up on a podium whilst eighteen year olds beg to stroke his chest hair?

'I haven't always been your dad,' he replies, smiling at me. 'What I'm trying to say is the tequila is good but, most of the time, what you really want is a nice orange juice or a cup of tea.'

I grimace. I don't want to be a bloody orange juice! My father senses my disgust because he knows me better than most.

'Or a lovely glass of wine with aromas of honey and peach . . .' He looks at me and holds my chin in his fingers, just as he did when I was little and I refused to listen to him. 'There is a lot to be said for old fashioned. It says endearing and lovable.'

'It says Miss Marple,' I say, and he laughs. I like my father's laugh. It is gentle and true. There is nothing false about him, and sometimes I wonder what it was that attracted him to my mother. Not that she is false, but she cares more about what other people think and her laugh can sometimes be for them. He gently pulls the end of my hair and I smile. I cannot imagine a time when he wasn't my lovely dad. He has always looked like this: tall, bald, with long arms, big hands and an oval face with deep creases that run from his nose to his chin. I cannot imagine him without us. We are his four seasons. I think I'm autumn, although maybe I'm winter. I seem to remember Emma getting upset about being winter.

I take a seat next to Katie and say hello to baby Alfie. He gurgles happily. Like his mum, he is a sunny little boy with a smile for everyone.

'He really looks like you, Katie,' Emma observes.

'Do you think?' Katie asks, pleased. 'Do you think he does, Harry?'

I look at Alfie. He looks like a baby, but he is a lovely one and Katie is lovely too. She is slim and polar-bear blond, with a peaches-and-cream complexion and an uncomplicated nature. What you see is what you get with Katie and she sees the positive in everything and everyone.

'He is beautiful, just like you,' I reply, and I am rewarded with a sunshine smile.

'Is everything ready, Daddy?' My mother's voice calls out. I cringe every time she calls him this. We are all over the age of ten, for heaven's sake. Lawrence exchanges a look with Katie, and I cringe all over again on behalf of my mother. Dad surveys his sizzling masterpieces.

'Yes, everything is good to go,' he replies, transferring the sausages, tuna steak and vegetarian sausages for Katie, on to two serving dishes. Mum disappears back into the kitchen for the salad although, by the look of everyone, we could do with hot soup.

Katie hands me Alfie and he is happy for approximately three minutes before he starts crying for his mum. I hand him back quickly. I am not good with babies, not until they are four years old and can talk to me. Josie says this makes them children. As I said, I am not good with babies. I am maternal, but not just yet. Having said that, I did have a couple of fantasies about the lovely dark-haired, brown-eyed children I would have had with Jason. Was I being presumptuous? Maybe, but when he moved in, it was out of love and not convenience. There was a chance of Jason being sent somewhere else with his job – we were hoping Italy – so any plans to buy somewhere together were put on hold. We were building a future and when we talked, there was definitely a we in there somewhere. Now I am beginning to doubt myself. Did I hear what I wanted to hear? I want to phone him and just check my facts; check that I am not going mad and remembering a life that wasn't mine. I want to ask him when he stopped saying I love you and meaning it. The weekend he met Sophie he phoned me three times and each time finished the call with a 'love you'. Guilt or indecision? Did I say something that swung it her way? I shall never know.

'Can I have another bottle of beer, Dee?' my father calls out.

'I'll get you one,' I say, and get up.

Mum swoops on me as I open the fridge, her small, now slightly podgy hands pushing the door closed. She has coordinated her nail varnish with the pink of her lipstick, which is also a theme continued in her choice of jumper. A sequinned poodle adorns the front. It's hideous.

'What are you looking for?' she asks accusingly.

'A beer for Dad,' I say, a little put out that she is acting as if I'm about to steal the contents of her fridge.

'He shouldn't drink so much.'

'Two on his birthday is hardly drinking to excess.'

I begin to open the fridge again, but she pushes the door and nearly severs my fingers.

'What are you hiding?' I ask.

'Emma says she wants the trifle to be a surprise.'

I raise my eyes to the heavens.

'Take the salad bowl and I'll bring the beer out, but I wish you wouldn't encourage him, Harriet. I don't want two alcoholics in the family.'

'I am not an alcoholic,' I protest, and then realise I sound as if I am one.

I take the salad and head outside.

Eventually, at the request of Katie, who thinks Alfie may develop hypothermia, we all move inside for dessert and presents. Emma does the big trifle moment. She has sparklers. Everyone oohs and aahs at the delicate chocolate swirls on top.

'Did you make them yourself?' I ask. Yes, I am being childish, but I can't help it.

Emma opens her mouth to speak.

'She's been taking lessons,' Alan pipes up. 'She's been at it for weeks now.'

Blimey, she did make them. That's what you do when you have too much time on your hands. That, and ironing handkerchiefs and pants. That's what she does for Alan. He is a man without creases.

Emma glares at her husband and a red blotch floods her neckline.

'Well, that's a lovely thought. Thank you,' Dad says, smiling.

Emma looks around the table and is back to being superior. Dad puts the spoon in and performs the ceremony of the first spoonful. We all hold our breath and wait for the gloop, but it doesn't come. Katie and Lawrence stifle a giggle. I look at my older 'I've got to be good at everything' sister. Her smile says she doesn't care.

Emma and I have never been close and our relationship never gets further than the time enforced by family gatherings, where we tolerate each other. She doesn't like it that I remind her of who she is and, according to her, actively conspire to ruin everything she does. This is a lie. Getting drunk at her anniversary party and snogging the golf professional was not a planned affront to her sensitivities, but rather a reaction to the thing he did with his fingers on the palm of my hand, and one too many glasses of champagne. She was disappointed in me, nearly as much as she is with Prince Charles, who refused her invitation to be the patron of her fundraising activities, and Alan, who could be a lot more dynamic at the golf club but isn't.

I don't like it that Emma talks in a posh accent and pretends. She pretends to be interested, she pretends to like people and she pretends to forget to ask Mum to her fundraising events.

'It's a traditional trifle with a fruit coulis instead of jelly,' Emma says haughtily.

'That's lovely. Isn't that lovely, George? Jelly is very common now,' Mum pipes up, and begins serving.

By the time I get home, I am exhausted from making polite conversation with Alan about the benefits of pensions, chasing the evil twins, who were wearing one each of my new boots around the garden, and the wrath of my mother after the present to my father was unwrapped. It was a new tent for his fishing. My mother thinks he spends too much time outside on his own and she cannot understand why he wants to sit in the dark for hours on end, instead of watching *Strictly Come Dancing*. My father adores my mother; it is clear in the way he looks at her, but I suspect his consistent adoration has been achieved by time away from her to dwell on it. Emma bought him a rare, limited-edition book and a framed photograph of her and the twins, whilst Katie bought him some thermal socks and a ridiculous-looking deerstalker hat. He will wear, it of course. If one of his daughters told him to hop on one leg for three days, I suspect he would consider it. It makes me feel safe.

I slump on the sofa with a cup of tea and consider a nice, hot, relaxing bath. First, though – Aaah, I have a message from Space Cowboy. Ye-ha!

Hey Belle
Shall we say Thursday 8pm?

I panic. It's a bit soon. I look in my diary. There is nothing there. I'm busy, I must be. My father's words come back to haunt me. I don't want to be the orange juice girl any more. She doesn't get the boy or the job. Okay, it's a yes.

This morning I leave Martha's *Guardian* and buy my own copy. Josie has promised to keep her eyes open for anything that might be of interest, but we both know that my CV says washed-up regional, rather than hot-off-the-press. I scour the Internet for tips on making myself ready for the job market but I can't help feeling I want to stay and fight my corner. The prospect of being pushed out of my job by a girl called Poppy is not something I want to consider. This girl goes when she wants to and not before time. Please don't let it be before time. Let me be fabulous first.

A bright pink Post-it note is stuck to my computer screen. The words 'Predictable Rocks!' are written in black marker pen. I smile. Stuck to my phone is another one, with the words 'Predictable is the new Black'.

'What are you laughing about?' Judith asks, and I jump out of my skin.

'Oh nothing, just Ed being Ed.'

'And that is?'

'Funny, a dickhead – I could go on,' I reply, smiling.

'He has a girlfriend, you know.'

Judith flicks her long blond hair. It looks as if it has been polished. Perhaps she has an army of little women who shine her hair with little cloths made of fairy wings.

'And your point is? Men and women can be friends, you know.'

'Not according to Harry, they can't.'

'Me?'

'No, Harry in *When Harry Met Sally*.'

I look at Judith and wonder what lies beneath those big baby-blue eyes. I have wondered for the last three years and the answer still eludes me.

'Judith, it's a theory that makes the film work, but this is real life. Surely you have male friends?'

'No.'

Judith wanders off to her pc and reapplies her lipstick as she waits for it to boot up. I watch her pucker up and then pucker up some more. It strikes me that in Judith's world there is no such thing as a male friend, because they must all fancy her.

I check my diary and realise with a sinking heart that I have to: 1. Attend a preview of three men with violins and moustaches reciting Chekov, and 2. Accompany a girl and her mother who have agreed to review a performance by a group of thirteen year olds calling themselves Precocious Puberty Presents. I also need to chase up images and listings for my 'what's on during the school holidays' piece. Josie emails me to tell me she is having a nightmare getting Gwyneth to agree to the images they want to use, has just been delivered a basket of muffins from George Clooney's people, to apologise about changing their interview date, and is moaning because she has to attend the *Elle* Style Awards ceremony tonight. I tell her I don't want to be her friend any more.

'Why?' Josie asks, laughing.

'Because here I am psyching myself up for two hours of listening to a group of pretentious thirteen year olds murdering a musical I have seen at least twenty times in the last ten years.' I take a deep breath. 'And you, Miss Green, are moaning about attending the *Elle* Style Awards with your gob full of George Clooney's muffins!'

Josie laughs loudly.

'Hey, everything loses its sparkle in the end. I have been going to the awards for years and it's boring now. I would much rather be having sex on a full stomach of my boyfriend's gorgeous home-made curry than listening to the same old public masturbation.'

'See, now you are just taunting me.'

Josie laughs again.

'So tell me. When's the big date?' she asks.

'Thursday night.'

'Oh my God!' Josie screams down the phone. 'What's his name?'

'Space Cowboy.'

'I mean his real name?'

'Clive.'

'Clive – the cowboy?'

'He doesn't look like a Clive, though.'

I don't admit to my own disappointment at the revelation of his name. What's in a name? He looks like a Raif. I could call him Cowboy, or Boy. He could call me Babe.

'Make sure you phone me before and after.'

'I will, don't worry.'

'I am so excited.'

'Me too,' I reply, because I am. My first date and it's all happened so quickly. Perhaps I won't need to have any more after Thursday. On Friday morning I may be cancelling my subscription. I may be late in, with my eyeliner smudged sexily under my eyes after a night of talking and sexual tension, my hair a little dishevelled from his hands – his impatient hands.

Girl Without a Date in Her Diary – Blog entry – April 4th

In a couple of days I meet my first DateMate. SC is a man of few words. His approach has been direct and to the point. If this is a clue to his skills in the flirting or foreplay area then perhaps I should cancel. I wonder how many women he has met before me and if it was them or him that didn't cut the mustard? What will he be like? It's hard to tell from a description, four emails and a photo. The photos are small on DateMate and often taken on holiday. In his, he is leaning on a motorbike with a parched desert behind him. As I said, it's hard to tell.

What is the etiquette for this kind of thing? Is it like speed dating with an allotted time to ask as many questions as you can? Do you, can you, what is your opinion on . . . ? It feels as if I am going on to the *X Factor:* 'It's a no from me! You lack charisma and style . . . Next!'

It doesn't feel like a first date. First dates are romantic and usually come after the initial meeting. This means you have already seen, spoken and liked them enough to say yes. You already know their smell and the colour of their eyes. I remember meeting J for the first time. He smelled slightly citrusy and his nails were all the same length and smooth as if filed. No, this is nothing like a first date. This is something completely different. It lacks something integral to the whole process of falling in love. Some people do, though. There are stories of people finding their DateMate soulmates. A friend of a friend of a friend met someone over the Internet and is now extolling its virtues to anyone who is listening. They are madly in love, she says. They met after thirteen dates. Hah, unlucky for some, she also likes to say. Thirteen dates? I haven't got time for thirteen dates! I haven't got that many outfits.

Girl Without a Date in Her Diary – Blog entry – April 6th

I'm feeling sick. What if we don't like each other? Do we throw our hankies on the table and leave, or do we paint a smile and stay? I'm thinking, stay for as long as you can bear it, because nobody likes to hurt other people's feelings; except, of course, my elder sister. I haven't got a hankie. Perhaps we should have a sign. If I fiddle with my ear, it's a good sign. If I check my phone, it means I like you as a person but you're not the one for me?

P.S. I can't call him Clive. Clive says grey underpants and holes in his socks. Clive says boring. Is it okay to change someone's name? Or not say it at all? I had an uncle called Clive. He used to put his hand in his pocket and rummage. He said it was his small change but it wasn't. Nothing jingled.

What star sign is he? What if he is a Scorpio or a Capricorn? I can't believe I didn't ask.

Good questions to ask either on or before a first date (with hindsight, I think it should be before):

What star sign are you?
Are you married?
What colour are your sheets?

After trying on countless combinations, I go for glamorous rock chick with jeans and heels. My first instinct was to wear flats, but I want to feel sexy and Space Cowboy is a six-footer, so it shouldn't be a problem. I try to tousle my hair but it looks more Edward Scissorhands than come-to-bed siren and I have to perform a last-minute rescue operation and brush it out. Now my hair is flying out at all angles, attaching itself to everyone's jackets. I nervously make my way through the pub. The noise level is high and it's busy with students and people eating pies and gravy around scrubbed pine tables. I feel sick with anticipation. What will he look like? Will he like me? Please let him like me. Stand up straight. It's going to be okay. It is. What's the worst that can happen?

I look around and a couple of men catch my eye but there is no one who looks remotely like Space Cowboy. My heart sinks. I have been stood up. Bloody typical! I turn to go, when I feel a hand on my arm.

'Harriet?'

I am expecting a Kiefer Sutherland lookalike with a light stubble and taut stomach, ready to whisk me off on his motorbike to LA or Bristol. This is not what I get. My stomach lurches to the floor.

'Cowb . . . Clive?' I ask, and nearly choke on the

words. He doesn't look sexy or dangerous. He is five foot eight with a large ornate belt that's too small for his pot belly. His heeled boots have spurs. Five foot seven.

'Shall we get a drink?' He turns and walks off, clearly expecting me to follow him. He has a Harley Davidson motif on the back of his leather jacket. I consider turning and running, but I can't bring myself to do it, because that would be rude. Yep – predictable with good manners.

'So, gorgeous. We found each other,' he says, displaying more confidence than he should.

'You take a good photo,' I croak.

He looks at least fifteen years older than he should. He definitely had more hair in the photo and less fat in the cheek area.

'Thanks, you're pretty good looking too.'

I am too shocked to speak and when the barman asks what we want to drink, I am lost for words. My mind is in free fall. I don't have a hankie or a sign. We never discussed signs. Clive looks at me. 'Let me guess, you're a vodka-and-pineapple-juice lady?'

'Wine, actually,' I reply, not sure if I should be laughing or not.

'White or red?' the barman asks.

'White,' I squeak.

'A pint of Fosters for me and a glass of the house white for the little lady.' He laughs at his own joke. I don't, because it's not funny.

'Actually, can I look at the wine list?' I ask the barman, and Clive the Cowboy raises his eyebrows.

'Large or small?'

That's a stupid question. We take our drinks and sit down at a table.

'So are you always this fussy?' he asks, and I look at him, not sure what he means.

'Can I have a look at the wine list?' he says, doing a bad imitation of my voice.

'I didn't say it like that.'

'You did.'

'So is this your first time?' I ask, changing the subject. I want to poke his eyes out but feel that perhaps his real personality has yet to shine through. Yes, personality is more important than looks or the way someone dresses, or the fact that they are an irritating idiot. Perhaps it's nerves.

'No, I've met about eight girls, but none of them has revved my engine – whereas you . . .' He starts singing: 'If I told you, you had a beautiful body, would you hold it against me?'

People look round and I want to slide under the table. I am in a nightmare I cannot wake up from. Somebody help me? Anybody? Ed's girlfriend Noush completes the horror by appearing at our table. I look around for Ed. If he is here I will never live it down. Please God, no.

'Harry, how are you?'

A Polish model with legs longer than my dad's ladders, Noush is so skinny I worry about her in high winds. She doesn't speak that much English, but I get the impression that their relationship isn't exactly based on lengthy intellectual conversations.

'Noush, what a surprise. Are you here with Ed?'

'Ed? No, he is . . . how you say?' she does a batting action with her arm. Her tiny breasts jiggle inside her T-shirt and I can see Clive is transfixed. At some point his good qualities have got to shine through – haven't they?

'Tennis?' I suggest. Noush shakes her head.

'Squash?'

'Badminton?'

Noush continues to shake her head and then smiles. 'Cricket,' she says.

'Oh, okay,' I say, surprised, because her miming skills didn't point to that and I didn't know Ed played cricket.

'Okay, bye,' she says, and is dragged off by other beautiful people into a night more glamorous than mine. Clive watches her go and I want to tell him to shut his mouth.

'Great arse for a skinny bird.'

'It's not very polite to comment on another woman's physical attributes,' I point out.

'Are you always this stroppy?'

'I am not stroppy!' I snap back, feeling as if my eyes will pop out of my head in indignation. Clive stands up.

'You know what, darling; this is not going to work,' he says, and walks out of the pub. His spurs make a noise like empty cans.

To say that I am shocked is an understatement. I look around to see if anyone noticed, but no one is laughing out loud. How dare he! How dare he walk out before me!

I am not sure whether to laugh or cry. I search faces for recognition but it seems nobody noticed my little bubble burst. The noise of the pub surrounds me like a blanket. I want to go home, but if I leave now, everyone will know. If I sit here for a while they will think it was meant to happen; that the guy I was with didn't actually walk out on me but probably went to the toilet. Eventually, I will be able to sneak off. I'll finish my wine and crisps first; then I'll leave. Shit, shit, shit. I had such high hopes. Tonight was going to be my night. Tomorrow was going to be a beautiful day full of hope and promise and . . . This slightly ludicrous thought makes me want to laugh out loud. What an idiot I am. I was so sure I was going to meet the One, that it was going to be that easy. A little optimistic, you might say. Stupid, would be my sister Emma's choice of words. It was funny, though. I phone Josie.

'Hi, I wasn't expecting to hear from you so soon. So

how is the cowboy? Putting his stirrups on?' Josie laughs at her own brilliance.

'Oh Josie, he was horrid, it was awful.'

'Was?'

'He's just walked out!'

'But you've only been there twenty minutes.'

'I know. I would have walked out myself after five, but I was worried about hurting his feelings – little prick.'

'I bet it was.'

'What?'

'Little. And I bet he wears a thong.'

I laugh at the thought and immediately feel better. A man with a guitar walks past the table and smiles at me. I blush slightly and smile back. He takes to the microphone and welcomes us all. His name is Chad. His shirt sleeves are rolled up to reveal muscular tattooed arms. He holds his guitar close with the gaze of a man in love. I am mesmerised. I tell Josie I have to go.

Chad's songs are sad and beautiful. The room fills with an appreciative audience and I am surrounded by people nodding their heads. Everyone applauds. When he finishes, I could go home, but what will I do when I get there? Watch TV? I get myself another drink. When I return, there is a girl sitting in the seat next to me. She smiles.

'Wasn't he awesome?' Her accent is American.

'Excellent,' I reply. 'Is this a one-off?'

'No, just every other Thursday. I'm Kath,' the girl says, 'and this is Kyle and Raj.' She introduces me to two guys standing nearby.

I hold out my hand and they shake it warmly.

'This is Kyle's sister now.' She points to a girl in a floaty dress and hobnail boots. 'She's awesome.'

I open up my second packet of crisps and tell them to

help themselves. The singer called Chad walks by and I swear we share a moment.

'Wow, that singer just gave me a look,' Kath says, and with the confidence of a child she follows him up to the bar.

I bet she has never done Internet dating.

'Another packet of crisps?' Raj asks. Raj smells beautiful.

Girl Without a Date in Her Diary – Blog entry – April 6th

Okay, so the cowboy didn't turn out to be the One. We were not going to ride off into the sunset and watch the stars appear around a camp fire. It lasted minutes, not hours, and that was too long. Did I say he walked out on me? Oh, the humiliation. I was ready to slink back home and cry into my hot chocolate, but instead I found myself enjoying an acoustic gig at the Jug and Mutton. There must be a lesson here. Don't waste time sitting in front of the computer talking to strangers. Get out there and talk to strangers. Tonight I shared a polystyrene tray of rubbish chips with a mad American and a beautiful-smelling boy called Raj. Raj was gay, but his friends weren't. There were lots of them there tonight. It was like being in a beer-soaked sweet shop. Unfortunately, I didn't fancy any of them, but I did learn about something called the string theory and that reindeer like bananas. I also learned that it's not as scary as I thought it would be to do something on my own.

Ed ambles over to my desk. He reminds me of an elephant. Not because he is big, because he isn't – in fact, he is a bit too skinny. It's the way he walks. You never see Ed run anywhere, or get upset, or angry. Ed is a bit of an enigma and I have no idea what drives him, if anything, other than his photography.

'Noush says she saw you last night.'

I am ready for this and have my credible story all lined up.

'Yeah, I was interviewing some guy who runs motorbike taster sessions.' I cannot look at him when I do this. If I lie to my computer it doesn't count.

'Oh, wow, I'd be interested. You'll have to give me his number.'

Bugger! I nod, and return my attention to my computer. This conversation is now over. He remains on the edge of my desk, swinging one of his legs in time to a tune I can't hear.

'Noush thought he was your boyfriend.'

'What?' I turn to him, my shock palpable. I can't believe Noush would think I'd be with someone who looked like that, someone who watched her breasts jiggle.

'Yeah, I told her it wouldn't be.'

I wait for more. There is always more.

'Because if you had a new boyfriend, we would all know about it. You start to bounce and I haven't seen you bounce for ages.'

'You make me sound like Bambi,' I reply, wishing I felt like bouncing now.

'More like one of those birds with the long stick legs.'

'What, a flamingo? They don't bounce.'

'No, they have long, pointy beaks and round bodies.'

'I don't have either.'

'Mmmm . . . pointy beak?'

I hit him hard on the leg and he jumps up from the desk.

'Fuck. That hurt!'

I smile sweetly.

'You just gave me a dead leg,' he complains.

'Let that be a lesson to you. Never mess with a woman who is without bounce.'

'You don't have to be.'

'What, are you offering yourself up?'

'No!' He sounds offended. 'I was actually thinking there must be loads of blokes who would love to go out with you.'

Sometimes I love Ed.

'So where are they? I was out last night and not one of them was interested. Okay, I wasn't particularly interested in them, except for the gay one, but that's not the point. I never get chatted up.'

'Probably because you're scary looking.'

'First predictable and now I'm scary looking? Thanks a bunch!'

'No, I meant that you look like you won't suffer fools gladly. You have that look.'

'What look?'

'That look.' He points to my face.

I don't even realise I am giving a look.

'How do I stop giving the look?' I ask, worried.

'I don't know.'

'Well, that's great. Now you've made me paranoid about a look I don't know I'm doing.'

'I'll tell you from now on. If it helps, your eyes go a little wide.' He attempts an impression of me. 'Jez, over here, mate.' He motions Jeremy over.

'Has Harry got a look?' Ed asks him.

'Yeah,' Jeremy nods.

'And how would you describe that look?' Ed perseveres like an interviewer on daytime TV.

'Like she wants you to jump up and down on one leg.'

Ed nods in agreement. They both look at me in a self-satisfied, knowing way.

'Bugger off, I have work to do,' I snap and stare at my brainstorming circle. Inside this circle are the words sexy and breath of fresh air. There are lines leading from it, with tiny satellite circles on the end of them. These are empty, waiting for my flashes of brilliance. What can I do to make the What's On page everything it isn't?

An hour later, the circles have been transformed into flowers and faces. I rest my head on the desk in frustration. Where is fabulous when I need it?

'Perhaps you should go to bed earlier?' Georgina's voice purrs. I am scared to look up, but I do. My face is burning. I smile weakly but Georgina's face shows no sign of amusement.

'It's g-g-g-good for inspiration to . . . cut out all stimuli . . . to zone out and . . . then you are more receptive to creativity.' The stammer makes it less convincing. Georgina raises her eyebrows to an unnatural level.

'Is that so?' she asks, and looks vaguely amused. She is the cat and I am the mouse.

'You know what I'm thinking, Harry?'

That Poppy Darling probably has inspiration oozing from her freshly oxygen facialised pores? That Poppy Darling exists on two hours' sleep? That Poppy Darling is already running around Soho House interviewing star guests in the way that only she can? I shake my head that no, I don't know what she is thinking.

'That Poppy will be good for us all.'

I stare into my computer like a child told there will be no birthday this year.

'When does she start?'

'We're hoping to have her first column ready for July's or August's issue.'

I close my eyes. I have just two or three months to come up with something better than an It girl with famous friends. Now I have two deadlines to keep me awake. How many days until Chloe's wedding? Not as many as I would like. I sigh. It's an exaggerated one.

I have begun to sigh a lot; quite loudly, as if I am trying to blow all the air out of my whole body. I didn't realise I was doing this until Judith began tutting. Sensing my unhappiness, she has invited me to attend her Sunday evening service, but I have declined. I may look in need of salvation, but God is not going to deliver on this one. I need something that says my section is a must read, although if nobody is reading the magazine, there isn't much point.

The office has a dejected, almost desperate air about it. Nobody says anything, but it's there; in the way we all stop talking when Georgina appears, the unspoken pressure to work through our lunch hours and the coffee changing from filter to instant. More insidious is the chocolate thing. Giant bars of Cadbury's chocolate are now a staple of our afternoons, because a sugar rush is the only high we can look forward to. I bought the minty bubble one and then Judith bought the biscuity one, and now it's an unwritten rule that the top of the filing cabinet is never without something chocolate. So as circulation and advertising figures fall, our waist measurements are doing the opposite. At this rate I will be as big as a house, which doesn't bode well for Chloe's wedding. I have enrolled in a gym, but have yet to go. Anyway, there is no point in starting until Monday – no point at all. This weekend is going to be packed full of empty calories – the ones that have no place in your life and do irreparable damage to your thighs, the ones that make you smile. We are talking cake and alcohol.

With half an hour to go before the weekend, I log on to DateMate for some light entertainment. There is a message in my inbox and despite my disaster with Space Cowboy I am intrigued. It's the second one from Wordsmith. I take another peek at his photo. Quirky looking, but in a safe way that people at a wedding would like. Second time lucky? No. No! I'm not putting myself through all that again. I'm going to trust in that old thing called fate.

As the train leaves Bath for Paddington, I sigh with relief. I am looking forward to a nice weekend away. The week has done little to ease my sense of unease. I can feel Poppy Darling's sweet minty breath on my neck as she waits for me to vacate my chair. Yesterday, as I closed down my pc and wished everyone a good weekend, I realised I have never hated my job, but have just gradually become disenchanted by my own diminishing drive and Georgina's lack of imagination. Between the two of us, we have ensured I have become like a stale old loaf, being made into the same sandwiches, day in, day out.

Well, I have decided I am not going to give it up

without a fight. Getting a new job somewhere else is not the answer. It's a quick fix and running away from what I care about; what I want. What happened to the modern-day Jane Austen doing her thing? Come on, Harriet, this is no time to be giving up. Hand me my bonnet: I am going to be the one who turns *Life to Live* around; not Poppy Darling whatshername. I am going to be the one who is responsible for saving not only my own page, but the whole magazine. Then I can consider my position. I want success to be a word that people (mainly Jason) associate with me. Harriet Peel? She may be predictable, but she is a sexy, successful predictable.

I walk with purpose, my head held high, through the ticket barrier.

'Miss? Miss?' a man's voice calls out. 'Miss!'

People are looking at me. I turn to see a rail guard chasing after me, waving his ticket machine. I colour with embarrassment.

'Your ticket please, miss,' he says with red-faced irritation.

'Sorry, I have it here somewhere.'

I spend the next five minutes searching through my handbag. People are looking at me and I feel like a criminal. I try to think sexy and successful. I smile my brightest smile. The guard frowns back.

'Ticket?'

'I have it here. I know I have,' I simper.

Twenty minutes later I am paying for my ticket again.

Everyone is already at the Dorchester when I arrive. We are here to celebrate Chloe's thirtieth birthday with afternoon tea. Chloe, who likes themes, insisted that this was a very *Sex and the City* thing to do (if it was based in London), and we are all dressed accordingly, with dresses, heels and the latest must-have handbags according to, and designed by, Chloe. Mine is decorated with appliquéd red satin roses and goes beautifully with my new cocktail dress with its full skirt and net petticoat.

The hotel is muted and tasteful, with palm fronds and gold-edged crockery. Josie is here along with mutual friends Vicky, Lucy and Chloe's sister Tamara and friend Zoe. There is lots of hugging and air-kissing amidst a cacophony of squeals and gossip. My traumatic week is soon forgotten as I catch up with everyone's lives. With Chloe and Josie in London, the opportunities to get together are few and far between, but it never seems to matter. We laugh and eat and my fitted satin bodice struggles with both.

'So come on, Harry, we are all dying to hear more about this Internet dating,' Vicky urges. She says it as if it's something dirty, like finding hair down a plughole.

'Josie?' I glare at her. It was meant to be a secret. I can't believe she has blabbed.

She shrugs her shoulders. 'It's on your blog.'

She has a point.

'But I don't want anyone else to know Girl Without a Date in Her Diary is me.'

'Your secret is safe with us,' Chloe promises.

'Tell Tamara about the cowboy,' Lucy urges. 'You're going to love this.' She nudges Tamara.

A good-looking waiter interrupts with offers of more champagne and prompts a shocking display of flirting. Unfortunately, it doesn't distract them for long and I eventually give in and tell them all about Clive the Cowboy. Their response is one of uncontrollable laughter and looks of horror.

'I think it's very brave of you, Harry. I have to admit, I wouldn't do it, even if I was desperate,' Vicky says.

'Me neither, but I love your blog. It makes me feel better about Jim. He may not be the perfect husband, but the alternative . . . urgh!' Lucy says, shuddering.

'Thanks,' I reply. This is making me feel so much better.

The laughter continues into a champagne-cocktail-fuelled night and by the time we get back to our boutique hotel, we can barely speak, let alone walk. It is not a dignified entrance.

The next morning we are all looking grey and worn, except for Chloe who is remarkably fresh-faced and full of energy. We sit down to breakfast, and talk inevitably turns towards the wedding; of shoes, hen-night options and colour schemes.

'I was thinking of a fairy cake tower.'

We all agree that is a marvellous idea.

'And arriving on a white unicorn, like Liv Tyler in *Lord of the Rings*?'

We all agree that this is a dreadful idea.

'Or on the back of pizza delivery boy's bike? How cool would that be?'

We all look at Chloe as if she has finally taken cool to the edge of crap.

'I assume Jason is still coming?' I hate myself for asking. I might as well stab myself with my fork.

Chloe nods. 'Sorry, Harry.'

'It's okay,' I say, because I want her to think it is. Chloe has always felt responsible for introducing Jason to me in the first place and blamed herself for my ensuing heartbreak. What's he doing? Where's he going? Who's he with? My questions were endless and my pain without boundaries. She was really good, bless her, and still is, but I don't ask any more. Except today. Today, I couldn't help myself. I guess I was secretly hoping that she would tell me he had changed his mind, broken his leg, or that Sophie's hair had fallen out.

'You'll be in love with someone else by then. I have faith in the power of DateMate to deliver,' Josie tells me with certainty.

'I'm not sure I want to do it any more.'

'Oh come on. It makes for a great read. The girls in the office love your blog,' Lucy says.

'Do they?'

'Callie said that it inspired her to go to a gig the other night.'

'Wow! And?' I ask.

'She said she hated it. The toilets were really dirty and it was a bit loud.'

'Come on, Harry. The single and disillusioned women of the world need you. What you're doing is a public service.'

'How do you work that out?' I ask.

'It makes them feel better, it inspires them. It says, don't give up yet, because I'm not . . . true love is out there.'

'I think you're building my part up a bit,' I say, although I like the thought of it.

Maybe I could persuade Georgina to give me my own column in *Life to Live*. Tips for dating for the modern woman? The thought makes me laugh.

'The cowboy was just a practice session,' Josie says. 'Now we need to look at our strategy, examine the mistakes and make sure it doesn't happen again.'

'You make it sound like a military operation.'

'Madonna didn't get those thighs by watching other people do Bikram Yoga,' she says.

'You've lost me.'

'It takes dedication to get what you want. The

foundations are there to make Operation DateMate successful. We just need to build on them.'

'I don't know,' I reply. 'I'm not sure if I can cope with another date like the cowboy.'

'Do you want a date for the wedding?' Josie asks.

'Yes.'

'Do you want Jason to be sick with jealousy?'

'Yes.'

'Then we need commitment. Yes, chef?'

'Yes, chef!'

'I think it might have been a mistake to have the full breakfast,' she says, looking a bit green.

'Wait!' I shout to the man with the whistle. My overnight bag is banging against my leg. It's getting heavier and heavier. I am running like the Elephant Man. A whistle blows and my train lurches into action without me. I stand and watch it go.

To my right is another train. People are watching me from the comfort of their seats. I gaze back into the first-class carriage. It's . . . no, it can't be. I am frozen in time as the noise of the station fills my ears, deafening me. I am staring but I can't stop. It's him. It's Jason, and he's with her! He is talking into his mobile whilst Sophie is reading a magazine. My blood runs cold. I need to get away, to run as fast as I can, but I can't move. I am stuck here, being tortured, and they are oblivious of my pain. I watch as their train pulls slowly away. My bag drops to the ground. My fingers are white from a lack of blood. They are numb. Everything is numb. I feel as if everything has congealed.

An hour later I sit on a train which is full of people. None of them speak. The noise of the train and buzzing of iPods fills the spaces. I close my eyes and will myself to sleep. Despite my best efforts, sleep is replaced with a myriad colours and thoughts. I drift in and out of memories.

I remember that first day as Jason walked me to the station to catch the last train home. As we walked, neither of us speaking, I felt the thrill of belonging. I knew at that moment that I would think of nothing else for the next forty-eight hours until I saw him again. I can't imagine feeling like that for someone else. It makes me feel sad and alone.

I watch the moving landscape as it changes from grey concrete slabs, red-brick houses and tiny square gardens, to rolling hills and swollen rivers. If I was so sure that Jason was the One, how can I transfer those feelings to somebody else? How many Ones are there in a lifetime? My mum and dad would say one. Chloe would say two. She spent five years in an abusive relationship, because he was the One. It didn't matter that he took drugs, slept with other women and stole money from her purse. He was her one true love and she was willing to stand by him. When he disappeared with her then flatmate, she thought she would die without him. We had to call her mother over from Florida, we were so worried. Then along came Tad. The second coming.

I want to be over Jason, but the withdrawal symptoms are still kicking in. My name is Harriet Peel and I am an addict. The biggest hurdle is Chloe's wedding. Once I get that over with I will be fine. I can draw a line under it all and get on with my life. First, though, I need to find someone. But how? Cohabiting or married friends either cancel your usual Friday night out, or prefer a quiet little country pub full of OAPs and families so that 'we can hear each other talk'. This is great, but no bloody good when you are trying to find someone. Don't get me wrong. I have no wish to return to my nightclubbing days, unless

I am completely trollied, of course, and Josie convinces me that it would be fun. She is always wrong. It never is, and without a week's wages of *Cosmopolitans* and at least one of us crying in the toilets, it seems a bit sad. But finding a single man out there, while everyone else is in love land, is not easy. Is Internet dating the answer? There must be thousands of single girls out there asking the same question. I can't be the only one.

Maybe the girls were right; maybe there is a readership for my Internet dating antics. Lucy's words about the girls in the office reading my blog come back to me. Would it really be so ridiculous to ask Georgina for my own column? If you don't ask, you don't get.

I open my eyes and look around to see if someone has heard my mind whirring. I ask the person on the opposite table if I can have a piece of paper from their notepad and begin to write.

Girl Without a Date in Her Diary – Blog entry – April 9th

I've just had an epiphany.

I slip into step alongside Georgina as she heads towards the meeting room.

'I wondered if I could see you after the team meeting,' I suggest brightly.

'Is it important?' Georgina snaps.

'Fairly.'

'I have another meeting after this.'

'It's just that I've been thinking about *Life to Live* and what you said about Poppy – about bringing new things to the editorial content.'

'And?'

'I've come up with an idea.'

I hold out a piece of paper.

'Pop it on my desk. I'll have a look at it later.'

'Great. Shall we meet tomorrow morning and go over it? I'm free in the morning.'

Georgina is not listening and I reluctantly join the others seated around the meeting-room table.

'Have you seen this?' Georgina slams a copy of *Bath at Large* on the desk. She looks at us and waits.

'"*Big Brother*'s Chantilly visits Bath Hot Spot,"' Jeremy reads out.

'*That's* the sort of thing *we* need,' Georgina growls, and sticks her finger hard into Chantilly's tanned face.

We all sit there like naughty school children caught smoking behind the bike sheds. Georgina listens gravely as Jeremy tells us of another drop in advertising revenue.

'We need a Chantilly. Okay, who is due to visit Bath in the next few weeks?'

'The two camp blokes from that interior design programme on Living TV,' I read from my list.

'It's hardly rock 'n' roll,' Debbie the designer points out, and everyone nods.

'We need a big sexy name to grab people's attention back to *Life to Live*. I am assuming Nicolas Cage is not banging our door down?' Georgina glares at me.

I shake my head and look to my pad.

'Does anyone know anybody famous?' she demands.

'I know someone who knows the man from the bank advert. You know, the one where they sing,' Judith pipes up, but everyone ignores her.

'I want young, sexy and famous!' Georgina booms.

Everyone looks down at their hands. Judith coughs. Georgina taps her pen. Judith coughs again.

'What about a showcase of emerging talent?' I suggest. 'Like those *Vanity Fair* spreads. We could photograph them in different locations. Ed would do a really good job on something like that.'

Georgina nods cautiously. 'Well, it's an idea. In the meantime, Judith, ring round and find any tenuous celebrity link to the city and I'll give Poppy a call. She may well have some little celebrity friends. Paris Hilton? Prince Harry? Harry likes rugby, doesn't he?'

She smiles and swishes out of the meeting room in a cloud of chiffon scarf and Black Orchid perfume.

Instead of watching TV, I spend the evenings editing and expanding my blog to form an imaginary column for *Life to Live*. When Georgina gives me the go ahead I want to be ready. I'm excited by it and it's given me a new sense of purpose. I imagine the executives at Living TV are lamenting over their falling viewing figures because I'm pretty sure it was me keeping them going on weekday evenings. When the phone rings, instead of rushing towards it hoping it will be Jason, I see it as an intrusion. For the second time tonight, I leave it to me in recorded form to tell the caller to leave a message. My mother's voice rings out, loud and unforgiving.

'Cooooeeeeee, Harriet! Have you heard the news? Another wedding to look forward to – Emma and Alan are going to renew their wedding vows. Isn't that wonderful? Of course, I said to your father that we should offer the garden as the reception area – we could hire a marquee. Perhaps you could ring around, or look on the Internet – we also need wine glasses. Oooh, it will be lovely; a little something to look forward to before Katie and Lawrence next year. Emma says she doesn't want any fuss, but I said nonsense, and we have already agreed to pay for the wine for the hundred or so guests.'

'*You* agreed, Dee! *You*, not *we*!' my father shouts out.

'George, shhhh . . . so, August bank holiday – put it in your diary, darling. Hope you had a nice time in London and haven't come back too depressed. I know it must be hard for you seeing the others . . . it was different when you were in your early twenties, but now you're almost thirty . . . and of course, Vicky and Lucy have children now . . . well, I am sure it was all nice.'

'Dee.' My father's voice calls out to her with a warning attached to it, and it makes me smile.

'August bank holiday, then. You could take a couple of days off and we could go shopping with your sisters for outfits. Bye, darling. Ring me. It would be nice if you rang us . . . we never seem to hear from you . . . you could pop round tomorrow—'

My answer machine cuts her off.

Renewing their wedding vows? What's that all about? Emma and Alan are a couple who pose the question of why do it in the first place. I can't believe she is going to subject us to another over-the-top gathering of her snooty friends. It's bad enough that we have to go through the yearly trauma of the twins' birthday party. Each is more elaborate and more horrifying than the previous one. Last year the theme was the Princess Factor, which was a precocious *X Factor* in satin dresses and tiaras. Six weeks before the party, we were all given a song to sing in front of Emma and Alan's twenty friends and their children. I did my best, despite the heckling, only for Sharon Osbourne, alias Emma, to tell me I lacked talent.

Now I have to find another outfit, which I can ill afford, and a man sooner than I thought. If I go on my own my mother will never believe I am not a lesbian. I log on to DateMate. I know I said I wouldn't, but desperate times call for desperate measures and now I have two dates to fill.

My mother offers me a piece of soggy cold omelette.

'They call it tortilla,' she tells me.

They have just returned from a holiday in Spain with their friends Gerry and Suzy. We sample the thin triangles of cooked egg. Precious, the dachshund, hovers at our feet waiting for scraps.

'It's not how I remember it,' my mother complains. 'What do you think, George?'

'Maybe it needs to be slightly thicker?'

'Do you think?' She pouts.

'Only a little. It's very nice. In fact, I think I'll have another piece.'

My mother nods, satisfied, and returns to the kitchen for a top-up.

'Everything okay, munchkin? You seem miles away,' my father says.

I provide a smile.

'Just thinking about work stuff and Poppy Darling taking a big chunk of my What's On page.'

I have briefly mentioned the situation at work and he is sympathetic, but my father is the first to admit that office politics are a world away from his own experience. A man with a passion for cherry woods and beech, he is more used to dealing with master craftsmen and young lads eager to learn how to feel the grain of wood beneath their fingers. He has no interest, or experience of, stupid It girls with miniature dogs and trust funds.

'I wouldn't worry too much. Girls like Poppy don't have longevity. Mark my words – she'll be a flash in the pan.'

'I don't know. Georgina seems intent on her joining *Life to Live*. In some ways, I can see what she's trying to do. The magazine needs someone to pull it out of the doldrums, but I was hoping it would be me and not a rich girl who doesn't give two hoots about the magazine.' I let out a sigh. Like sand slipping through my fingers, my earlier determination feels slightly diminished by too much time spent thinking about it.

'The thing is, I really think I could make a difference, Dad.'

'And you will.'

'You sound so sure.'

My father smiles at me. 'I am. Aren't you the girl who put a sticky pad under your egg for the egg and spoon race?'

I smile at the memory.

'And I seem to remember you camping outside the

Sphere offices for a summer job placement. I had to bring you a flask because your mother was convinced you were going to die of hypothermia and she would be in the national newspapers for neglecting her children. And what about that award? That didn't come from thin air.'

'Thanks, Dad.'

'No need to thank me. I'm just reminding you of what Harriet Peel can achieve when she puts her mind to it.'

He is right, of course. I need to fight for what I want; not just wait for it to land on my lap. When did I become so complacent? When did I stop wanting the best for myself? An image of Jason standing in my kitchen the day he moved in springs to mind. He had just replaced my framed print of Van Gogh's *Almond Blossom in Bloom* with a blown-up photo of the Hong Kong skyline on the wall.

'I was talking to John today,' he said, surveying the scene with satisfaction. 'He said that when I get my next overseas posting he could probably get you a job writing for one of the ex-pat newspapers.'

'Doing what?' I asked. I hadn't even considered leaving *Life to Live* then.

'I don't know, journalist stuff, I guess. That's good, isn't it?'

'It's great.'

He kissed me then. We kissed a lot.

'It's going to be so good. Living the dream, baby. I can't wait. John promised me a little promotion this time.'

'Hey, that's great news.' I shared the vision of his meteoric rise within the diplomatic service, of us living in a swanky apartment funded by the Government, of being together who knew where. It was an exciting prospect. I had only been to Greece and LA. I looked at the Hong Kong skyline.

'Honey, where did you put my Van Gogh?'

'I put it with the stuff going to the charity shop.'

I hated that photo of Hong Kong.

'Are you going to stay for dinner?' my mother asks, pouring herself a large gin and tonic.

'No, thanks, I'd better get back,' I reply.

'For what?' she asks.

Good question.

'Stuff.'

'Ooh. Have you got yourself a boyfriend?' my mother asks excitedly.

'No.'

She gives my father a look that says, 'See, I told you.' I should have lied. Is there still time?

'Stay for dinner, munchkin. It will be nice,' my father says.

I nod. Why fight it?

I settle back in the blue-and-pink patterned sofa and rest my feet on the square pouffe thing. Dad flicks through the TV channels and I look through a copy of *A World of Organs*.

'It's your mother's,' my father explains. 'She wants an organ for Christmas.'

'George, why is there omelette in the dog's basket?' Mum shouts from the kitchen.

I hover at the edge of Georgina's office. She is talking and laughing loudly on her mobile. She motions me in with her hand and I tiptoe in. This is hard; tall people don't do tiptoeing particularly well. When she finishes, she is smiling.

'That girl is outrageous. She has me in stitches every time I talk to her.'

She writes something on her notepad. I wait.

'That was Poppy. She's promised to look through her address book for me. Apparently she was being told off for using her mobile on a flight to New York. That girl has balls.' She laughs. 'Watch out world, here comes Poppy.'

I gulp and fix a smile on my face. My horoscope this morning said, beware of the Scorpion and steer clear of conflict. Is Poppy a Scorpio? Has she a sting in her tail?

'What can I do for you?' Georgina asks.

'I just wondered if you have had a chance to look at my column proposal,' I ask hopefully.

'No, not yet.'

I wait.

'I'll look at it later.'

'Maybe I could talk you through it now?' I persevere.

'Harry, I'll look at it later,' Georgina says without looking up from the piece of paper that has suddenly focused her attention away from me.

I nod and smile, and decide to bide my time. I figure if I ask her every day, then at some point she will break and look at it just to shut me up. I go back to my desk and wait for another day. Feeling a little disappointed at the lack of progression, I fill each cheek with chocolate. I can get six cubes in one, but only five in the other. Does this mean I have one cheek smaller than the other? I stuff more chocolate in my cheeks, and stick two small Post-it notes to my top lip. My squirrel impression is ignored by everyone except Donald. He is here for one of his six-monthly meetings and with his blue blazer and polka-dot neckerchief he looks as if he has just parked his very expensive and shiny white yacht outside. Judith said it's named after his wife Debbie and has a waterbed. He looks at me from the corner of his eye and I can see him mentally deciding that the reason his magazine is losing money is all down to employees spending too much time impersonating animals. The prospect of finding my P45 on my desk comes ever closer.

My phone rings and I pick it up with as much enthusiasm as I can muster.

'Harriet speaking. What's On.'

'The end of the world, by the sounds of it.'

'Hi, Katie.'

'Are you okay?' she asks with real concern. My younger sister cares. She cares about everything, from the plight of hedgehogs crossing the road, to whether someone has been mistreated whilst picking the contents of her unwashed bag of seasonal leaves. She is one of the nice, sweet people.

'Yes, I'm fine – work is getting me down a bit, that's all.'

'Oh, I don't miss that at all. You should get pregnant, Harry. Being a mum is great.'

'You sound like Mum,' I reply.

Katie is one of those lucky people who have an angelic baby who sleeps through the night and gurgles happily throughout the day. My older sister Emma delights in predicting that this will not last. Just you wait, she says with glee.

'So what have you been up to?' I ask.

'I've just had a visit from Emma, and I needed some light relief. She has been preaching the gospel of child rearing according to Emma Benbow, and I'm exhausted.'

'Like what?'

'Um, let's see. You shouldn't give in to your baby – that you are the boss and you should let them cry – that swaddling is the best thing, that I am too soft and I am laying the foundations for a child with no respect. I felt a bit depressed after she left.'

'And follow these rules and you too could have your own devil children who wake people up in the middle of the night with a torch directed in their eyes,' I counter.

The memory of being blinded at two o'clock in the morning by the devil twins still haunts me.

'Oh gosh, I'd forgotten that. Your scream woke everyone up.' Katie laughs. 'That was Christmas. You weren't with Jason then, were you?'

'No. He was in the Seychelles with Sophie.'

'Hey, someone better will come along.'

'I know,' I reply, because that's what people expect me to say; to be positive and sooooo over him. The trouble is, that in the same way you know a low-fat wrap is a better, healthier option, you still want one of those sausage rolls you know have been made with the scrapings from the floor. I'm like an ex-smoker and it only takes the slightest whiff of him for the cravings to begin all over again.

'I assume she told you all about the renewing of their wedding vows thing?' I want to change the subject. Sometimes I can do the 'I am over him' thing really well. Now is not one of those sometimes.

'She may have mentioned it.' Katie laughs. 'Apparently, she's going to have a string quartet playing a piece of music especially commissioned for the occasion.'

'Oh, God! Why? If they love each other, then that's great, but why can't they just keep it to themselves, maybe hold hands every so often. Why do we need a bloody chocolate fountain and a violinist to tell us how devoted they are?'

'She's having a chocolate fountain?' Katie sounds shocked.

'No, I think it's lemon syllabub.'

Katie laughs and Alfie makes a little meowing sound, like a kitten.

'So what have you got planned for the weekend? Anything exciting?' she asks dreamily, like she does when we go shopping and she says she is just looking.

'Nothing really, just mooching,' I reply. 'What about you?'

'Lawrence's brother has invited us down to their place in Devon for the weekend. They have a baby a few months older than Alfie, so that should be really nice.'

I suck in the sigh that wants to escape, the one that says a thousand things, including, how lovely, I wish I had a boyfriend who had a brother with a place in Devon. We chat about nothing much for another ten minutes before she says she has to go and meet a friend in town for coffee. I stare at my computer and yearn for a lovely weekend of cream teas and sex, although Katie says this is not what it used to be since Alfie.

Chloe sends me an email asking if I mind sitting at the same table as Jason and Sophie. She tells me it's a nightmare trying to keep everyone happy and she will do her best to get me on a separate table. I tell her I don't mind at all. What else could I say? Then I panic. I have approximately thirty weeks to find a date. With a sneaky look around the office, I check there is no one around. Judith is out on a photo shoot, and everyone else has popped out for lunch. I log on to DateMate.

> *Wordsmith – don't judge a book by its cover . . . likes autumn landscapes, going to festivals and listening to music. I am looking for a girl to read to, and to enjoy the odd impromptu weekend away, where we talk about music and books until the small hours.*

He does sound lovely. He likes to read, so he must be fairly intelligent, likes to go to music festivals, but can also do the romantic weekend away. In short, perfect. He isn't particularly good looking, but more interesting, in a sexy, geeky way. This is a man who will woo me into bed with his knowledge of books and music; who will wear a quirky suit to Chloe's wedding and make Jason feel inadequate. Jason hates people who are more intelligent than he is.

Should I? Ooooh, I don't know. I ring Josie.

'Go for it. I've been thinking about Operation DateMate and I think you should go out with as many men as possible. It's a numbers thing. The more you go out with, the greater the chance you have of finding the One. Simple, really.'

'It's easy for you to say that,' I reply.

'Remember what I said about Madonna. Success takes strategy and commitment, and honey, if I could do it for you, I would. Just think of it as material for your column. Has Georgina said yes yet?'

'No, but I'm working on her.'

'Great stuff. Gotta go, I've promised Ben I'll go shopping for cutlery with him, although heaven knows why. It's daft. I mean, he's supposed to be the one who doesn't want to do that sort of stuff.'

'It's nice to do things like that together.'

'Is it? I wanted to go bowling. Buying cutlery is the sort of thing you do when you're getting married.'

'You are.'

'Mmmmm . . .'

Before I go home I email Georgina and attach my proposal.

With Josie's words about Operation DateMate ringing in my head I decide she may have a point. Madonna didn't become one of the world's most successful recording artists by eating Chinese take-out and thinking about it. Angelina didn't get to be babe-licious by sitting at home watching TV. No, they both got out there and worked out until their bodies were the best they could be. A strong, can-do body equals a strong, can-do mind. It also makes you more attractive to the opposite sex; particularly the sporty types. In short, it's a win-win situation. I see myself going on a Rocky-type journey, struggling in grey baggy sweatshirt bottoms, only to emerge victorious with the roar of the crowd behind me and a good-looking man waiting for me with his arms outstretched at the finish line. Running seems to be a good thing to start with and I am pretty sure even I can run a couple of miles. Easy-peasy! Judith recommends a circular route around the city. She says it's a good distance for beginners, so this weekend is the start of my battle against the odds and my 'I am not going down without a fight' strategy. The strong get out there and win. The weak go home and eat Doritos.

I set out with my iPod and Madonna-like baseball cap. Five minutes in and I think I have sprained my ankle. I stop and wonder if I should go home. Maybe I need to do some stretching to warm up. I drink some water and do some stretching-type manoeuvres. I have no idea if I am doing them correctly, but I look the part. I start again, this time with a gradual jog, and my ankle feels okay. Halfway round it starts raining. I carry on shuffling forward, determined to kick start my efforts towards a new me. Then my body gives up. It begins to reprimand me for being bloody stupid; that we still have a mile to go. My shuffle becomes a laboured walk, followed by another attempt at a shuffle, followed soon after by another walk. A hand on my shoulder is enough to make me scream. Very loudly. The scream is accompanied by a flurry of punches aimed at nowhere in particular.

'Fuck! Ow, Harry, it's, ow fuck, it's me, Harry. Stop!'

I stop. Ed is shielding his face with his arms.

'What the hell?' I yell at him.

'I saw you from the cricket field. I called out but you didn't hear.'

I pull out my iPod earphones.

'I was running.'

'You looked as if you were doubled over.'

'I was just catching my breath before the next ten.'

'You look like you're freezing. Come on. The game's been rained off. It's tea and cake time. Come inside and warm up.'

'What are you doing round here?' I ask.

'I belong to the local cricket team. We play every other Saturday.'

It's weird, Ed's lived in Bath for a couple of years now but I have never seen him out and about and we've never really mixed outside work. From what I can gather, he spends most of his time going back to London with Noush. I guess while I was with Jason it didn't seem right to meet up. Actually, thinking about it, I've only been out with the people from work a handful of times over the past couple of years. We used to go out for tapas every Thursday night. Maybe we should again.

'Come on. You can rescue me from the nice ladies who insist on mothering me,' Ed urges.

Tea and cake sound a much better prospect than limping home, and it's better to take these things one step at a time. Best to rest now and not overdo it. Ed leads me to a cricket pavilion where warm tea is served by equally warm and accommodating women. They fuss and feed me fruit cake while we wait for the rain to stop. When it does, everyone cheers and I watch as Ed and his team-mates take to the field. I have no idea what's going on, but even I can appreciate men in white being energetic.

I clap loudly until one of the women tells me that Ed has just been bowled out after two runs. It could have been better, she tells me gently. He might have just lost them the match.

Ed returns to the pavilion and shrugs his shoulders.

'You were very impressive,' I say, and we both laugh.

He looks very different in his whites. Quite good looking, really. I hadn't thought about it before now. Ed is just Ed at work. It's a shame Jason knows him, otherwise he would be the perfect wedding date.

'You have a brother, don't you?' I ask.

'Yes, younger.'

'And has he got a girlfriend?'

'Yes. Got engaged last week, actually. Why?'

'Just wondering.'

'Wondering what?'

'Wondering if I should start dating again.'

I clap enthusiastically as a tall man with a tan enters the field. He has a rather nice bottom.

'That's the other team,' Ed informs me.

'But I can still applaud perfection.'

'Well, if you want a date, some of the boys out there are single.'

'Are they?' I scan the field. There are some rather lovely men out there, and not one them is drunk. Maybe being active is the new going out.

'Probably not your type, though,' Ed adds.

'Hey, Ed,' the cricketer with the rather nice bottom calls out. He makes his way over with a winning smile.

My failure to set the tarmac alight and lose one hundred and twenty pounds in the process is pushed to the back of my mind. I smooth the damp frizz that is now my hair, pull back my shoulders and remind myself that I am sexy, soon to be successful, and free next Saturday.

'Hi, Phil,' Ed says. Phil smiles at me and I do my best to appear friendly, but mysterious.

Ed begins to talk cricket scores and I listen intently, apparently fascinated. At some point during the conversation I zone out and start thinking of what to have for tea tonight. I decide on a tuna pasta bake and resume my 'how interesting' look. Ed and Phil eventually stop talking overs and unders and gaze out towards the field to watch the game. I use the opportunity to kick Ed. He frowns at me. Introduce me, I mouth.

'Oh, Phil. This is my friend Harry. We work together. Harry was out for a run—'

Enough Ed, enough.

'And Ed, bless him, was worried about me getting wet out there.' I laugh as if rain is my best friend.

'Ah, a runner. I'm always impressed by people who can. Never been able to myself. How far do you run?'

I shake my head. 'Seven K.'

'Wow, that's good,' Phil enthuses and Ed coughs.

'I'm training for the half-marathon,' I add for effect.

'Are you?' Ed asks.

'Yes,' I lie.

'Shall I get us a cup of tea?' Phil asks.

'That would be lovely, Phil,' I reply, and ignore Ed shaking his head.

I have a dream involving a field and two men. They are fighting over me. One has a book, the other a cricket bat. The one with the book wins with a barrage of big words and carries me triumphant to his yurt. We have sex by candlelight on a sheepskin rug. He reads to me when I cannot sleep and then wakes me up with passion and poached eggs, but not at the same time.

Girl Without a Date in Her Diary – Blog entry – June 2nd

I have come to the conclusion that you have to put the effort in and be a tiny bit ruthless to get what you want, otherwise people will just come right up and steal it from under your nose. This is relevant in all aspects of life, from jobs to that last Stella McCartney dress in Top Shop. Does this also apply to men? I put this to my friend E, who is one. He said that yes, making an effort, but appearing not to, is the key to success. Men, he said, think about other stuff and are often blind to the tactics used by the clever female to snare them. I put this into practice at the weekend.

First up was a cricketer with a pert bottom. I learned as much as I could about cricket, then, when appropriate, I positioned myself to make small talk about the delights of the game. It worked – to a degree. An hour and a half later and I am bored rigid. Not only did he play cricket but he also went diving, hill climbing, and mountain biking, played golf and belonged to an orienteering group. My desire to feel his left buttock was exhausted by the stories of his exploits and successes. Eventually, I made my excuses and went home.

June 8th

Not to be put off, and following on with my sporting theme, I figured sitting in a stadium full of three hundred-plus men, watching other men in shorts, sounded a lot more promising than watching men rub their balls from the safety of a cricket pavilion. With this in mind I attended my first game of rugby. Unfortunately, this didn't go without a hitch. Surrounded by passionate men and a field full of bulging thighs was enough to make me lose my step and fall in front of a full stand. A huge cheer went up and a group of large men rushed forward to help me up. I suspect I should have whimpered a bit and played the helpless female card, but with half a cup of lukewarm tea over me and my hands and knees covered in wet mud, I responded by rushing off to hide. Don't let this put you off. Rugby players and their fans are worth investigating. I especially liked the bit where they lift one of the players high up into the air to catch the ball. It was breathtaking stuff. It made me think of ballet dancers. Another option? Perhaps . . . They have big thighs. My friend said they have rotten feet and don't eat a lot. I cross them off my list. Swimmers? Broad shoulders and skimpy trunks . . . early morning training sessions . . . mmmm, not so good. What about triple jumpers? They're tall.

I need to join a club. God, I'm exhausted just thinking about all this. I must have expended at least three thousand calories on nervous energy.

June 9th

Exhausted by my sporty options I returned to good old sedentary email. This doesn't mean I have relaxed my attitude to making an effort. I'm just doing it in a different, less energetic way. I have researched my potential mates, picked out the ones that statistically match, and reacted accordingly with my emails. This means I am now talking to a guy who likes to take coastal walks and read books. Instead of my usual chatty but wholly irrelevant style, my reply mails have been littered with references to my love of the wind in my hair, the salt on my lips and literary references. We are meeting up next week. Ten out of ten for Peel.

P.S. The trouble is it feels a bit premeditated and not really how I wanted to find someone. Am I being naïve thinking that romance can come about from a shared joke or a mutual love of Cherry Bakewells? According to my friend J, yes. She is of the opinion that romantics are always disappointed. This is disappointing in itself and I'd like to prove her wrong. We shall see.

I hop to the phone, one shoe on, one shoe off.

'Oh, you are alive?'

'Hi, Mum. Look, I can't talk. I'm going out.'

'I just phoned to see if Emma sent you the list of presents?'

'Presents!'

'For the renewing of the vows. There's a list.'

'Presents? She wants presents?'

'Harriet, stop getting hysterical. Men don't like women who can't hide their problems.'

'Mum, I have to go.'

'Where are you going?'

'Nowhere interesting.'

'Who are you going with?'

'No one.'

'What do you mean, no one? Why are you being so secretive?'

I know that she won't let it go. She is like a terrier with a bone. I let out a sigh. What the hell.

'I have a date.'

'Oooh. What are you wearing?'

'Jeans and a blouse.'

'You should wear dresses and skirts more. Men like women to be feminine, and Harriet, remember to laugh at his jokes, but not too loudly.'

'I don't think he's the sort to tell jokes.'

'What sort is he?'

'The clever sort.'

'Then remember to pronounce your words properly.'

The venue is a new gastro pub showcasing its new jazz evening. I am not a fan of jazz, but Georgina is, and she wants me to write a review. Right now, I will cut off my right arm to a jazz riff if she wants me to. Does jazz have a riff or a rhythm, or neither? As I ponder this question to a background of a cello, saxophone and a woman singing some doo-be-doos, a man walks into the pub and looks around. He is tall and wiry, with dark hair. He has a long, narrow face, and when he spots me, he smiles, his large ears shifting slightly. Dressed in jeans, a blue shirt, suit jacket and brown shoes that have been polished to within an inch of their life, he looks like a teenager dressed in his dad's clothes. He is not what I was expecting. The picture in my mind was of someone dressed in an old Glastonbury T-shirt, Converse trainers and a surf sweatshirt; someone with a graze of facial hair and a VW camper van in the car park. How did I get that wrong? So much for my statistical analysis and carefully considered emails.

I smile back and remind myself that I am open to new possibilities. Perhaps it's time I expanded my mind and horizons.

'You must be Belle of the Ball?' His laugh lingers a little too long. He is nervous, like me.

'I am. Harry. Pleased to meet you.'

'Hi, I'm David.'

We shake hands and my handshake is firmer than his.

'I'll just get myself a drink,' he says.

I fix my smile back in place as he returns and sits down. His arms and fingers are long and take up most of the table. I am pretty sure long fingers mean something about intelligence and sexuality. I prepare myself to be seduced with lots of interesting facts. He looks clever, so I figure he must be.

We make small talk; he has two brothers, his parents are retired, he loves music, cheese and his spaniel, Dotty. He talks in quiet, measured tones. I like his confidence and although he is not quite what I expected at first, I find his intelligence quite attractive and more than a little fascinating.

'So, music wise. What kind of thing do you like?' I ask, trying to find some common ground.

'I bought the Sorrentinos' CD the other day.'

I rack my brain but the name means nothing to me. Are they the next big thing? If he's a regular at the festivals he must know his stuff. I feel the pressure to confirm my own credentials in the cool, hip department; a trap I often fall into when confronted by people cooler than me. It is only recently that I have recognised that this is the very thing that marks me out as being the uncool one. Unfortunately, this new inner knowledge doesn't stop me.

'I went to Glastonbury a few years ago, but I'd love to go again,' I say. I have a pocket-sized daydream of us going together and sharing a luxury yurt.

'Oh, I've never been to Glastonbury – no, it's mostly literature festivals I go to. I'm not really into rock music. The Sorrentinos are a three-piece who do a lot of the classics, from opera to music hall but without a musical accompaniment. Fabulous stuff. This is great, by the way. I like a bit of experimental jazz.'

My fantasies of comparing CDs in the early hours of the morning float out of the window, along with a few frantic saxophone solos. I cannot think of one area where our musical tastes converge.

'Is that okay?'

'What?' I try and rewind, but find I lost it somewhere between Salman Rushdie and a Chinese violin virtuoso.

'If we go on to Barnaby's Bookstore? You're not averse to surprises, are you?'

My laugh is as unconvincing as my answer.

'Surprises; I love surprises, but isn't it a bit late for Barnaby's to be open?'

David touches the side of his nose, which for some reason annoys me. My old French teacher used to do it. I hated French. Probably because I wasn't very good at it.

The fresh air hits me, and after two large glasses of wine I realise I am a little tipsy. I should have eaten before I came out, but the phone call from Mum put me behind and I ran out of time. She has texted me twice already. Since Katie showed her predictive texting, we are now not only subjected to long phone calls, but also three-page text messages.

The bright interior lights of Barnaby's spill out into the darkness of the street. David is the perfect gentleman and opens the door for me. About thirty people are standing amongst the bookshelves talking quietly and drinking wine. All eyes turn to us as we enter and I feel as if I should make an effort to warrant their attention, like singing a loud ta-da or putting my hands up the air. A woman resembling a vampire and a small, strangely proportioned man rush over to us. They fight over who will clasp David's hands first.

'David, you look so well, come in, come in,' the woman gushes. She has a red gash as a mouth and is dressed in black figure-hugging wool, grey opaque tights, a grey pashmina held together with a huge silver flower clasp, and shoes that belong to the Wicked Witch of the West. They usher David in and I allow myself to fall behind.

'It's sublime,' the tiny man says, his extraordinarily large head shaking in excitement. He turns to me. 'What did you think?'

What do I think of what? Life, the universe, how Madonna manages to do those split things, why I have been dragged on a first date to a book event with people I have never met before?

'Of *Dragons in the Mist*?'

Aahh, so we are talking about a particular book. Mmmm . . . now do I pretend, or tell the truth? Pretend.

'Fabulous.'

David turns and smiles. I smile back, not sure if he is impressed or if he knows I have no idea what the little man is talking about. We are handed glasses of lukewarm wine and surrounded by people with insincere smiles. Why has he brought me here? People close in around David and I feel at a disadvantage, especially when the little circle I have been sucked into begins talking about people I know nothing about, but somehow feel I should. After half an hour of listening to their attempts to outdo each other in their knowledge of obscure literature, I make an excuse about going to the ladies. Instead, I gravitate – or rather, sway – towards the nibbles table. Now this is more like it: parmesan twists, olives, crisps, bruschetta, cheese, more wine. I hover and pick at the food. The vampire woman has her arm in David's and is monopolising his attention. I wait for them to finish. Then I get bored. I take my little plate of posh pastry things into the bookshelves where I peruse the titles on offer. I feel like a kid allowed in a shop after hours. It's great. I begin to read a book about a woman who travels to Peru.

I should go back – just a couple more minutes. God, I can't believe she did that in those temperatures, and without toilet roll? Oh, that's awful.

'Aaah, so this is where the real party is?'

I turn round and survey the intruder who has entered my little bookshelf world. Dark jeans enclose long limbs, and a printed T-shirt is loose against his stomach. He is very good looking, in a floppy, long-haired dog kind of way. He also makes eating olives look incredibly sexy. Grrrrr. I want to flick my hair or something. I blush instead and put the book down as if I have been caught stealing.

'So you know this lot, then?' he asks.

'No, I came with someone. Someone who seems to know everyone in the room,' I reply. 'Whereas I don't. Hence my escape.'

'Is it just me, or could this be better?' he asks and removes a book from the shelf. He has long fingers and skin the colour of honey.

'No, I think you're right. It could be. The food is good though.'

'The food is great. These things are usually good. Some of the authors they have are amazing and you get to meet some really interesting people.'

'But not tonight,' I venture.

'Not tonight. These people don't dance.'

'Dance?'

'Okay, have a look out there. Can you see any of them dancing, getting drunk, and laughing out loud? Do you want to spend more than fifteen minutes of your life with them?'

I peer out from my shelf at the collection of serious beards, pale skin, women in hats and scarves and nodding heads. He is right; these people don't dance – they talk, consider, talk some more, and if they do laugh, it is in that superior self-righteous way they usually reserve for people who haven't read *War and Peace* and don't watch subtitled films on a Saturday night.

'So you come to a lot of these things, then?' I ask.

'I try to when I'm in town, although I was dragged to this one by my brother. He fancies one of the girls who work here.'

'So which one is the author?' I ask.

When he points to my date for the evening, I find I am lost for words.

'David Smethic. Expert on Welsh coastal erosion, bird migration and author of *Dragons in the Mist*,' he tells me.

'I think I need another drink,' I reply, and make my way to the drinks table. Mr Floppy Hair follows me.

'I'm Nate, by the way,' he says, and clinks my glass. Wine slops on to the carpet. We both look down. I put my foot over the stain and he smiles.

'Harry,' I reply, and I can't help wishing that he was my date for the evening. Tall, with a thin face and hazel eyes, he is really rather beautiful.

The woman with the big red mouth taps her glass for the room to hush. Nate smiles at me. I smile back up at him, then look down at my shoes in case he can see what I am thinking. The woman makes a long speech about how wonderful David is. He has the good grace to look embarrassed, and I can see him scanning the room. When he spots me, he smiles. He has a nice smile. Everyone claps politely and he begins to read a long passage from his book. It sounds very intense. Everyone begins to fidget, but David has retreated to his own dragon-filled world. I start to play with two breadsticks. Nate follows suit and sticks two round crackers to his eyes. I attempt to stifle a giggle and as David talks on, we play a game of a hundred and one uses for nibbles. With Nate next to me, egging me on, I stick the breadsticks up my nose.

For some reason, everyone, and I mean everyone, turns to look at me. David is holding out his hand in my direction. I stare back with a breadstick in each nostril. Everyone is quiet, except the snort from Nate as he tries to swallow a laugh. He is the only one who wants to; everyone else just looks at me as if I have just made a rude gesture to the Queen.

Gradually people return their gaze to the star of the show. David doesn't miss a beat, and quotes something. It must be funny because everyone laughs, and it is clearly at my expense.

'Nice one,' Nate whispers. 'I'll give you a ten for entertainment value.'

'Thanks,' I reply, wishing I felt better about it.

As the evening draws to a close and a straggle of people queue to have their books signed, I consider leaving under cover of my embarrassment. Unfortunately, my conscience gets the better of me. I pay for my copy of the big weighty hardback with the airbrushed picture of a dragon on the front (that's more gone from my wedding-outfit fund) and join the queue. When it's my turn, David looks up at me and I am not sure what I see in his eyes. Disappointment?

'I'm sorry, David, it was really nice and everything, but I guess I . . . I'm so . . . well, thanks for a lovely evening,' I stammer.

I wait for him to tell me it doesn't matter, that it was mildly funny and perhaps we could do something next Saturday. He doesn't. Instead, he removes the book from my hand and signs it with a flourish. I consider saying something else, but decide it's best if I don't. His face tells me it's best if I don't. As I leave the shop, Nate gives me a little wave, but doesn't rush to ask for my phone number. Why would he? A woman who sticks breadsticks up her nose is not the sort you want to spend the rest of your life with. I blame it on my mother. If she had shown me more attention as a child, if she hadn't phoned as I was getting ready, if she hadn't got on to the subject of buying Emma and Alan a second wedding present . . . Yes, it's all Mum's fault. She has sent me six text messages. I text back that I am okay. Within ten seconds my phone rings.

'Was he nice?'

'Yes.'

'What does he do for a living?'

'He's a writer.'

She makes a noise that I take to be approval.

'So, will you be seeing him again?'

'I don't think so.'

'Why?'

'I just don't think I will.'

'You didn't swear, did you?'

'No.'

'And he didn't ask to see you again?'

'No.'

'And you say he was nice?'

'Yes.'

'Well, these writers are a bit stuck up sometimes. Barbara went to see JK Rowling. Queued up for four hours, she did, and then got moved on by the security people for taking up too much time. She was only asking her what she thought of Michael's idea for a book.'

I lie in bed and feel bad about David. We didn't have much in common, but I was willing to give it another go. I feel responsible for ruining what might have been a nice evening. My remorse lasts for approximately two minutes before I start thinking about the lovely Nate and fantasising about going to the wedding with him. I phone Josie.

'I've just met someone.'

'Wow. Hurray for whatshisname. What is his name?'

'Wordsmith – David. It wasn't him.'

'You've lost me.'

'The guy I met whilst on the date with David. His name is Nate . . . oh Jose, he was lovely, and funny and tall.'

'But?'

'That's it. There is no but.'

'There's always a but.'

'Well, there wasn't this time. We talked, I fancied him, end of story.'

'So you're not going to see him again?'

'No.'

'That's the but. We need to talk about your flirting technique.'

'I don't have a technique.'

'Exactly.'

Girl Without a Date in Her Diary – Blog entry – June 17th

. . . so when I get home I open my book to see the heart-rending message my date has left for me. 'To my darling H – it wasn't meant to be' or 'To H, a brief light in my life'? There is no message. That was it – not even a kiss.

So there goes another disastrous date. I will never be able to go into Barnaby's again. Never! The nibbles were good, though, and perusing the bookshop after hours was great. It could have been worse. Actually, no, it couldn't.

But you know what? Author evenings are a great way of:

1. Spending an evening with free drinks and nibbles.
2. Expanding your literary knowledge.
3. Potentially meeting new men (who can read).
4. Choosing early birthday or Christmas presents.

I'm having a miss-Jason night. The evening seems empty and I cannot fill it alone. I have tried listing possible ideas for my column but my mind is busy with other things. I miss him and it sucks. Saturday and Sunday mornings are the worst. He would inhabit them with his mess and half-asleep bad temper, lying on the sofa, eating a bacon sandwich and watching rubbish TV. Sophie probably insists they go out for brunch. Does he like that about her?

I think of the guy in the bookshop. Nate. He was nice. Why couldn't I meet someone like that on DateMate? I indulge in a little daydream of bumping into him coming out of a bookshop. He tells me that he has been searching the city for me. I play hard to get and tell him I'm busy until next week. It stops me thinking of Jason.

The phone rings and I make a wish.

'Who's next on Operation DateMate?' Josie asks.

'I give up.'

'You can't give up. Now, I've had a look through some of the profiles and there are some great ones out there. You just have to spend a bit of time searching. DonnyD sounds wonderful. He likes a fuller-figured woman and dancing. I've always wanted to try a bit of Latin.'

'Why are you looking through DateMate when you have a gorgeous guy at home who adores you?'

'I'm just helping you.'

'Oh yeah? And DonnyD?'

'I think it's healthy to see what else is out there, and there's no harm in looking.'

'You're mad, Josie. You love Ben.'

'But we don't have sex as much as we used to.'

'I think that's normal, isn't it?'

'It's not romantic and dirty any more.'

'Romantic and dirty?'

'Yeah. You know.'

I don't, and now I am not sure what I've been missing out on.

'It's just not the same. Perhaps we've reached the end of the road?'

'Josie, are you looking for excuses to stray?'

'No.'

'Every relationship has its ups and downs.'

'I'm bored. I need some excitement.'

'Then buy a vibrator and a French maid's outfit.'

'What's the harm in emailing a few guys? I'm not going to sleep with anyone.'

'That's what Jason said when he went on that weekend to Manchester.'

'This is exactly why you have to give DateMate another go. Come on, Harry. All you need is one nice guy. Just a good-looking, funny, sexy guy who is taller than Jason, can cook a roast dinner, is successful, drives a car with a leather interior, is loved by your grandma, run-of-the-mill type.'

'Like Ben?'

'Oh hah bloody hah!'

'Love you.'

'Get back on that computer!'

What does my horoscope say?

> *Your new moon is full of promise at work and at play . . . With this in mind, don't regret a hasty decision and instead embrace the possibilities. Venus, the goddess of love, is looking your way . . . Make a note of the twenty-ninth. Be ready and beware of thinking you can do it alone. Money is a problem this month but don't despair, your positive nature will see you through.*

What does that mean? Would giving up on DateMate be a hasty decision? Is Venus doing her thing over the Internet or on the high street? Maybe I should hover outside every bookshop in the city. Why am I going to be short of money? I go to bed worrying and then wake up remembering my new moon full of promise. New moons are there to be exploited. I bet Angelina hasn't wasted any of hers. I resolve to wring mine dry. Georgina had better watch out. My new moon is heading her way.

Georgina is not in. I sit at my desk and ponder my next move. I can't send her any more emails and her in-tray is like a black hole. I pick up the phone.

'Barbara. When is Georgina back in?'

Barbara is Georgina's personal assistant. She is like a Rottweiler with broad shoulders and a loud bark.

'Wednesday.'

'Can you slot me into her schedule?'

'She hasn't said anything to me about a meeting.'

'No . . . but I want to surprise her with something.'

'Surprise? What sort of surprise?'

'That would ruin the surprise.'

'I don't know.' I can hear Barbara sucking the air between the gap in her front teeth.

'Please, Barbara. I promise never to steal your love heart Post-it notes again.'

Thankfully Barbara laughs. She must be having a good day.

'All right. Two p.m. You've got half an hour.'

'That's all I need. You're the best, Babs.'

'Don't call me Babs.'

'Sorry, Barbara.'

I make the finishing touches to next month's What's On page and reward myself with a little sneaky look at DateMate. I'm not going to do anything. I'm just looking . . . just in case, because you never know.

Clown and poet seeks muse. Can I be the pearl that kisses your neck, the circus of your dreams, the darkness . . . ?

'What the hell is this?'

Shit! I shut the web page down as fast as my fingers will allow.

'Oh no, let me read more. What was that, and who was that guy?' Ed asks. His eyes are wide with surprise and amusement; whilst mine are wide with the shock of being discovered.

'Bog off. It's none of your business,' I reply, feeling the flush creep its way up from my neck to my cheeks. It settles like a hot flannel. I fiddle with a folder to avoid looking at him, but I have no idea what I am looking for. I have gone blind with embarrassment.

'Are you online dating?' Ed looks at me, his eyes still wide.

'Bugger off, Ed. I'm busy.'

'Not busy enough to stop you looking up weird-looking poets.'

I laugh then, because he was very weird and his poems were pretty awful.

'Come on, bring the page up again.'

I reluctantly log into the website again and allow Ed to flick through some of the profiles.

'Wow, some of the girls on here are gorgeous.'

'Yes, but you only get head profiles – they might be three hundred and thirty pounds, with very small heads,' I offer.

'Oh my God! Look at this guy! He is seriously scary – and, get this, he thinks he is very attractive. The bloke is a freak, and who's this optimistical daydreamer . . . is that a real word, optimistical? This is great.'

I shut down the web page.

'Oh Harry, I was just getting into it.'

'Go away. I need to do some work.'

'But you still haven't told me what you were doing on there.'

'If you must know, I am looking for someone to take me to Chloe's wedding and I thought this might be a good start. Some of the men on there are nice – seriously – and it saves all that getting to know each other rubbish that takes months. I haven't got months.'

'I'll go with you.'

I look at him as if he is joking, but he isn't.

'You're being serious.'

'Of course I am. A good-looking, great-on-the-dance-floor, popular with grannies, amenable type of guy like me would be the perfect date for a friend's wedding.'

He's right.

'That's very sweet of you, but I want someone I can kiss and be a little in lust with. Jason is going to be there and he knows you.'

'So what are you saying? That the thought of you being

a little in lust with me is so out of the ball park he wouldn't fall for it?' Ed looks hurt and I am not sure if he is being serious or winding me up. A smile plays at the corner of his lip. I decide to change the subject.

'You use the train quite a bit. Do they stop at Chippenmartin at the weekend?'

'Not sure, why?'

'I'm going to my sister's and my car is playing up. I don't really want to drive.'

'I could give you a lift.'

'No, it's all right. I'll get a train.'

'Don't be silly. I'm driving up to London for the afternoon anyway. I can drop you off and pick you up.'

'Are you sure?'

Ed nods and smiles.

'You are lovely.'

'So they say,' he says, and wanders off.

Maybe Josie was right. He could be my emergency plan C.

Judith sidles over to my desk.

'What's the difference between an atheist and agnostic?' she asks.

'Why?'

'Jeremy says he's an agnostic.'

'It means he believes but doesn't practise.'

'Aaaah.'

'Judith, what do you think of us all going out for a drink together one evening? What about next Tuesday?'

'I have church on a Tuesday, but you could all come to that if you want. It's not overly religious.'

'Do they have alcohol?'

'No!'

I consider this and wonder if I should be more open-minded about what constitutes a good evening out.

'But we do have sausage rolls and singing.'

'I'll put it to everyone,' I reply.

The emails back are overwhelmingly in favour of tequila slammers and nachos, and we take a rain check on the day, which we'll decide later. Before I leave, I print off another copy of my proposal and when Barbara is on her lunch break, I sneak into Georgina's office and pop it on the top of her in-tray in the folder marked 'urgent pending' along with a few strands of black fur. I read somewhere that black cats bring luck and their fur can act as a conduit. Margot's cat Sapphire now has a small patch where the hair is shorter.

The M4 motorway is grey and monotonous. I look up at a sky full of white tissue paper clouds. A plane flies low and I watch its progress over the green and yellow hills of the Somerset countryside. Tiny dark figures spew out from its insides. Parachutes open and they float down, swaying from side to side. This is something I will never do. I want to, but not enough. My fear of heights will prevent it. I want to keep my job. Will my fear prevent that too?

'You okay?' Ed asks.

'Yes, why?'

'You were scowling. Here, have a gummy bear.'

Emma has invited the family over for a renewing of the vows strategy meeting. I wasn't quick enough with an excuse, and Emma, like everyone else, knows I have nothing to do on a weekend these days. My life has changed in so many ways since Jason left. We were always so busy, going away for weekend breaks, socialising with his friends, doing family stuff, that when Chloe, Vicky, Lucy and Josie all moved away with their respective partners, it didn't seem to matter too much. I was too busy to notice the gap. Now the gap seems huge and I am not sure how to fill it. Even going to the odd gig on a Thursday hasn't meant a miraculous change to my social life, so here I am, with Ed, who is dropping me off before going on to meet some friends. He is suffering from a hangover and his flagging energy levels prompt an extreme right turn into a drive-through.

'Urgh, you're not really going to?' I ask, feeling a little superior.

'Yeah. I haven't had one in years.'

'Nor have I,' I say almost wistfully, before reminding myself that they are evil and not conducive to an Angelina-like physique. Brenda from WeightWatchers would tell me that for one hamburger, I could eat a never-ending amount of vegetables. For one cheeseburger I could properly eat for a whole week and still have points left for a treat.

'A Big Mac is calling my name,' Ed announces.

'What, fat boy come and get me?'

'Chicks dig a couple of love handles.'

Ed leans out of the window and places his order. A girl with yellow hair and matching skin smiles at him. Her teeth are very straight, like tiny white bricks. Her smile makes her vaguely pretty. I lean forward and smile too. Her face returns to the sullen and disinterested we started off with. She should smile more often.

'Don't think I'm going to give you any,' Ed says, accepting his bag.

'I don't want any,' I retort haughtily.

'Last chance.'

'Nope.'

He parks the car.

'I fancy some fresh air.'

We lean against the car. I am strong for about two minutes.

'Give me a bite,' I demand.

'A moment on the lips, a lifetime on the hips,' Ed sings, holding his burger out of my reach.

'Just give me a bite.'

I reach out and try to grab at his hand. He leans into the car and I lean in to him, tickling him under the arm. He doubles up and I take my chance to grab the burger. As I run off across the car park he attempts to grab at my jacket. Once at a safe distance, I stand, turn towards him and stuff it into my mouth – the whole thing. I begin to laugh, then choke and spit. A sliver of gherkin flies from my mouth and lands on the pavement, narrowly missing somebody's trainer. The owner of the trainer is, oh my God . . .

'Nate?'

'Harry?'

I look into the face of someone who has crept into my thoughts more and more lately and I realise that he is the template any aspiring DateMate has to match. He hasn't shaved this morning, but his hair looks shiny and clean. It curls at the end. I had forgotten how lovely he was in the flesh. I swallow hard, and again, then I cough.

'You okay?' he asks.

I nod, swallow and cough some more. He waits for me to finish and I can see Ed smirking from the corner of my eye.

'So what brings you here?' Nate asks. He sucks lazily on his strawberry milkshake.

'Oh, I'm on my way to my sister's. What about you?'

'Airport. I'm doing some work in Israel.'

'Gosh. For how long?'

'I'm not sure. It just depends on the situation when we get there.'

'What do you do?' I ask, and release the cough that's been threatening to choke me.

'I work for a charity supplying medical expertise to areas that need it.'

'Wow.'

'I'd better get going. It was nice to see you again.' He looks to Ed expectantly.

'Oh, sorry, this is Ed.'

'Nice to meet you, Ed.' Nate holds out his hand. They shake with vigour. 'Well, you two have a good one.' He smiles. He has a lovely smile. I watch him as he walks to a car that's seen better days. I turn round to find Ed smirking at me.

'What?'

'You have mayo around your mouth,' he says.

I feel my stomach hit the floor. That's that, then.

When Emma asks why I am not eating much of her specially made gazpacho, I do not tell her that cold soup is the work of the devil and I have already succumbed to one of his successes earlier. No, I tell her that I am saving myself for the main culinary surprise. The surprise being that there isn't one. She brings out a notepad and the twins are told to go and watch a DVD. It is *The Princess Bride* and I hope that nobody will notice my absence after I slip away to go to the toilet. I just settle myself far enough away from the twins, when Emma's dulcet tones bellow through the house.

'Harry, we are all waiting for you!'

I skulk back in and resume my place. Emma coughs to indicate the meeting is in session. Even baby Alfie is given a stern look when he begins to cry. Katie shrugs her shoulders in an apology and attempts to soothe him. Her boyfriend Lawrence is not here, and I want to know if he has a written note to excuse himself.

'We were thinking of Drakes Hotel for the reception,' Emma informs us. She looks to Alan for his nod, but he doesn't give one. He smiles at us all instead. Once fixed in place, I suspect his smile won't move for the rest of the afternoon.

'But Mum and Dad offered to have it their garden,' I remind my sister. She glares at me and we both fall back into childhood staring games. Who will look away first? It will be me.

'We' – Emma looks at Alan for solidarity – 'thought that numbers might prohibit that particular option.' She says it with a touch of disdain, and I want to grab her hair and pull it, just as I wanted to when we were younger, but never did.

'Drakes. That's the posh one, isn't it?' My mother sounds impressed. 'Margaret's daughter stayed there and said a cappuccino was five pounds.'

'Five pounds!' my father says, frowning.

'It did come with biscuits.'

'I should bloody well hope so.' He shakes his head, clearly disgusted.

Emma coughs for attention.

'You can all stay the night. It will be a treat.' Emma draws a line across her notepad.

'For those who can afford it,' I say.

'What's that supposed to mean?' she demands.

The rest of the family remain silent and place their usual bets.

'I can't afford Drakes, Emma. I've got Chloe's wedding a few weeks afterwards. Wouldn't it be nice to have it at Mum and Dad's?'

'It would be lovely, Em. Dad could do a barbecue,' Katie pipes up enthusiastically. I smile gratefully for the back-up. It's not like her to take sides.

Dad shrugs his shoulders noncommittally, but I can see he likes the idea.

'It would mean reducing the numbers,' Emma says, clearly irritated by this little blip in her plans.

'I thought it was meant to be an intimate family kind of affair.'

Emma ignores me and continues on to the entertainment.

'There will be a violin ensemble as guests arrive and the twins will be singing a duet after the speeches.'

'I was thinking of having my hair cut into a bob, like Victoria Beckham,' my mother interjects. Emma falls silent.

'So, anyone for a game of Snap?' my father asks cheerfully, and we share a smile.

The rest of the afternoon is spent listening to my sister talk pretentious shit, and with me holding my tongue. When Ed arrives to pick me up, it is not before time.

'So, you ready to go?' I ask, grabbing my coat and bag.

'Oh, Harry, let the boy take a breath. Cup of tea?' Mum asks.

'That would be great, thanks,' Ed replies.

Much to Emma's irritation, Mum is acting as if the kitchen is her own. She noisily opens and shuts cupboards looking for cups and biscuits.

'Use these mugs,' Emma instructs, closing the door to her best china. The mugs are the ones she uses for workmen.

'The boys are in the living room, dear,' my mother says, and Ed smiles his best 'mums love me' smile. He transfers the smile to me as he pushes past to get to the living room.

'Very tall, isn't he?' my mother gushes. I ignore her and follow him in. He makes himself comfortable next to my father and begins to talk cricket. I cough very loudly.

Ed turns. 'You're giving me the look,' he says.

'The look?' my father asks.

'She has a look. You must have seen it. The one that says, right now she is expecting the sun, the stars and the moon. The one that says if she doesn't get them gift wrapped to go in five seconds, she will break your legs. It's similar to the one that says dance. Dance or I will shoot.'

'Aah, that look.' My father chuckles, and I frown at him for colluding with someone who talks so much rubbish.

'Do the guys on DateMate know what they are letting themselves in for, I ask myself?' Ed laughs.

I want the ground to swallow me whole. Please swallow me whole. Please! I close my eyes, and then open them again. No, I'm still here and my father is looking up at me in surprise.

'Internet dating? Is that sensible, darling? I hope you are being careful.' The lines on his forehead look more pronounced and I want to reach over and smooth them down with the palm of my hands.

'I'm being careful, Dad, you don't have to worry.'

'Internet dating! Who's Internet dating?' My mother appears.

'Harriet is,' Alan says, not looking up from the TV. I want to walk over and slap the bald patch that is appearing on the top of his head; the one he tries desperately to hide.

'Harriet? Well, I don't know what to say,' my mother says. Now there's a first.

She looks at me with something akin to respect and I don't know whether to feel pleased or horrified.

'Of course, as horrible as it is, and not that I want any of my girls to have to resort to it, it's probably for the best.'

'Why?' my father asks, looking irritated.

'She would be the first to say she hasn't had much luck

so far. And she's not getting any younger. She's the only one left.'

'This is not *Pride and Prejudice*, Dee,' my father answers.

'Don't be clever, George. My point is she needs to do something, and it's nice that people who wouldn't normally get out can meet up and chat.'

Oh God. I want to go home.

'Mum, Internet dating is not like that. It's very different these days. Professional, normal people use it, not social inadequates whose only relationship has been with a gerbil.'

'Gerbils? What's the matter with you, Harriet?'

As I die my slow and painful public death, Ed is keeping his head down, slurping his tea.

'I think it's a great idea and it's what people do now,' Katie says helpfully.

'Even so. You need to be careful. There are men out there who groom you to meet them.'

'That's paedophiles, Mum. I'm twenty-nine.'

'And that's why it's good you're doing something, dear. Time is running out. Remember, your Aunt Susan started going grey at thirty, and that was it. She ended up with Colin. It was a waste of a good woman.'

'You haven't put your real name on there, have you?' Emma asks with panic in her voice.

'You can always say it's someone who looks like her,' Alan reassures her.

'Ed, coat.' The tone in my voice tells him something, because he moves quickly.

At the front door, my father hugs me close. Behind him the rest of the family wait. We always do the waving from the front door thing.

'You don't need to do Internet dating. Someone who

deserves you is out there somewhere and he will know that you are special, without you providing a list of measurements and likes and dislikes.'

'Thanks, Dad. I'm just doing it so that I have a date for Chloe's wedding. I don't want to go on my own.' I am surprised when my voice falters and I get the sudden urge to cry.

'Just be careful, sweetheart, and if you can't find anyone, I'll go with you. I may not be the youngest swinger in town, but I can dance a mean Funky Gibbon.' He hugs me close and kisses the top of my head. I smile and swallow my tears away. His jumper feels prickly on my face, but I stay there, feeling drowsy in the warmth of his arms. I can hear his heart beat.

'Thanks, Dad.'

Emma is standing behind him, her arms folded over her substantial bosom. Her face is a mask. We do the fleeting hug thing, with the continental kisses she likes, but I never get it right. She smells of freesias and hairspray. The pearls make her look like the wife of an American president. I thank her for a lovely time. I should have left it at that, but for some unknown reason I get the urge to do the right thing.

'I'm sorry about earlier, Emma, but I really can't afford the hotel.'

'You afford what you want to afford,' she says, bristling in her Alexon two-piece.

'What's that supposed to mean?'

'It means it would be nice to have support from the whole family.'

'It would be nice if I had a rich husband who could pay for a whole bloody weekend at Drakes. It would be nice if I didn't have to work for a living to pay my rent!'

'This is my big day, Harry.'

I want to ask why. Why do we all have to endure another one of Emma's big days? Her first wedding, the girls' christening, wedding anniversaries, her twenty-first, twenty-fifth, thirtieth and thirty-fifth birthday, her election as big cheese on the parish council, her first prize at the flower arranging . . . the list goes on. Why do we have to endure her gazing into Alan's watery eyes and telling him she will continue to obey and whatever else it was she promised to do the first time round? Will he believe her this time?

I will sign an affidavit, and swear that she is a good wife and mother, an upstanding pillar of the community, an expert on hors d'oeuvres and the reason Marks & Spencer saw an upturn in profits last year. I will do anything not to be subjected to another bloody self-obsessed party, where everyone talks with their best telephone voices and I am told not to drink too much.

'Another big day?' Now why did I say that?

'Just because you—' she begins, and I know what is coming. I put my hand up to stop her.

'Don't even go there.'

Ed coughs loudly to remind us that he is a reluctant witness to the continuing battle between me and my sister. Mum loves to tell the story of how Emma drew on my two-month-old face with a felt tip pen, of how she cut the tail off my donkey outfit the night before the nativity play, of how she didn't talk to me for two months after Katie and I did a rendition of 'Dancing Queen' at her wedding. Apparently I was old enough to know better. I have a lifetime of stories about Emma and me at odds with each other. According to Emma, it's because I have what Mum's friend Janice calls a fancy job; I think I am better than her. I don't, really I don't. If she would listen to me, I would tell her how rubbish I am at it.

'Are you two always like that with each other?' Ed asks, as we drive home. I nod and follow the tiny rivers of rain on the car window. I think of my sister and wish it wasn't like that. I don't know what it is; something strange happens when we are together and the old samurai swords come out. The wounds are often superficial, but sometimes they cut deeply. I let out a big sigh. Today wasn't one of my best.

'So what are you up to tonight? Trawling the Net for some unsuspecting male?' Ed asks.

'I can't believe you brought that up.'

'I'm sorry, I didn't realise it was a secret.' Ed looks at me sheepishly and passes me the gummy bears.

'So what are you doing? Seeing Noush?'

He nods. 'I guess so.'

'You two seem good together.'

Ed nods again. 'Yeah, we will probably settle down on a farm where I make organic cheese and live off the obscene amounts of money she makes from modelling, and our long-limbed, long-haired, multilingual children will go to school with Lily Allen's kids.'

'Yeah?'

'Nah.' Ed turns to me and laughs.

My thoughts turn to Nate and I wonder if he has a girlfriend and if they plan to settle down on a cheese-making farm. I bet he likes a Wensleydale. No run-of-the-mill, mild Cheddar for him. Oh no. This is a man who probably goes fishing for his tea and eats his catch simply; with a splash of olive oil, lemon and a hunk of crusty bread. I bet he never uses a recipe book. I imagine he likes pickled onions, too.

*

Josie has sent me a fake moustache in the post. It's meant to be a disguise; just in case I see Nate again. I put it on and spend the rest of the morning talking in a French accent. It amuses me if no one else. The unexpected absence of Georgina means that the office is unusually relaxed. An email was sent out to say that she was incapacitated with a migraine and hoped to be back by the end of the week. Barbara says it was brought on by an allergy attack. This is disappointing and means my hoped-for Wednesday meeting will not happen. What did my horoscope say? Make a note of the twenty-ninth. I look at the calendar. The twenty-ninth is next week. I can't wait that long.

The arrival of a flushed-looking Jeremy stops me banging my head on the desk. His usual cool exterior has been replaced with sweat.

'Follies have withdrawn their advertising.'

'What? Why?'

'They said they're going to try *Bath at Large*.'

This is not good news. There have been minor moves to the 'other side', but our major contributors have remained loyal.

'Who have we got to replace them?'

'That's what I came to tell you, no one. You now have a great big gaping hole in your page with an hour to go before sign off.'

'And?'

'This is bad, Harry. Donald is signing off and I don't want him to know, not until I find someone to replace them. Is there anything you can use as temporary filler?'

'Leave it with me,' I reassure his panic-stricken face, and he nods, already grateful for the miracle I am not sure I possess.

'Why are you wearing a fake moustache?' he asks.

'It's a long story.'

'It suits you.'

'Thanks.'

My mind is blank. What do I do?

Oh my God! What sort of stupid-arsed question is that? What I do is use the situation to my advantage. This is the bit where Rocky wins the match. Bif, bof and she's down. I can hear my heart beating. It's too fast. I'm going to have a heart attack and nobody will ever know that I can do better. Calm down. It's the right thing to do. Be brave. My palms feel hot and clammy. I rub them together. Deep breath . . . I open the secret file that contains my edited blog entries and swallow hard as my hand hovers over my mouse. Select. Cut and paste . . . I look around as if I am about to bring the country to its knees with my actions. I begin to type.

Donald is brown and wrinkled like a walnut. He is bored and he sighs a lot. I look around the office as he scans over my page with surprisingly clear blue eyes. They are startling in their intensity and remain the only thing not affected by the sun, his advancing years and a diet of whisky and soda. I am not sure whether he knows what he is looking for, or if he is just doing a good impression, but I am hoping the latter. As far as I can make out, he has never been an editor in his life, but bought *Life to Live*, and five other regional magazines to complement his burgeoning leisure empire. He looks up and frowns. I hold my breath.

'A Girl With a Date in Her Diary? I like it.'

'Without a Date in Her Diary,' I correct him. 'Without.'

'Good, good.'

I feel a little lighter. Donald looks up at me with a frown.

'Were you wearing a fake moustache earlier?' he asks.
I nod.

Girl Without a Date in Her Diary – Blog entry – June 28th

My horoscope today said that I have to take risks and embrace the sun in my moons – both professionally and in my love life. I have a limited window, apparently. It didn't say anything about the twenty-ninth, but maybe different astrologers see different things. With this in mind I have done something brave at work and put my reputation on the line. I have also agreed to another date – tomorrow with High Flyer.

I spend a lot of my time working but would love to find someone to sweep me off my feet and away from the four walls that restrict me. I love the outdoors and eating out al fresco. If you are a girl who likes to travel and explore new places, then you may be the one for me.

He has suggested we meet in a village pub a couple of miles out of the city. I have a good feeling about this. My sun and moons are ready. Picture the scene:

We will share a bottle of rose wine and as the sun disappears, wonder where the time has gone. Reluctant to go home he will suggest dinner, where the soft candlelight will make me appear unusually beautiful. By the time C's wedding comes round we will wonder what life was like before we met. We will laugh a lot and hold hands. He will be funny and entertaining in a group. He will offer to design Mum and Dad's extension (he is an architect). At the wedding, we will smooch on the dance floor, and he will tell me I am beautifully constructed, as J (my ex) glares at us from the corner of the room and his girlfriend refuses to dance because she will have a snag in her tights. Later, we will holiday in Italy and picnic on a remote hillside with seven different cheeses, olives and red wine. We will toast DateMate and laugh at the absurdity of it all. Can you believe we met on Internet dating, darling? No, but I am so glad we did. Where shall we go next week? Give Brad a ring and see if they fancy EuroDisney.

An early morning mist hangs gently beneath a pale watercolour sky. The streets are empty except for a few people unlocking the doors to shops, putting out containers of flowers and picking up litter. It is the calm before the storm. I can't remember the last time I was up this early on a weekend. My date is obviously a morning person. I am wearing a short-sleeved, knee-length floral dress and a pair of brown boots. The sun is yet to burn through and it's still slightly chilly. I am glad of the last-minute addition to my outfit of a tiny navy cardigan. A road sweeper whistles as he passes. His smile is toothless. I feel a little like I should be dancing in the middle of the road like Mary Poppins and singing about a wonderful day.

My date for the morning is the only person in the café. He must have been waiting for them to open up. I smile, pleased that he looks pretty similar to his photo.

'Stuart?'

He stands up and I am not sure if his surprised smile is a good or a bad sign.

'Harry?'

He is dressed in jeans and a taupe sweater. Slightly taller than me, which is always good, his blond, layered hair curls slightly at the ends. He reminds me of a golden retriever dog. When I was young, my Auntie Deirdre had one and I remember thinking it was nice and I would like one when I grew up. I fiddle with my purse.

'Shall I get you a drink?' he asks.

'Cappuccino, please.'

I watch him go. He is nice. Apple pie nice. You can't go wrong with an apple pie. Talking of food, I look at the breakfast menu. I am getting hungry. My Stuart pie walks back with two coffees.

'You are just as pretty as your photo suggested,' he says, and I laugh like an embarrassed schoolgirl. Hell, I like him already.

'But I can't imagine why a lovely girl like you should need to go on a dating website.'

'I didn't need to – I just thought it might be a nice way of meeting people. I don't really do the club thing any more, and evenings spent in trendy bars seem to be dwindling as well.'

'Never did the bar and club thing,' he says.

'What, not ever? Not even when you were at uni?' I ask, a little surprised.

'No, I was into model airplanes. I spent most of the time with the model group I belonged to.'

I nod, and try not to jump to any conclusions.

'And do you still play . . . fly model airplanes?'

'No, gone on to bigger and better things. I fly balloons now.'

'Wow – hence the name High Flyer.' I laugh at my own stupidity. And there was me thinking High Flyer meant successful, frequent-flyer air miles, hotels and exciting destinations. 'So, balloons. How exciting. Do you have your own?'

'Our company sponsors one, so my mate Geoff and I can get out most weekends. It's a real escape from sitting in front of a computer.'

I nod, in an interested way.

'I went on a balloon safari last year,' he offers like bait. I know I am meant to be impressed and I am. It's the animal part. I love animals. I can talk David Attenborough as good as the next person, probably better. And I do. The next half-hour passes pleasantly with exchanged stories of giraffes, antelopes, elephants and the lifecycle of the mole (my contribution) and I am relaxing.

'Another coffee, or perhaps some breakfast?' I ask. Croissants are romantic food and I have my eye on a rather large one. We could share it. No, forget that. I want my own.

'Actually, you know I said I flew balloons, well, I thought it would be really nice, and a little romantic if I took you on a flight today. That's why I wanted to meet early. Early morning flights are the best.'

I am surprised, and it obviously shows.

'Is something wrong?'

'No, no. What a lovely idea,' I stammer.

My profile says I am a go-getter action-type girl. Now is not the time to say I am terrified of heights.

The noise frightens me. It's loud, very loud. The basket is big, which should reassure me, but it doesn't. I am already feeling claustrophobic.

'Are you cold? Did you bring a jacket?' Stuart asks, looking concerned.

'No.' My teeth chatter. Icy-cold fingers of fear dig their nails into my arms and I shiver again. Like a true gentleman, he places a fleece round my shoulders. Normally I would be touched by this gesture of chivalry, but right now I hate him for making me do this. I jump out of my skin as the flame fires up into the balloon. Stuart's friend Geoff smiles at me encouragingly and I grimace back.

'You are going to love this,' he shouts above the noise, and I nod because I want to believe it will be true; that after the fear has gone I will be like a bird up there, flying high. How high? HOW HIGH? No, it's best I don't know.

'Ready?' he asks, and I nod, because this is all I seem to be able to do right now.

The basket jerks and then jerks some more. Then it sways and jerks again. I feel the laws of gravity deserting me and I hold on to Stuart for support. He smiles like the hero he imagines he is. I am not looking over the edge, but I know from the way that I can't see trees any more that we are going up, that we are now too high for me to climb out and go home. It is hurting my jaw I am biting down so hard.

'Wooohooo,' Stuart shouts, and I admire his enthusiasm – I really do, but right now I wish he would just keep his wooohooos to himself, because I am counting my breaths and keeping them slow, slow, slow – breathe, that's it, slowly. Oh God. I hyperventilate.

'Are you okay?' Stuart shouts.

'We might have to go back,' I shout back.

Stuart laughs and hugs me. Oh my God, what if they take me to an abandoned farmhouse and kill me? What if this is what Stuart and Geoff do? The panic increases.

'You do look a little peaky. You'll be fine, though. Once you get used to it, you'll love it.' Stuart hugs me again. I resume my counting, but it is not helping.

'Just take a peek over the edge.'

I shake my head no.

'It might help. To see rather than feel. Get your bearings.'

Geoff nods. I peek over the edge of the basket and scream. I scream so loud that I cannot hear Stuart. His mouth is opening but I cannot hear him. He shakes me and I stop screaming and start crying.

'I have to get out. You must take me back down.'

'Don't be silly. You've just had a shock. It will be great. You will love it. I promise.'

If he tells me I will love it one more time I will push him overboard.

'No, I'm sorry, I really am, but you must take me back down,' I shout as firmly as possible.

'But that's ridiculous,' Stuart replies, clearly annoyed.

'Please . . . you need to take me back down . . .' I am on the verge of hysteria. 'Now!'

'But we've just got up.' He glances at Geoff who shakes his head in bemusement.

I am crying now, and shaking, and praying. Judith would be impressed that I have finally found God. If I get out of here I will tell her that I think she may have a point. She will like that. I realise that I am talking to myself, but someone needs to calm me down and Stuart is looking horrified.

'Look, I think you need to calm down,' he shouts, his voice hard.

I can feel the sweat running cold down my back. Counting is not helping and my breathing has a mind of its own. It is working against me, threatening to suffocate me rather than save me. I want to be sick.

'I don't think you realise the gravity of the situation. I am not someone who regularly makes a fuss. When I say I need to get down and get out of here, I mean it. Please. Get me down, NOW!'

Stuart is not looking at me as if he has found true love.

Eventually, I feel the jolt of the ground. I thank all the gods in the universe – including Judith's. Geoff helps me out and I fall to the ground like a woman who discovers an oasis amidst a desert. I laugh, aware that I am sounding a little hysterical. I don't care. Right now I'm just happy to be alive.

When I find my land legs, Stuart is glaring at me, his arms folded.

'I need to go home,' I stammer through chattering teeth.

'I'll walk you back,' he mutters.

'It's okay, I'm—'

'Come on,' he demands and marches off across the grass. 'I'll see you later,' he calls to Geoff who looks a lot more forgiving than my date for the day. I try to convince Stuart that I am okay on my own, but he refuses to concede and continues to walk. I look around and consider my options. We have landed in a field, but I have no idea where. I reluctantly follow him, barely able to keep up.

Half an hour later, without a word spoken, we reach civilisation.

'I'm okay here, thanks,' I say.

'If you're sure?'

I'm not, but I can't stand another minute of this.

'I'm sure, thank you.'

'I'm sorry you didn't like the balloon,' he says, but I get the impression any real sympathy for me was left two miles away.

'Me too,' I reply.

He nods, seemingly satisfied he has done everything he could. I turn and begin walking towards a row of houses.

Bastard. Selfish rotten bastard.

The earlier sunshine has disappeared and there is a chill in the air. I continue walking, cold and dejected, trying to recognise a familiar landmark. I think I know where I am. Maybe not. Now that the sickness has passed, I am also extremely hungry. I look at my watch. It is eleven thirty and I haven't eaten anything. My feet are hurting, but not as much as my pride. Oh God, where the hell am I? I'm not going to cry. I'm bloody not!

'I don't suppose you know where I am?' I ask a man with a walking stick and a deerstalker hat.

'Bath,' he says rather unhelpfully and walks off.

'Thanks a bunch,' I mutter.

My stomach growls loudly as a substantial barrel-shaped woman with an empty wicker basket passes. She has a Barbour jacket and a walk that says she knows where she is going. I follow her from a safe distance. We turn a corner and I sigh with relief. There are people; lots of them and they are surrounded by food.

The farmers' market is my saviour. There is hot tea and stalls of food waiting for me to sample their wares. I am so hungry I feel sick. Chilli olives, tiny cubes of goat's cheese, a slice of salmon and dill flan, squares of dark cardamom chocolate and a hunk of walnut bread are devoured gratefully. I become emotional over large flat cap mushrooms and buy some cheese, chutney and an apricot tart. The market is full of people with arms and bags full of large dark green leaves, French loaves, bags of blood-red oranges and home-made chutneys. Children's hands reach up and remove tiny squares of iced sponge and women listen intently to a man talking about his large lemons. I wander through the striped canopies and begin to feel more human. My near-death experience is almost forgotten as I hand over money in exchange for brown paper bags full of fresh home-grown produce. I have no idea what I will do with it all but I feel inspired by red chard and a circular soot-covered cheese called Black Betty.

A stall with ciabatta bread, olive oils and large strings of brown toasty garlic bulbs entices me over. A man with a beard and a red handkerchief tied round his neck hands me some pale bread and points to a small dish of oil.

'Go on, dip it in there, it's not strong.'

I dip and place the golden drenched bread into my mouth. The oil slides on my tongue and touches my taste buds with something smooth, smoky and almost sensual.

'Wow, that's gorgeous.'

'Good, huh? It's the roasted garlic.'

'And the bread. It melts in the mouth. How do you get it that soft?'

He laughs as I dip another piece in the oil.

'Come and find out. We do a bread-making day course. You'll like it.' He smiles like a pirate.

'You should never be afraid to use garlic in your cooking. It can transform the mundane into the wonderful. Crush it beneath your hands and smell. Isn't that amazing? Go on, come closer . . . that's so good. Isn't that good?'

Is it me or is he making garlic sound sexy?

I sign up for the cookery class immediately and walk home happy. I may not have a date but I do have a string of beautiful garlic bulbs and enough food to invite Chloe, Tad, Josie and Ben over for Sunday lunch.

I bet Angelina doesn't get garlic breath.

Girl Without a Date in Her Diary – Blog entry – July 1st

Let's talk about farmers' markets. I have never made the effort, preferring instead my local supermarket for a one-stop shop. Disgraceful, huh? My loss. Now I am a convert. If you are down in the dumps, the fresh, funny-shaped vegetables and smiling faces of the stall holders will lift your spirits. You can even talk to people, if you like. I did and I liked it. It is a place for the senses. Touch, smell, and taste your way around. Then go home and cook something you've never made before. Invite a friend round or, if you have more than one, make it a dinner party. Saturday sorted.

I also tried my hand at bread making. Something else I can recommend to all you foodies out there. All that kneading is a very therapeutic experience and quite sensual; especially with a man called Patrick behind you, clasping your hands, forcing them into the dough, his breath on your neck . . . maybe I'm making it sound more sexually charged than it was, but I enjoyed it. His loaf rose beautifully. He said it was all in the wrist action.

P.S. Other foodie things to do can be found in my GWAD column in *Life to Live* magazine.

P.P.S. Men go to cookery classes. Just thought I would mention it.

P.P.P.S. . . . Did I mention *Life to Live*? To find out how I got on with my latest Internet date, buy it, read it, then tell your friends about it.

Georgina opens her drawer, takes out a small rectangular packet and swallows a couple of tablets.

'Are you feeling better?' I ask with as much sympathy as I can muster.

'Bloody allergy. I don't understand it. I thought I was only allergic to cats, but there must be something else here. I'm going for tests.'

'Aah, well . . .'

My explanation is cut short by Georgina slamming a copy of *Life to Live* down on her desk.

'Now, would you mind explaining what this is?' she barks at me.

The What's On page stares back at me.

'Since when has this page become a forum for girls looking for men?'

'I thought—'

'You thought what?' Georgina interrupts.

'That it might be funny?' I offer painfully. Of course it wasn't, not in the slightest, but I thought . . . What did I think? What the hell did I think?

'I wanted sexy and posh with cocktails. It's a What's On column, not an opportunity for you to include a "funny" story from a girl who—'

'But it has recommendations,' I protest.

'Men who read books, and free fucking nibbles!'

I have no answer. I feel crushed, like a tiny ant beneath her wide-fitting court shoes.

Georgina closes her eyes and takes a deep breath. I wait, and shrink further into the floor. Her eyes are like slits when she opens them. I stand there, my feet stuck to the carpet. I imagine a future of telling anyone who will listen that I ruined my life with a stupid idea. I will then drink a bottle of gin, before taking to the stage and singing Celine Dion songs at a late-night karaoke bar.

'We needed something to fill the space, and I had to act fast. I've been writing a blog and the feedback has been positive. I thought it might work well in a column.'

'And do you think it does?'

'Yes.' I am brave. I am a lion. I am taller than her.

'This', she points to my piece, 'is not *Life to Live*. Hopefully, Poppy's column will be in our next issue.' The words are weighted, heavy with insinuation and hidden messages. My shoulders droop slightly. I pull them back.

'Couldn't you at least give my column a chance? See what happens, and if it doesn't work, then go with Poppy.'

'This is not *Sex and the City*, Harry.'

'No, but it isn't Paris Hilton's Best British Friend, either.'

I swear Georgina snorts like a bull waiting for the charge. She talks through gritted teeth.

'Poppy will appeal to our readership. She will appeal to people who appreciate the finer things in life and whether you like it or not, she will be the new face of *Life to Live*. Now I suggest you leave my office while you still have a job.'

She sneezes loudly, and for one brief moment I consider telling her about the cat hair. Then I change my mind.

As I walk home an old woman passes me. She is hunched and slowly dragging a plastic white Scottie dog along the pavement by a lead. She has no one to tell her that this is not a real dog. This will be me in twenty years' time; I am convinced of it.

Josie is upset. I know she is by the appearance of a box of Krispy Kreme doughnuts.

It's good to have her here, although I won't be saying this by the end of the weekend. She is untidy and I am her Hoover. It used to work well when we were living together full time; there was a consistency to her untidiness, which meant it was spread out and prompted a kind of acceptance on my part. Now, she is like a hurricane, whirling in and then whirling out again, leaving me with the devastation and an empty muesli box. Anyway, that comes later. She has only been here a few hours, and right now I still love having her here. She brings some much-needed laughter and life into the flat.

'I don't know, Harry. Is Ben the One? I mean, how do you know?'

'But I thought you did? You said the first time you slept with him he was the one you were going to marry. It was all very romantic.'

'That was a long time ago, now we have a new sofa,' Josie laments, sticking a currant on her tongue. It looks like a fly.

'What's the sofa got to do with it?'

'We were just sitting on it the other day and I thought, is this it? A brown leather sofa and watching Will Smith films!'

'But you love Ben?'

'I know I do. But would I love someone better? I hate Will Smith films.'

'But that's what love is all about. Compromise and spending money on household goods.'

'Yes, but Chloe adores Tad. I mean, she worships him. They are a really romantic couple, and me and Ben . . . well, I don't think I adore him. Is it just habit with us now? Should we really be rushing into this? Should I be with someone called Half-Man-Half-Biscuit?'

'No, and you're hardly rushing it, Jose. You've been together for five years, and living together nearly two. I don't understand your reluctance to commit.'

I shake my head in despair. Josie loves Ben and he loves her. Okay, he likes Will Smith films, is excruciatingly shy when it comes to strangers and social situations, and is never going to be the next Bill Gates, despite an IT job, but he puts up with her never washing up a thing, the fact that she hates cooking, and her ability to spend half their grocery budget on magazines. He is also very funny, and apparently his shyness doesn't apply in the bedroom. I don't understand why she is dithering. Ben is not perfect, but then nor is she, and I am fast coming to the conclusion that the perfect man doesn't exist. But then I also come to the conclusion quite soon afterwards that if he does exist he will not be waiting like a stale loaf of bread on DateMate. He will have been snapped up by somebody blond with a pointy nose job and enhanced breasts; someone who can't keep her dirty paws off other girls' boyfriends. Someone who promises free tickets to rugby matches, and a lifetime of blow jobs. Okay, breathe. And again. Once more.

Bitch!

We spend the weekend talking about Josie's love circle (it can't be a triangle because there is no one else involved). We also drink quite a few raspberry martinis, eat anything that is over ten per cent fat, shop for things we love, but don't need, and surf through DateMate. Josie loves it, and I have to stop her registering and stalking Half-Man-Half-Biscuit. He is not even that nice.

On Monday morning I find the bathroom has been hit by the Josie bombshell, with damp towels draped everywhere and my favourite Space NK goodies left discarded with their tops off and in places where I can't find them. As I wander through to the kitchen, I expect to find her eating the last of my muesli, but everywhere is quiet. She has left a note to say that she has caught the early train back to London for a photo shoot with the people from Gucci and has threatened to return sooner, rather than later.

As I potter around the kitchen restoring things to order, I am surprised by how much I miss the noise and chaos. Having her here this weekend has served as another reminder of how much I miss someone filling my life with TV programmes I don't want to watch, trips to the cinema on a rainy Sunday afternoon with a giant packet of Revels chocolates, and out-of-tune songs drifting from the bathroom as all the hot water is used on one shower. I miss Jason.

I am choking on Coco by Chanel. Poppy Darling, or Poppy Demuth Lanvers, as she is officially known, wafts around in a golden cloud of the stuff and it's giving me a headache. She is visiting the office to 'meet the team'. She was meant to be here yesterday but cancelled half an hour before she was meant to arrive. Today, she floated in an hour late. She is sitting on my desk, sipping carefully on a skinny latte, and pretending not to notice Jeremy and Ed gazing at her with their tongues hanging out. She is, as I feared, pretty, in a posh, pony kind of way, with long colt-like legs encased in leggings, large kohl-rimmed eyes, full, glossy lips, and a teased mess of blond hair. A huge pink designer bag sits next to Jimmy Choo-clad feet, and her charm bracelets sound like tiny bells whenever she moves her arms, which she does, a lot. Poppy is exaggerated in everything she does, from the way she talks, walks and thinks.

'You want some gloss?' she asks, handing me a shimmering pink tube.

'No, thanks,' I reply, to which Poppy raises perfectly groomed eyebrows. I don't think I have ever had groomed eyebrows. My plucking skills could be improved and I am pretty sure one is thinner than the other.

'It will make you look sexy,' she says, reapplying her own. Her lips look like still-wet, varnished plastic. She looks at herself in a jewelled compact and pouts. Like Jeremy and Ed, Judith can't stop staring. Like everyone else, she is in love with Poppy Darling.

'Is it time for lunch yet? I spotted a divine little restaurant on the way over.' Poppy barely conceals a yawn.

'It's only eleven thirty.' I don't point out that she has only been here for half an hour.

'As I was saying, this is where your article will appear.' I show her the spread on my computer screen.

'Fabulous,' Poppy responds unconvincingly. 'Aah – I know what we can do,' she squeals, jumping off my desk and pulling at my arm. 'Sweetie pie, I am going to give you a make-over. You need a little Poppy glamour in your life.'

Actually, your bloody Poppy glamour is already buggering up my job and any dreams I had of doing something of note, so move your bony arse away from my desk and leave me alone to do the one thing I thought I was okay at.

Of course I don't say this out loud. Instead, I gently pull away from her Chanel, Rouge Noir grasp with a fixed smile that says, I think you are charming. Unfortunately, Poppy is used to getting what she wants and she digs those four-inch heels in.

'Come on, leave that. Weeeee are going to the ladies! You need a man in your life, and I –' she points to herself – 'I, darling, can make it happen!'

I look at her in surprise, and she shakes her gorgeous large head, her hands placed on the oversized patent-blue belt cinching in her tiny waist.

'Oh Harriet dahhling, don't look at me like that. You are not getting any, that's obvious for all to see.'

'Have you been talking to Ed? He's been talking that bouncing rubbish, hasn't he?' I demand.

'No, he hasn't said anything.' Poppy looks over at Ed, who suddenly pretends to be checking his camera. She reveals big white teeth and licks her lips. I am surprised her tongue doesn't stick to them. 'He's very cute.' She lingers a while in her imagination, before turning back to me.

'So come on.'

'No, I have work to do. I can't just disappear.'

'Why not?' Poppy regards me as if I am being difficult.

'Because I have deadlines and Georgina will not be very pleased if I just disappear.'

'Oh, don't be so boring, Harriet,' Poppy says, with irritation.

'I'm not being boring, Poppy,' I say through gritted teeth. 'I can't just leave work for a make-over.'

Poppy loses interest in me and turns away.

'Judith?' she asks, and Judith is like a puppy dog being told she is going for a walk. They disappear off towards the toilets like new best friends, leaving me to wonder if I can get away with locking the door and leaving them in there overnight.

I search around in my not-so-designer, but cheaper rip-off handbag and finally locate my compact mirror amongst the tissues, chewing gum, spare keys, plasters and paracetamol. Do I really look like someone who is clearly not waking up at the weekend to a gorgeous pair of buttocks and a six-pack? I look closer. Poppy is right; I do not have the glow of someone who is in love – or, at the very least, in lust – with anyone. My reflection becomes a little hazy and I blink away the tears. So Poppy gets to have sex and my column. Something is wrong here; very wrong.

Poppy appears again just before three p.m., to say goodbye.

'Fabulous shopping here,' she says, gathering up her bags.

I smile, because I am too tired to do anything else, and today has been a struggle of gargantuan proportions. My headache has travelled to behind my eyes and I am looking at my computer screen through slits.

'Next time, though, I am going to insist on a full make-over with make-up, hair and some retail therapy. I don't care what you say. You are in serious need of some Poppy glamour.'

'I'm not that bad!' I complain.

'No, but a present always looks nicer when it's gift-wrapped with a ribbon. I can transform anyone. All my friends ask me for advice.'

My head is thumping. Poppy leans over my desk, exposing tiny breasts. She kisses me on both cheeks. I have to hold my breath against another assault of perfume.

'Be good, sweetie. You know . . .' she gazes into the distance and I wait for the piece of wisdom I know will follow. 'I am so excited by this writing thing. It's going to be such fun. I was thinking, now I'm a writer, I really should write a children's book too. My friend Talia says Sophie Dahl and Madonna have done it, so there is no reason why I can't, and Daddy knows a publisher.' She stares back into the distance. 'The amazing adventures of a little girl called Poppy.'

Well, it's inspirational.

And with a 'Ciao, sweetie pies', Poppy totters off, waving to everyone as she goes. I feel awful. My head is throbbing. I feel nauseous, and my skin is breaking out into a rash. There is a possibility I am allergic to Poppy Darling and you know what they say about allergens. Don't expose yourself to them, and begin making a list of ways you can eliminate them from your life.

I feel the need for some fresh air and make an excuse about doing a review in town. I look through my own list of What's On and head towards the Marlborough Museum. A handful of people wander from room to room, their voices reduced to a whisper, their footsteps echoing on the polished floorboards. There is an air of serene politeness here and I feel the need to tiptoe. Even my mind is whispering. A large round bronze statue of a woman sits on a pedestal, her one bosom large like a swollen fruit. Her lips are protruding and full. A group of giggling school children point at her lack of knickers and are ushered on by their teacher. I hover in front of canvases and attempt to find something to relate to. Squares of colour draw me in and I peer in closer.

'It's kinda strange, isn't it? How a red square can hold so much fascination.'

I turn round and Nate is sitting on a wooden block. His ankles are crossed, his jeans loose. A paperback lies open on his lap. How did I miss him?

'Are you stalking me?' I ask.

'I could ask you the same.'

'I thought you were in Botswana.'

'Israel. We never made it. Things were too volatile over there.'

He is looking at me and I would pay a million pounds to know what he is thinking. My horoscope never said anything about a tall handsome stranger. Think sexy. Think confident. Think fabulous. Think tall.

'How are you?' I ask, because it seems a good place to start and open-ended questions are the way forward.

'I'm good. And you?'

'Yes, good. So you're a fan of contemporary art?' I ask.

'Yeah. I also love the fact that you can lose yourself a little in a museum.'

I nod.

'Is that why you're here?' he asks.

'I needed time out from work.'

'What do you do?'

'I write the What's On column for *Life to Live*.'

'Right.' He nods. 'My mum reads that.'

We are the only people left in the room, except for a man sitting on a chair by the entrance. He is reading a book and listening to our conversation. I look down at my shoes. I have nothing of interest to say. Nothing! Just when I need it the most I am without conversation. I am also without perfume, a make-over and high heels. Today was a slob day. Hair scraped back into a ponytail, the merest hint of mascara, jeans and trainers. Only this morning I was dismayed at the dark circles under my eyes and the grey pallor of my skin. I told myself it didn't matter today. Oh how wrong I was. I catch the eye of the man with the book. Is he thinking dull? Six or seven people drift in and begin talking softly about the paintings.

'So I guess you didn't see the author again?' Nate says.

'No.' I smile at the memory. I relax a little and lean on

to the sculpture of the woman. I wonder what he kisses like. Slow, with his hands cupping my face. He has long pianist fingers. They would fit mine.

'Ed seems nice, though.'

'He's not—'

'DO NOT touch the exhibits.' The man's voice booms through the room. I jump out of my skin. He is pointing my way with a long spindly finger that probably gets lost up his nose every night. Everyone is looking at me – no, staring at me as if I, too, am an exhibit. They begin to whisper loudly. I flush beetroot red and try to smile it off. Great! That's just great. Now I feel like a naughty schoolgirl and not sexy at all.

'Well, it was nice to see you again,' I say and hurriedly move along to another room of exhibits. Shit! Shit! I stare at a painting of a woman by a lake but the image blurs in front of me. I should have stayed. I should go back. But what would I say? Oh, I just wanted to look at the red square again? This is ridiculous. What is wrong with me?

When I emerge back on to the street I am temporarily blinded by the bright sunlight. I blink like a mole resurfacing. Nate is there, waiting. For me?

'Did you like the woman by the lake?' he asks.

I nod. We both seem to be lost for words. He rolls his paperback in his hands.

'I figured if I was going to be a stalker I should do it properly and follow you home.' He smiles.

'You might have a bit of a wait as I'm going back to work.'

'Aaah.' He nods. 'Do you have to?'

'I should really . . .' My gaze is still fixed to the pavement like chewing gum. He will think I have social interaction issues.

'Can you spare another hour?'

I hesitate. My horoscope also said, 'Be very careful of those that promise you the world. They have hidden agendas.' Is Nate promising me the world?

'I want to show you something. Come on. You'll like it.'

Is he going to take me into a dark alley and pull his trousers down? That might be wishful thinking on my part.

'It's another museum. One that has probably missed your radar.'

Oh well.

As a hazy summer sun disappears, and our shadows become longer, I forget Poppy Darling and her size-six bony backside sitting in my seat. I remember other sunny days; when I was happy, and walking beside somebody else taller than me.

When I was a child I used to go fishing with my father. On the way we would always stop at the baker's and buy three crusty cheese rolls (two for him and one for me), salt and vinegar crisps, and a couple of cans of Fanta orange. Sometimes he would sneak in a couple of iced buns and I would pretend I hadn't noticed the surprise. With our flimsy carrier bag of supplies we would make our way to the river bank to find our perfect spot. I never knew the criteria, but my father would suddenly drop his bag and turn to me with a, 'Crack open the Fanta, munchkin.'

I must have been only about nine or ten; after that it was discos and boys, but just for those two summers, it was Dad. I loved the tiny triangle of green he called a tent. It smelled of damp and plastic, and as it buckled under the weight of the rain and became sweaty with the heat of the sun, I grew like the sweet peas in my father's greenhouse. Whilst he sat in silence waiting for a bite, I would lie on a blanket, chewing sweet strands of grass, my legs crossed behind me, reading books about girls who danced, rode ponies or had brave adventures.

I look to the man by my side. He yawns. 'Sorry.'

'It's okay. Late night?'

'No, nothing as exciting. I don't sleep too well.'

'You should try camomile tea.'

'Tried it all. I am currently on a regime of warm milk, cinnamon and a giving-up-smoking CD.'

'You smoke?' I ask, surprised. He doesn't look like a smoker.

'No, but it's the whole hypnosis thing. Figured it's worth a try. So tell me about *Life to Live*.'

I don't want to talk about my job. I want to talk about his sleeping habits, his morning habits and any other habits he has in between. I decide that it might be in my best interests to hold back on that particular line of questioning and stick within the safe parameters set. He probably has a girlfriend habit and I probably don't want to know.

An old man wearing tweed trousers pulled high up to his waist and polished brogues answers a large blue door with a giant knocker. His hair forms a white ring round his head. The skin on top shines under the glare of an ornate glass lamp that hangs from the high carved ceiling. His jowls are long and droop heavily over his shirt collar.

'Good afternoon. Good afternoon to you. What a lovely surprise. Yes, what a surprise.'

'William.' Nate shakes his hand warmly. I hesitate behind him. The man smiles at me with yellow teeth.

'William, this is Harry. Would it be okay if we had a look around?'

'Hello, hello, how nice. Come in, come in.' He ushers us in with the sweep of an arm. 'Yes, yes. Come in, come in. Tea? Tea!'

'Tea would be lovely.'

I follow Nate into the four-storey Georgian house. The man opens a large white door and beckons us in. I walk into a room full of boxes and floor-to-ceiling wooden shelves. It's like a library but without the books. Instead, there are advertisements from magazines filling every space, filed in alphabetical order by year and month. They span nearly a century. I flick through old adverts from the fifties and sixties and marvel at how things have changed for us; how much freedom of choice we have now. It is a treasure trove of history. William brings us tea and we spend half an hour listening to him talk about his most valued items. His voice is rich and velvety and I feel myself relax into it. My one remaining granddad is a miserable old bastard who hates everyone and everything. He smells of turnips and wet dog. If he was more like William, I might visit him a bit more.

Nate flicks through a box. His eyelashes are long and I find myself wondering what we would do on a first date. He looks up and smiles at me. I look away, self-conscious of my thoughts. He is still watching me. Say something . . . say something.

'I didn't know about this,' I say to fill the space.

'Places like this are found by accident. I wander a lot – especially when I can't sleep. It's amazing what you find. William here is open every Wednesday and Saturday afternoon. Sometimes he has biscuits. All he asks for is a small donation for the local hospice.'

'It's great.' I make a note to include it in my column.

We thank William and head back outside.

'Thanks for bringing me,' I say.

'My pleasure. If—'

'You forgot your scarf, young lady,' William shouts out from the door.

I wrap it round my neck and we do the whole goodbye thing again with William. His goodbyes, like his hellos, are twice as long as anyone else's.

'William's nice,' I say and Nate nods.

We stand awkwardly, watching the passing cars. Somebody has put washing-up liquid in the fountain outside. It spills foam and I wave away a bubble.

'I guess I should be going,' I say.

'Me too,' he says, but makes no move to go. 'It was nice,' he says. He is so close I could lean over and kiss him. One step and it would be so easy. He opens his mouth slightly and I hold my breath. A bubble floats in front of his face and we both laugh. He glances at my watch. I wonder why he doesn't wear one. I wonder a lot of things about the man standing in front of me.

'I have a meeting in ten,' he says.

I check my watch.

'It's five to.'

'I'd better get going. I'll . . . I'll probably see you around,' he says in a panic.

'Yes, see you . . . around.'

We head off in opposite directions until I realise I am going the wrong way and have to turn around.

Girl Without a Date in Her Diary – Blog entry – July 25th

My sister is renewing her vows and my friend is getting married. Me? I am trawling through an Internet dating site hoping to persuade someone that it would be in his best interest to accompany me to both and act as if he is very much in love with me, despite only knowing me a few months. My panic to find this person was made worse recently at the local shop. Like every busy girl with some inches to lose, I was looking for something quick, easy and calorie-free. Whilst I was there I did something that made my blood run cold. I picked up a miniature bottle of wine. As I stared at the little bottle in my basket it hit me. I not only needed a date for the wedding but I needed someone to stop me falling head first into spinsterhood. I put the bottle back on the shelves and ran. Then, at the same time as the cashier, I realised I hadn't paid for my low-fat tuna pasta with sweetcorn and had to run back. A jail term was narrowly missed, but only because the cashier didn't really give a shit.

Will I wake up one morning with a couple of hairs growing out of my chin and stop shaving my legs? Do spinsters still exist? Will I be the last one in modern times prompting BBC Points West to do a little report on me when I die? The last spinster in the UK died last night from an overdose of cough medicine and fruit cake.

Shaken to the core, I logged back into my Internet dating site and made twenty men my favourites within the hour. Inspired by a recent trip to a museum I primarily chose artistic and creative types. I quite fancy an artist; someone who would be a little bohemian, a little temperamental and genius-like. I imagine myself naked on a sofa – a muse. He would paint my thighs thinner and bottom smaller, obviously, and I would be the inspiration to his sell-out shows at Tate Modern and MoMA.

Talking of museums, I highly recommend them: for expanding your mind and a little peace and quiet. It's a great way to while away a few hours and they usually have a nice little gift shop for those shopping urges and a café for the sugar ones. I suspect that if you meet a man in a museum then you are on to a winner (unless his trousers are too short and he mutters to himself as he goes around). He is more likely to be cultured, creative, sensitive and interesting. This is a sweeping statement, but even if you find a stupid man who looks great and kisses like a dream, all is not lost. Everybody has a talent. Some are just better with their hands than their brains. You don't have to listen to him.

'It's so bloody frustrating.'

'Harriet, language,' my mother reprimands.

'But I'm the one who puts the work in!' I reply sulkily. 'I'm in the office at eight every morning whilst Poppy Darling is in Ibiza, sunning her skinny little body. She doesn't even have to get up in the morning if she doesn't feel like it.'

'She is obviously good at what she does, otherwise your boss wouldn't have gone with her,' Emma says, avoiding my eyes. If she looked my way, I would surely turn her to stone.

'It's not because she is good, it's because, according to Georgina, we all want to read about someone rich and pretty,' I spit back.

'Well, I still don't know why you thought publicising this Internet dating thing was a good idea. I would have thought you would have a little more pride.' She closes her eyes briefly and breathes in through her nostrils. They flare slightly.

Aaah, so this is what this is all about. Emma is worried that I am sullying the family name; that her ladies at the tennis club will have something to gossip about.

'Nobody knows it's me,' I retort, savagely tying the ribbon round another stupid box.

'Can you be careful with those,' Emma says, with a stony face.

Sometimes she pushes the boundaries of sisterly love and it's at times like this that I dislike her intensely.

We are all sitting around her dining-room table, stuffing tissue and tying ribbon. Why she thinks her lady guests will want a funny little soap with lavender bits stuck on the top, when they could have had a champagne truffle (my suggestion), is beyond me. One of the twins – Victoria, I think – appears from her Nintendo DS and hovers behind me, looking over my shoulder. Her breath smells sugary and sweet.

'Mummy, Harriet isn't doing it right.'

'I know, darling, now it's time for bed. Off you go.' Emma turns her face towards the living room, and shouts. 'Alan? Alan! The girls need to get ready for bed. Make sure they do their French verbs and clean their teeth.'

Alan doesn't answer, but, like a slug in the garden, we know he is there.

'How is it going with the dating thing? Are you going to bring someone to Emma's do?' Katie asks, checking her phone. She hates being away from her boys but hates saying no to people even more.

'I hope you are not thinking of bringing a stranger you met on the Internet and exposing our family, and MY friends, to someone we know nothing about?' Emma looks horrified.

'Oh shut up, Emma,' I snap.

'Don't tell me to shut up.'

'Well, you're being ridiculous.'

'Excuse me. So says the girl who has lost all semblance of reality. I mean, what the hell is wrong with you? You are being so irresponsible.'

'Irresponsible?' I ask. I can't help feeling a little pleased at the thought.

'Yes, irresponsible, and you might think it's okay to throw caution to the wind in your desperation, but to expose the family to it all . . . it's unforgivable.'

'Girls,' my mother interjects a little half-heartedly.

'What do you think of it all?' Emma challenges.

My mother hesitates. We all wait.

'I think it's quite nice for Harriet to get out more, and she isn't getting any younger, Emma. She isn't like you, and this Internet dating thing . . . your father's right, we should support her, and it will be nice if she brings someone.'

I cough to remind them that the person they are talking about is actually still in the room. Katie giggles, Emma looks at me as if I am a homeless person who has inadvertently crept into her house, and Mum turns to me with a look of pity she reserves for anyone whose first language is not English.

'It's a shame that tall friend of yours is with that model,' she sighs. 'The nice men have their pick of the beautiful women.' Mum puts her hand on mine as if I am a lame dog.

'Not that you're not beautiful, darling, but you know what I mean.'

'I know what you mean,' I reply.

When Josie said she was coming back sooner rather than later, she wasn't joking. This time, though, she's here to stay. She has left Ben and moved back here permanently. When I say 'left', I am not sure if she has officially left him. They still talk on the phone, and there were no tears when she arrived on the doorstep with her suitcase, but Josie has said she needs time to think. She has warned Ben that this may take a few weeks, or even months, but the outcome will be that she will find herself. Personally, I don't think this is entirely true, because I don't know anyone who is more in tune with themselves than Josie. She knows where she is going, always has done, and doesn't compromise on anything, especially accessories. Sometimes a tendency to vary between sizes fourteen and sixteen depresses her, but she looks to the positive and embraces it all with a belt, some great eyeshadow and a wide, engaging smile. No, Josie doesn't need to find herself; she just needs to make up her mind. In the meantime, I am trying not to get upset by her untidiness, her annoying habit of eating my apples and discarding them half-eaten, of leaving the kitchen like a bombsite in the morning, her loud snoring, pinching my spot on the sofa, and forgetting to replace the milk. I am not sure if I have become less tolerant, or if she has just got worse, but if Ben can cope with this and still love her, then I think she should snap him up before he cleans the romantic, lust-fuelled dust from his glasses.

At some point yesterday, probably after half a bottle of wine, it was decided that she clearly couldn't be trusted with such a decision and it was passed to a crystal. The woman in the crystal shop assured us that it would be sensitive to issues of the heart. It looked like a pale pink lozenge and felt cool to the touch. The note that came with it promised answers and a boyfriend. I spent another fifteen pounds on a purple stone designed to bring clarity and success. When I asked if this covered all areas of life, including love, career and money, the woman behind the counter considered me with aquamarine eyes and calmly suggested that I might be expecting quite a lot from a crystal.

Back at the flat Josie held the crystal on a piece of thread like a hypnotist's watch and went cross-eyed watching to see which way it leaned. Left for no, right for yes, or was it the other way around?

'Is Ben the One?' Josie asked.

The crystal didn't know either.

'Here, let me have a go,' I insisted.

I swung the crystal and asked the question.

'Will I ever see Nate again?'

'What was yes again? Left or right?'

Neither of us could remember.

'What about, The Big Beef?' Josie asks.

She has been on DateMate for over an hour.

'Man boobs and fake tan,' I reply.

'ScubaDoo?'

'Wears lycra shorts, when he really shouldn't.'

'LustforLife?'

'Read his profile – he's looking for a kinky kitten and a no-holds-barred experience. I suspect inviting him to a wedding isn't quite what he had in mind.'

'Mmmmm, okay, what about Twinkle Toes? I am a romantic Spaniard with a fire in my belly and my heart. I am looking for a lovely girl to dance with me. Beginners should apply. Look at him, he's drop-dead gorgeous.'

Curiosity gets the better of me and I peer over her shoulder.

'One of the better ones,' I muse. 'But he knows it, and I'm not sure I want to be with anyone who rates themselves as extremely attractive.'

'Not for you! For me!'

'Jose, aren't you a little too young to be having a mid-life crisis?'

She clicks back on to LustforLife.

'Can you be a size-sixteen kitten?' She begins typing.

Big cat who loves to be stroked. Ready to be tamed.

'Jose!' I grab the mouse from her hand.

'Oh, come on, it will be funny.'

'No!' I walk away with the mouse.

'Don't be so boring.'

For once I don't care about being boring.

'Harry! You're not my mother!'

'No, I'm not, but right now I'm the best you've got and somebody needs to be sensible.'

'Okay, okay. I won't do anything. But you need to. We have just a few months left to get you a date. Come on. Look, Ordinary Boy sounds nice?'

'Ordinary Boy hasn't got a photograph,' I reply, not interested.

'Looks aren't everything and he sounds perfect for you.'

'Does he?' I reply sarcastically.

'I think you should send him a message.'

'No, I've got to phone Mum.'

I have been avoiding her calls, because life seems crowded enough without being dragged into the ongoing politics of Emma's vow renewal. The food was the latest upset. Mum wanted to contribute her salmon quiche and her special, celebration chocolate fudge cake, but Emma has refused. With her reluctance to give an inch, and Mum asking everyone what was wrong with her cooking, it took Katie to smooth the way. Now Emma has agreed to let Mum make the cake, in addition to the caterer's dessert of strawberries with elderberry sorbet and tiny shortbread biscuits. I am pretty certain I know which one Dad, Katie and I will go for – and Alan, too, if he can sneak away to the shed to eat it.

'We thought you'd emigrated,' my mother says.

'Josie says hi.'

'Aah, when's she getting married to that lovely boy?'

'I don't know. Everything's been postponed. She's back here for a while.'

'Why? What have you been saying to that girl?'

'This has nothing to do with me,' I protest.

'When Marlene got divorced, she tried to drag the whole close with her. Tony and Val had that trial separation because Val got some funny ideas into her head. Thought she was missing out, started wearing tight jeans.'

'I rang because I wanted to ask if you would make one of your delicious celebration cakes for my birthday.'

'Oh, darling, that's nice . . . I would, you know I would, but I haven't got the time. Your sister is thinking about having the reception at theirs. Apparently Drakes are being funny about the catering, so we're going shopping for some new conservatory furniture and a marquee.'

I make a joke about whether there was also going to be a new extension built and a helicopter landing pad installed, but Mum told me that jealousy was a destructive emotion. She is right, of course, and I feel bad. So bad that I ring Emma to talk hors d'oeuvres and then sigh with relief when she isn't there.

Chloe drops in on her way back from a weekend at her sister's and we use it as an excuse to visit our favourite restaurant, La Cirque. As we um and ah over the menu she reveals that she is hoping to wear something by Vivienne Westwood, teamed with a pair of outrageously high red platform shoes and Tad will complement her with a pair of specially made red shoes with engraved steel toe caps. We are suitably impressed and squeal with excitement. Josie adds that if she ever gets married, then she will be wearing something similar from Target Discount stores and the groom will be going to Clarks for a pair of shoes he can wear again for work. She adds that as bridesmaids we will all be wearing badly fitting peach satin that is guaranteed to show any cellulite and muffin bellies.

'Not that Chloe has an ounce of fat on her,' I point out.

Her cheekbones are more pronounced and she is pale and ethereal looking, like a blonde Liv Tyler in *Lord of the Rings*.

'You're losing too much weight,' I tell her.

'I would highly recommend getting married for weight loss,' she replies.

'I'll keep it in mind when the next person asks me.'

'So what happened about arriving in the Batmobile?' Josie asks.

'Tad lost interest. Now he wants us both to arrive on a London bus,' Chloe says, popping a green olive into her perfect rosebud mouth.

'For the wedding menu, we were thinking sausage and mash, with jam roly poly for dessert?' Chloe suggests.

We nod in agreement.

'And I was wondering if I promised not to dress you in peach satin whether you both wanted to be my bridesmaids.'

We shake our heads, no.

'Oh, come on,' Chloe whines.

'No! The only reason a girl asks her friends to be her bridesmaids is because it's the only time she can guarantee that she will be the prettiest one there. You don't need to do that, Chloe, because you are always the prettiest; and anyway, I for one am not going to subject myself to being dressed as an overgrown flower fairy,' Josie declares.

'So you're saying I'm not the prettiest one?' I protest.

'When Chloe is not around you are.'

I don't even bother to be upset. I have never been the

prettiest. Not at school, at university, or at work. I have never walked into a room like Chloe or my sister Katie and had people turn in admiration. This isn't a problem. I suspect there is a huge pressure to being beautiful. People want to be disappointed. Jason said I had a look about me. When I scrunched my nose up at him, he told me it made me interesting. Interesting? What the frigging hell does interesting mean? It's not beautiful. Sophie is beautiful, which leads me to believe that interesting can only take you so far. I would like to be beautiful. Just once; I want to be beautiful the day of Chloe's wedding.

As the waitress clears the plates we look at the dessert menu we had earlier vowed to resist. Do I or don't I? I am trying to be good. In my fantasy, beautiful means size zero. The conversation turns to the wedding guest list and I ask Chloe if Jason is still going. I want her to say no. If she does, then I am off the hook. I can be as fat as I want and go on my own.

'As far as I know, yes. Although, apparently, he had a falling out with Sophie last week.'

I don't want to know. Sod it! I do.

'Oh, why was that?'

'Old habits die hard,' Chloe says enigmatically. 'It's all back on now I think after Sophie read him the riot act.'

I nod and decide that I don't want to hear any more.

'I'll have the toffee fudge pudding with ice cream please,' I tell the waitress.

With Georgina not open to further discussion about the column I am at a loss to know what to do next. Josie said that this was the time to get another job, but I am reluctant to give up just yet. I need a cunning plan, or a miracle. Moons full of promise clearly don't work that well.

'You look depressed,' Judith observes, as I stare into space.

'I'm okay,' I reply, hoping she will leave me to it. The hum of the photocopier is reassuring. There is consistency there. I concentrate. Back and forth, back and forth. Judith flicks her long blond tresses over her shoulders. She is staring at me but I am being hypnotised by the green light. I wish she would go away and leave me to it. I'm hoping that at some point a flash of inspiration will change my life for ever.

'Have you thought about God?' Judith says, with a look of pity.

I gather my still-warm copies from the tray.

'If I am honest, no, but I suspect his diary is pretty full right now with people who are starving or being tortured, and despite what I feel at the moment, I can't report Georgina to Amnesty International, nor can I admit to not eating when there is a packet of Oreo biscuits on my desk. But thanks anyway.'

I walk away leaving Judith to wonder what people being starved or tortured has got to do with God.

Georgina heads me off at the water cooler. She is all fabric and frown, and I try to look efficient, shuffling my papers as if they are important.

'Have you heard from Poppy?' she asks.

'No,' I squeak.

Georgina's frown deepens, her skin mimicking the gathers in her elasticated trousers.

'She's in Ibiza,' Judith calls out from her section. Georgina's reaction is to look at me for a second too long, like it's my fault, before walking back to her office. I breathe.

'She's been in Ibiza for weeks.'

'Her family has a place there,' Judith says in a whisper.

She sidles over like a baby alligator and flutters post-Poppy glitter eyelids at me.

'She's invited me over. She says it's beautiful. She says that as you watch the sunrise come up, you can see inside yourself . . . She says you can feel God.' Judith's voice is wispy and light.

'Jude, I hate to shatter your illusions, but I suspect Poppy is probably high on something that isn't Jesus when she's watching the sunrise come up,' Ed says. He picks up his camera bag from my desk. He looks tired and worn, as if he's spent the night on someone's couch.

'Don't call me Jude!' Judith spits, and flounces off.

Ed shrugs his shoulders and turns to go.

'You okay?' I ask.

'Yeah, bad night.'

'You should stay away from beautiful women,' I suggest.

He smiles and walks away.

An email from Georgina on my computer screen with a red exclamation mark attached to it pops up. My heart lurches.

Dear Harry,
I am always looking at ways to develop our staff and I thought it might be nice for you to write another column for next month's edition. Although I have had my reservations about the 'Girl Without a Date in Her Diary' column, I was impressed by your enthusiasm and quick thinking last month. See it as an opportunity to shine. It will be a fitting platform for us to lead into Poppy's column later. Unfortunately, we are running out of time. Wednesday by eleven a.m.?
Kind regards,
Georgina

Now, I am well aware that this is because Georgina cannot get hold of Poppy or her column. Our It girl is probably swinging her arms up in the air to some Balearic beats wearing a tiny chiffon thing from D&G; her only thoughts are probably where she has left her shoes and whether she will sleep with the DJ. And who can blame her? So, I have been called upon to fill the gaping hole Georgina has in next month's copy. I could tell her to poke it, but that would be stupid. No, I am going to play the game. It will also look good on my CV. One copy is a fluke. Two copies equal experience of writing a monthly column. I email two yeses. One to Georgina and the other to someone called RiverTing on DateMate. I have four months. Now is not the time to get cold feet and RiverTing is an artist. I drift into a daydream that involves me being Carrie Bradshaw-like with a leotard top on and my artist boyfriend sprawled over my leather chair telling me about his creative juices.

'Darling, a show in New York, why that's great. Posh and Becks want to buy one of your pictures. One million pounds? That's amazing, darling. You are so talented. A picture of me? Oh darling . . . let me just finish this article.'

GWAD – *Life to Live* column

I'm thinking summer, I'm thinking flip-flops, I'm thinking riverside. This sudden interest in water has been inspired by what I am hoping will turn out to be the love of my life, or if not that, at least a date for my friend's wedding. Walks by the river are always a good thing to do, especially on a first or second date and I am quite partial to a delightful Tea Barge run by an equally delightful lady called Martha, who makes the best cakes and has a tortoise called Fred. What could possibly go wrong when you are beckoned in with a smile as welcoming as the tea and vintage, floral cushions.

The river is versatile and free. Here is a list of other river-inspired things you can do:

- Hire a barge with your friends for the day. Lie on the roof in an itsy-bitsy bikini; but only if you have an itsy-bitsy body to go with it. If you haven't, then go for intelligent instead and read a book.
- Walk the eight miles to Welford-on-Avon. With all the calories you have used up you can treat yourself to lunch. Get the train back. There is no need to be obsessive about exercise.
- Carry a parasol. Because where else could you get away with it?
- Hire a punt and sit there looking gorgeous whilst a friend does all the hard work. Suck seductively on an ice lolly so that any available man who happens to go by will have dirty fantasies about you for the rest of the day. He will then track you down and declare his undying love a week later.
- Cycle along the river with the Grunt and Grub Club and see Lycra as it should be worn – with big thighs and impressive proportions.
- Alternatively, start jogging, but never call it that. It's running, and remember to smile at fellow joggers. One of them could be your future boyfriend. Fit people like other fit people. You can develop a leg injury later on.

My Riverside Encounter

Oh well, *c'est la vie*. (That's me trying to be positive about another disaster.)

Girl Without a Date in Her Diary – Blog entry – August 2nd

I should have known. When I asked my date for the day why he was Internet dating, he replied something about needing to look beyond his world as it was . . . to search for what lies inside, to explore and surprise himself. RiverTing didn't believe we have one love, but have the capacity to love many things in different ways. According to him, the world is a multi-coloured thread of people and nature.

Which was fine. I'm okay with all of that, but it was his jeans and his fingernails. They were dirty. His T-shirt was unironed and his scuffed boots looked as if they were about to fall apart. He smelled of man. Stale man. Maybe it's an artist thing. I wasn't too keen on the dreadlocks either. He was nice though and I figured I could get used to the dreadlocks. It's kind of cool, and not very me, which appealed enormously. I began to like the thought of shocking friends and family with my new, dirty, but very cool artist boyfriend. And he had a gallery. That impressed me. This is where we arranged to meet.

The gallery turned out to be a barge. It was dark green with the words 'Artist's Muse' painted along the side in elaborate red letters. The paint was dull and cracked like a blister; the roof full of fire wood, various plants, a bicycle, a kite and an old piece of wood painted with the words 'The Riverboat Gallery.' A wind charm made up of torn strips of coloured material and cutlery tinkled in the wind.

I stepped carefully over pieces of carved and strange shaped wood. It smelled of stewed carrots.

'You live here?' I asked. I didn't mean to sound so shocked, or for my voice to be quite so high pitched. I sounded like my mother.

'I can't imagine ever going back to dry land; to living in a house, paying a mortgage, council tax, mowing the lawn, being a slave to capitalism.'

'No,' I replied, and wondered if he could ever imagine cleaning.

I tried to think unpredictable and exciting, but all I could think about was that here was a man who made papier-mâché seagulls and had a dirty sofa. My entire muse-like fantasies went floating down the river.

I look across at Josie, who nods.

'Do it,' I tell Suzie.

The procedure is painless, and I feel curiously liberated. I am now a girl with a funky fringe, and I will soon have hazelnut tones expertly layered through my hair to give texture and shine. Since Poppy's visit, I have been worrying about my lack of fabulous and have decided this is the reason I have had to resort to Internet dating. If I am exuding 'no sex – given up', then it's no wonder I can't get a date in the normal world. Would you pick up the tin with the faded label from the supermarket shelf? No! Well, not unless it was on special offer. And, if I am honest, I am also a little worried about hitting my thirtieth birthday. Josie didn't help. After telling me not to take any notice of an empty-headed piece of fluff called Poppy, she then agreed that having the same hair style for six years was a little boring and nobody did mousy brown any more. I was fast becoming a relic.

'I've loved reading your page recently,' Suzie says, expertly snipping away. 'The GWAD bit about Internet dating. It was funny. One of my clients works in the bookshop at the top of Milton Street. She said that they had loads of enquiries about forthcoming author events. It made me laugh thinking of all those women lurking amongst the bookshelves.'

I blush, pleased that not everyone hated it.

'I really admire her, doing the Internet dating thing. It made me think differently about it. Who knows, I might give it a go myself.'

'And I love her suggestions of things to do. They made me laugh,' a woman with half a head of ringlets pipes up.

'Have you been reading her blog too? I can't believe she didn't like that RiverTing. He sounded really cool,' one of the hairdressers shouts across the salon. This prompts another discussion.

'Oh no, he wasn't the one for her. She wants a man with the grrrr factor.'

'Shiny hair and clean underpants.'

'Got to like the arts.'

'Tall and dark.'

'Funny.'

'But sensitive.'

I feel a curious sense of pride. People are reading my column and my blog. Who would have thought it?

'So, who is it?' Suzie asks.

'Oh, just someone I know.'

'Tell her I have a brother who would love her.'

'What does he do? Does he own a good suit? Does he own his own place? Any dangerous or stupid hobbies?' Josie pipes up from behind her magazine as Suzie goes off in search of a brush.

'Josie!' I reprimand.

'What? You won't ask. You let that bloke Nate go. I mean, if it was left to you we wouldn't be getting anywhere.'

'I didn't let Nate go. He wasn't interested. If he was, he had plenty of opportunities to ask me out.'

'Perhaps he's shy. Have you thought of that?'

'Well, it doesn't matter now. I probably won't see him again. He said something about going away again.'

I think of Nate and wonder where he is. Saving lives somewhere? I bet he has a girlfriend. Guys like that always have a girlfriend. Suzie brushes the hair from my shoulders. I survey my reflection. It's me, but a glossy, shiny new version. I like it. I can't help wondering if Nate would.

'What do you think?' I ask Josie, swirling around needlessly.

'You look fantastic.'

'Really? I don't look sensible or boring?'

'No.'

'Or like a spinster?'

'No.'

I give Suzie a bigger than normal tip. Chloe phones as we are leaving for some S&L (Shopping and lunch).

'Sorry, Harry. I hate to pressure you, but you have to confirm if you are bringing someone to the wedding in the next three weeks.'

'That's a yes,' I reply.

'You've found someone?' Chloe asks. The surprise is evident in her voice.

'No, but I will,' I say optimistically. With this hair, how could I fail?

Josie bursts in and lands on my bed. The duvet folds in under her weight and I am engulfed by balloons and flowers.

'Happy, happy birthday!' she screams, and thrusts a gift-wrapped box into my hands. I wipe the sleep from my eyes and look at my bedside clock. It's six bloody thirty!

'I couldn't wait,' she says excitedly. 'Open it, open it.'

I deliberate over the box slowly, aware that my audience expects a build up. Inside pink tissue paper is a gorgeous charm bracelet with silver hearts and tiny pale green stones. I hug her close and put it on.

'Thanks, Jose. It's beautiful.'

'I bought some champagne as well.'

'Shall we have a glass of bucks fizz to start the day?' I suggest, attempting to get into the spirit of things, but Josie shakes her head.

'No, I'm going back to bed,' she says, and shuffles back out of the room. Now fully awake I open the cards she has placed on my bed. There are the predictable floral cards from Emma and Mum, the girlie ones from Josie and Chloe, a rude one from Ed, an Alfie hand print from Katie and Lawrence, and . . . my heart stops. Well, it doesn't stop, but it sure as hell feels like it. I study the front of the card as if it holds a clue, but it doesn't tell me anything, except that he knows what will make me laugh. I open it carefully, as if beautiful butterflies will fly out and fill the room.

Happy Birthday.
Have a great day.
Hope you are well.
Jason xx

It is not as my heart hoped: a plea to forgive him, to let him back into my life. What would I have done if he had said any of those things? Placing it carefully on my bedside table I pull the duvet over my head.

'Two butternut squash risottos, sausage of the day and root vegetable mash, one sea bream, one chicken Caesar salad with dressing on the side and no parmesan, and one salmon . . .' The waitress looks up and waits for confirmation. Mum, Dad, Katie, Lawrence and Josie are all talking over each other. The only person listening to her is me, which is exactly what everyone expects. Harriet the sensible. I nod in confirmation.

'Can we have some jugs of tap water? And, Mum, do you want sparkling?' I call out. 'And one bottle of sparkling,' I confirm.

It is my birthday. I look around the table, listening to the hum of the various conversations going on around me. My mind wanders to the past, to a birthday when Jason and I went out with Mum and Dad. He held my hand under the table as if for reassurance and I can remember thinking that I loved him. When I return to the present I feel a little lost. Wouldn't it be nice if—

A kiss lands on the top of my head.

'You look beautiful tonight.'

I look up at my father's kind face and smile.

'I just thought you should know,' he says.

'Thanks, Dad.'

Any thoughts of Jason are swept away by a chorus of 'Happy Birthday'.

Tomorrow my diet will really start, but tonight I savour the taste of my last dessert till after the wedding. *Looking Good* magazine has said it will take me at least six weeks to achieve a beach-perfect body. This, I assume, is similar to a wedding/make old boyfriend jealous and new boyfriend faint with lust, perfect body.

'Harriet, tell everyone the story of Emma's thirtieth birthday party,' my mother calls out loudly. The gin and tonics have kicked in, bringing a flush to her cheeks and flamboyance to her hand movements.

'Which one?' I ask, knowing which one.

'When you fell over on the dance floor.' She laughs loudly at the memory. Katie doesn't help matters by choking on her banoffie pie.

'It's not really that funny,' I respond, shaking my head.

'What do you mean, it's not funny? It's hilarious,' Josie

calls out at the end of the table.

'I slipped on a rogue strawberry from the gateau. End of story.'

Mum will not let it go, and tells the story with comedic additions from Katie, and Josie, who wasn't even there, but heard the story in stages, as I leaned over the toilet bowl the next morning.

'I don't remember this?' Lawrence says, looking puzzled.

'You and Dad were having a cigar outside,' Katie says, smiling. 'That was the night you proposed, remember?' She squeezes his arm and he pecks her on the nose.

I drink my coffee and settle into the glow of my nearest and dearest. What kind of man would fit into my close-knit little world? Nate? Someone I haven't met yet?

I lie in bed and think of Jason. I think of him a lot; not quite as often as I used to, but enough for it to hurt still. The birthday card has prompted a mixture of feelings. Is he trying to make contact? Does he regret leaving, or was it just a nice thought? I think of him happy without me. Is he happy? Do they work well together? Does she play with the curls at the back of his neck, or massage his calf muscles after his weekly rugby? Does she ignore the fact that he grunts loudly when playing with his Ninterdo Wii, or does it annoy the hell out of her? What is she like? Whenever I ask Chloe, all she will say is that she is nice, but in a different way to me. This is not helpful, but I guess I will find out at the wedding . . . which wedding? The wedding I don't have a date for, not the other one I also don't have a date for.

The table plan is apparently being fought over next week and Chloe has promised to do all she can to keep a chair free for 'one other'. I am not sure if this is a good or a bad thing. If I don't find the 'one other', there will be an empty chair next to me. Here is no one, it will say, like a bright beacon of loneliness, and Jason will feel sorry for me. Oh God. My stomach churns with the thought, and sleep continues to be something that will happen at ten o'clock the next morning at work. I need a date. I get up into the quiet darkness of the flat and tiptoe out into the lounge. Josie has left the computer on and the blue screen lights the room in an eerie glow. I feel as if I am being watched by a thousand men who promise me the moon and expect the stars back. With a cup of tea, I sit on the sofa, switch on the TV and flick through the channels, hoping for some distraction from my busy mind. The world of the insomniac opens up and I switch between *Country File* and an episode of *Neighbours* from 1989. I am not watching, though; I am thinking of the wedding, of Jason, of Nate. I switch off the TV and gravitate towards the computer. I have a message from Ordinary Boy. Hang on, I have three messages. I look into my outbox. Josie!

Today was the day I had planned to tell Georgina that my column is working; that people are actually reading it. Instead, I am drinking double espresso in a bid to stay awake and praying that she doesn't appear and notice my lack of activity and the fact that my blouse is not ironed. At least I'm not wearing it inside out any more. An hour's sleep is not good for me, but it's my own fault.

There is no excuse for emailing people you don't know until the early hours of the morning. It is the action of a sad person; the sort of person who likes their Internet Second Life better than their own. I feel sick with tiredness and cannot function. My yawns threaten to suck in anything that comes within a hundred metres of my desk. I file my copy and with little energy to do anything else I begin daydreaming of a different life. This life would involve me writing my column for *Eve* or *Marie Claire*, and a range of Sunday supplements. I would be called upon to go on Breakfast TV and comment on the dilemmas facing the modern single woman and Internet dating. It would be a demanding job, but one I would thrive in. Editors would insist on working with me, because I am the best there is. After losing two stone with the help of Madonna's trainer, I would be unrecognisable as the girl who thought her career was over before it had begun. Every evening I would go home to my riverside flat with its designer sofas and trendy, mood lighting, where my gorgeous, lovesick boyfriend would be waiting. Now, this is where my daydream goes a bit haywire because the boyfriend has no face.

I log on to DateMate and click into my inbox . . . ah, this is the one I want.

> *What is your favourite colour?*
> *Ordinary Boy x*
>
> *That's a rubbish question.*
> *Belle x*
>
> *I have a list.*
> *Favourite food?*
> *Favourite book?*
> *Favourite holiday destination?*
> *Favourite film?*
> *Carrot or the Stick?*
> *OB x*
>
> *Are you being serious?*
> *Belle x*
>
> *I thought we should make more of an effort to*

do this Internet dating thing properly. Answer the above questions and I will know everything about you and make my decision accordingly. OB x

You are joking?
Belle x

Yes
OB Xxx

I consider asking him if he can dance, but then change my mind. We might not even dance at the wedding; we will probably be too busy making use of the Russian goose pillows and wondering what it would be like to have sex underneath a sink with red lighting. This thought makes me smile. He swears when he has sex. He will insist we do it in a lift, down a dark side street, in the back of a taxi. He will talk football with Alan and tell Emma that her syllabub is delicious as he slips his hand under the table and runs his hand up my thigh, before brushing his fingers lightly over my knickers. I imagine he is slightly unshaven and his hair is too long. His hands are slim and he can play any instrument he puts his mind to. Oh, that's Nate. Who was I thinking about again?

My phone goes and makes me jump.

'Harriet.'

'Georgina.'

'What are you doing?'

'Um, I was just about to do an interview with –' Girls Aloud? Beyonce? Bono? Nelson Mandela? – 'The Wurzels,' I reply.

'The Wurzels?' Georgina repeats.

'Three blokes who sang about a combine harvester about twenty years ago.'

'I know who the bloody Wurzels are. I just wondered

why you were interviewing them.'

'Because they are doing a barn dance night at the racecourse and I—'

'Forget the Wurzels. Have you heard from Poppy?'

'No. I've left a couple of messages on her mobile but I think she's in Ibiza.'

'Still!'

'I might be wrong, but I think she was planning on emailing her piece over.'

If she is, then she needs to do it in the next twenty-four hours. Georgina sighs heavily over the phone.

'I have something ready to go,' I venture.

I can hear her breathing through her nose. She is still suffering from her allergy attack and I feel bad; for about two seconds. Then I remember that she is making me fight for something I know I can do well.

'Okay, hopefully Poppy's will come through, but if not we'll have to go with yours instead.'

'Great, I'll get on to it straight away,' I reply. There is a tight feeling in my stomach. I feel as if I'm going to burst, like a jack-in-the-box. I imagine a flurry of balloons and streamers floating out of my mouth with my laughter.

Girl Without a Date in Her Diary – Blog entry – August 15th

I had my hair cut. It looks good. I can tousle now. Unfortunately, looks are important in the dating game. It's a harsh truth . . . look rough and past your sell-by-date and you will attract something similar. Angie and Brad? I rest my case. No, I'm not obsessed, I just can't think of anyone else.

My friend J says that if you look as if you can't be bothered, then you're asking for it – not to be bothered. Perhaps that's been my problem – my peripheral vision has been so focused on a particular someone that I have forgotten how to be bothered. It got me thinking. No matter how rubbish you feel, there are certain rules to follow if you are single but don't want to be. (This doesn't apply to those sisters who are happy being numero uno – you can stay in your tracksuit bottoms.) If you are not having sex, there is no reason to advertise the fact by not shaving. Make an effort at work (a high percentage of relationships begin in the workplace) and use the time you would have spent cuddling up with someone to go to the gym and get that body into shape. This is a good opportunity to change your look completely. Just go for it. Hair – make-up – the lot.

So it's all about looks, I hear you ask? Shallow Hal? No, but I have come to the conclusion that it helps to maintain the illusion of fabulous. And let's be honest – putting aside my feminist protests and conviction that beauty is skin deep, I want to make myself attractive to the opposite sex.

Saying all this I am in a quandary. My latest interest on DateMate hasn't got a photo. No photo! Yes, you heard me right. No photo! Am I bothered? You bet I am!

Am I mad continuing our correspondence, or am I being romantic? I keep thinking, *You've Got Mail.*

I'll keep you posted.

Did you see what I did there?

'You bought me coffee and you're smiling?' Ed says suspiciously.

'So?'

'It's making me nervous.'

'Why?'

'Because I've got used to you scowling, and now you're grinning like an idiot.'

'See these?' I wave two envelopes in front of his face. 'These are fan letters. Can you believe it? Two people have written in to say they love the column.'

'Your mum and dad?'

'No! I'll have you know they are complete strangers.'

'That's great, really great.'

'And Georgina has asked for another column.'

'A good day for Miss HP and the world. See, I knew Georgina would see sense— ooh, talk of the devil, and she is sure to appear. Look busy.'

Georgina swoops over like a huge eagle, her red-polished talons ready to either gouge my eyes out, or collect my masterpiece. I hold it out proudly, feeling confident that my eyes will live to see another day.

'Poppy came good. I've just got her email. Thanks, but we won't be needing your piece now,' she says.

I am stunned.

'I have fan letters,' I say weakly.

Georgina glances at my envelopes.

'How quaint.'

I am crushed.

'Thanks for all your hard work, Harry. I appreciate it, of course. Can you do me one last favour? Can you do a quick edit on Poppy's piece for me?'

I look at her blankly. If I launched myself at her and tackled her to the ground, would I be hailed as a hero or never work again? Georgina doesn't give me a chance to find out. The fabric of her dress billows like a tent behind her as she disappears into her office, leaving me crushed and blind. I switch on my computer and begin to type.

'Make me smile, Ordinary Boy.'

Mum, Katie and I wait for Emma to emerge from the fitting room. It will not be the first time; we have been 'helping' her to choose an outfit for what seems like days. When I said this, Emma informed me that we had actually only been out for three hours and twenty-six minutes. We were instructed to be ready by nine thirty, so that we could be ready for the shops opening at ten. After a night of tossing, turning and worrying about my job, my future, and pretty much anything else that needs worrying about, I overslept, and my requests for a much-needed coffee to urge me into existence were met with a stern look and an exaggerated sigh. Emma only conceded because Katie simpered apologetically that it might be nice to have a cappuccino.

The Better Bride smells expensive. We are the only customers in the calm, cream-carpeted oasis with tasteful flower arrangements and gushing, overattentive, clearly on commission, sales assistants. Now bored, Katie and I are flicking through the dress rails and Mum is trying on hats. Emma appears from the fitting room wearing another pastel creation with an expensive price tag and a lining. Each outfit has had varying degrees of appliqué or embroidery, to presumably justify the price and make up for a lack of imagination and style. This one is in mint green, with padded shoulders and a matching chiffon scarf. Emma is keen to cover her bottom and fleshy arms, but this is not doing either.

In front of the floor-length mirrors and harsh lighting, she appears vulnerable. She tugs at the material and surveys herself from all angles, as if one of them will provide a surprise revelation. Emma is not pretty like Katie, but she is striking, and today I want her to feel good about herself, because not everyone can be the Katies and Chloes of this world. Emma may not have a size-ten figure, but she has long slim legs, a fabulous complexion, striking features and a really lovely smile – when she remembers to use it.

'You look lovely, but I think I prefer the last one,' I suggest tactfully. Emma looks like a long and lumpy broad bean pod.

'Why?' Emma asks, turning to the left and then the right.

'The cream of the last outfit complemented your colouring and, overall, I think it was a better silhouette,' I say, congratulating myself on an unexpected show of delicate manoeuvring.

'Is it my bum or my thighs?' Emma demands.

'Neither, I just liked the other one.'

'But I like this one.' Emma frowns at me. 'What do you think?' she asks the shop assistant with the large calf muscles and heavy perfume.

'I also think Madame looked lovely in the cream, and perhaps the lilac.'

'Me too; it's the cream or the lilac,' Katie says, pulling out a full white meringue with net petticoats. She holds it against me.

'I liked the cornflower blue,' Mum says.

Emma disappears back into the changing room.

Katie and I look at each other, grab a dress each and pick a changing room before the sales assistant can stop us. Five minutes later, Katie emerges in an elegant long satin sheath and I have struggled into a strapless number with swathes of fabric falling from the bust-line.

'Oh, my God, you look beautiful,' Katie says all misty-eyed.

'So do you,' I say with a lump in my throat.

Emma coughs behind us. She has her hands on her hips and a frown on her face.

'Oh, Madame looks fabulous,' the sales assistant says, producing a hat to match.

'Stunning,' Katie says, and I nod in agreement.

'Are you sure?' Emma asks.

'The lilac brings out the colour of Madame's eyes.'

'She has her father's height and large feet, bless her, but thankfully she has her mother's eyes,' my mother says.

Reluctant to take the dress off, I continue to swirl in front of the mirror.

'And one day your prince will come,' I promise myself. 'And he will be tall with dark hair, defined calf muscles and a big—'

The face looking through the window is a familiar one. The girl with him isn't. Nate peers in closer. His recognition is like a spark. I expect him to smile but he doesn't, he just stares at me as if I will disappear in a puff of smoke. Right now I wish I could. My twirling dies down to a sway. Our eyes are locked. The girl with him is talking and pointing to something in the window, but he is not listening. I am rooted to the spot as everything fades around me. All I can see is him. He is still looking at me. I wave weakly with my fingers. He waves back with his, and the girl looks at him with a question. He says something and she nods. What did he say? They walk away and I feel like a bride left at the altar.

'Who was that?' Katie asks.

'Oh, just someone I know.'

'He looked nice.'

'He is, very nice.'

'Can't you ask him to the wedding?'

'I don't have his number. And I'm not sure I could cope with the rejection if he said no. Anyway, that was probably his girlfriend.'

'Shame,' Katie says and lifts the dress over my head.

'Are you still doing that Internet dating thing?' Mum interrupts.

'Kind of,' I say beneath swathes of petticoat.

'That's nice, dear. Just remember not to have your head in the clouds the next time you meet someone. Look at your sister and how beautiful she looked a minute ago. That could be you.' She places a creation of yellow feathers on her head. 'What do you think of this?'

'It looks like a canary on your head.'

'And that's your other problem: sarcasm.'

'That wasn't sarcasm, Mum.'

'And trying to be clever. Men don't like that, you know.'

With oversized glossy paper bags stuffed with tissue paper and the promise of looking beautiful, we go for a late lunch in one of Emma's favourite bistros. Mum looks to the waitress proudly as Emma makes a big thing about smelling, swirling and tasting the wine, and then tells me off for eating all the bread.

By the time we all leave, a glass of wine means that I am entirely convinced that I have had a wonderful day. I even go as far as to suggest we do it again when Emma goes shopping for the twins' outfits. I am trying hard to be positive and supportive about this renewing the vows thing. This lasts for approximately another five minutes, until Emma tells us that instead of a disco, guests will be split into teams and expected to take part in quizzes, including guess the wine region, and name that composer. I wonder if I will go down with suspected food poisoning on the day.

Keen to get back to little Alfie, Katie is dropped off first. Emma and I stay for a cup of tea at Mum and Dad's. My father is watching the cricket, but seems pleased to have his solitude interrupted with our chatter and display of collective purchases. The kitchen smells of burned toast.

'Did you mow the lawn and fix that shelf?' my mother asks.

'Yes, Dee,' he replies.

I leave Emma and Mum upstairs discussing outfits and join my father in the living room. The curtains are drawn to keep out the glare of the sun from the TV screen and I am reminded of the fishing tent. He passes me a chocolate biscuit and we dunk, listening to the ginger-sponge-like tones of the commentator.

'You let your mother buy a yellow bird for her head,' he says.

'It was out of my hands,' I say.

'Well, if there is a woman who can carry it off, it's your mother.'

There is a lot of clapping. The sunburned audience and my father are pleased. I have no idea what's going on, but it's oddly soothing and I am in no hurry to get back to my flat.

'You look tired, munchkin,' he says, ruffling my hair. He is the only person who can get away with it.

'I couldn't sleep last night.'

'Why?' He looks worried.

'Oh, just the usual.'

He turns the TV down.

'I've told you before, girls like Poppy will come and go, but girls called Harriet are there for the long term. We gave you that name, and an education, for a reason.'

'I know.'

My mother appears, humming out of tune. The yellow bird wobbles on her head. My father looks at her with an affection softened by the years and she responds by telling him off about something. This is the way they are. Every Christmas he takes advantage of a few Babychams and playfully hugs her, forcing her to sit on his knee for the Queen's speech. With a high-pitched squeal she tells him to leave her alone, slapping him on the arm. She is laughing when she does it. Emma and Alan don't laugh. If they do, then it's behind closed doors. Perhaps they cry with laughter when they get home. I like to think so. Families are funny things. Am I because of them, or despite them?

Even a couple of peach Bellinis cannot rouse Josie out of the Bendrums (the doldrums but Ben-sized).

'Ring him,' I urge.

'No!'

'Why not?'

'Because I'm now at the point where I've been rejecting him for so long that I'm not sure if he wants me any more.'

'Talk to him, Josie.'

'No!'

'But if neither of you makes the first move, you're going to lose him.'

'Then so be it.'

'You're so stubborn.'

'And your point is?'

I shake my head and order a couple more drinks. The bar is busy with groups of people meeting for after-work drinks. Josie surprised me by arriving at the offices of *Life to Live* with a long face and a need for cocktails. Her boss told her she was depressing everyone and instructed her to take a duvet day. This made her even grumpier. When I introduced her to Georgina, she practically growled.

'Have you seen Mr Bookshop lately?' she asks.

'Nate? No.'

'If he was with a girl looking in the window of a wedding-dress shop then I suspect he's not on the market anyway.'

'Yeah, you're probably right.' I sigh. My disappointment is acute. 'But I do have Ordinary Boy.'

'The guy without a photo?' Josie shakes her head.

'Looks aren't everything.'

'Are you mad? You won't be saying that when he turns out to be a five-foot-two weirdo.'

'Love conquers all,' I say with drama.

'For a grown woman who should know better, you talk so much friggin' rubbish it's unbelievable.'

'Where's the romantic in you?'

'She's shopping in IKEA, looking at matching crockery and wondering what happened to her life.'

'What time are you leaving tomorrow?' I ask.

'Ten.'

'And you're going to stay the night?'

'She's insisted.'

'It will be nice,' I offer.

Josie looks at me and I shrug my shoulders. I try, but the positives are hard to find. Josie's mother is a neurotic mess. Since Josie's father left fifteen years ago, she has been consumed with bitterness and a need for alcohol. She used to be a talented concert pianist, but now sits at home drinking away her memories and playing 'Monday, Monday' by The Mamas and the Papas on full volume so that the neighbours regularly complain.

We order a couple more Bellinis, which seems a strange thing to do considering the circumstances, but Josie isn't her mother. She talks about the father she refuses to see, but thinks about every day, and I thank someone for being so lucky with my own parents.

Now I don't know what makes me think that I am better than I was yesterday, or the day before that, but there is something. I looked in the mirror this morning and thought, yeah! That was it, just, yeah. Was it my horoscope?

> *With your ruler Mercury highlighted and a build-up of planets in Aquarius, opportunities in work and romance are yours for the taking. Enjoy being the centre of attention and ditch the shoes and attitudes that don't fit any more.*

Or was it the women in the hairdresser's, or the thought of Josie's mother sitting in her flat drinking away her regrets? Maybe it was the rubbish joke and subsequent emails from Ordinary Boy, one of them telling me that he thought I was pretty wonderful. Perhaps it was the copy of the *Guardian* newspaper Ed placed on my desk this morning. Whatever it is, I feel full of fight. I take a deep breath and make my way to a brave new world.

Georgina is sitting behind her desk. She looks remarkably brown, but she hasn't been on holiday and she obviously didn't wear gloves. I cough to clear my throat, because suddenly it has gone dry. I place the *Guardian* article on her desk.

'Media Monkey is speculating on the identity of Girl Without a Date in Her Diary.'

'It's four lines.'

'From little acorns grow . . .'

'And it isn't translating into sales.'

'But I think you need to give it time . . . time for word to filter through.'

'I don't have time, Harry. Now did you want me for anything else?'

'Look, I know you're still keen for Poppy to do her own column, but I think…'

What was I thinking? What was it I'd rehearsed to myself in the bathroom mirror this morning? My mind has gone blank and my hands are clammy.

'I think that maybe, there might be . . . I think that there *IS* room for both of us . . .'

This is a little white lie. I am pretty convinced that Poppy will lose interest soon and I want to be the one left standing.

'Harry, sit down.'

Georgina flicks through some papers on her desk, and I strain to see if the words 'notice period' or 'remove from premises immediately' are there. She looks up and smiles thinly.

'Poppy's column was, well, let's just say that, on closer inspection, it wasn't ready for publication. It needed a good edit, and as you know we have run out of time. I have decided to go with your piece for this issue.'

'You have?'

Georgina nods gravely. I refrain from punching the air in victory.

'This is a temporary measure.'

'You won't regret it, Georgina.'

'Poppy's column will go in the next issue.'

I am not listening. I am dancing my way back to my desk.

The restaurant is busy and Judith and Jeremy are sulking. Judith cannot understand why nobody wanted to attend her church evening and Jeremy is sulking because the rest of us are taking too long to decide what dishes to have.

'Why can't we just have three potato dishes, two prawns and two lamb skewers?' he complains.

'Because we need something green in there. I think we should have a couple of salads.'

'I'm not paying for salads,' he replies sulkily.

'We need garlic bread,' Ed pipes up and smiles. He is clearly enjoying the indecision.

'I think we need more Sangria to get through this,' Josie suggests.

She has come out on our first work night out and can't quite believe that my work colleagues can produce a magazine every month, when making a decision on what to eat is clearly impossible. Is this why we stopped going out before? I bang the table for order.

'Okay, here's the plan. We each get to choose two dishes. You can't choose the same as someone else's. That's it. On top of that, we order garlic bread and a couple of salads for everyone.'

Everyone pauses and makes a mental decision as to whether to argue or agree. They go for the latter and joviality is restored. The waitress smiles gratefully and we top up the Sangria. Despite the niggles, we are having a nice time and I'm glad I made the effort to organise it, even though it took us so long to finally have a night out together. I am becoming quite the social butterfly. I'm going to the Jug and Mutton for an acoustic set tomorrow night, attending a cookery class with Josie on Saturday morning, and there is an author event Monday evening. My diary is looking like my What's On page. Talking of which, my column looks fabulous, even if I do say so myself.

The food arrives and we all stop talking. Jeremy, Ed and Derek the accountant immediately grab the garlic bread.

'Excuse me,' Judith raises her voice, 'Grace, we need to say grace.'

'You are joking,' Jeremy says with his mouth full.

'Do I look like I'm joking?' Judith asks.

It all kicks off again and Josie and I get a fit of the giggles.

I don't want to leave this funny set of people. Maybe I won't have to. I cross my fingers and text everyone I know to buy a copy of this month's *Life to Live*.

We all have a hangover the next morning. When the phone rings, I have to hold the receiver away from my ear as some old dear complains that her garden party wasn't featured in last month's issue. She uses words like incompetent, ineffectual and useless: things that would normally upset me, but not today. Today my head may be thumping but everything else is good.

'You're bouncing?' Ed says.

'I am!'

'Another date?'

'There might be.'

'So who is it this time?'

'I'm not telling you.'

'He's a six-foot-three fireman, with a blind dog and a degree in philosophy?'

'No.'

'A dangerously handsome brain surgeon who gave up his practice in Harley Street to help the poor in Africa, before returning for the launch of his bestselling book charting his emotional journey saving orphans?'

'Nope.'

'A five-foot-nothing singer, with a pert bottom and a penchant for wearing cream suits?'

I shake my head.

'Voice-over movie guy?'

I look at him and wonder what goes on in that strange mind of his.

'I'm not sure what he does. If he is successful, he doesn't like to show off about it.'

'So, he's on the dole and spends his days busking and spraying graffiti on railway bridges.'

'I doubt it.'

'What does he look like?'

'I don't know that either.'

'Do you know anything about this guy?'

'Enough to know I might want to take him to Chloe's wedding.'

'Aaah, but can he dance to "You're the One that I Want"?'

'I have no idea, but I hope not.'

'You'll regret it later. Who wants to go to a wedding with someone who can't do a good *Grease* impersonation?'

'Me.'

'And that, Harry Peel, is where your life is going wrong.'

He walks off and I read my email from Ordinary Boy.

Time we met?

I check my horoscope and reply with a very enthusiastic yes.

GWAD – *Life to Live* column
Deirdre McKay offers me a biscuit. We are sitting in her living room with its headache-inducing patterned carpet and dust-covered ceramic trinkets. She is dressed in eighteenth-century costume and through the French windows I can see a man in the garden. He is dressed as a soldier. I am trying to concentrate on what she is saying, but my gaze keeps wandering to the nutcase stabbing a stuffed sheet hanging from the washing line. Deirdre follows my gaze.

'That's my husband Bob. He's practising for a battle scene,' she explains, with a touch of pride in her voice. I nod, as if this is all normal behavior for a teacher and traffic warden living in a semi-detached house. This encounter got me thinking. What makes the perfect man and the ideal relationship? Is it being with your best friend, laughter . . . money? Is it someone scraping the ice from your car on a cold winter morning or making you laugh when you don't want to? Is it good sex or a good sweater? Will my next date provide the answer?

Talking of which, I've bought some scones and clotted cream. I don't know why. Actually, I do. I think it may have something to do with a clotted cream fantasy I have, which is very similar to my lift fantasy – which means, for lots of reasons, it's never going to happen. But, by taking them, I am opening up the possibility, just like I do every time I take the lift instead of the stairs, and that makes me feel just a teensy weensy bit dangerous, and in my world, that's as close as it gets.

When I am not thinking clotted cream in my knickers, I am thinking a romantic picnic with champagne, tiny, sweet strawberries, and a glimpse of slender ankle – mine, not his. My feet and ankles are probably my best point, which means I shall be using them to my advantage with a pedicure and some new, rather posh flip-flops. I am leaving nothing to chance. When Angelina bagged Brad, I'm pretty sure she didn't have rough skin on her heels or missed her bikini wax. Oh, come on, I don't believe Angie is perfect all the time. When Brad is out filming on location I bet she lets it all go; her tattoos disappearing underneath a layer of thick dark hair. Will my date look like Brad? My guess is that if he is doing Internet dating, he doesn't. Do I care? No. I imagine that as Angie is hirsute, Brad is a little bit boring.

My date checklist and preparation:

- Ask your friends what your best points are, then buy something that highlights them.
- Tidy your flat, because you never know.
- Oh and hide all those embarrassing CDs, and display books that make you look interesting and intelligent.
- Don't eat garlic for at least 48 hours before the date.
- Buy a new bra with lift and cleavage.
- Pop a little self-tan on to make you look healthy and sun-kissed. White thighs are never good unless you're a size 6!
- Turn the music up – Dance yourself dizzy and

boogaloo an hour before the date to get yourself in the mood and in a happy place.

- Banish any thoughts of your ex-boyfriend.
- Think Angelina. Think sexy and mysterious.
- Don't expect Brad. My mum always tells me to lower my expectations and she might have a point. It's better to be pleasantly surprised than disappointed.

During the date:
Ah well, this is where it all goes horribly wrong for me which means I am the last person you should be listening to. You're on your own. Good luck!

When I was younger, I had a pen pal. She was a girl called Brigit and she went to the ballet and had a horse called Noble. When I finally met her she didn't have a beret, or tiny feet in black patent shoes. She didn't dominate a room with her superior breeding and angel-blond curls. In my mind she was all of these things, but in reality, Brigit was an awkward girl with lanky brown hair, buck teeth and crippling shyness. She was probably really nice, but I remember being disappointed. I had told all of my friends about her and she let me down by not being the person I wanted her to be. Internet dating is a bit like having a pen pal.

Ordinary Boy is gorgeous and when I say I cannot fully articulate my relief that he is, then you should believe me.

I try to look sexy rather than slumped, in a blue-and-white-striped deckchair. Alec (that's his name) walks towards me holding two ice creams. He licks his hands as the ice creams begin to melt. I wave and his boyish features break out into a smile. His teeth are perfect. I am dazzled by them. Dressed in jeans, flip-flops and a white shirt that complements his cinnamon skin, he looks younger than he is, although this might have more to do with the incredibly long eyelashes, or the dark glossy hair that occasionally falls in front of hazelnut eyes. He could be a little taller, but then couldn't most people. It's a cross I have to bear. I just won't be able to wear high heels. No big deal.

We have found a perfect spot in the ornamental flower garden. Partially shaded from the hot sun by a pretty, fragrant bush covered in small white flowers, just far enough away from the musicians playing in the band stand, and secluded just a little, so that it feels cosy and intimate.

'Here you are, gorgeous,' he says, handing me an ice cream. 'I asked them to sprinkle some pink bits on for you and to cover it in strawberry sauce stuff.'

I hate strawberry sauce stuff.

'Oh, how lovely,' I simper.

'Do you want a blow back?' he asks, pointing his cone at me like a finger.

'A what?' I ask, wondering if this is where I find out he is a pervert and wants me to have sex with a member of the band while he watches.

'You get the last of my ice cream.'

I am still not convinced, and I frown, worried about what I am about to let myself in for.

'Trust me.'

Now the old Harry would run a mile at those two words, because everyone knows they are the most dangerous words anyone can ever say to you. The new Harry will say, what the hell?

'Okay, open your mouth,' he instructs.

I do as I am told and he bites the end off his cornet, before placing the other end into my mouth. I have to open it wide to accommodate the cornet's width and cannot imagine that it is particularly attractive, but I am trying to hold on to those 'what the hell' thoughts. They are the thoughts of someone who is sexy, irresponsible and sucking the marrow out of life; or rather the ice cream.

Alec blows hard, and a cold shot of ice cream hits the back of my throat. I am filled with the fabulousness of it all and the need to choke. I go with the latter and Alec pats my back until I recover.

'Wow, that was amazing,' I respond with a raspy voice. Alec nods, smiling at his success. I develop a headache and spend the next ten minutes coughing.

The sun covers our faces with hot hands and we sit there, eyes closed, listening to the band and an enthusiastic trombone.

'This is nice,' he says lazily, and I respond with a low murmur.

'You're nice.'

'Thanks,' I reply.

'In fact, I was a bit worried that you would be . . . well, not my type . . . a bit on the mad side.'

'But I'm not, I'm quite sensible,' I respond and experience the usual disappointment that comes with the word.

'Yeah . . . It's cool.'

I refrain from jumping up from my deckchair and performing a victory run – doing a high-five with the trumpets, hugging old ladies and kissing small children on their heads.

'Why did you think I would be mad?'

'Because I had this idea that most of the women who do Internet dating are.'

'But I bet they're not.'

'There are a few who should be accompanied or at least sedated, but on the whole everyone seems pretty normal. My mate Tom has just subscribed.'

'I think it's great.' So says the girl who thought Internet dating was the act of a desperate woman a few months ago. In retrospect my view of it has changed. Writing the blog and the column has made me realise that it doesn't have to be all about finding the One. It can just be a great way to try different things and go to places you wouldn't normally experience sitting at home, feeling smug because you haven't succumbed to DateMate. I wasn't looking for the One, but a date for a wedding and I'm happy to say that Alex is a contender for both.

Outside the flat we spend a few seconds hovering on the step, making small talk. Alec rocks on his feet with his hands in his pockets.

'I've had a great time,' he says.

'Me too,' I reply.

'Great weather.'

Kiss me! Kiss me!

He leans forward and plants a kiss on my cheek. I smile and it is enough for him to try one on the lips. Hurray! He tastes of vanilla ice cream.

'I'd love to see you again,' he says.

'That would be good.'

'What about Tuesday night?'

'I'm busy. I could do Thursday, though.'

'Thursday it is, then. Do you fancy an Indian?'

I smile inside.

'You know what, if I am honest, I don't. Do you mind if we do something else?'

'No problem. Franklin's?'

'That's a bit expensive.'

'Let's live a little.'

He kisses me again and leaves me grinning from ear to ear like an idiot.

'You've been putting your plastic recycling out on the wrong day,' Martha Gennings's voice snaps me back to reality. I swing round. She fills the door frame like a dark, avenging angel.

'Sorry, I have a friend staying. She forgets which week it is.'

'Well, if we can all make an effort to remember in the future.'

I nod and squeeze past the small space she has left between herself and the door frame. She smells of throat lozenges.

'He is perfect!' I squeal to Josie who is painting her toenails a hideous shade of orange.

'How perfect?' she asks.

'Pretty near perfect.'

'Near?'

'As near as it gets right now.'

'Is it near enough for Chloe's wedding?' Josie asks, screwing the top back on her nail varnish.

'Yes.'

'If he's nearly perfect, what's he doing on DateMate?'

'He's recently split with his girlfriend and most of the places he goes out to involve people she knows.'

'Okay, I can go with that. And there's nothing wrong with him?'

'No!'

'Hurray, I'll get the hair dryer.'

'You've lost me.'

'To dry my nail varnish. We need to go out and celebrate. Harry, my dear, our search is over.'

'What if he doesn't ring?'

'He will. He kissed you, for goodness' sake.'

We spend the evening drinking champagne cocktails at our favourite bar. Fuelled by champagne and with the back-up of my old partner in crime, I am doing a good impression of being a social butterfly and loving it. We spot Noush looking like some kind of rock 'n' roll angel in grey skinny jeans and a see-through chiffon top. I don't know what it is, but I always get the impression that she is never having a particularly good time. She is one of those people who look to the door when they are talking to you. I call her name in a high-pitched girlie voice and wave her over. She turns and waves back, but instead of coming over, she disappears into the crowd. Someone and somewhere better to go.

Determined to get herself out there, Josie does a good impression of flirting with a guy, but I can tell her heart is not in it. Instead, she checks her phone periodically when she thinks I'm not looking.

Back at the flat we change into our pyjamas and feast on peanut butter and toast.

'It's hell out there,' Josie observes.

'What?'

'Being single – it's shit.'

'Mmmm . . . It's not as much fun as it used to be.'

'No wonder people are Internet dating.'

'You don't need to. You've got the lovely Ben.'

'I'm not sure I have any more.'

'Of course you do.'

'You know, Alec reminds me of Jason,' she says.

'When did you see him?'

'When you were snogging him on the doorstep. I was spying from behind the curtain.'

'He doesn't look anything like him,' I say, a little put out.

Josie pulls her knees up to her chest. She looks like a freshly scrubbed child with her rose-pink cheeks, fluffy pink slippers and hair pulled into a slightly wonky top knot.

'Okay, if Jason was to walk back into your life, what would you do? Would it be him or Alec?'

'That is an unfair question,' I reply, waving my toast

at her. 'And anyway, I've only just met him.'

'But you always know on a first date if someone is a contender or not.'

'Did you know with Ben?' I ask controversially,

Josie licks her fingers of peanut butter and ruminates on the question.

'Yes.'

'And is he still a contender? Will he make it to that all-important last round?'

'The phone vote isn't through yet.'

'I don't understand you, Jose.'

'That's what Ben keeps saying.'

We sit together, barely an arm's length apart, but our minds drift off to other places. The TV is on, but neither of us is watching.

'Noush is really very beautiful,' Josie says.

'She is,' I reply, and sigh. Tonight, though, my sigh is different from the sighs that have passed my lips over the past few months. This one is a sigh of happy resignation; because Noush may have cheekbones that make photographers weep with desire, but today I have been kissed and the latest issue of *Life to Live* is going to hit the streets with another one of my columns.

'Beautiful, but not perfect. She has an extra toe on her right foot.'

'Nooooo!' Josie reacts with exaggerated shock horror.

'See, it's all relative,' I say, with my new glass-half-full outlook.

We both get up and wander towards our rooms. I think of Alec and try to remember Jason. The details of his face are lost to me, but I remember his hands, the smell of shampoo in his hair, the tiny scar on his knee, the frown he woke up with and the smile he gave me an hour later. Alec is nothing like him.

*

Bypassing the 'does he, does she like me' bit means we have pressed fast forward and got to the 'relationship' stage quite quickly. Three weeks after first discovering Alec on DateMate we are officially a couple and I have met his friends. He has also agreed to go to Emma's second wedding fiasco. I have yet to obtain my sister's approval and submit security checks on him, but my mother's curiosity will override any doubts Emma might have.

There are moments when I think that we might have benefited from waiting before rushing headlong into all this, but I put that down to the old Harry being safe and sensible. When he takes my hand or looks at me with those chocolate eyes and tells me I have the most kissable lips, none of it matters. I am someone with a date in my diary.

My phone rings and I pick up with a sing-song hello.

'This happiness thing is getting on my nerves.'

'Who's upset you today? P Diddy? Madonna?' I ask. Josie is still grumpy.

'No, bloody, stupid Manda Frington.'

'Who is Manda Frington?'

'Some rubbish actress demanding a Chanel vintage couture dress. The same one I promised to Tania Heading.'

'What, *the* Tania Heading?'

'Yes.'

'See, you don't get that with a woman who is running a series of posh jumble sales. She just wanted a cup of tea. So to what do I owe this pleasure?'

'I was sitting here, bored, with a double chocolate-chip muffin. My hopes of finding answers to life, love and the universe within its chocolatey depths are not going to be realised. What time are we going out tonight?'

'Eight.'

'So, this is the nice friend Alec was talking about? The one we saw the other night?'

'Yes, Alec says he is very keen. He said he liked your smile and the size of your breasts.'

'Did he?'

'Yes.'

'Wow, I like him already.'

'Are you sure you want to do this?'

'Of course I am. He was hot, and I'm footloose and fancy free,' Josie declares. 'What's there not to be sure about?'

As Josie and the friend get to know each other, Alec and I sit too close together. People are probably vomiting around us as we speak. Tonight is the night. I can feel it and I have bought new red and black underwear especially. I am almost faint with longing. My suspicions that Josie is not experiencing the same are confirmed in the ladies' toilets.

'Sorry, Harry, but I don't feel too well. I'm going to go home,' she says. I put my lipstick back in my bag and promise to make it up to Alec. He is not happy.

When we get back to the flat, Josie is near to tears.

'What's wrong?' I ask, confused.

'I miss Ben,' she complains, collapsing on the sofa. I put my arm round her and draw her in close. 'Everyone I meet is always a poor substitute. I end up thinking, oh Ben wouldn't do that, and Ben would say that. I thought I wanted the excitement and romance of someone else; that I was somehow missing out, but I realised that, tonight, all I'm missing out on is me and Ben, and the way it's so easy between us.'

Hurray, at long bloody last.

'Oh Jose, you need to ring and tell him.'

'I can't, I think he's seeing someone else.'

'Why?'

'Just from a couple of things he said, and now he's stopped ringing me.'

'Don't jump to conclusions. Look, if you want him enough, then you need to tell him.'

'It's too late,' Josie wails, and fat tears roll down her perfectly peachy cheeks. 'Sorry for ruining your night of hoped-for hot sex.'

'It's okay. I probably wouldn't have slept with him tonight anyway,' I lie.

'I bet he's a groaner.'

'Jose!'

'What? Don't tell me you haven't thought about it.'

'I haven't.'

'What was Jason?'

'He was a crescendo. What about Ben?'

'Ah, ah, ah, ahhhhhhhh.'

'How can you let that go?'

Josie shakes her head and, for some reason, I think of Nate. Have I let that particular fantasy go? I think that at some point I probably did. He had a girlfriend and as much as I wanted him to, he didn't ask me out. No, it's time to move on – from Nate and from Jason.

Judith peers at me through her fake glasses. Today she is working the competent secretary/conference organiser look, with her hair pulled back into a sleek ponytail, crisp white blouse and a below-the-knee pencil skirt. She is on the Saving Me, Saving You committee – which is, as she never tires of telling me, a nod towards the Abba song, 'Knowing Me, Knowing You'. Tonight she is heading off to a conference in Lancashire to celebrate her virgin status and to have sing-songs with other like-minded people.

There is a raffle and she is trying to flog me a ticket. I have succumbed and bought two. The promise of winning the first prize of a hymn-and-hand-holding holiday in Wales is too much to miss.

'So, how did you meet him?' she asks. 'Him' being Alec.

'Oh, through a friend of a friend.'

'What, Josie?'

'No.' I am unwilling to lie to someone who has a direct line to God.

'What does he do?'

'He's a postman,' I say proudly, as if he delivers babies instead of letters.

'How quaint.' Judith raises her eyebrows. That's the second bloody time someone has used the word quaint and I resent its sudden presence in my life. I growl and Judith moves away from my desk, having clearly lost interest. I don't care. My glass is half full, and even the decision to replace the fresh milk in the communal office fridge with those horrid, long-life mini cartons doesn't affect me. This morning I have a boyfriend with a six-pack. I also took a call from the *Chronicle*. They wanted to interview Girl Without a Date in Her Diary for a piece they're running on Internet dating. Riding high, Harriet Peel. Riding high.

My phone rings.

'Harry, can you liaise with Poppy about the next issue? I want it ready in good time.'

'Of course.'

'Good,' Georgina says, apparently satisfied. 'Your column – I liked it, but, well, we discussed it, and I did say that it was temporary; preparing the way for Poppy's.'

'You still don't like the thought of running the two columns?'

'I want to launch Poppy as a breath of fresh air – as the

way forward. I think another column will dilute that.'

'But the last set of figures showed an increase in sales. Surely that has to account for something?'

'And you attribute that to your column, do you?'

I feel the sideswipe like a slap to the face. I grit my teeth and count to five.

'No, I'm not saying it's all down to that, but the feedback has been good. We've had a lot of positive emails, and this morning I took a call from the *Chronicle*—'

'As I think I said the other day, I think you've done a great job, but now we have to look to the future. I have high hopes for Poppy's column. Perhaps we can discuss this again in six months' time,' she says.

I feel the anger rising up inside me. Georgina waits for my response but I have nothing to say. If after all this she wants Poppy, she can have her. I don't intend to be here in six months' time.

'Great, I'll get Poppy to give you a call,' she says, and puts the phone down.

My phone rings again but I let it click into voicemail and continue typing the word BUM.

BUM, BUM, BUM.

I try to concentrate on the owner of the restaurant, a prematurely bald man in his thirties with a sharp suit and even sharper line in rubbish. I can see his mouth move but my ears have shut down. I am sure his new menu and refurbishment is exciting and well worth the thousands spent, but all I can think of is Poppy stealing my column space.

With the speeches over we are all invited to take the opportunity to talk to our hosts over coffee. Everyone gets up and hovers around the table with tiny cups of coffee and their perfectly honed networking skills. I escape to a long rectangular window and look down on to the street below. People are busy, hurrying from one place to another. A girl with a beret has stopped in the middle of the street. The busy people are forced to walk around her. She doesn't care. She is talking into her mobile and someone is making her laugh. I want to be that girl. Alec doesn't phone much.

'Are you all right?' the woman from the tourist board asks. She is my height, with ash-blond hair scraped back into a clip, and a face devoid of make-up. Her eyes are kind behind coloured rectangular-framed glasses. She looks genuinely concerned, and I consider crying, but manage to hold it back with a cough.

'It might help to talk about it,' she offers kindly, but I shake my head.

'No, I won't bore you with the details.'

'Sometimes, other people's problems make you feel better about your own, and you will be doing me a favour. I can't be any more bored than I am by all of this. Come on, let's go into the bar and grab ourselves a decently sized cup of coffee.'

Karen has a large brown wart on her chin. She is nice and funny, and urges me to talk about it. I protest a little bit more before telling all.

Karen looks at me as if she has heard it all before. I consider telling it again, with more emotion and an anecdote about being beaten as a child.

'That's tough,' she says eventually.

I wait for a revelation, for advice, for confirmation that I am right to be angry.

Karen shakes her head in despair and looks towards the window. She is deep in thought and I don't want to disturb her. I wait and try not to fidget. She turns towards me.

'Shall we get another coffee?'

There is something about one-upmanship in the world of emotional trauma. Karen tells me about never pursuing her dream of running a ski chalet in France because her husband didn't want to. The husband is now an ex-husband because six months ago he went off with her ex-best friend. My issue with Poppy doesn't really compare, but she was right; talking about other people's problems does make you feel better about your own. As we leave, she hands me her card and scribbles a number.

'It sounds to me as if you need to call it a day with this boss of yours. I have a friend who works at *Circling* magazine. You should give her a call.'

'Thanks, I might just do that,' I reply. Talking to Karen has made me even more determined to do something. I don't want to be like her, regretting a life affected by the actions of others.

I lie in bed thinking about Alec, but I dream of Brigit. She is at Chloe's wedding and her face has been painted like a clown's. Black mascara-tinged tears stain her white cheeks, revealing pink blotchy skin underneath.

Girl Without a Date in Her Diary – Blog entry – August 31st

Tomorrow is September, which if statistics are to be believed is the most popular month for weddings. This has prompted me to wonder how you know if the man you're with is the One? Is it when he proposes and you don't hesitate to accept?

- My friend said it was.
- My other friend said it made her worry that he wasn't.
- My mother said she always knew.
- My sister said there was no such thing.

- My other sister said that a pregnancy test confirmed two things for her.
- A male colleague said that he wasn't into men but if he was, he would want one who did the housework and cooked like his mum.
- The woman in the post office said she was still wondering after thirty years of marriage.
- Madonna said something similar.
- Angelina looked into those baby-blue eyes and saw beautiful babies.

Emma has forgotten that she is the bride and is acting like a royal wedding coordinator. Her cheeks and neck are flushed and she has a list. She barks orders at anyone over sixteen and carrying a tray; even the guests are not safe from her overcritical eye. She has discarded her matching jacket and forgotten about not wanting to reveal her thick fleshy white arms, one of which is pointing to a guest without a glass. A nervous-looking waitress rushes off to rectify the situation. Emma was born to do something where you need a clipboard and one of those walkie-talkie things. She is clearly in her element. Alan, on the other hand, is looking uncomfortable in a grey suit, and a new hair cut. He doesn't look like a man who has rediscovered a passionate love for his wife.

We have all survived the renewing of the vows, and are now being rewarded with an impressive buffet supplied by The Olive Tree – caterers to royalty and people with too much money and tiny hands. Everything is in miniature and designed to fall apart as soon as you pick it up. All I can think about is getting through this and getting home. This is the night. Well, technically it will be the second night, but the first wasn't quite what I had in mind. I figure practice makes perfect.

As evenings go, it had been as good as it gets. A nine

out of ten. There have been other evenings in my past with a perfect ten, but they are the ones I'm trying to forget. It started with champagne cocktails followed by a funny one-man show, dinner at Thai Palace, another champagne cocktail and a relaxed wander back through the streets of Bath to his flat. We held hands and talked, and every so often Alec would stop and kiss me. The nearer we got to his flat the longer and more passionate the kisses became. By the time we got back to his front door, I was dizzy with the need to get naked. I tried to calculate the last time I had and concluded that it was far too long, but any nerves I thought I might feel were curiously absent. He made it easy for me, chatting and joking and I felt comfortable in his presence. I just had to be there and be fabulous. And I felt it. When he undressed me with his eyes I felt a frisson of excitement. I felt desirable and wanted.

His tiny third-floor flat was a bit of a disappointment. Clothes covered the floor and bed and dirty crockery was piling up in the kitchen. He apologised and quickly made an effort to clear up. As he did, I took the opportunity to flick through his large collection of film and computer games. In between *The Godfather* box set and *Warcraft – The Game*, there was a framed photo of Alec and a girl. She was tiny with a snub nose and a curly mass of strawberry-blond hair. They looked good together. I peered closer.

'That's Charlotte. My ex.'

I nodded and moved on. I wanted to know more but figured tonight wasn't the best time. I kissed him to remove the memory and we fell on to the now made bed. Our passionate kissing soon resumed but something had been lost in the time it had taken us to get here. It wasn't right and the fireworks I was hoping for were rained off.

It was all over in a matter of minutes. Instead of cuddling up afterwards, we both lay there, staring at the ceiling, lost in our own thoughts. I couldn't wait to get away, back to my own bed, and made an excuse about an early start.

I console myself with the thought that sometimes you have to work at these things and have high hopes for a second attempt. It was probably me; out of practice. Josie was right, though: he is a grunter.

The polite murmur of wedding guests rises in volume as the Lady Mayor arrives.

'You okay?' I ask Alec and squeeze his hand.

He rewards me with a dazzling smile.

'How are you, munchkin?'

My father has food on his tie.

'Okay.' I nod, smiling brightly.

'How are you finding the Peel family, then, Alec?'

'Well, your eldest daughter hasn't had me ejected yet, so I guess it's going well,' Alec replies.

'Give her time, give her time.' My father chuckles.

Alec smiles politely. The sound of Alfie's giggling briefly distracts us. My father looks around at the assembled guests. I follow his gaze out towards ladies jostling for space and attention with their hats. He is looking for my mother. A yellow bird is spotted bobbing up and down and he smiles.

'This is nice,' he says, turning back to us.

'Isn't it? Emma's done really well,' I respond. It feels as if we are playing parts in a Jane Austen BBC drama. I feel stilted and, as voices drift around us, I feel the pressure to fill the space. Alec seems unaware.

'You have food on your tie,' I say to my father.

'Saving it for later.'

We laugh and fall into another awkward silence.

'So have you any brothers and sisters, Alec?' my father asks.

'Two brothers.'

We wait for more but Alec has clearly said all he wants to say. I get the sense he doesn't want to be here and I feel irritated by his lack of effort. My father nods at something. I am not sure who is struggling the most, him, Alec or me.

'George, George?' my mother's voice calls out like a school dinner bell. For once I am grateful. My father smiles ruefully and disappears.

'Do you want another drink?' Alec asks.

I nod. I wonder how many he has had and then feel guilty for caring. I squeeze his hand reassuringly again before he goes.

I smooth my grey linen short-sleeved dress and straighten my hat and back. I don't feel as good as I want to. I feel dumpy and frumpy. The outfit would have worked better with heels. I walk around the periphery of the striped, manicured lawn generously sprinkled with pristine people. They are drinking champagne and eating the strawberries that Emma was so adamant in having, although I am glad to see a fair number of them are sampling my mother's celebration chocolate cake. A long table draped with crisp white linen is covered in food and purple irises, chosen to complement Emma's outfit. Like her, they are tall, erect and perfectly arranged. The sound of a pianist playing complicated classical masterpieces can be heard through the doors leading out on to the terrace, and a large white marquee has been set up for the evening's entertainment.

A podgy, freckled hand grabs at my arm.

'This is my middle one,' my mother coos, dragging me into the middle of a group of women immaculately dressed in varying shades of pastel. Her yellow feather head piece wobbles like a comedy bird.

'Aah, so this is the one with the baby?' a woman with perfectly arched eyebrows asks.

'No, that's Katie, the pretty one over there. Harriet here hasn't got any children – well, not yet, anyway. We have a new young man, though, don't we, dear? So who knows. This time next year we may be having a double wedding.'

I cringe and smile as if I don't care.

'This is the one who writes,' she adds, raising her eyebrows towards the sky.

'Hardly, I just produce the What's On page for *Life to Live*.'

'Oh, that's the one with the girl who is Internet dating.' A woman smiles at me, but I don't feel the warmth.

'Yes, I know the one.' The woman with the eyebrows laughs. 'It's quite amusing. I like it, but poor girl. Where did you find her?'

'She's a bit of mystery, really,' I reply, smiling in what I hope is an enigmatic way.

'My daughter loves it. She says it's about time they had a bit of humour in there; personally, I'm not so sure,' another woman says. She pats at already abnormally smooth hair with a hand that is wrinkled and covered in brown liver spots. I decide I don't like her. Emma appears from nowhere like a school mistress behind the bike sheds. She's probably worried that either Mum or I will make fools of ourselves. Unfortunately, I cannot say that she is without cause to worry, because we all know that she has past evidence on her side.

'Harriet, perhaps you and Mother would check on the girls for me?' Emma says, guiding us away from the group. I take her hand. 'You look lovely today,' I say.

'Do I?' Emma replies, and I witness one of only three occasions when my elder sister reveals a chink in her formidable armour.

I squeeze her arm. She hesitates, but whatever is on her mind will stay there. I am left with Mum wittering on about some Lady so and so who has a recipe for monkfish. My mother hates fish, but today she loves it.

'Isn't this wonderful?' she gushes, arms outstretched. 'Wonderful.'

Content that the twins are not performing human sacrifices on the other small children, I leave my mother with Auntie Barbara and wander off to find Alec. I find him leaning against the door of the TV room. It's full of kids watching *Herbie Goes Haywire*. I touch his shoulder gently and he turns, smiling weakly.

'I was just going to come and find you,' he says, handing me a glass of champagne.

'Are you okay?' I ask.

He nods unconvincingly. 'What time can we politely disappear, do you think?'

'Is it really that bad?' I ask. 'Actually, don't answer that.' I laugh, hoping he will.

'I just want to get you back,' he says and nuzzles his head into my neck.

Laughter drifts in through the open window. I can hear my mother's above everyone else's. I start to move towards the door but he grabs my hand.

I can hear Katie call my father, and Alfie crying. I feel torn. Alec pulls me towards him.

'Let's find a little corner. Come on, no one is going to miss you.'

On at least two occasions I have fantasised about having a quickie at one of Emma's parties. I imagined lying on a pile of coats in the spare bedroom, my knickers pulled to one side, my dress pushed up to my waist, a fur coat soft on my thighs. I would reappear with my cheeks flushed, eyes bright, and my lipstick hastily reapplied. Right now, though, and this is something I don't quite understand, I am not in the mood for hot, frantic sex. I want to be with my family, enjoying the sunshine, cuddling my little nephew, laughing and joking with Katie and Lawrence, checking on my father. Perhaps I should have come on my own.

I kiss Alec on the lips. They are soft and warm.

'Come on. I promise we'll go soon.' I take his hand and we head back out to the garden. The sunshine blinds me. I blink and refocus on shades of sherbert pastels. My ears fill with the sound of people talking, glasses tinkling and plates being scraped. A plane is flying overhead leaving a white trail in an azure sky. I look to my side and smile at Alec. Everything is perfect. I look down at my shoes. They are new. They were over my budget and I didn't want them. I wanted the high ones. Who am I today? I look towards the lawn and wave to no one in particular. A couple of people look round to see who I am waving to, but my attention has already shifted and I am walking and holding on tight to my gorgeous new boyfriend.

As the sun disappears and the clouds threaten rain we all transfer to the marquee where long speeches threaten my will to live. Alec seems quiet and I try to fill the spaces. He goes to the bar and leaves me wondering. Have we already said everything? Have we nothing else to laugh about? Our humour is out of sync and I feel like an old sitcom where the laughter is delayed. He is lovely, though. Part of me wonders if Mum was right. Should I lower my expectations? Is my romantic ideal based on films and books with no relevance in the real world? Am I always looking for something that doesn't exist? The one that fits perfectly? This thought makes me feel a little sad. I don't want to let go of that particular dream; or feel as though I have compromised on something as important. How many people do let go?

I look around me and try to work out who has found their dream mate and who hasn't. My gaze rests on Katie and Lawrence. She has her back to him, with her head resting against his chest. He kisses her hair as they sway to the music. It makes me smile. It makes me believe for a little longer that it does exist.

My father fills Alec's seat and we watch as Mum hits the mini dance floor to perform the twist with Auntie Barbara.

'What happened to the string quartet?' I ask.

'Apparently Alan put his foot down. It seems he likes a little eighties disco.'

'Are you sure?'

'That's what your mother told me. Alec seems a nice lad.'

I nod.

'I think your mother is hearing wedding bells.'

I laugh. 'It's early days yet.'

'Is it? I knew by day ten that, despite my best efforts not to, I was going to ask your mother to marry me.'

'But how often does that happen? You were just lucky.'

'Yes, I was.' My father looks wistfully at the dance floor. My mother's cheeks are flushed and her hat is crooked. 'She was different to all the other girls – she had a spark to her. We were so different, but I knew she was special – that what we had was worth holding on to. She was, and still is, my best friend.'

'Wow,' I say, almost disbelievingly. I have never heard my father speak about my mother like this. There are tears in his eyes and it makes me feel vulnerable. He looks at me and smiles.

'I'm not saying we are perfect, no relationship is, and I may need the odd break from her relentless enthusiasm for life, and get irritated by her maddening refusal to consider things outside her world, but we have always, always laughed together. When things have taken a turn for the worse with the business, etc., and we haven't known if we would lose the house or not, your mother has always been there to make me smile and not take myself, or life, too seriously.'

I don't know why I am crying, but I am, and my father hugs me to him.

'I'm sorry, munchkin; I didn't mean to upset you.'

'You haven't, it's just . . .' I cannot finish my sentence. I think of Jason and Alec. I think of Nate, the one I secretly hoped for. Is Alec second best? We just need time, that's all.

My father hands me his white cotton handkerchief.

'Look, I don't know about this Alec chap, but what I do know is that I want you to be happy, and lucky enough to be with someone who will take your hand and make you smile, even when life isn't being kind to you. If he is that person, then I look forward to spending more time with him and putting him through the fishing-trip initiation test.'

I hug my father. 'Thanks, Dad.'

'You know, you are a very special person and you deserve someone who knows that; in the same way that your family and friends do.'

'I don't think Emma does,' I reply, laughing through my tears.

'People show their love in different ways. Your sister is fiercely loyal, and when the chips are down I believe she will be one of the first to be there with a comforting casserole. You know she is actually only truly herself when she is with you and Katie. She feels safe with you.'

'Do you think so?'

'I know so. Now are you going to dance with your old man?'

I shake my head. 'No, I think Alec and I are going to head back.'

'That's a shame. The party was just starting.'

I kiss him on the cheek and refuse to entertain the thoughts that seem intent on entering my world.

Emma is flushed from the dance floor. I realise she is a tiny bit pissed. She drapes her arms round me.

'Thank you for coming. Thank you . . .'

She transfers her attention to Alec who looks at me with panic in his eyes. I shrug my shoulders. There is nothing I can do to help.

'Thank you,' she points to him, 'thank yooo, Alec. I have to say, I was a little worried . . . you hear stories, don't you?' Emma is slurring her words. 'But if you have stolen any of my friends' purses, then nobody has noticed yet!' She laughs loudly.

'I'm joking. Of course I'm joking. You must take care of Harry here . . . not like that little shit she was with before. Did you like the food? Does it bother you that Harry is taller than you?'

I attempt to pull my sister gently away, but her grip on Alec tightens. He looks as if he might scream.

'Aaah. Here she is – my lovely wife.'

Alan appears like a guardian angel. Emma releases Alec and drapes herself round her husband.

'Easy does it, bubba,' he groans.

Bubba? What's that all about? I'm not sure I want to know.

'Let's get you a coffee, shall we?' he suggests.

'You know I quite like you, really,' Emma slurs, ruffling his hair. She makes loud kissing noises.

I do love my sister when she is drunk. She will have no memory of it tomorrow, of course. I think that's the only way she can cope with it.

Alec and I are quiet on the way back, making small talk for the benefit of the taxi driver. I stifle a yawn.

'Are you coming back to mine?' Alec asks.

'No, I think I'll go home.'

I feel tired and I want to be on my own.

'We could have a lie-in tomorrow morning.' He winks at me.

'Do you mind if we take a rain check? I'll give you a ring.'

Tomorrow Josie is stalking Ben and I am already planning what I will do with a much-needed day on my own.

Alec looks surprised and frankly, so am I.

Girl Without A Date in Her Diary – Blog entry – September 4th

I'm still thinking about the One. My father says he knew straight away. What does it mean if you don't? Can people grow on you? Renewing your wedding vows . . . is this a way of reminding yourself that he is the One? Whenever they do it in *OK!* or *Hello!* it usually means a divorce is imminent; either that or they have a jacuzzi to pay for.

When I look at my father and mother, I see good old-fashioned true love. That doesn't mean they are perfect, but underneath the mundane day-to-day stuff you can see it. There is a certainty there. When

I look at others, I see something else and I wonder if they are just as happy, or if they look at my parents and wish they had done things differently. My parents are my template. Is it too much of an ask for something similar?

So, back to weddings. I am thinking of a Caribbean hideaway for mine. Just the two of us. I am not sure I could cope with the guests and the talking to them part. We would be married by a minister dressed in shorts and then spend a honeymoon touring America in a convertible car. We would share the driving and he would play the guitar and wear a Stetson. He might even grow a moustache for a while. There would be lots of sex in motel rooms and breakfasts of pancakes and eggs. The second week we would tour Europe where Brad and Ange would invite us to their chateau in France for roast partridge and soft Brie.

Other stuff to do when you have found the One:

- Write I Love You on a steamed bathroom mirror.
- Order a pizza with one topping for him and one for you.
- Visit DIY stores and talk colour.
- Have a heart-shaped bikini wax.
- Make toast love hearts.
- Do a spinning class together. The bikes are so close you can hold hands. Aaah.

I watch as Josie struggles to squeeze everything into her bags. She arrived with one, but is leaving with three. Two girls looking for love is a recipe for disaster and during her time here there has been too much filling the void shopping. Hopefully, now that she is leaving, our respective bank balances will have time to recover before Chloe's wedding.

'I'm going to miss you,' I say, passing her a box of muesli with a bow on it. She walks over and hugs me. I drown in a sea of breasts and Happy by Clinique.

'I'm going to miss you too, hun,' she replies, releasing me back into fresh air.

Josie is going back to Ben. Not before time, I say, but there were moments I thought it wasn't going to happen. Ben made Josie suffer. He wanted assurances that she was sure, that if she came back, then they did it properly and built a life together. There was going to be no more one leg in London, the other back in her old life here in Bath; no more reluctance about buying furniture for the flat or changing the subject when the wedding word came up. Josie simpered, begged, sent him flowers and eventually got down on one knee and asked him to marry her. He said he would think about it, and Josie reacted with a blow that sent him flying backwards. He broke a finger protecting his fall and his mother said that she would boycott the wedding. They both couldn't be happier and the old gregarious and enthusiastic Josie is back.

'I'm really, really going to miss you,' I repeat, because watching her pack is bringing a lump to my throat. I had got used to hearing her singing in the shower, waking me up at six in the morning, and coming home to bags full of expensive Selfridges goodies to feast on, whilst she chatted about her celebrity-filled day. Her mess, and the month's rent-worth of magazines that make the living room look like a doctors' surgery, have been oddly comforting.

'Hey, it will be fine. You've got Alec now.'

'But it's not the same.'

'Well, it should be.'

'No, I meant who is going to talk rubbish until the early hours and tease me about . . . well, about being me? Who is going to make me peanut butter and banana sandwiches when I am feeling miserable and know that it only works with white bread?'

'I know what you meant, and I still think that you should be getting all that and more from your man; if he is the right one,' Josie says, and shrugs her shoulders as if it is out of her hands. I don't know how to feel. Angry, or sad? She holds me at arm's length. Her face is full of regret.

'Hey, I am happy for you, really I am. If he makes you happy, then he makes me happy. He is gorgeous, nice and not Jason, and that's good enough for me. I didn't mean anything . . . I guess I just . . .'

'What?' I ask.

The buzzer goes, and the taxi driver's voice threatens to let the whole building know he is outside. We hug again and I help her outside with her bags. She gets in and winds the window down.

'I'll come and see you in a couple of weeks' time,' I say. I blow her a kiss and wave as the taxi drives off and disappears.

The flat is quiet and empty without her. I wander from room to room aimlessly, picking up things and putting them back where they belong, and then wishing I hadn't. Alec rings and promises to be here in ten minutes. I should be happy but I feel empty. Like the Easter eggs I got when I was little. Break them open and there is nothing there.

Judith looks radiant.

'How was your weekend?' I ask, and I am treated to a tale of holding hands and a celebration of good against evil.

'You could feel the love in the room,' she swoons.

'I bet you could.'

'You're horrid, Harry. The men there don't want sex.'

'Okay.'

I resume the task of editing Poppy's column.

> But then the Russian invited us on his yacht. He was a bit old and smelled of mouthwash, but he was dripping, literally dripping with gold. Merry Carter was there, Daveed Canatoph and that woman from *Brothers and Sisters*, the one who has really glossy hair. The canapés were divine, but Francesca and I declined and had a Bellini cocktail instead. After reading that article about how Lindsey got to be size zero we are on a diet of pineapple and nothing else.

Poppy's article is a mess. The juicy tit-bits, or fascinating glimpses into a world so different from mine, are far and few between. Putting aside my own personal feelings about all this, I am bored after the first paragraph, but, if that's what Georgina wants, that's what Georgina can have. It says a lot about what *Life to Live* is going to become if this is going to be the linchpin of its future success. No, I'm better off out of this. I need to let it go and get another job. I have registered on recruitment websites, but I'm still reluctant to take the next step and go for interviews. It feels like I'm giving up. The thought depresses me further into the carpet, which needs a good clean.

I make enough changes to Poppy's article to make it publishable and email it over. Have I really lost out to this . . . this rubbish? 'Somebody save me!' I say louder than I originally meant to.

'Only you can save yourself,' Judith says.

I momentarily dream that my pen is a poison dart and will render her temporarily unconscious when thrown into her retreating backside.

Oh my God – literally! Judith is right; not that I would ever tell her that, but she is.

Georgina removes her giant red-framed glasses and lets them hang against her chest.

'Thank you for sending me Poppy's column. I'm glad to see you have better success in getting hold of her than I do. So what can I do for you?'

'Georgina, I know you are keen to go with the Poppy column, and if that's the way you ultimately want to go, then fine, I will accept your decision, but—'

Georgina puts her glasses back on and surveys me like someone looking through a microscope. I refuse to be intimidated.

'How many readers will really identify with Poppy and her empty world? A couple of young girls who dream of being footballers' wives? I might be wrong, but as far as I can see, these are not the people who read our magazine. Our reader is predominantly female – these are the girls who read the books that Richard and Judy, or Oprah recommend. Why? Because they trust them. They will trust Girl Without a Date because she is like them. She is someone who is trying to make her way and not always getting it right; someone who can come up with some alternative suggestions for spending their precious time, things that maybe they hadn't thought of.'

I stop for a second. Georgina stares back at me.

'They want to know if she finds her man, because everyone loves that search for romance. What incentive is there to read about a girl called Poppy who will only spread her legs for the richest man, and has no interest in what Miss and Mrs Average do when they are not working their socks off to earn the money she gets transferred from her father's account?' I take a breath. I should probably shut up. 'The day of the It girl is long gone. Our readers want real women they can identify with, and that transcends the ages. The magazine has lost its way because it has forgotten who its readers are.'

I take another breath. My cheeks are burning, my breathing is rapid and my temples are throbbing. I think I might pass out.

'Have you finished?' Georgina asks. Her eyebrows are raised with surprise. Amusement or outrage? I am not sure. This might be the time when I run as fast as I can towards *Bath at Large*'s offices, with a promise that I will take a pay cut, that I will do anything, if they will just give me a job.

'I thought it was important to tell you how I feel.'

'Thank you, Harry. I will, of course, give considerable thought to everything you have just said. Now, if you will excuse me, I have a conference call to take.'

I close the door carefully behind me. Ed is waiting for me.

'You have that look. I'm guessing it didn't go too well in there,' he says.

'No. I think it might be time to get another job.'

'You can't leave. Who would arrange our next night out, keep me amused, and monitor Mr Stair Runner?'

'Poppy?' I suggest.

'I doubt if she gets out of bed for less than a grand and the promise of a rich Russian.'

I grumble all the way to the town centre. When we arrive at our destination, Ed begins to take photos of a man painted silver and pretending to be a statue. I attempt to interview him but it's not going well. He has a squeaky thing in his mouth and thinks it's highly amusing to squeak rather than talk.

'You know what?'

The man looks at me. He is evil. Behind that silver make-up lies a dark heart.

'You're not funny. Now you can speak to me like a grown-up or you can carry on squeaking. If you choose the latter I will leave and go and have a cup of tea. Something I wanted to do as soon as we met.'

Ed whistles in what I assume is appreciation.

'Hey, don't let it get you down,' he says as we walk back to the office.

'It just makes me so mad. I told Georgina what I thought because I really care about the magazine and she looked at me as if I was talking gibberish. It just confirmed that it's the end for me at *Life to Live*.' I feel a little tearful.

'Oh come on. She'll come round.' He hugs me into him. This just makes me want to cry more.

'Do you fancy a drink?' he asks.

'What, no Noush tonight?'

'Noush and I finished a little while ago.'

'Oh.'

'It's okay, though.'

'What happened?'

'We just wanted different things. Come on,' he hugs me again, 'I could do with a drink.'

Alec is visiting his mum in Florida. I'm sure he wouldn't mind. He knows I go out with work colleagues and this would be no different. I could do with letting off some steam. I feel a few 'f words' coming on.

'Okay.'

After a pub meal and too many drinks, Ed and I return to my flat for a cup of coffee. We sit on the floor, our backs resting against the sofa, staring into the beige carpet I wish I didn't have. I fantasise about polished floorboards and trendy tufted rugs.

'So, how's it going with the postman?' he asks.

'Okay.'

'Just okay?'

I don't reply.

'Am I detecting doubts?'

'He is lovely and gorgeous and . . .'

'And?'

I am not sure what the 'and' is, and I feel uncomfortable thinking about it. I expect too much. I'm lucky to have someone like Alec. Like an Etch-A-Sketch, I wipe my mind clean.

'He is lovely and gorgeous. End of story.'

The music washes over my bare feet like a wave and I wiggle my toes in time. Ed watches them as if they are performing mice, but he seems miles away.

'Are you okay?' I ask, because I get the distinct impression that he isn't, although my distinct impressions are a bit blurred at the moment. Perhaps I am drunk. He closes his eyes briefly and runs a hand through his hair.

Then he reaches over and kisses me. I am stunned.

'What was that for?' I ask, feeling a little shell-shocked.

'Oh come on, Harry. You must know how I feel about you?'

'No . . . no, I didn't . . . don't,' I stammer.

Suddenly we feel too close and I get up to . . . to do what? To make a cup of tea. That's it – I'll make a cup of tea. I wander into the kitchen, trying to work out what just happened. Ed follows me.

'You're right, we are friends, but I can't deny my feelings for you, Harry. Noush wasn't the girl for me and I'm pretty sure Alec isn't the guy for you. Come on, we get on really well . . . we—'

I put my hand up to stop him. I am not sure I want to hear any more.

'Ed, don't . . . please. Look, I think we had better forget about the tea.'

Ed nods and looks at me like an injured dog. I don't know what to say. I didn't see this coming. Should I have?

'You're lovely but, Ed, this is a bit of a shock.' I attempt to ease the situation but I just want him to leave. I need some space. 'And I'm with Alec.'

'He's not the one for you. You know that, but you just don't want to admit it.'

'Go home, Ed.' Suddenly I am sober and very tired.

As I lie in bed I think back over the last few months and what I might have done to give Ed the impression that there was a chance. I feel as if someone has revealed a secret identity; one I never suspected. Ed may as well have just turned out to be Batman. I guess I never thought of him in that way. He had Noush, and at first I had Jason, which meant we were always in the safe zone. Oh God.

My night is an unsettled one and I wake up feeling out

of sorts. When Alec texts me I feel guilty; as if I have cheated on him.

Girl Without A Date in Her Diary – Blog entry – September 14th

How do you know if the line between friends and being something else – something more – is a thick black one or a bit blurred? I am all for a bit of flirting, but with the proviso that we both know it is just that: a bit of harmless, friendly flirting – the sort that makes the world go round. In my limited experience, when friends have crossed that line and slept together it rarely works and something is lost. Saying that, I also know of someone who was in lust with her best friend for years and just waited until said friend realised what was good for him. They have been together five years and are among the happiest people I know. They are an example of it working, but I suspect the majority of people recognise that what they love about their friends is not what they would love in a relationship. I might be wrong. Maybe your past friendship will be the foundation of a happy life together. The trouble is, if this doesn't work out, then you are more than likely to lose this friend for ever.

This also got me thinking about having the courage to take a risk. It's a hard thing to have the guts to tell someone how you feel, both personally and professionally, especially when there is a large part of you that knows it would be easier to play safe. Fear of failure is what stops us doing things; from saying yes to someone, to fighting for what you believe in, to striving for something more. I guess it's all about grabbing a moment. First you have to recognise it and accept it for what it represents. Then you have a decision to make. You can either take a deep breath and say the words you've wanted to say for too long, or you can turn and walk the other way. I make it sound like I know what I'm talking about, but unfortunately what you know and what you do in the heat of the moment are often completely different things.

If you do want someone, or something, then go for it. In the words of my lovely dad – what's the worst that could happen? You fall flat on your face?

And what if you do? You get up, wipe the dirt from your chin, and know that you didn't let a moment go and then spend the next ten years regretting it.

So, back to where we started. A friend recently told someone how he felt and as much as I think he might have got his moment wrong, I now admire him for his courage.

If you're having the same dilemma of should you or shouldn't you, I think you should! You never know.

Ed and I avoid each other for the remainder of the week. Actually, that's an assumption. I am avoiding *him*, and I am guessing he is doing the same because, apart from a fleeting glimpse of him leaving the office, I haven't seen him. Part of me feels angry at him for complicating matters; part of me feels sad because I might have lost a friend.

I realise I am burying my head in the sand and refusing to think about all the things I feel uncomfortable about, but despite being a woman and able to multitask, I do feel that one thing at a time is the way to go at the moment. So, instead of dealing with matters of the heart, I focus on my search for another job. I remember Karen at the restaurant and take a look at *Circling* magazine's website. It's impressive and in London, which is where I should have gone in the first place instead of wasting my time here at *Life to Live*. I decide to take the plunge and leave a message for the editor and then register with another recruitment agency, who reassure me I have transferable skills. This is helped when I get a surprise email to tell me I have been shortlisted for the Regional Press Awards. Girl Without a Date in Her Diary is in the running for best newcomer. Oh my Lordy Lord. Who would have thought it? I excitedly scan through the email for details:

This 'prestigious' awards ceremony will take place at the Guildhall where guests will be treated to a seven-course menu by celebrity chef, Michael Bayonne. Your compère for the evening is local celebrity, Tania Collins.

It's like the bloody Oscars; well, almost. I phone Josie and Chloe.

'Red shopping alert. I need a dress to kill and shoes to match.'

The girls accept the challenge and we arrange to go out Saturday.

'Shopping at Brown's, then off to Marlow's for mussels, chips and champagne for lunch,' Chloe suggests, and I can't think of anything better.

I don't phone Georgina because she will know and I'm not in the business of gloating. But maybe I will be if I win.

When Alec rings later that night and asks me if I have any news, I forget that I haven't told him.

'Why didn't you ring me?'

'Sorry, I guess I just got carried away in the excitement of it all.'

I realise I have also been avoiding Alec. He leaves me messages and my response time has doubled. Since Emma's wedding, things feel different. The boxes were ticked and I was congratulating myself for a job well done, but now I'm rubbing them out, wondering what all the rush was for. I was looking for a date for the wedding, not the One. But Alec is one of the nice guys and I need to give us a chance.

'And partners? I assume we get an invite too?'

'Oh, I don't know.'

Should I tell him I was thinking of going with Josie?

'Can't wait to see you on Saturday. I've missed you,' he says.

'Me too,' I reply, but I feel as if I am lying. 'Oh, I can't do Saturday. I'm going shopping.'

We have our first argument. It isn't a major one but I am accused of always putting other stuff first. I feel bad, but not bad enough to rearrange my shopping trip.

It's raining outside and instead of going out for a lunchtime flit around the shops, I take a little peek at DateMate. Since meeting Alec I haven't used it. I convince myself I am looking for purely recreational purposes, but I still jump like a guilty person when the phone rings.

'Harry. Hi. It's Candice Lamb, editor of *Circling* magazine.' She pauses, presumably to let the information sink in.

'Oh, Candice. Thanks for getting back to me.'

'Harry, it's my pleasure. Your column has been noticed. We love it here. I'm really pleased you got in touch to let me know you're available.'

Wow!

'We love you so much that I think we might have a home for a Girl Without a Date in Her Diary. Somewhere she can really spread her wings; a place where the cultural diversity is enormous and doesn't include an old woman dressing up as Jane Austen. We might have to shorten the title, though. A Girl Without?'

What can I say?

'Just think, Harry. You could reach a potentially huge audience.'

I should say something.

'Don't say anything right now. Have a think about it. In the meantime, I'll email you some promo stuff about the magazine. Believe me when I say it's one hell of a ride. We can talk about the boring stuff like a moving allowance and other benefits later. Anyway, gotta go, I have a photo shoot with the shortlisted Turner Prize line-up and Malcolm McLaren. I'm calling it Art and Anarchy in the UK.' She laughs. 'How great is that?'

'It's—'

Candice has already gone. I put the phone down and look around. Did anyone else hear what just happened?

I sit staring at my pc for a long time. My keyboard needs cleaning. Should I use a cotton bud? Is it a hot bed of germs? I read somewhere that the average keyboard has more germs than a toilet seat. Is that true? Have I just been headhunted?

'Jose, Candice Lamb has just telephoned. She said she wants me to edit their What's On pages, AND, they love my column.'

'That's amazing! Congratulations.'

'Thanks.' I feel a little star struck. This is how they must feel on the *X Factor*.

'Hey, you know the best thing?' she says.

'What?' I ask.

'You'll have to move to London, and that means you will be closer to me and Ben! Hurray.'

Move to London? God, yes . . . What about my little flat with its rubbish carpet?

'I need to think about it.'

'What is there to think about? It's a no-brainer,' Josie says, but even she knows I can't break the habit of a lifetime.

I have been invited to *Circling* magazine to meet the team and despite my reservations about working and moving to London, I decide to go. Everyone is paper thin, including Candice. I suck in my belly and cheekbones. They are enthusiastic with their 'hi's, 'yeah's and sincere, 'I'm listening with really interested head nodding's. Candice takes me to lunch. Her skin is taut and her dress is expensive. I wait as she rummages around in her giant black patent Chanel handbag.

'I'm desperate for a ciggie. Come outside with me,' she instructs.

It is drizzling. Umbrellas are launched, while others brave what they feel isn't really rain at all. They forget that the tiny drops of moisture will settle on top of their clothes and their hair, creating layers that will eventually break through. I shiver uncontrollably as my body adjusts from the reassuring warmth of the restaurant. Candice seems oblivious of the cold as she puffs away.

'So the thing is, Harry . . .' She takes a long drag. I watch as the smoke disappears into the damp air. 'Join us and you will have the opportunity to work with an amazing team. We will live, love and work together.' She throws her arms up into the air and laughs. It comes from the back of her throat.

'Live together?'

'When I say living together, I don't mean literally, but we will be spending a lot of time in each other's company, being creative, pushing the envelope . . . the air will be full of inspiration. It's up to you to breathe it in, Harry.' She takes another drag and flicks her cigarette to the floor.

I look at the stump, disintegrating in the rain.

'It will also be a shockingly huge salary.' Candice laughs again. It is a dirty laugh. I join in, but mine is clean and missing something in execution.

I watch as people huddle together, talk into their phones and disappear into neighbouring restaurants and coffee shops. When I was a child I imagined the city to be full of beautiful people with tiny snub noses, thin legs and wide, almost round blue eyes. They would all stand with one leg slightly forward; hand on hip and slightly leaning backwards. They would smoke cigarettes in long black lacquer holders. The men would wear check trousers and have wide foreheads. I imagined myself as one of them: catching a train to a new life, waving to my sisters through the smoke. For some reason the trains were steam driven. If I worked for *Circling* magazine I would be one of the beautiful people.

I imagine a flat with wide polished floorboards, huge pieces of art on the walls and a wardrobe of designer cast-offs left over from fashion shoots, although I might need to lose a bit of weight first. My evenings and weekends would be spent attending glittery literary launches, London Fashion Week, going to bars with *über*-cool artists, singers and models. Their coolness would rub off on me and eventually nobody would remember the old Harry. I am standing on the edge of something.

Actually, I am standing on the edge of a pavement, in the rain, and I'm friggin' freezing. I shiver.

'Oh, darling, you're cold. Come on, let's be naughty and have dessert. The lemon meringue is divine here.' Candice takes my hand and drags me back into the restaurant. The white tablecloths look crisp and clean against the brown leather. The waiters are dressed in black; the hum of conversation is politely reassuring.

With my wedding waistline in mind, I refuse dessert and go for coffee instead.

'Open wide,' Candice instructs.

'No, I'm okay, really.'

'Open your mouth.' Her voice is soft and silky. She is smiling and coaxing with her spoon. 'Harry, it's good to try new things.'

She places a spoonful of pie into my mouth. 'Now tell me that isn't fabulous.'

It isn't. My mum's is better. Candice takes another spoonful of dessert.

'I imagine your mind is bursting with questions to ask me.'

I try and think of one but my mind is blank. Candice doesn't seem to care. She appears to have forgotten she has asked the question in the first place.

'Isn't this fabulous?'

I nod. It is. It is also a tiny bit scary.

Alec meets me at Chalk Farm tube station. I am making the effort to be the perfect girlfriend and lowering my expectations. A night out with Josie and Ben might help him to feel a little more included in my life.

'How did it go?' he asks, hugging me to him.

'It was good.'

'And?'

'I don't know. I need to think about it,' I reply. My head is full of what ifs and I need time to process them all and consult my horoscope. That's something I haven't done for a while.

Josie and Ben are already in the pub when we arrive. They have news.

'We've just put a deposit down on a flat!'

'Oh my God, that's fantastic.' I hug Josie to me.

'I know. I'm finally a grown-up,' she says. 'Next I'll be looking at fridges and checking their energy ratings.'

She seems pleased at the prospect, but Ben and I shake our heads. Josie is like a cat; you can only domesticate her so far.

'Come on, let's get another drink to celebrate our flat and your job offer.'

Josie and I leave Ben and Alec to talk football as we order more drinks and some food at the bar.

'You two next,' Josie observes.

'No,' I say a little too quickly. Josie looks at me.

'But you seem good together?'

'Yeah, we are,' I reply.

'But?'

'I don't know. Maybe I'm expecting too much and this is as good as it gets. I just have a sense that there is something missing.' I feel as if I am betraying Alec but the need to voice my concerns is overwhelming. It's like a release to say it out loud. Perhaps now that I've said it, my concerns will go away.

'Maybe it's not something that's missing, but some*one*?'

'I don't get what you mean.'

'Do you feel like you did with Jason?'

'My relationship with Jason was different. I was besotted with him and I was absolutely convinced that it was the big love thing and then he went off with someone else. Clearly I can't be trusted with gauging relationships.'

'I think you know. You just need to listen to your heart,' Josie says, patting hers. 'The thing with Jason has made you forget how to trust it.'

'Since when did you become such a romantic?'

'When Ben and I bought that sofa! I love that bloody thing. We snuggle up and it's the comfiest, most beautiful thing in the world. I love it and I love him for bringing it into my life.'

'Wow, you're going to make me cry tears of joy in a minute.'

'Sofas are the new diamonds. Mark my words.'

Josie hugs me. We walk back to the table where Ben and Alec are animated in conversation and I feel incredibly lucky. I have good friends, the prospect of a new job, recognition for my work on the column, and a relationship where I am in control of my emotions. I am walking tall. It's all good. Maybe I'm thinking too much about the Alec thing. He's great and we're good together. What more do I want?

'So, how are things with Ed?' Josie asks.

'Oh, that's a bit of a disaster. We either look the other way or walk in the opposite direction.'

'That's a shame. I like Ed.'

'Me too,' I say. 'I miss him, but part of me wonders how we are going to get past this.'

'How funny life is. A few months ago we were looking at an empty chair at a wedding. Now you've got men falling over themselves to sit next to you. All you need now is for Jason to get in contact and Chloe can assign a whole table for you. Harry and her men.'

I laugh at the thought.

'Part of me quite likes the thought of going on my own now,' I suggest.

'You *are* joking?'

'Half joking.'

'What are you two laughing about?' Alec asks.

'Life and sofas,' I respond.

'Maybe we need to get a sofa?' Alec replies and I laugh because I assume he must be joking.

As we spend the rest of the evening talking and laughing, I forget the job offer, Ed and all the head and heart stuff. I concentrate on enjoying the here and now. Tomorrow is decision day and it can wait.

Alec and I walk in silence towards the tube station. We are both lost in our own thoughts and I am quite happy not to share mine. As we turn the corner I am transfixed by a jacket in the darkness. Is it him? Is it Nate? My heart skips a beat. I haven't seen him since the wedding dress moment. For all I know he could be married by now. I look around but he seems to be on his own. I instinctively let go of Alec's hand.

'What's the matter?' Alec asks.

The jacket turns and it isn't him. What would I have done if it was? Nothing. That's what I would have done. God, what's the matter with me? Life is complicated enough and I'm with Alec now. Looking for someone I used to have a crush on is the action of someone who . . . should be single?

'Sorry, I thought I saw someone,' I say to Alec and smile. He takes my hand and draws me into him.

'You know, talking to Ben and Josie got me thinking. Maybe we should think about moving in together. What do you think?'

'I think that if we don't get a move on we are going to miss the last train home,' I respond lightly and begin to run.

'Hang on, wait for me,' Alec calls out.

It takes me a few seconds to realise I am probably running too fast.

Alec is snoring lightly and I resent his presence. I lie in bed counting sheep and listening to the pitter patter of rain on the window. Someone is playing music upstairs. I hum along and fill my head with something other than the nagging thoughts. Candice is expecting a decision by tomorrow. The panic twists my stomach into knots. I am stuck in the well of indecision and it's dark down here. The pipes fill up with water and a door is slammed shut. The music is turned off and the silence settles like a blanket of snow. I am wide awake. I think of other things, nice things; things that have nothing to do with jobs and men. I check the time. It's late and I should be asleep. I close my eyes and then open them again. This is no good; I need to make a decision.

I could stay at *Life to Live*. It's what Georgina expects me to do. Safe, sensible, and oh, so predictable Harry. No. It's time to go. It's time to surprise myself. I'm going to take the job at *Circling*. I'm going to be dynamic and . . . what's another word that's like dynamic?

I shove Alec in the ribs and he stops snoring.

You would think that now I've made a decision, I would feel on top of the world. You would think. The trouble is I am now wondering if it is the right one. I keep putting off ringing Candice and my day is suddenly full of other things I have to do first, like grocery shopping. I have taken a day's holiday. I'm not in the mood for Georgina and Poppy and I need some head space.

The supermarket isn't helping my decision-making process. The vegetable section is the worst culprit. Desiree, Charlotte, Jersey Royals and King Edwards tell me they are perfect for mash, roasting or salads. Shiny red and yellow peppers vie for attention against the dark, matt green of courgettes. I gaze at them for a while, transfixed, before turning to the mushrooms. Chestnut, shiitake, oyster. Tomatoes are safe. Plum, cherry, on the vine. I give up and head towards the ready-made meals.

'Hey, you.'

Nate stands there looking beautiful with an aubergine.

He is like a glass of water in the desert and I want to drink him dry. Tanned, unshaven and wearing sunglasses in the supermarket, he looks like a rock star with a vegetable.

'Hey.'

'It's been a while. How are you?' He takes off his

sunglasses to reveal dark purple smudges under his eyes. I want to rub them away and promise him sleep.

'I'm good, and you?'

'Yeah, good.' We stand there, him with his aubergine; me with my low-fat pasta bake.

What is it about us? I always feel as if we should have lots to say to each other, but never do. It's as if we are waiting for our parents to push us forwards. Go on, Nate. Talk to the nice lady.

'So, how was the wedding?' he asks.

'Oh. Awful.'

'God. I'm sorry. Are you all right? Is Ed okay?'

He looks truly concerned. I suddenly realise why.

'No, no, it wasn't my wedding. It was my sister's. Actually, it wasn't hers. She's already had one. This was a renewing of the vows thing.'

'Aaah.'

'The last time I saw you, you looked as if wedding dresses were on the agenda?' I suggest, remembering the girl who was peering into the window of the dress shop.

'My sister.'

'Aaaaah.' My heart lifts. Is this my moment? The one where I should be taking a deep breath and being brave?

'Your dinner doesn't look very appetising.' He points to my basket.

'That's because it isn't.'

'I can do pretty amazing things with an aubergine.'

'Should you be advertising that in a supermarket full of uptight women? You're likely to be mobbed.'

'I was actually hoping that you—'

My mobile rings.

'Emma? Hi. This is a nice surprise,' I say, because it is. Emma never rings me, and I am astonished that she even has my mobile number.

'My sister,' I mouth to Nate. He smiles.

What Emma says next is a lie and I end the call before she can tell me any more. It is a lie, because it can't be true.

The house I grew up in seems smaller. The stone appears grey and uninviting, the door in need of paint. I hesitate before ringing the bell. A part of me wants to turn and run, but I have nowhere to go. Emma opens the door and ushers me in without words. She looks grey. I walk into the living room, and can barely look at them. They are all there, motionless; waiting for someone to break the spell of inertia and disbelief. My mother gets up and hugs me close as if her life depends on it. She feels fragile and tiny, like a child. When she eventually pulls away I look into a face that is confused and lost. I feel numb and the tears don't come.

'Oh Harry, we tried to phone you.'

'I had my phone switched off,' I reply.

'It was so sudden. He was in the garden, trimming the edges of the lawn . . . I'd been nagging him to do it for ages.' My mother's voice breaks in perfect time with my heart. 'He was humming, just like he always does . . . and then . . .' My mother crumples before me and Katie springs up and gathers her up, leading her back to the sofa.

I look around me. They are all waiting for a reaction, for me to say something, but I can't. My father is dead and I am lost.

The moment I heard the news has gone. I remember Nate being in my flat and making me sugary tea. He made phone calls and drove me here. His voice was calm but I don't remember what he said.

My father had a massive heart attack and was dead before they got him to the hospital. He never regained consciousness for my mother to tell him it was all going to be okay, that she loved him, that we all loved him. Did he know? When he was alone and gripped by an unrecognisable pain, did he know that we would crumble without him in our lives? Perhaps it's best he didn't, because if he did, he would never have left us. The pain is like a clenched fist inside my stomach. I hurt, but the feeling is reassuring. I am not sure I ever want it to go, because that would mean forgetting.

The next few hours are a blur as Emma insists that we all eat, whether we are hungry or not, and the details emerge. She suggests Mum goes back with her, but Mum is adamant that she doesn't want to leave the house. Katie and I agree to stay so that Emma can get back to the girls. Whilst the rest of us sit comatose, unable to function, she has made copious cups of tea and dealt with the flurry of phone calls and the stuff that no one else has the stomach to deal with, including phoning the funeral home and arranging for the doctor to visit. It is she who talked to him and agreed on a course of sedatives for Mum. Emma has been amazing, just as my father said she would be, and it is this that finally makes me cry. When I do, I cannot stop and it is Emma who holds me close until the sobs subside. She promises to be back in the morning and leaves Katie and I to check on Mum as the sedatives take hold. We spend the rest of the evening talking until, exhausted, we look for the sanctuary of sleep in our old bedrooms.

*

When I wake the next day, I am ten years old and waiting for my mother to shout that breakfast is two minutes away. I am on the periphery of sleep and wakefulness. It feels safe and warm. I lie quite still. There is a dressing table and a rug I don't recognise. The dressing table has a china figurine of a girl with a dove. There are magazines on an upholstered stool; presumably for guests to read. *Good Housekeeping* and *Fishing Monthly*. I remember and cannot breathe. An unwelcome shaft of sunlight breaks through the curtains and settles across me. I close my eyes to it. I don't want sunshine today.

Emma is in the kitchen, making what looks like a casserole.

'She won't eat otherwise,' she says, answering a question I don't ask. I sit at the table and rub my eyes. They feel swollen and full of grit. Emma passes me a mug of coffee and resumes her cooking.

'Where's Mum?' I ask, taking a sip of the hot liquid. It burns my tongue.

'Still asleep. The doctor said she would probably be out of it for a while.'

I nod. 'And Katie?'

'Gone back to collect Alfie. Then she's coming back.'

I try not to look out of the window, into the garden my father loved; the place he spent his last hours. Did he feel the autumn sun on his head and wish he had worn his hat? What was playing on his wind-up radio? The cricket? *The Archers*? *Gardeners' Question Time*? Whose voice was filling his head? Was he planning next year's planting? Courgettes, maybe, and more of the cherry tomatoes my mother loves? Did he make a note to replace the spade with the split handle? Was he wondering if it was time for a cup of tea and a chocolate digestive? Did he know in that moment, when the pain came, that he was going to die? The tears roll slowly down my cheeks, warm and unwelcome.

'I can't believe he's gone,' I say.

Emma stops. 'Nor can I,' she says, looking into the saucepan. She adds more pepper and resumes stirring.

Georgina answers the phone and I am momentarily lost for words.

'Aah, Harry, I was going to email you. Can you pop into my office around ten? There's something I want to discuss with you.'

'Georgina, I . . . I'm sorry, I'm not going to make it in today. My . . .' The words stick in my throat. 'My father died yesterday.'

There is silence. I feel comfortable in it. There is no need to say anything. In fact, I wish there were no more words; that people would just nod and walk away.

'I'm so sorry,' she says. 'Give your mother my best wishes. Take all the time you want, and if there is anything I – we – can do, then please call.'

'Thank you,' I say, and end the call before she can say anything else.

I phone Candice and tell her I can't accept the job at *Circling* magazine. She tells me that the job is mine and she will keep it open for me.

'Call me in a month,' she says and I wonder if it's possible to feel any differently than I do now in the space of four weeks.

Judith phones and leaves a message on my mobile. She tells me that my father has gone to a better place, that he is happy. She says that her group will pray for him tonight and for some strange reason I am glad.

*

The church is full and it makes me feel better. My father was loved, not just by us, but by many. There are the apprentices he has taught over the years, old drinking pals, friends who rented the same villa in Majorca with my mother and father, year in year out, familiar faces from the village they have lived in for over thirty years, relatives I didn't expect to see so soon after the renewal of Emma's vows, and members of his beloved fishing club. The organ drowns out the sound of polite whispering. My hands and feet are cold.

I cannot think of him in the mahogany coffin with the perfect white roses. They are too perfect. He would have hated them. His favourite was the double Tangerine Dream variety. It is too late in the year for them. He was cutting them back when he died. Next year they will return, stronger and more beautiful. I look up to the ceiling. The music is too loud. He would have hated this. I look across at my mother who is shrinking between Emma and Katie. The black is sucking the little colour she has left in her face and her hair seems to have turned from blond to ash overnight. The vibrancy has gone, leaving in its shadow a frightened woman who cannot be left alone.

He would have squeezed her hand and then laughed when she pushed him away, annoyed that he wasn't going to make it to Laura and Geoff's next weekend. He would have told a funny story to put everyone at ease and would have made a rude comment about the vicar. He would have told me not to worry. What's the worst that could happen, munchkin? he would say. I swallow hard.

The organ stops and the vicar clears his throat. He talks as if he has known my father for years, but we all know my father only set foot in a church when he had to.

Emma takes to the lectern and uses words like proud, dependable and values. She reminds me of a ship figurehead. Her voice breaks and we all wait in silence for her to continue. Somebody coughs and Alfie begins to grizzle.

'. . . But the most special thing about my father was that we could rely on him. We could rely on him to be there for us and make it all okay, to make us feel beautiful when we didn't feel it, and to make us laugh, even when we didn't want to. My father was a very special man and I wish I had told him so.' The tears run without restraint and my sister falls apart. A man with white hair and a moustache rushes to her side and helps her back to her seat. Katie is sobbing heavily beside me. I take hold of her hand and squeeze it tightly. My Uncle Bob's figure at the lectern is blurred through my own tears and they fall easily as he reads 'The Human Season' by Keats. His voice falters and I, my father's winter girl, wonder how life can go on. It must, I know it must, but I don't know how.

As we make our way out into an appropriately flat, grey day, I notice Ed, and I am grateful for his support. He approaches me as we wait for my mother to read the messages on the wreaths. I shiver with the cold and Josie hugs me into her. I am glad she is here.

'I'm so sorry about your father, Harry. He was a lovely man,' Ed says.

'Thank you,' I say. This is all I can say to people. Thank you, thank you, thank you. I shall drown in thank-yous. It is nice that people care, that they want to acknowledge my father, but I am struggling with the grateful smile and the serenity part. I am trying hard not to scream.

'I hope you didn't mind me coming? I just wanted to pay my respects,' he says, averting his eyes to the job of moving a leaf with his shoe. His shoes look new.

'No, of course not. It was nice of you to come. You are more than welcome to come back to Emma's afterwards.'

'No, I'd better get back. Are you okay?' He looks sad

and I want to touch his face with my hand; to reassure. I want to tell him it's okay, but it isn't and I am tired of saying it today.

'Thanks for coming,' I say, and move away to join my mother.

Emma has given me and Josie the job of distributing the sandwiches and mini quiches we made earlier. Today I am more than happy to be instructed, and I go about my tasks on automatic pilot. Katie is keeping Mum busy with baby Alfie. His infectious giggle and attempts to walk provide a welcome diversion and a safe topic of conversation for the constant stream of well-wishers. There are cards with flowers on. They are muted and polite; like the people who nibble on the sandwiches and talk in low voices. Alec asked if I wanted him to come today and I could see the relief in his face when I said no. I know he feels uncomfortable with my grief and his distance is marked but, if I'm honest, it suits me. I don't want to have to worry about anyone else's feelings apart from my mother and my sisters.

'Mum is staying here tonight, and I've made a room up for you too,' Emma says as I accept a tray of tea and coffee to pass round.

'Oh, thanks, but I'll go home,' I say, surprised.

'No,' she puts a warm hand on my arm. 'I don't want you to be on your own tonight, and I'd like you to stay.'

'Okay, thanks.'

Later, when everyone has gone, I sit next to my mother as she stares into a glass of brandy and tell her what my father said to me at Emma's reception.

'Your father always was a soppy bugger,' she says, smiling through her tears.

*

When I return to work, everyone tiptoes around me, trying to be kind. I feel suffocated by their sympathetic smiles and well-chosen words. I try to make them feel better whilst the voices in my head scream something else. The alternative is worse. At least here, the phone calls and emails provide a temporary respite to the darkness that sits at the back of my brain, beating a rhythm, waiting.

'Do you want some company this weekend?' Vicky asks.

'That's really sweet, but I'm pretty busy . . . can't get away, loads to do,' I reply.

'Do you want to come over this weekend? We could do Sunday lunch at the pub?' Josie asks.

'That's really sweet, but I'm pretty busy . . . can't get away.'

'Come shopping with me?' Chloe suggests.

'That's really sweet, but I'm pretty busy.'

'We could go to the cinema?' Alec says.

'That's really sweet, but I'm . . .'

I draw the curtains. A note gets pushed through the door. 'Are you okay?' it reads, 'I can make beans on toast, provide mind-numbing anecdotes and whisky cocktails. I can also be very quiet in a corner. Nate x.'

That's sweet. I go to bed.

I'm tired, but I can't sleep. I clean every corner of my flat and rearrange my wardrobe twice. All of my clothes suddenly seem wrong and are now in dustbin bags destined for the charity shop. Then I run out of things to do and panic at the space in my head. Alec is away watching football up North somewhere, Emma and Alan have taken Mum away for the weekend, and Katie and Lawrence are visiting his parents. I feel lost. The walls of my flat are pushing down on me. I lean against the wall and sink down on to the floor, my head between my knees.

The door buzzer goes and for a moment I am not sure where I am.

'Harry?' Nate's voice rings out.

I am frozen to the spot. My breathing becomes shallow, in case anybody hears.

'Harry, it's Nate.'

I don't want to be with anyone and I wait for him to go.

He comes back the next morning and again in the afternoon. I have phoned in sick. Nobody asked why. I ignore his persistent knocking and listen for the silence that will follow.

It's late and the rest of the world is asleep, but I have every light on in the flat.

'Harry, I know you're there. Are you okay?' Nate calls out.

I wait for him to go and count to a hundred. I just want to be left alone with my comfy socks and blanket. I want to reduce my heart rate and fall into a deep sleep like a hibernating animal. When I was a child my father brought home a baby hedgehog. We made a little bed for him in a cardboard box and called him Mr Pincushion. We tried to coax him with cat food and milk but he wasn't hungry. I woke up in the middle of the night to see my father crouching over the box, the hedgehog in his hands. I got out of bed and poked Mr Pincushion. He was a stiff ball of pins. It was my first experience of death. Early next morning we watched from the bedroom window as my father buried him in the garden. I had nightmares for months afterwards that we had made a dreadful mistake and Mr Pincushion was trying to dig his way out. Oh God . . .

*

The pain, when it comes, is like a body blow. My stomach hurts with the effort of holding it in and my breathing trips as I gasp for air. My tears fall like a salty avalanche. I hold on to the pain with both hands. I am frightened of losing my father, of forgetting the kindness of his eyes. I am frightened without him; of being on my own. Exhausted, I take one of the tablets the doctor has prescribed and sleep.

'Miss Peel?' The voice is not one I recognise.

'Miss Peel, can you hear me?'

Of course I can hear him. I tell him he can't dig there because that's where Mr Pincushion is. My mouth opens and forms the words, but they are not heard. I try again.

'Okay, guys,' the voice says.

There is banging. Who is banging? I shift and drag myself up and out of the syrupy darkness. There is another bang and a crack. I look round in panic. Four firemen burst through the door into the room. I jump up, wrapping the blanket round me as if this will protect me.

'What the?'

I feel slightly drunk, as if everything is in slow motion. It's like coming out of anaesthetic. Firemen? There are firemen in my flat!

'Miss Harriet Peel?' one of the firemen asks, and I nod. Nate is right behind them. What's he doing here? I try hard to concentrate.

'Is there a fire?' I ask, looking around in case it's in my kitchen.

'No, miss, there isn't. Are you okay?'

'Yes. Would you mind telling me what's going on?'

'I thought you had . . . I thought.' Nate trips over his words.

'We understand from this gentleman that you have recently suffered bereavement. Nobody has seen or heard from you for days. There was a concern that you had . . .'

I look to Nate. He looks white as a sheet.

'Well, we can see you are okay. Have a good day.' The fireman shakes his head as he leaves. The question about my welfare is replaced by one about the nearest place for a coffee.

'What about my door?' I shout, but they have gone.

'I'm sorry, Harry,' Nate says. He shakes his head as if he can't quite believe what's happened. That makes two of us.

'You thought I would kill myself?' I ask. I shake the fog from my brain.

'You're grieving, Harry, and sometimes that can . . . people can fall into depression . . .'

'I'm not depressed, Nate.'

'Harry, it's okay to be depressed, to grieve.'

I sigh heavily with impatience.

'My father has died, but I am coping. Now, if you will excuse me, I would like to carry on coping.'

Nate takes a step towards me and holds out his hand.

'Don't do this on your own, Harry. Let me help?' His voice is gentle.

'And what do you propose to do?' I demand angrily. 'Tell me it's going to get better in time? Well, I don't want to hear it. I don't want to forget and get on with my life. I just want people to leave me alone.'

'I know what you're feeling.'

'You don't know how I'm feeling,' I spit back. 'I'm fed up with people who know so much, when they don't. They don't know how it feels to be without him . . .' A sharp stab of pain makes it difficult to breathe.

'Harry?'

I feel tired and deflated. The anger has disappeared as quickly as it appeared.

'Nate, it's nice that you care, but really, I hardly know you. Go and save some other damsel in distress.' I am so very tired. My limbs feel heavy. I just want to be left alone. I look out of the window. Somebody in a tourist bus looks back at me. She takes a photograph. I stay there and watch Nate walk down the street. His hands are in his pockets, his head is bowed. I feel bad but only for a moment. Right now, I haven't got room for anyone else.

The words on the screen are not making much sense. My heart is not in it because they will just be fillers for Poppy's column. Georgina has asked for another column, just in case and rather than refuse I send her the two that I was working on when I was full of hope for something different. I have no interest whether she uses them or not. I am filling gaps and filling time. I know I should ring Candice but a new job just seems too much to cope with at the moment.

At some point, life has continued the way it always has, but for me this is the hardest thing to cope with. I am still not getting on with my life. I can't move forward, nor do I want to. I think of my father and cover my eyes, pressing into them with my palms. I don't want to see or imagine. I don't want to go to sleep, where nightmares or insomnia fill my nights. I don't want to be alone but I don't want to be with any-one either. Alec has kept his distance and I haven't pushed it. I feel as if we are growing apart but I feel helpless to do anything about it. Part of me thinks we were heading that way anyway. I don't know. Everything feels blurred.

I catch Judith's eye. She is smiling and I smile back. She has taken to buying me coffee and talking in a soft, sugary voice. It is making me uncomfortable.

'I thought you might like this,' she says, placing a card on my desk.

I know what it is before reading it. I have had a hymn card on my desk every Monday morning.

'Thanks, Judith.'

'Sorry you didn't win the best newcomer award. Personally, I think you should have won it.'

I had completely forgotten about the award ceremony. I had a little black dress to wear. I seem to remember wearing it to the funeral instead.

'Thanks, Judith, that's very sweet of you.'

'You didn't miss anything, though. The ceremony went on for ages and Tania wotsername was rubbish. I could have done a better job. You know she had an affair with Bob Richards, don't you?'

I shake my head.

'So, what's with you and Ed?'

'Nothing, why?'

'You just seem weird with each other.'

'We're fine.'

'You haven't slept with him, have you?'

'No!' I say, shocked.

'Good, because solace cannot be found in the arms of another.'

This is a ridiculous statement. Of course it can, but for some unknown reason I can't find it.

I head out at lunchtime and find a table at my favourite café. I've been coming here quite a lot lately. I get my fix of being with people but without the pressure to talk to anyone. Today the café is full and people are on fast forward around me. I remain in my protective bubble. Sometimes they bounce against it. I spoon the chocolatey froth from my coffee. It dissolves in my mouth and I drift off somewhere else. I don't see Ed arrive. He sits in the chair opposite me.

'You okay?' he asks.

I nod, avoiding his eyes. Instead I stare into my coffee.

'Look, I might have ballsed up, Harry, but I still care, and I hate it when you are sad.' He covers my hand with his own. It feels warm. The tears fall. They tickle my cheeks as they run slowly down towards my chin. I remove my hand and wipe them away.

'Sorry,' I say.

'It's okay.'

I nod.

'Do you fancy a walk?' he asks, and I am grateful for the gesture. He has a good heart.

We walk along the canal in companionable silence. The breeze makes the trees rustle and the ducks swim faster.

'Mr Steps fell up them last week,' he says eventually.

'Up them?'

Ed nods gravely.

'Tripped two steps from the top. Broke two toes, apparently.'

'Oh, God. Poor thing.'

'Mandy from upstairs says that he insisted on dragging himself up those last two before the ambulance took him away.'

We both begin to laugh and then feel bad for doing so.

The nights are getting shorter and easier. Sometimes I can go until three thirty a.m. before waking up. Alec hardly stays over any more and I can't remember the last time we had sex. I have been putting off the inevitable, but as I lie here now, listening to the dawn chorus and wondering what the day will bring, I remember something my father said about not being able to imagine his life without my mother.

I realise that I have never felt that about Alec, that I knew on the way back from Emma's wedding and then again when I saw Nate at the supermarket. He was never going to be the One, but I convinced myself that it didn't matter. When I first met him, I loved the fact that he was gorgeous and into me, but what I really liked about him was what he represented. For a moment in time, I was Harriet Peel, a can-do-anything girl with possibilities. I was a girl with a boyfriend and I was going to walk into Chloe's wedding knowing all of this. Now I realise that I don't need to be with someone to make me who I am, to make me happy. I want to be with someone for the right reasons. Life is too short to be without love.

It is still dark outside but I get up and make a lasagne to take around to Mum's later. I'll ring Alec in a bit. It's too early to do it now.

I'll have some breakfast first. And I'll just do the ironing, and the housework, and maybe sort out my wardrobe. I have so much to do. The phone rings. It's Alec. I panic. What do I say? I'm not prepared, I'm not prepared . . .

'I was going to ring you,' I say.

'I saved you the trouble.'

We both remain static in the silence. I take a deep breath.

'Look, Alec,' I begin.

'It's okay,' he interrupts.

'I think you are gorgeous and lovely, but . . .'

'I understand.'

'You do?' I ask. Perhaps he can enlighten me.

'Of course I do. You're in love with someone else.'

'I am?'

'I always got the feeling you were thinking of someone else when you were with me.'

'My dad,' I reply flatly.

'No, before you lost your dad. I always felt as if I should be looking over my shoulder. Look, no worries. I've got to go, that's the door. Take care, Harry.'

'But—'

'Charlotte wants me back,' he says suddenly.

'What do you mean?'

'I mean, I'm getting on with my life.'

'You could have at least waited,' I say indignantly.

'Waited for what exactly? For you to realise that I'm not the one for you? Come on, Harry, how can you be upset with me?'

'I don't know – I just can.'

Alec laughs.

'You are a great girl and you're going to make someone a very lucky man.'

The tears fall down my cheeks.

'And Charlotte is a lucky girl,' I sob. 'Really lucky. You are so lovely.'

'Bye, Harry.'

I am still blubbing ten minutes later.

For a baby, Alfie is beautiful. He gets better and less scary with age. If I drop him, he now has enough bulk and a fully formed skull to survive. My mother coos over him. Unlike the rest of us he seems to love the high-pitched noise she makes. He is the light of her life.

'So, you're not seeing that Alec any more?' Emma asks. She fills a cafetiere with hot water and, rather surprisingly, gets the best china out.

'No,' I reply sadly.

'He seemed a nice boy,' my mother says. The skin on her face doesn't seem to fit any more. Her fingers shake a little, sometimes.

'He was nice,' I confirm. 'I'm not sure Dad was too impressed, though.'

'Your dad liked him. What was not to like? He just wanted the best for you, that's all. He had this theory. It was all about having a twinkle in your eye. Like our Katie. When she met Lawrence she had a twinkle.'

Katie laughs. 'What happened to that guy who called the fireman out?' she asks.

'He sent someone round to fix my door and I got a bunch of pink roses and a box of home-made chocolate-chip cookies, but I haven't heard from him since.' I look at my fingers and think of his. They would have fitted mine. 'I was pretty horrid to him.'

'That's a shame. There's something quite romantic about having your door broken down.'

Emma places a plate of biscuits on the kitchen table. The silver and green box promises a generous covering of the finest Belgian chocolate and an experience of pure luxury and indulgence. I brace myself.

'And you say the cookies were home-made?' Katie asks, picking two gold foil covered fingers.

I smile, remembering the large disks that looked like cow pats. They weren't that bad.

'He sounds like one to keep,' Katie says, handing Alfie a chocolate finger.

'Unfortunately, he's the one that got away,' I reply ruefully.

'Why not phone him? Tell him how much you loved the cookies.'

'I don't know his number. In fact, I don't know anything about him. It's strange, I don't even know his second name, but in some ways I feel as if I have known him for ever. Does that make sense?'

Katie nods and sighs. Emma sighs too, but hers is a different sigh.

'What about that lovely Ed? I liked him,' Mum says.

'He had that model girlfriend,' Emma points out.

'Not any more,' I tell her.

'There you go, then,' Mum says, looking pleased with herself. 'You want to get yourself in there before he gets snapped up.'

'Mum!' I respond in mock horror.

'What? He liked you. We could all see that. And he's a good lad. A bit lanky, but tall, and tall is good for you, Harriet. There are not many men of his height around.'

'Good job, owns his own flat,' Emma observes.

I am not even going to respond. She pours the coffee and we go back to our separate thoughts. Except for the hum of the fridge, the kitchen is quiet. I tap my feet against the chair until the look on Emma's face tells me to stop. It is so quiet. From my flat there is a constant hum of traffic and people chatting as they walk past. Here, there is just silence. A vast white space of nothing. That's why the twins are so loud. Emma complains of headaches and the scuff marks on the floor.

The twins come rushing downstairs talking over each other. They hug their grandmother.

'Girls! Please. I have a headache,' Emma complains.

My mother is looking out to the patio doors. A man is raking leaves. He is Emma's 'man that can'. His name is Bert and he does everything and anything for a crisp ten-pound note.

'I should go back,' my mother ventures.

'There's no need,' my sister says.

'Well, if you're sure?'

My sister smiles and I wonder if she gets scared in the middle of the night and wakes up drenched in sweat. I wonder if Alan whispers in her ear. It's okay, darling, it's okay.

'What are you doing tonight? Anything exciting?' Mum asks.

'I'm actually out with Ed tonight.'

My mother smiles.

'Mum. Ed and I are friends.'

'It would be nice to have an engagement party this year. We need something to cheer us up,' my mother says.

And that's when I know she will survive.

Josie and I are justifying spending a fortune on our outfits for Chloe's wedding. We had no other alternative, we will wear them again, these are timeless items that every girl should have in her wardrobe, we have to invest to accumulate, and you get what you pay for: we look stunning. The reasons know no limit. I have gone over my budget and bought a duchesse satin dress in the palest of pinks. It has a fitted waist and a full skirt. I have teamed it with matching four-inch babies with the thinnest of heels and the pointiest of toes, and a clutch bag in the shape of an oyster shell. I am happy to be persuaded that it's an investment purchase, which is what we always say to each other when we know we really shouldn't be spending this much money. In between congratulating ourselves, we discuss Alec.

'I can't believe you didn't wait until after the wedding to do something about it.'

'I'll go on my own.'

'Let's have a think. What about I pay for an escort? It can be an early Christmas present?'

'I've decided. I'm going on my own,' I repeat.

'But there's still time. We'll have to pull our fingers out, but—'

'Jose, I'm fine about it.'

'But what about Jason?'

'I am okay about Jason.'

'So he's not the one Alec was talking about?'

'I've hardly thought about him over the past few months.'

'Have you heard from Nate?'

'No.'

'We need to find a way of getting hold of him. I could run off a list of charities in the area.'

'If he was interested, he would get in contact.'

'He baked you cookies. What else do you want?'

'But I haven't heard anything since.'

'He probably thinks you don't like him.'

'Well, it doesn't matter now. I probably won't ever see him again. Anyway, I quite like being on my own at the moment.'

'That's what everyone says when they can't have the one they want.'

'But I mean it.'

And I realise I do.

I arrive at Chloe's hen night with a bottle of champagne and a banoffee pie. It is home-made; not by me, but by my mother. She is methodically going through the whole *Good Housekeeping* dessert book, ticking the recipes off with marks out of ten and comments. Her number comes up on my mobile.

'Hi, Mum.'

'Darling, I was just checking you had remembered the banoffee pie.'

'Yes, thanks. I have it here in a carrier bag.'

'Is it secure?'

'Yes.'

She has started worrying about the small stuff, and her rate of phone calls has increased tenfold.

'Give that sweet girl my love.'

'What are you doing?' I ask. Between us we ensure Mum is busy. I am ticking off every public garden and tea room in the area, Katie is taking her swimming with baby Alfie, and Emma is taking her to keep fit classes. Emma hates it and complains about the staff, common people's germs and the facilities at the local leisure centre on a regular basis. Mum loves it. She already knows everybody's name.

'I'm at your Auntie Barbara's,' Mum says in a whisper. 'I worry about her, you know. Between you and me I think she has lost the plot a little since your dad died. She keeps talking about life being too short. She's flying off to Lanzarote next week. She keeps telling me I should go, but I don't know.'

'You should. Look, I've got to go. I'm in Chloe's hallway.'

'Okey dokey. Love you.'

'Love you too.'

I'm pretty sure we did it before, but now, saying I love you at the end of a phone call has become an unwritten rule.

The evening is spent watching re-runs of *Sex and the City* and eating. The first hen night was spent at London's finest. I missed that one. Tonight, the usual suspects have gathered together with some of Chloe's work colleagues and Tad's family. I don't know everyone but the company is easy and the food is good. We drink too much champagne, laugh too loudly and talk too much rubbish; and, for the first time in a long while, I realise I am not grieving. The black shadow of guilt that passes over me is sudden and unexpected, but it is enough. I excuse myself and go to the toilet. I close my eyes and try to recapture a memory of my father. It doesn't come.

When I return, Josie rubs my arm.

'It's okay to have a nice time,' she reassures me. I smile gratefully, feeling lucky that I am surrounded by friends who know and love me. It's enough.

My mobile rings.

'Hello,' I catch the panic in my voice.

'Harry?'

I move the phone away from me, 'I'm just going to take this call in the garden,' I say and rush outside, nearly tripping over a plant pot on the way.

'Harry? Are you there?'

'Jason.'

My heart is beating so fast, I can barely speak.

'How are you?' he says in that lazy way I had forgotten.

'I'm good,' I reply. All the clever, interesting things I dreamed I would say are forgotten as I shiver in the darkness and wonder why now. 'So, what have you been up to?'

'The usual – working, went to New York a little while ago, which was amazing, my sister got engaged.'

'Oh, give her my congratulations.'

'Thanks . . . so, are you? Engaged or anything?' he asks, and I know I should lie. I promised Josie that if Jason ever rang, I would.

'No, I'm not with anyone,' I reply, and then, because I cannot help myself. 'What about you?'

I hold my breath.

'No, Sophie and I split up a little while ago.'

'Oh.'

'Look, I've got to go. I just wondered if you wanted to maybe meet for a cup of coffee or a drink sometime.'

'Yes, why not? It will be nice to catch up,' I respond casually.

'Great, I'll call next week. Bye.'

'Bye,' I say, and hold my mobile to my chest. He phoned. Jason phoned.

'Everything okay?' Josie asks when I walk back in.

'Yes,' I reply slowly. I feel drugged. 'That was Jason.'

'Wow,' Vicky says. 'Is that good or bad?'

'I don't know.'

A Girl Without a Date in Her Diary – Blog entry – October 22nd

Breaking up is hard to do. Actually, it's shit, even if you are the one instigating it. I have experienced both, although, to be honest, me ending a relationship has only happened twice – well, once and a case of not being entirely sure who technically finished it. My friend, on the other hand, is an expert in breaking up with men. She does the 'there isn't anyone else, I just want to be friends' thing really well. They accept it, even though in the back of their minds they know she is telling a porky pie. Being the dumped is horrendous; especially if you didn't really see it coming. This happened to me. I didn't see the other girl waving her crotchless knickers in the background, or realise that the reason my boyfriend was losing his temper so much at everything I did, was because he was justifying his actions. He was looking for that final argument; the one where I would say, 'What the hell is wrong with you?' and he would reply with a 'Nothing, it's you . . . it's us. We are just not working . . . I'm leaving.'

Do you go back to an ex? It's one of those questions that divides us all. My friend J says no, whereas my friend C says yes. If he is the One, she says, then look to the future and not to the past. I'm where I always am: on the fence, dangling my legs and looking at the cows and thinking how pretty they are. Carrie in *Sex and the City* is a 'give the man another chance' girl, even when she has the gorgeous Aidan. I have to admit that this is when I have briefly come off my fence and wished, like her, that Big would ultimately prove to be the One. Like so many, I waited years for it to happen and I cannot help drawing similarities to my own life. Will my Big – or rather, my not so big, but average and perfectly formed prove to be the One? Or should I ask him to step to one side because he's blocking my view?

My one rule on this is that break-ups can only be make-ups with a grand, romantic gesture. Actually, thinking about it, let's not limit ourselves to exes. Romantic gestures should be a part of any new relationship, primarily during your first months together. Demand them, and don't, like me, moan at the mess they've made when one happens. With this in mind, I'm thinking romance, first dates and making up.

- Take a tour bus and sit on the open top. Snog and take photos of each other for the duration.
- Go for brunch at the Riverboat Café. Order the poached eggs on muffins and try the seductive hollandaise on the lip trick. I am reliably informed that it's a winner every time.
- Share a hot tub in the Royal Spa Hotel. The candlelight is great in there and good for hiding those imperfections and cellulite.
- Lie in the park and star watch. This is not a good idea if there are drunks around.
- Get matching tattoos.
- Eat tiramisu.

I have enrolled in a poetry workshop. Timothy Langton Dowds is our tutor. He wears a black floppy hat and dyes his beard. I know he dyes it because his picture on the course programme showed a grey beard. It is also an alarming shade of black and I wonder if he has saved himself the embarrassment of buying hair dye and used shoe polish instead. He talks mostly about himself with a low gravelly voice punctuated by annoyingly long pauses. Then he talks of iambic pentameters and rhythm of speech.

'Okay? So you have an hour to write your own poem. Remember what I've said.'

Timothy goes out for a coffee and a cigarette. The two poets and four non-poets of the class begin scribbling frantically. I stare into space and doodle. My brain is empty of inspiration. I text Josie, then try again. Think, Harry, think of anything . . .

Jason didn't phone the next day or the day after that. Sometimes I wonder if I dreamed it. It doesn't matter as much as it did before. My life is very different now to the one I was living. I am a member of a book group; I go cycling with the Grunt & Grub Club, and dancing with my mum and sisters. Sometimes I go out with Ed. We have got over the difficult friends/sex/love thing. At least,

I thought we had. Then came the prawn balti incident.

There we were, enjoying a prawn balti, and before I know it, it's getting too warm and my vision goes blurry.

'Are you okay?' Ed asked. I wasn't, as a matter of fact, and when I stood up to go outside for some fresh air, the floor seemed to give way. I could hear Ed's voice reassuring me, but I couldn't see him. When the ambulance men carried me out on a funny chair I tried not to think about how embarrassing it all was. Ed held my hand until the ambulance man told him he was in the way. He sat with me for four hours in Accident and Emergency. They told me I had a vascular something, which sounded dramatic but actually meant I had fainted. Was I drinking enough water? Was I under stress? Did anyone see my knickers through the disposable robe?

I am frightened of dying in the middle of the night, on my own. Ed slept on the sofa again. He is too big for it and could hardly walk the next morning. I made fried egg sandwiches and we watched *Animal Rescue*. And that's when I told myself that most girls would kill for a man like this. I mean, we were practically a couple anyway and maybe Mum was right: I had high expectations. Too high. My romantic dreams were just that: dreams. Wasn't Alec a case in point? Jason had gone quiet, and Nate? I look out for him every day, and I am always disappointed.

Okay, I need to pick a word and start with that. I look around the room and everyone is writing and crossing out. My doodles fill the page. In amongst them is Nate. Not him, obviously, but his name, surrounded by love hearts and flowers.

Timothy wafts in smelling like an ashtray. He looks over one of the girls' shoulders and nods. He whispers something and she laughs too loudly. I bet her iambic pentameters are perfect. I scribble on my notepad. Roses are red, violets are blue, Timothy smells and so do you.

Oh, joy of joy. We get to read our pieces out. The middle-aged woman with the pale blue jumper surprises us all with a poem about self harm. Joseph, the good-looking poet and only eye candy in the room presents a piece on coming out. Carol reads out a piece on being beaten as a child and then bursts into tears. Colin has written about a life without love and Jasmine, the other poet, has written a poem on torture in Iraq.

'Harry, isn't it? So, Harry, what's the title of your poem?' Timothy asks, wiping his mouth with a handkerchief.

I clear my throat.

'Chocolate Chip Cookies.'

Timothy peers at me from beneath his wide brim. He licks his lips. Is he thinking of the cookies or getting ready to devour me with some choice words?

'Okay, let's hear it, shall we?'

I take a deep breath and read my masterpiece. When I have finished there isn't a dry eye in the room. This is a lie. When I have finished, there is just a stunned silence. Then Colin begins to clap until Timothy glares at him.

As we leave, Colin rushes up to me. He is slightly breathless.

'I really loved your poem,' he says. His voice is a monotone.

'Thanks.'

'And you have really nice hair.'

'Thanks.'

'Do you want to go out for a drink?'

'Oh, that's very sweet. Thank you, but I can't. I have to get home.'

'That's fine. What about tomorrow?'

'Sorry, Colin.'

'Saturday night?'

'I have a boyfriend,' I say in desperation.

'What's his name?'

I miss a beat.

'Jason, I mean Ed.'

Colin narrows his eyes.

'Jason was my ex. I get confused.'

He seems satisfied and walks towards Jasmine.

'Fuck off, loser,' she retorts.

The middle-aged woman in the blue jumper says yes.

I guess I should feel flattered that he asked me first.

'I'll have the nude.'

I always go for nude.

'Sorry, can I change my mind? I'll have the purple,' I apologise.

The girl who is doing my manicure smiles. She is used to smiling. I wonder if she has a menu of smiles. My mother is also smiling, so is Katie. Emma was smiling, briefly.

It is my mother's birthday and we have all gathered at the Bath Spa Hotel for some pampering and complimentary champagne. The twins are wiggling in their seats. Emma's reprimanding voice is consistently low in tone. It says 'I am calm and in control.' I have my doubts.

'It's a shame about Chloe's wedding,' my mother says.

'Why?' Katie asks.

'Harriet having to go on her own.'

'I'm okay with it, Mum, really I am.' I look at my nails. 'Can I change my mind? The purple might be a bit much. I'll go for that pale pink.'

'What's got into you?' Emma asks.

'She heard from Jason,' Katie says.

'What? Jason, Jason?' Emma asks, looking surprised. 'Girls, sit still.'

'Yes, that Jason,' I reply mournfully.

'Is he still with that Sophie girl?'

'No, apparently they split up.'

Emma nods knowingly.

'Your father was always very suspicious of men who don't eat their crusts,' Mum says.

'That doesn't make him a bad person,' I say, a little annoyed. How did she remember that, for heaven's sake?

It was the big introduction. Dad, this is Jason, the One; Jason, this is my dad, who will always be the other one. I made a picnic and Jason left little bread angles of crust on his plastic plate. I hurriedly gathered them together and used them to feed the ducks. Fishermen hate excitable ducks. We left.

'So, he won't be going to Chloe's wedding with Sophie?' Katie asks.

'No,' I reply.

'Which means he could potentially go with you?' she suggests.

'Harriet wouldn't be that stupid! To slot back in after everything he did to her?'

If I agree then I am potentially lying. I really am okay with going on my own, but there is a small part of me that longs for the fairy-tale happy ending when I get there. The one where I walk in wearing my lovely dress, my love-me, lust-me and everything-else-me shoes, and he is there with his back to me. 'Dancing Queen' is playing in the background and the person he is talking to spots me and says something . . . He turns. He cannot believe his eyes. I stand there surveying the room. I look stunning. He is staring, mouth open. I barely flicker my interest as he walks over and takes my hand. Cue Ray wotshisname singing something beautiful. It's so perfect I feel myself welling up.

'Are you crying?' Victoria asks, waving her legs in the air.

'No,' I growl.

'Victoria, close your legs.' Emma turns to me. Her face is serious.

'Just be careful.'

'I will,' I say, irritated. 'Changing the subject, I propose a toast. To the girls' tour to Lanzarote.' I hold up my glass carefully, trying not to smudge my nails, and everyone follows suit. The twins raise their orange juice. My mother giggles, 'Your Auntie Barbara and I are hardly girls,' she says.

It's nice to see her laugh. Despite her 'I'm okay now, you really don't have to worry about me' mantra, she is clearly and painfully lost without my father.

As we leave, Emma falls into step beside me.

'I'm sorry if I sounded full of doom and gloom earlier. Sometimes I forget. If you love Jason, just go for it. Don't worry what anyone thinks, just embrace the possibility,' she says.

I look at her and wonder how many more times my sister is going to surprise me.

'Is that what you did?'

'No, and that should be reason enough,' she says sadly. I reach out to hug her, but she pulls away.

'Girls! Will you stop that! I'm getting a headache.'

After a trip to my father's grave, we say our goodbyes with lots of hugging and kissing. Since my father died we take a lot longer than we used to, and sometimes I get a double hug in the confusion. Their perfumes are as familiar to me as my own; their smiles and laughter cherished and precious. If I worked in London the opportunities would be few and far between. Candice has sent me an email telling me again that the job is mine if I want it. She's given me another week to decide.

*

The meeting room is full of the sound of amiable chatter.

'Okay, everyone, let's get what I hope will be a short meeting underway,' Georgina says. 'I would like to welcome Kiki back from her travels. She will be resuming her role as fashion director, leaving Judith to concentrate on features.'

Kiki smiles serenely. She has cheekbones to die for and bangles that could make it happen with one blow to the back of the head.

'And I would also like to welcome Ed,' Georgina says. 'I thought it would be nice to invite some of our more trusted outside contractors and colleagues from different departments. I see it as a two-way process where they can see how we work, provide feedback, and perhaps put forward some ideas.'

'I'm putting the sexy back,' Ed says with a straight face.

'We are not doing sexy any more,' Georgina replies, as if he is being serious. 'We are doing innovative, clean, informative and challenging.'

We all nod seriously.

'So, what have we got?' Georgina booms. 'Kiki, now that you are back, what do you suggest?'

'I was thinking gold, jewels, autumn colours, opulence, richly embroidered fabrics, burnt umber, sapphire against a backdrop of muted, moist-laden greens and bruised skies,' she says. Her hands move as if she is laying it all out before us. She licks full, rose-red lips and makes the word muted sound dirty. I imagine oral sex is her speciality. As she talks, she looks at Ed from feline eyes. I wonder if he is imagining what it would be like to sleep with her. I begin doodling.

'That's great. Well, the good news is, sales of the

magazine are on the up, and that is down in no small part to our new column from—'

Ed coughs. I look up and everyone is staring at me. I stare blankly back.

'Girl Without a Date in Her Diary has been a huge success. People are buying *Life to Live* again. It appears you were right, Harry. Our female readers want to find out what happens to our intrepid serial dater; even our male readership is intrigued. They all want to know who she is.'

'But I thought you went with Poppy's column?' I ask, confused. Has Georgina lost the plot? Surely she remembers rejecting my last column.

'No, we used your column again.'

'You've lost me.'

'I suspect that, with everything else that was going on in your life at the time, you didn't notice. I changed my mind, and the word on the street tells me that I made the right decision.'

I don't know what to say. 'Liar' springs to mind. I know perfectly well that what she means is Poppy took too long to write her columns. Well, it doesn't matter now. What matters is that my column is a success.

'I was wrong. It seems people love the column.' Georgina is smiling.

I am smiling.

'I have letters and sales figures to prove it.'

I am still smiling.

'I don't know why I didn't think of it before. It wasn't the girl; it was the story that was the problem. So, for the next issue, Poppy will be working to the same template but in reverse. She's young, hip and has the essential glam factor. In the same way our readers indentified with your column; they will aspire to be the girl Poppy is. She will be the antithesis of the Girl Without a Date in Her Dairy.

She will be the girl with so many dates she doesn't know what to do with them all.' Georgina looks rather proud of herself. I look around the table. Ed is playing with his pen, Judith is sitting pious-like with her hands clasped on the table. Kiki is playing with her hair. Jeremy smiles weakly.

'As for the What's On column, I thought we could expand it, with more interviews, etc.'

I don't know what to say. I am momentarily stunned.

'What do you think?' Georgina asks.

Everybody looks to me. There is a sense of anticipation and dread in the room.

'I think it stinks!'

Everybody except Ed continues to look at me. They are deathly quiet, waiting for Georgina to react. I look around the table. They think I have lost my mind. I look at Ed. He is fiddling with his shoes. A smile plays on his lips and I can see he is struggling not to laugh out loud. It makes me want to laugh too, and then I do. The shock turns to relief as everyone joins in. They think I am joking. This makes me laugh even louder.

Georgina tells me she is sorry that I am leaving,

'Is it a question of money?'

I could say yes and demand an exorbitant sum. I want floorboards. It would pay for them.

'No, it's not about money. It's a question of integrity.'

'I can understand that.'

That's not the answer I was expecting. I bite the skin from my bottom lip.

'The reason I am sorry to lose you, Harry, is because of your integrity. I have always been able to rely on you.'

'But that was my downfall. You saw me as the boring, predictable one.'

'Predictably good; not boring. Your reliability is your

strength, not your downfall. It's a shame you can't see that. You were right; we had lost touch with our readers and, unlike them, it took me a while to catch on to Girl Without a Date. It was a great idea and you worked hard to make it happen. When I asked you to fill Poppy's space I knew I could rely on you. You're a great team member. I'm just sorry you're not going to be here to see it go that one step further.'

I am shocked and a little bit annoyed. I also have nothing to say. No, actually, I do.

'I'm sorry, Georgina, but that's just rubbish.'

Georgina stares at me and waits for me to continue.

'Being a head-down, hard-working, reliable member of the team gets you nowhere. I never wrote that column for Poppy to take over. I wrote it for me. The team sucks.'

I slam the door. Jeremy claps but not loud enough for anyone to hear. Judith looks at me with pity and self-righteousness. I kick her bin over. I am a vigilante, fighting for justice and I am taking no prisoners in this dark, unfair world. Grrrr . . . The phone rings.

'Hey, it's me.'

Vigilante becomes pussycat. Purrrrr . . .

'Hi,' I breathe.

'How are you?' Jason asks.

'I'm good.'

'That drink? Are you free Thursday night?'

'No.'

There is a pause and I enjoy the brief moment of power.

'But I can probably do Sunday.'

'Great. Sunday night it is,' he says enthusiastically.

I throw my stress ball across the office and a flip-board goes flying. The whole office looks up from their computers. I hold my hands up in the air.

'Sorry, sorry.'

I walk home feeling disorientated. I thought I would feel a sense of euphoria, but I don't. It just feels weird. My mind is a whirlwind of possibilities. I don't see Martha Gennings coming out of the door. We both shriek and have our non-existent black belt karate chops to the ready.

'Oh, it's you,' she says, lowering her hand.

She is wearing blood-red lipstick and a midnight-blue velvet jacket.

'I was hoping to see you. How are you? I noticed a few more bottles than normal in your recycling lately.'

'I'm fine, thank you.'

'Good, good.'

'And your mother?'

'She's very well, thank you. Going anywhere nice?' I ask.

'As a matter of fact, I am. I'm off to the theatre. Do you go to the theatre much? No, I imagine you're doing clubs and things . . .' she trails away. 'Aah, I forgot to say, I read *Life to Live* the other day. I'm not sure about this girl who does the dating advice thing. Where on earth did you find her?' She hovers by the door. This is the longest conversation we have ever had.

'But she is quite popular with the youngsters. Oh, remind me to give you the rest of my vegetable box. Lots of strange things in there this week. I thought you might know what to do with them. You creative types know about red chard. Toodle ooh.'

The night air fills the lobby and she is gone. Her perfume lingers for a while. I am still not sure if I like her or not.

My mother rings from Lanzarote and she sounds a little tipsy; Josie rings from IKEA, threatening to start meatball warfare if she doesn't find the way out in thirty seconds; Chloe rings and says that if I change my mind about bringing someone then she needs to know forty-eight hours before the wedding, and Ed rings and I agree to meet him for a quick drink before I go to an event at the literature festival. In the end, he comes with me, although I would have been okay on my own. After a lacklustre performance by a novelist best kept in his writing shed, we walk back in companionable silence. As we walk, I think about a lot of things, such as what was it like to live here in the eighteenth century, do I have enough milk for tomorrow, and how do I feel about Ed? Then I think of Jason and wonder why I said yes to the drink. I should have said no. I don't tell Ed.

Girl Without a Date in Her Diary – Blog entry – October 29th

As the dark winter nights draw in, I am thinking about three things. Making do, the rubbish on the TV and being a lesbian.

Let's start with making do. Why do some people make do and others don't? Is it something you are born with or a behaviour learned from parents or the playground? I'm trying to work out if it's better to make do. Does it mean your expectations are lower? If so, does this have the knock-on effect of meaning you become easy to please, and that, in the long run, you say, 'That's just about okay and I'm going to go with it'? People who make do seem to be happy enough . . . aah, you see, there's the sticking point for me. Happy enough? Enough for what? A lifetime? If I made do and lowered my expectations, would I find it easier to be happy with my lot? And if I did, would I be like the cat that got the cream or would I always wonder what if? This is a tricky one. At times like this I think of our old friend, Angelina. Now I know for a fact that Angie has never made do. Although it could be argued that she doesn't need to. With a body and lips like that, who needs compromise in your life?

This brings me neatly on to being a lesbian. (It has been reported in the press that Angelina has dabbled.) Personally, I prefer men, but a few times this week I have thought that perhaps it would be easier if I fancied my fellow female. Or would it? Is the perfect female as hard to find as the perfect man? I looked around me, at friends and work colleagues. There was no one I particularly fancied. On the train the other day, though, there was a very beautiful redhead with freckles and skin the colour of milk. If I was to fancy a girl, then she would probably be it. Then she laughed and it was horrid. She also had a habit of sniffing a lot.

So, after a lot of pondering I came to the conclusion that making do or becoming a lesbian are not options. If, like me, you are also single, then I suggest you switch off the TV and use the time constructively to lure the One. This is the romantic dream One, not the making-do One.

- Make an apple pie and open your window. Any man within a two-hundred-metre radius will sniff those sweet aromas and think again about the girl who lives nearby. This will be no good if the men who live nearby are perverts. You might also want to wear a cardigan because it's cold outside.
- Hot-foot it down to Stained Ltd and learn how to make a stained-glass window. It's always good to have an interesting skill.
- Talking of interesting skills. Book into a

pole-dancing course. I have tried, but tall people with gangly legs don't look so hot hanging from a pole. Think orangutan.

- Head towards the Royal Spa Hotel and leave the cold weather behind in the sauna or heated outside pool. I heard on the grapevine that the English rugby team spend their free time there. Just be careful that your make-up is water resistant.
- Looking for affection? Then cuddle a cat. The local cats' and dogs' home are always looking for people to provide a bit of affection for their moggies. It's also a good thing to get the aah factor from the one you are lusting after.

I am scrubbed, exfoliated, polished, moisturised and spritzed. My underwear is new and my sheets are clean. I am ready for anything. There is no use in making rash statements like 'I won't sleep with him', because I know from past experience that as far as Jason is concerned, there are no guarantees.

I walk through the bar, scanning the tables for a sight of him. He's not here. I feel a familiar sense of disappointment. Silly, silly me to think things were different. I turn to leave. Just as I reach the door, I feel a tap on my shoulder.

'Where do you think you're going?'

I turn towards that familiar dark hair and olive skin. He is smiling, and so am I.

'Hello, baby girl,' he says, and kisses me on the cheek. I don't recognise the aftershave, but I do recall the feel of his lips on my skin. He stands back to survey me. 'You look great.'

'Hello, Jason. Long time, no see.' This is me attempting to sound casual.

'Yeah, I guess we have a lot of catching up to do,' he says. 'I took the liberty of ordering a chilled bottle of New Zealand and a bowl of pistachio nuts.'

'You remembered.'

'Of course I did.'

We talk easily. We have a past to refer back to. Jason is the one who knows that I have a tendency to talk in my sleep when stressed, that I have a thing about mice and anything else that scurries quickly, and that I love cheesy-topped rolls. He also knows the amount of milk I have in my tea and is unfazed by my habit of leaving pistachio nut shells in the bowl instead of putting them to one side. I hate things on tables. It's untidy and he understands this. We have stories to remember and mutual friends to catch up on.

Another bottle of wine helps the process and I barely remember the hurt. When he goes to the toilets I watch him go, and for a moment I am reminded, but, like a tiny splinter, it is soon forgotten when he returns and kisses it better. His smile is for me and I can only recall how much I shone in its brilliance.

I tell him about the new job at *Circling*.

'Congratulations, baby. Beautiful, and now brilliant and successful. I always knew you would be.'

'Did you?'

'Yes, you know I did.'

'I just thought you wanted me to be.'

Jason laughs. 'Still the same Harry.'

I laugh with him, but he's wrong. I'm not the same Harry.

The air is still and the sky full of stars. Our breath forms puffs of dragon smoke.

'Thank you for a lovely evening. It was nice to see you again,' I say. I am playing it cool; so cool I'm positively arctic.

'We should do it again,' he replies.

I don't answer. Should we?

'What about Sophie?' I ask.

'She was never you.'

I try and see through him but my X-ray specs aren't working. They never were where Jason was concerned. Highly perfumed people wander past and an ambulance siren plays in the distance. We stand in the moment and I remember another time when I thought someone would kiss me and he didn't. Why did I let Nate slip through my fingers? When I needed someone he was brave enough to be there. When he said something, I believed him.

Jason kisses me gently, fleetingly, and I wonder if this is how it felt before.

I cannot sleep. What happens now? I guess that's up to me. I get up and look out of the window. Nate is somewhere out there, perhaps unable to sleep just like me. I go downstairs into the kitchen and make a lasagne. I now have six in my freezer. When I do eventually feel tired enough to sleep, I dream of a man wandering the streets. He is looking for me.

My mother's smile is a forced one. She is doing well; really well. I want to wrap her in a blanket and put her on my sofa in front of feel-good Audrey Hepburn movies.

'Ready?' I ask.

She nods.

'It's going to be okay.'

'I know,' she replies and takes one last look around. The removal men are working around us. The house looks bigger without the furniture in it. There are shadows on the wall where framed photos of us at school, university and weddings sat. I used to be embarrassed by them, but now I realise they were just a demonstration of how proud my parents were of us all. I miss my father every day, but today seems particularly hard. I put my arm round my mother and gently move her towards the door. We stand on the pavement, watching the men struggle with a sofa.

'I'm doing the right thing,' she says.

'Yes, you are,' I reply with conviction. 'Your new flat is going to be lovely.'

She nods and I love her so much I want to cry.

When we arrive, neither of us is in any hurry to get out of the car. The flats are nice, situated in a new development overlooking the canal. They are close to amenities and her friends. She will only be eight miles away from me.

'When do you start your new job?' she asks, turning towards me.

'Next week,' I reply.

'We're so proud of you, you know.'

I gulp; and she laughs.

'Hark at me. We? I? You know what I mean.' She taps my knee.

I smile. We look out on to an empty road. They have done a nice job on the shrubbery.

'You'll get to mix with lots of *Heat* magazine types; the sort your father said had one eye on the door.'

I feel crestfallen.

'Look at that face! Come on, it will be fun. You won't care which way their eyes are pointing. As long as one of them is on you, it doesn't matter. You might find yourself a nice young man.'

'I don't want a nice young man.'

'Of course you do.'

We watch a man with white hair and beige trousers wash his car.

'My old mum used to say it's too easy to say what you don't want.'

I have no idea what she is talking about.

'She also used to say that broccoli would make my hair curly.'

The man with the white hair surveys his work. He has a small travel Hoover and a packet of boiled sweets in the door pocket.

My mother and I stand outside the flats and look up at the cream stone chosen to complement the surroundings. An elderly couple say hello and disappear into the communal entrance hall.

'I hope it's not full of old people.' Mum snorts a little too loudly, and follows them in.

The flat is new and waiting for furniture to bring it to life. She wanders over to the patio doors and presses her nose to the window.

'I think I'm going to buy a hot tub for the garden.'

'Are you?' I ask, surprised.

'Hot tub parties are all the rage now, apparently.'

I am glad Emma is not here.

I wish my father was.

I feel like the new kid in school. My new job is sparkly and the people are scary. I am given a week-long induction with various team members before being let loose on my own pages. I feel justified and more than a little inclined to phone Georgina and blow a raspberry. The new job has meant early mornings, late nights and lots of camomile tea to ease my fractured nerves after a day of commuting in and out of the big city. It's an army assault course every day, testing my agility and mental capacity to withstand the horrors of human nature at close range. People smell. Sometimes they sneeze and I imagine air-borne viruses swimming up my nose. Someone shoves me and I breathe in a lungful of dust as air rushes through the underground tunnel. I tell myself that I will get used to it. I join the swell of bodies making their way to work, and then join them again to go home.

We are like migrating birds doing the same journey day after day.

After two weeks I am in a routine, timed to the last minute. I arrive in Paddington with twenty minutes to continue my journey. This gives me five minutes to get a coffee and then another fifteen to get in to the *Circling* office. I have no minutes to spare. If I want to pee, then it has to wait. I figure it's good for my pelvic floor; something Katie, Emma, Vicky and Lucy all seem to be obsessed with. Apparently time invested now is time well spent for the future when the maternal instinct kicks in. Sometimes I wonder about having children. In my mind, the age of thirty-four sounds about right. That way I will have become entrenched at *Circling* and secure enough to take a year off. Who would be the father of my children? Aah, this is where I come undone. I'm not entirely sure. I should know. I know I should know. When I imagine my life ten years on, it's a bit hazy.

I have come to the conclusion that the predominantly female workforce at *Circling* magazine is from a different planet. I try hard to fit in but I miss the easy way of *Life to Live*. You can smell the ambition here; along with the sickly sweet strawberry of the caffeine drinks. The girls here speak in acronyms, work late, party even later, don't eat and their outfits are mismatched. I feel out of it because I am not wearing knee-length socks, neon nail varnish, patent-leather ankle boots and a woollen hat. I had convinced myself that top-to-toe black was cool. Here, it's just safe. I am frightened of colour that doesn't match. At some point, though, I am going to have to go with it. Timing is the key. Leave it too long and they will all nod their heads knowingly; too quick and I will get it wrong. Gradual is the key. Today I have bought a turquoise hat. It looks stupid, but tonight I will wear it around the flat to get used to it, and tomorrow I will wear it to work – if I feel brave enough.

'I'm sorry, but I'm not sure about that hat.'

We were talking about rabbits but it appears Josie couldn't control herself any longer.

'You mean I don't look like someone from the pages of *Elle*? A style leader who will ultimately start her own fashion movement?'

'No. You look like . . .' she begins to laugh, then snort. 'I'm sorry, Harry, but you really shouldn't wear hats.'

I rip it off my head and stuff it in my handbag.

'Can we get back to the rabbits? Are you sure it's a good idea?' I ask.

Josie stops laughing and blows her nose loudly.

'Yeah. Chloe's always wanted a white rabbit, and they're the dwarf kind, so they're not that big.'

'But two?'

'We can call the boy rabbit Tad and the girl one, Chloe. How cute is that?'

'I still think it's a weird thing to give as a wedding present.'

'Not if you dress them up as a bride and groom it isn't.'

'Have you lost your mind?'

'Stop changing the subject. Have you heard from Jason?'

'He phoned yesterday.'

'And?'

'He's working away, so I'll probably see him at the wedding.'

'You're being very cool about it all.'

'I feel cool about it.'

'What does that mean?'

'I don't know, but I'm hoping for a bolt of lightning or

an appearance from my guardian angel, because it's making me feel uneasy. I don't do cool.'

'And Ed?'

'Ed's fine.'

'Nate?'

'Nothing.'

'Did I tell you that we've set the date? It's not till next year, so you have plenty of time, but you might want to get back on to DateMate. The three men in your life are clearly amounting to nothing.'

'I'm in no hurry to rush into anything. I'm doing okay on my own these days.'

'Doing okay? How rubbish is that? You don't hear Angelina, Nicole – I could go on – you don't hear them saying, "I'm doing okay".'

'That's because they're in love.'

'Exactly my point!'

'So am I.'

'Who with?' Josie screams and everyone in Starbucks looks round. Everyone! A baby begins to cry.

'I have to get back.'

'Don't you dare leave me hanging,' Josie demands.

'Byee.'

As I walk back to the flat from Bath Spa rail station I look at the faces of people who don't know me, but who are somehow familiar. It's a bit like being one buffalo in a country of thousands – I was thinking Argentina. I would know by instinct which herd I belonged to. This is where I live. This is my street and it feels good to be home. Every morning I walk this route and I feel a thrill. I have room to dance. In London I was one of many in a travelling swarm. Here, I feel safe. A few months ago I would have hated that word. It epitomised everything I despised. Now? Now I'm not so sure.

GWAD – *Circling* magazine column

It's that time of year when we put on our woolly jumpers, eat hot, buttered crumpets and wear hats that flatten our hair so that we can't take them off without a trip to the ladies' toilets. Turn to page six for my woolly-tastic range of hats to make you look seventies chic (always a good look for this time of year with all those polonecks, furry boots, long scarves and cord flares).

Here are my top tips for other things to do in November . . .

- Start knitting everyone you know a scarf for Christmas.
- Get a vegetable box delivered and make home-made soup. Leave out the cabbage, though.
- Go the Marlborough Arms with a friend and play one of their board games.
- Head for the cinema. Going on your own is rather liberating and you don't have to share your popcorn. Page 2 for films to see this week.
- Hold a retro fondue party. If you haven't got a fondue set, then just use a saucepan and some skewers. If you haven't got any friends, use a bowl and a microwave.
- Go to Minerva's for a shot of hot chocolate. Just remember to check your teeth afterwards. Chocolate teeth are not attractive.
- Or do what I'm doing – make a microwave cake in a mug and eat it in bed.

My evenings, and, more and more, my weekends, are spent reviewing events. I am still trying to find my way around, and if I find a venue within the hour I see it as a success. When I get there, I spend another hour/two hours with people who walk past me and pollute the room with their air kisses. Another two hours are spent on the train home with the evening drunks and I am lucky if I get home before two a.m. If I do have Sunday free, it is spent sleeping. The majority of invitations to go out after work have been turned down due to sheer exhaustion of being the new girl. When I have accepted, I am drunk after three Mojitos, and then resent a night spent on Lizzie's sofa. It's not made for tall people.

Lizzie is nice. Like me, she still has her foot firmly entrenched somewhere else and goes home at the weekend to see her boyfriend. We sometimes go to lunch together and congratulate ourselves that this is the stepping stone to greater things. Lizzie wants to work for *Vogue*. I wanted to once, but now I don't know. I am not sure about the others in the office. Like Candice, they are surface people and there seems little love for anyone or anything outside their world. It all feels very fragile and transient.

Ed tells me that *Life to Live* is still the same, that

Poppy's column is not setting the world alight. There have been letters of complaint, the readers want to know about Girl Without a Date, Poppy has missed next month's deadline, and Georgina is pulling her hair out. Do I want to know? Of course I do! I was right to leave *Life to Live*. Here, my column is appreciated and doing really well. Candice seems pleased with what I am doing and the hard work is paying off. I may be knackered and still unsure of where I'm heading, but I'm the one in the driving seat with the cool shades on and the map, and I'm pretty sure I'm going in the right direction.

'Where are you?' Katie asks.

'I'm just arriving back in Bath. I've been at a new exhibition at the V&A.'

'How exciting.'

'It was.'

'You sound tired.'

'I am.'

I can barely talk. My mind has shut down. I lean my head back against the head rest. The train jerks to a stop and people are standing and jostling past me. I join them and fight for my own personal space.

'Lawrence and I were hoping everyone would come to dinner on Wednesday.'

'Next Wednesday?' I flick through the diary in my mind.

'It's my birthday?'

'Oh, God, Katie, I'm so sorry. My brain is fried.'

'It's okay. Really it is.'

Katie would say this, even if I said I didn't give a damn about her birthday.

'I'll put it into my diary.'

'Great. Bring Ed if you want.'

'No, I don't think so.'

'Why not?'

My phone goes dead, which is just as well because I don't have an answer to her question. Ed is waiting. I know he is. He is waiting for a sign that says we have crossed the line from friends to something more. I don't give him that sign because something is stopping me. But what? Jason? Do I want to take another chance with him? This is crazy. Ed is lovely and sweet and we enjoy each other's company. What am I waiting for?

This weekend is the first weekend I haven't worked, either in London or at home. It's the only way I can keep on top of things and get to all the events I want to write about. Mum has persuaded me against my better judgement to spend my free time Christmas shopping. She has already bought Katie a perfume for less than ten pounds. It's called Tropical Dream and Katie will smell like a Bounty bar. Mum has always liked her bargains.

When we were younger our outfits rarely matched. If there was an orange plaid skirt that was marked down because of a missing button, then it was ours. Who cared that it clashed with everything and the replacement button didn't match? It's not about the money, but the thrill of the chase; of being smarter than the average shopper. She will proudly tell Katie exactly how much the perfume cost and that the raspberry Pavlova she has promised to make would have had raspberries in it, but the mango was on special offer.

She is wearing a new fake fur hat. It is a huge, round creation that covers her hair and ears; leaving little space for her face. It looks like a seventies Afro made of rabbit fur. I want to keep stroking her. I am carrying a three-foot-tall plastic reindeer. Its nose is red and when plugged in, it will glow brightly. Mum has bought it for Emma's garden. It's not going to fit in the car, I know it isn't, and I told her this when she bought it, but she wasn't listening. She was talking to the sales assistant about the mystery that is low-energy light bulbs.

'Did you go out with Jason?' she asks.

'Yes.'

'And?'

'It was nice.'

'And how is Ed?' she persists.

'He's fine. In fact, I'm seeing him tonight.'

'Seeing a lot of him these days, aren't you?'

'A fair bit.'

'He likes you.'

I nod.

'Quite a lot, by the looks of it?'

My mother is fishing.

'I'm not sure about quite a lot. I think he's fond of me.'

Fond? What a quaint word that is.

'Nice lad. A touch on the gangly side, and those feet . . .' She opens her eyes in mock horror. 'What are they? A size thirteen? Your Auntie Barbara always says you can tell a lot from the size of a man's feet.' She laughs to herself. We gaze at a cream coat in a shop window. The mannequin looks down at us haughtily.

'Not very practical,' Mum says.

'But very beautiful,' I say.

We wander on.

'Yes, he's a nice lad, that Ed . . .' Mum says to her reflection.

She is trying to wear me down. If she says it enough times I will agree. I know the tactics, but I will resist for as long as I can.

'The perfect man,' I say.

'Aaah, the perfect man,' she says, and nods in a knowing fashion.

We stop for a coffee and hang our handbags off Rudolph. We take it in turns. I go to the loo, then she goes to powder her nose. Then it's back to the serious job of the day – shopping.

Despite jewellery not being on our list, we stop outside a jeweller's shop for too long. Mum oohs and aahs over the size of rubies and diamonds. She likes to window-shop and will hover for extraordinary amounts of time if allowed. I am more commando-style. Let's get in . . . and then out . . . go, go, go. Chloe hates this; so does Katie. They both like to float around for hours but I guess it's easier if you're a perfect size ten and the whole shop would look great on you. Josie is like me but goes one step further and refuses to try anything on. She has this theory that changing-room mirrors are designed to make you look like shit, so that you buy more in the hope of transforming yourself into gorgeous. Most of our shopping time is spent taking things back.

My mother sighs over a diamond-encrusted watch. 'I had a perfect man once.' She sighs again.

'What? Dad?'

'No, Jonathan Reed was my perfect man. We'd been courting for two years. He went shooting with my father, bought my mother flowers and had a good job in a bank. My parents and everyone else thought I would be mad not to accept his marriage proposal. But I didn't. I accepted your father's instead – three months after meeting him.'

We move from the jeweller's and stop in front of a department store.

'My father was so disappointed in me, it broke my heart. He said your father ruined my life. Oooh. What do you think of that?'

'It's horrid. So Ed is not the one for me? Is that what you're saying?'

She has chipped away and snared me in.

'Ed is a nice young man. I like him, your father liked him, and he thinks the world of you; but all of that means diddly squat. Does he make your stomach flip? Does he make your eyes twinkle? Does he cause you to experience an indescribable urge to have his babies?'

'The thing is, Mum, I don't want anyone. I don't need a boyfriend.'

'No darling, you don't. But it's nice to have one.'

Five hours and twenty shops later, Mum calls it a day and leaves me to babysit Alfie. I check my watch and decide it's not worth going back to the flat. I am meeting Ed here in an hour. We are going to the cinema to see *Sex and the City*. He doesn't want to go but I have promised to go with him to see the next Batman film. We are the perfect couple.

I wander into a bookshop full of Christmas shoppers. I resent their intrusive presence. Bookshops should be empty so that you can while away an hour browsing undisturbed for nothing in particular. I do this for ten minutes before realising that I do want something in particular. I need something to read on the train to and from work. Something intellectual, but entertaining, or something trashy and full of the sex I'm not having. Here's one. I pick up a book marked 'raunchy read' and open it up at page five. I laugh out loud.

'Filthy.'

I turn around, startled, and snap the book shut.

'That's what my sister says, anyway. She says it's full of people doing it in stables and fields.'

I put the book down as if it is scorching my hands.

'Hi.'

Nate's face breaks out into a smile. I remember the smile. It's a whopper with bells on.

'How are you?' I ask. My heart is beating so fast I fear I might faint.

'Good, good. What about you? Are you still working for that magazine?'

'No, I work in London for *Circling* magazine now.'

'Great. Never heard of it, but that's great.'

I give him my blurb on *Circling* and make my job sound more glamorous than it is. His eyebrows are raised and he is nodding.

'And are you enjoying it?' he asks, when I have finished.

'Yes,' I respond cautiously.

'Is that a "yes" yes, or is that a "yes, not sure" yes?'

'It's early days yet.'

'What are the people like? I imagine it's full of creative media types with their noses up each other's bums?'

'Something like that.' I laugh.

'I can't imagine you working somewhere like that,' Nate says and I am not sure if this is a compliment or an insult. He looks into my eyes as if he is looking for a chink in my DNA.

'You're looking tanned.' I change the subject.

'I've been in Brazil for several weeks. I've just got back.'

'Wow, what were you doing there?'

'Child poverty is a real issue over there. All a bit grim, really. We took a team of paediatricians over. It's a small ripple in a big sea, but hopefully we can make a difference.'

'That's very commendable. I'm impressed.'

He raises his eyebrows. He looks offended.

'No, really, I am.'

'Oh,' he says, looking surprised.

He suits a tan, and that shirt. The jeans look good too. He has nice teeth . . . he is really rather . . . I mooch. This entails me swinging my body slightly and hanging my head to one side. It's a daydream thing and probably not that attractive. Then I get that snap thing again; the one that tells me to wake up and smell the coffee. I realise I am looking at a moment; one that requires seizing. This is one of those moments where my horoscope would be talking about Venus in Mercury.

'*Very* impressed, actually.' I sound more confident than I feel.

'Can I impress you some more over coffee?'

About bloody time! Where are those trumpets?

Our cappuccinos and a small round table separate us, but I feel uncomfortably close to him; too close. If I leaned even closer I would be able to kiss him. What would he kiss like? His bottom lip is fuller than his top lip. He has a wide, expressive mouth that breaks out into a smile easily. It is surrounded by a dark shadow of hair that forms the ghost of a moustache and goatee beard. I tap my fingers on the table. They are itching to reach out and touch his lips. I imagine pushing my fingers into his mouth; imagine him sucking slightly, biting.

'Harry?'

'Sorry. What?'

'I said I'm glad I saw you. I was worried about you.'

'Thanks. Look, I'm sorry about before. I was just . . . I was missing my dad, and I was angry; not at you, but at the world in general. I am truly sorry.'

'No apologies needed. I was just being an idiot. I'm the eldest of five kids. My own father died when I was sixteen and my mother took it really hard. She tried to take her own life and she was on medication for a long time. I guess I've always had to be there, acting the hero.'

I feel a little sick. I seem to vaguely remember shouting at him that he had no idea how I felt when Dad died. Oh God. He must have thought I was a real bitch.

'Being a hero is good,' I say, smiling.

'But not everyone needs one, and if I'm going to make a career out of it, then I need to at least get some tight-fitting lycra and stop crying over films.'

'Women like men who are man enough to cry.'

'I'll keep that in mind when you upset me.'

'The cookies were great, by the way.'

I leave out the bit about writing a poem about them.

'I'm glad you liked them. I can make other things too. I'm also quite good around the house. I can mend things; I do the washing-up and have a good memory for birthdays.'

We both laugh in that flirty way that says a thousand things. Then I remember Ed and panic.

'Everything okay?' Nate asks.

'Yes, I'm meant to be meeting someone, that's all. I'd completely forgotten.'

'Oh, sorry, I didn't mean to keep you . . . there's me, chatting away, and you've been trying to get away.'

'No, I'm having a great time,' I say quickly.

We both look at the table. Our hands are close. Two centimetres and they would be touching. I am at that moment again. Don't mess it up this time, Harry.

'Actually, my friend won't mind if I rearrange . . . if you wanted to . . . we could, I could stay a bit longer.' I suddenly feel embarrassed.

'That would be great. If you're sure.' He looks pleased.

'I'm positive,' I lie, and send a quick text to Ed. I feel

bad, but not as bad as I probably should. Nate's smiling face is enough to make me believe I did the right thing. I'm taking my moment and running with it.

We talk, order another coffee, talk a bit more, go to a bar, talk, eat Italian, talk more and drink whisky chasers. He walks me home and I invite him in for coffee because it's the polite thing to do. As I unlock the door I reassure myself that it is just that. A cup of coffee – nothing else.

He tastes of whisky and coffee and I cannot get enough. I am drowning in his saliva. He is hard. I can feel it through my skirt. We don't say anything. He closes the door behind him and grabs me, pushing me against the wall. My hands are gripping his hair as he kisses my neck and brushes my hardening nipples with his palm. I fumble with his shirt buttons and he grabs my hand.

'Harry?'

'Don't talk.'

I cover his mouth with mine. He attempts to pull my blouse off but it gets stuck on my arms. I have to help him before he pulls my arms out of their sockets.

'Sorry,' he mumbles, pulling his jeans off. His skin is warm. He pushes me against the wall and pulls my bra cup to one side. Oh my God! His fingers pull at the fabric of my knickers and he pushes them down to my knees. He lifts me slightly and I gasp. I cannot see or hear anything. All of my senses are centred on one place. I dig my nails into his skin. He removes my hands and holds them instead.

I am laughing with relief. I haven't laughed like this for a long time. Nate squeezes my hand and groans.

He kisses me gently on the lips. I smile and open my eyes. I see him and no one else.

Girl Without a Date in Her Diary – Blog entry – November 18th

How do you know if somebody likes you? I read somewhere that it's all about mirroring body language. If they mirror your gestures, or the way you sit, then it's a positive thing. Personally, I think I would find it a bit off-putting if someone scratched their eyebrow or crossed their legs when I did. Perhaps there's a delay thing with it. I always forget to monitor this sort of thing when I'm on a date.

If he kisses you then I guess that's the ultimate positive signal. I like kissing. When I marry I will insist on a lifetime of snogging with tongues. Too many married couples forget to snog. Their lives become busy with other things, but I think it should be a rule in any relationship to stop for at least a minute's snogging every day. It's such an intimate thing. When you haven't kissed for a long time you wonder if you will ever get the hang of it again, but I think it's like riding a bike. Within minutes, you're off and away. I have fantasies of doing it in the rain without an umbrella.

GWAD – *Circling* magazine column

Let's talk about sex! How do you know if you should or shouldn't? It's a tricky one. There are rules to be followed, but if you watch any good film, then the heroine nearly always gets the man, despite sleeping with him on the first date. But I have to remind myself that this is the real world and we are governed by the number four. Fourth date and then wait four days for the call. I did a survey around friends and work colleagues. Apparently this is rubbish. It's two dates and one day. No, it's ten dates and seven days. Why are there no bloody rules when you need them?

Things to do whilst you are waiting for that call:

- Learn how to appliqué. Why? Why not?
- Blow up twenty balloons. When he does call, release them into the air. You might want to check with your council. Apparently it's litter. How very unromantic. Maybe buy some white doves.
- Book yourself in for a body overhaul including pedicure, manicure and facial. If you have already slept with him then it's a bit late for all this, but it's still a nice way to pass the time.
- Invite your girly friends over and eat humous, garlic bread and garlic chicken. Enjoy the freedom of bad breath.
- Join a gym. Use the time constructively. A toned thigh could be the deciding factor for him.
- Take a flower-arranging course. A good way to save money on the cost of your wedding.
- Chuck out any big and comfy knickers you may have lurking. There is no need for him to know the truth.
- If it's a long wait, learn a language.

Katie is disappointed that I will not make it to her birthday. Candice reassures me there will be others and doesn't notice my flinch. I should have refused, but Wednesday comes and goes and instead of spending my sister's birthday with her I am making small talk and smiling brightly with people who are on my get-to-know list at a party for an artist with attachment issues and shifty eyes. I attempt to circulate, but blank stares and polite conversation mean that within twenty minutes I am back where I started. I am circulating in circles. My fellow colleagues, Pip, Darcy, Patrick and Lindell, seem to have this mingling thing down to a fine art, and when they are not clinging on to each other, laughing hysterically, they are smooching with the great and the good who have gathered to congratulate us on our latest issue. Lizzie is off sick and the laughs are few and far between. I feel as if I am a child peering into a glass Christmas bauble; the one hanging from the branch that's too high to reach. The colours turn and shine in the lights, but rarely fall on me. I look at my watch.

'Having a good time?' Candice drawls.

'Great. I was just checking to make sure I can get the last train back.'

'Did I mention the Franco viewing tomorrow night?'

I scan my mind, but tiredness is making it hard to think straight. I have been up since five thirty this morning and I am not looking at getting back home until the early hours.

'No, I don't think you did.'

'I need you to go and be me for the night. I have a social engagement I can't cancel.' She has her hands on her hips, with one eye on the door.

'Sorry, Candice, but I can't. I have something planned for tomorrow night. It's been in the diary for months now and I don't want to cancel.'

'I really need someone to go to this thing, Harry.'

'But this is my best friend's hen night.' I don't tell her that this is Chloe's sixth hen night.

'It's a shame, and I understand you don't want to let your pals down, but that's what happens. We make our choices to live in this mad, crazy, coke-fuelled world.' She laughs loudly, showing big white teeth, 'and sometimes, sweetie, we have to accept the consequences. Old relationships inevitably fall by the wayside.'

Coke? That explains a lot.

'But . . .' I attempt to argue my point. These are not old relationships – these are the people who are important to me. I don't want to be like most of the people here; clawing their way up the career ladder and stepping on people's heads as they do so. I can't remember the last time I spent any real time with Chloe and Josie – or Mum, come to think of it. She tells me it's okay, but I don't want it to be just okay. I like being with her. One of the more positive things that came out of my father's death is our now very different relationship. We laugh a lot together and she understands more than I ever gave her credit for. She's not only my mum, but she's also one of my best friends.

'You have to make a choice, Harry. We all do,' Candice says and opens her arms to a woman with a crocheted teapot on her head.

My feet are killing me. I find a quiet spot and phone Katie. She has had a wonderful time. I was missed.

I wait for my train and remind myself that I am living the dream: working for a national glossy, drinking in trendy city bars and enjoying people's reaction when I tell them what I do. I am Harriet Peel, going somewhere. Even Emma's friends are impressed. The beautiful people look hollow and faded in the darkness. Their heads are down. Everyone wants to go home.

I check my phone again. Nothing. Nate hasn't rung. I feel sick with my own stupidity. I look to the timetable. My train is half an hour late. I ring Josie.

'You all right?'

'It's been ages, and he hasn't rung.'

'I have to admit I'm surprised. I thought he would.'

'Me too.'

'Maybe it was just the wrong time for him. Have you thought he might have a girlfriend?'

'Oh God.' I think I might throw up.

'I don't know, I'm just thinking of reasons why he has apparently gone off the boil.'

I scan my mind for memories of our night together. There were opportunities for him to say something about not being available. He would have said. I'm convinced of it.

'No, he hasn't got a girlfriend,' I say.

'Then why?'

'He obviously had second thoughts.'

Josie doesn't say anything.

The heating blasts out from the vents at my feet, but I

am still cold. The carriage is empty except for me, and a couple in full evening wear. The woman is asleep on her husband's shoulder. He wraps his jacket round her shoulders and squeezes her into him. The gesture is tender and missed by her. I think of Nate and the day my father died. My mobile bleeps and I search through my handbag. My heart lurches into my mouth. It's him, it's him . . . It's Ed. Reliable, perfect Ed. I decide to ring him tomorrow. Right now I need to sleep a while. In five hours' time I will be back on the train, going the other way again.

The next morning I book myself in for a ten-thirty meeting with Candice. I have a half-hour slot, but it only takes eight minutes for me to tell her that I am not right for the job and to hand in my notice.

'Are you having a breakdown?' she asks, eyes narrowed.

'I don't think so,' I reply.

'Then pray tell me why you are giving up one of the most sought-after jobs in the industry.'

'Because losing my father taught me that life is too short and I thought by taking this job it would mean that I wasn't throwing my life away; that I was doing something dynamic and exciting and . . .' I fiddle with my ring and take a deep breath. 'It's been really good working for *Circling*. I've realised that I love what I do and I am really good at it, but not here. You need someone who can commit to the magazine one hundred and fifty per cent and, right now, my family are too important to push to one side. My father also taught me that time is precious and I should always be true to myself. I need to find another way and stop doing what I think I should be doing rather than what I want to do.'

'You know anti-depressants work wonders. Prozac is a miracle drug.'

'Thanks for giving me this chance, Candice.'

She waves me away with her hand. 'Well, if you change your mind . . .'

As I leave the office I am pretty sure that's not going to happen. I feel as if I have lost ten pounds in weight and then a miracle happens in Selfridges' changing rooms when I realise I have. Hurray!

Beautiful waiters in trendy black expertly weave their way around tables, carrying large round trays of steaming hot food. The room is infused with garlic and basil. As we walk in, people look up from their plates. They cannot help staring at Chloe, who unlike most brides-to-be is positively glowing with pre-wedding preparation. It's been a month of exfoliating, body polishing, and a hint of tanning salons, saunas, steam rooms and yoga. Her body is ready to surrender itself to Tad for a lifetime of caring, sharing and all that nonsense.

'You know you're heading for a fall, don't you?' Josie says from behind a menu. She flips it over to desserts and nods, apparently pleased.

'Why?' Chloe and I ask in unison.

'Because Tad will see this image of perfection and expect it for the next twenty-odd years.'

'No. He says he's quite looking forward to me falling apart. Apparently, he's always had a thing for overweight women with hairy armpits.'

'Wow . . .' Josie and I murmur.

'And Russian accents . . . And big navy knickers . . . a little bit of body odour . . .'

'I think you should stop now,' I suggest.

We order a bottle of champagne. The big day is close. The last hen night will take place the night before at Chloe's mum's. That's going to be a sedate affair, with her mum's roast lamb and *Barefoot in the Park* on DVD. I am looking forward to going to the wedding . . . on my own.

'To hairy Russians in big knickers.'

'To one-night stands.'

'Josie!'

'Oh, come on. You have to think of it as a positive. You said yourself it was pretty fabulous and the day you get married you will look back and remember. Then you will think, great sex, but he wasn't the One.'

This makes me feel sad.

'You had a one-night stand?' Chloe says a little too loudly. The whole restaurant turns round. I choke on my focaccia.

'I didn't know it was going to be a one-night stand.'

'You kept that quiet.'

'I felt bad enough about sleeping with him on what wasn't technically even the first date. It started off as a cup of coffee.'

'I don't understand why you feel bad,' Josie says.

'I don't know. Because I'm meant to be a nice girl.'

'Sometimes even nice girls have to throw their knickers to the ground if it feels right.'

'It did.'

'Then it was the right thing to do. Don't feel bad just because he didn't contact you afterwards,' Chloe says helpfully.

I hug my very pretty friend. She's right. It was a moment in time and a very nice one at that. Hell, maybe this is the start of a new me. Use-and-abuse-them, no-commitment Harry. Casual sex could be the way forward. That way you get the good stuff without relinquishing the TV remote. I do know one thing, though – my mother was right. I definitely had a twinkle in my eye the next morning.

'I propose a toast. To Harry for having the guts to walk out of two jobs!' Josie declares.

We all clink glasses.

'Have you any idea of what you want to do next?'

I shake my head. 'None at all. But whatever it is, it will have to be fabulous.'

As I walked out of the *Circling* office I knew I had made the right decision. It wasn't the right thing for me. What I do next, though, is anyone's guess.

'You look great, by the way. I love the fact you're wearing heels now,' Chloe adds.

'I am officially embracing my height. It's one of the advantages of being single.'

'Another toast. To four inches of pleasure.'

'To long cardigans being the new doll fit.'

'To black being the new black.'

'To brunette being the new blonde.'

'To winter being the new summer.'

'To unemployment being the new leisure time.'

'To iced buns being the new *pain au raisin*.'

'Are you sure about that?' I ask.

'Definitely,' says Josie.

We dance until our feet hurt, laugh until our jaws ache, and go back to Chloe's where we eat marshmallows dipped in melted chocolate.

The next morning I wake up with a hangover, Josie snoring and Tad filming us for a new documentary called *Girls Unravelled*. I tell him it's not funny. He tells me it's going to be a Cannes Film Festival selection winner.

On the first day of my unemployment I pretend I am on holiday and get up late.

On the second day I have a facial and read a book from front to back.

On the third day I do some Christmas shopping and go to Bingo with Mum.

On the fourth day I invite Katie and Mum for lunch and make a cake.

On the fifth day I go swimming and eat falafels.

On the sixth day I clean my kitchen cupboards and paint my toenails.

On the seventh day I panic.

Shit, I haven't got a job.

'I haven't got a job!'

Ed looks at me for a second and resumes poking at his egg. We are in our usual café eating breakfast. There is nothing fancy or healthy about O'Mally's, but it is warm and welcoming. The Gut Buster breakfast is the best cure for a hangover/depression/cold/being unemployed and any other ailment that is made better with a little cholesterol.

'There are slimy bits in this egg. Do you think it's cooked?' he asks.

'Yes, it's fine . . . What am I going to do?'

'Are you sure? The white should be hard.'

'Yes, I'm frigging sure!'

'I was just asking! Have you approached *Bath at Large*?'

'Yes, but they haven't got anything. I guess I could temp for a while?'

'It's worth a try. I'm not going to get salmonella, am I?'

'No, you're not going to get salmonella,' I say wearily and push my plate to one side. Ed swipes my leftover sausage.

Minty comes over wiping her hands on a stained apron. She has worked here for ever and her hair is the same colour as the cooking oil.

'Everything okay?' she asks.

I glance over at Ed who looks down into his breakfast. Coward!

'Everything is good, thanks,' I reply.

'Haven't seen you in here for a while,' she says.

'No. I had a job in London. Had, being the operative word. You don't happen to have a job here, do you?'

Minty laughs.

'I'm being serious.'

'I'll ask the boss, but you want to get back to that magazine. Me and the girls need to know what happens. Did she get her date? You know they've replaced her with some God-awful tart obsessed with how much money and Botox everyone has. I don't know anyone in my street that has Botox.'

'No, but you've seen plenty that need it,' Ed observes, wiping his plate clean with a slice of buttered white bread.

'You need to stop talking and get this girl back at *Life to Live*. The What's On page is not what it used to be. You used to make me laugh with your funny little suggestions. Clever, it was.'

Minty clears our plates. 'Can you cook an egg?' she asks.

'Better than whoever's cooking the eggs now,' Ed mumbles.

'Wet the bed, did you?' Minty retorts and Ed smiles. Minty has always given Ed an extra fried slice and bacon. She disappears into the kitchen. I empty my mug of milky tea and sigh heavily.

'It's not a bad idea. You could go crawling back to Georgina and ask for some work,' Ed suggests.

'No. Absolutely no way.'

'I have a friend who works for *Regional Historian*. I could ask them if there's anything.'

'Thanks.'

'You could sound a bit more grateful.'

'Sorry. Thanks. You're a good friend.'

'A good friend?' Ed asks, searching my face for something I don't possess. I look into kind eyes. Nate hasn't phoned. It would be so easy.

'Yes, friend. The very best friend.'

Ed nods and I can see him deciding something. A couple come rushing in, bringing the cold air with them. He kisses her and they cuddle into each other as they decide what to have. A pang of something like jealousy makes me sigh again.

'I'd better be getting on,' Ed says.

'Do you fancy the cinema later?' I ask.

'No. I've got loads of stuff on today,' he replies unconvincingly.

I nod, understanding.

'See you around, though. I'll let you know about *Regional Historian*.'

'Thanks, Ed.'

We go our separate ways and I would be a liar if I said I didn't wonder, just for a second, if I have made a dreadful mistake. I check my phone. Nothing.

'You are bootiful. My God, I have never seen such grace. Eeema, you are a horse, a how you say? A thoroughbred.' Pablo is all over Emma like a rash. She is giggling like a schoolgirl.

Josie makes a loud humph sound, but Pablo and Emma are oblivious.

'This is rubbish!' she complains.

Ballroom dance classes seemed a good idea at the time. Now, I am questioning our presence here. People are tutting at us. I have already apologised to someone for backing into them. My dancing skills are as good as my shopping trolley ones. Mum loves it, though, and for that reason I am sticking with it, despite Pablo's comments that, 'It eeze a shame rhythm does not run in the family.'

Pablo claps his hands loudly. His trousers are too tight round his pert buttocks; his shirt is opened too low.

'Ladeez, this is ze last one. Let'sssssssssssss rumba, bumba. Hey!' He claps his hands again and stamps his foot to the floor.

We all take our positions and try to remember the steps. Emma and my mother are naturals. Katie is a good learner. Josie and I are embarrassing.

'I can't believe you persuaded me to do this, Dee,' Josie complains. 'Fat girls shouldn't rumba. It's not natural.'

'Fat girls should always rumba, Hosie.' Pablo takes her hands and spins her around. 'No man likes a skinny minnie. You have sex, Hosie.'

'That's none of your business,' Josie says indignantly.

'No, I mean you are sex . . . how you say? Sexy. Yes, you are sexy, Hosie.'

'Oh, thanks.'

She turns to me and covers her mouth with her hand.

'I am sure he's Twinkle Toes from DateMate.'

'Did he just touch Emma's bum?' I say, shocked.

If he did, Emma has chosen to ignore it. She is definitely wearing more make-up than she was last week.

At the end of the class we head into town for something to eat. There is a queue for tables but Josie waves her business card and we are ushered through by someone with legs thinner than my wrists.

'I wouldn't normally like these types of places, but Diana said the wine list was quite impressive,' Emma remarks, looking around to see if she can see 'someone/anyone' she knows.

'I thought it was you!' Judith appears at our table like a blonde goddess. She is with someone who has a beard and long hair and a rather strange taste in jumpers.

'How is life in the big city?' she trills.

'I'm not there any more.'

'Oh.'

I can see Judith mentally challenging herself to leave it there. She won't, though.

'Did they get rid of you?'

'No, I left.'

'Gosh, that's very brave of you.'

'I think it was stupid, rather than brave. No job and rent to pay. What was I thinking?' I laugh it off.

'Well, when I said brave, I meant stupid.' Judith laughs.

My mother squeezes my hand. It is warm and reassuring.

'Well, I'd better go. John and I are meeting our church group. John's a recovering alcoholic, aren't you, John?'

John nods, before being dragged away to be saved.

'You've done the right thing, darling,' my mother whispers to me. 'If I'm honest, I was worried about you, and you know you can always come and live with me until you get yourself sorted out.'

I'm touched. 'Thanks, Mum. That's really sweet.'

'Not for ever, mind. Dorothy upstairs said she let her son move into her last house and he stayed for fifteen years.'

'Are you still planning on going to Chloe's wedding on your own?' Katie asks.

I nod.

'You should take that Poppy girl with you,' my mother says. 'She seems a nice girl and she was only saying the other day how much she liked weddings.'

Unemployment is not all it's cracked up to be. I'm panicking. What on earth am I going to do? Another week and I'm no nearer to finding another job. I just can't seem to find anything that makes my tummy do that flip thing. Talking of which, I still haven't heard from Nate. I am trying to forget about him and I know it's something I'll get over, but I feel stupid and sad that I misjudged the situation. I thought we had something. In direct contrast I have had quite a few texts from Jason who seems keen to meet up again. My reluctance to say yes has been rewarded with flowers – three bunches of them. I don't have that many vases. I gave some to Mum. She thought they were lovely, but then unlike me she loves carnations. I would have gone for peonies or lilies: something with attitude. I feel slightly disappointed. Take a little time and effort to match the flowers to the person, and *voilà*, you make someone feel extra special. It's not that hard to do. Does Jason see me as carnation type of girl? Well, he's definitely lost a few points for that. Now if he had gone to Tiny Gilespie on Walcot Street, then the arrangements might have swung the whole thing.

The world stops for a moment and I realise I am having a moment. Not a love moment, but more of a life one. Why on earth didn't I think of it before? I know so much about the city I live in. I know the places to find the cute tin flower pots for the lavender on your kitchen shelf, or the haberdashery shop that will transform a pair of jeans into something SJP would lust after. I know where to find cashmere jumpers in mouth-watering colours and the reasons why a girl should try the Blue Note Bar or take a second left past George Street. Over the past year I have met so many interesting people who are now my link to what is happening in the city. If there is a celebrity book event then Sadie from the book club will tip me off early – if there is a restaurant that's doing amazing things and a special lunch deal, then Ricardo at the cooking school will give me a call – and God, why didn't I think of this . . . Chloe knows all there is to know about what's hot in the fashion world, whilst Josie is my celebrity gossip source. I have all this knowledge at my fingertips and nowhere to put it. My blog readership is increasing but . . . I stop writing and look out of the kitchen window. Am I mad?

'Am I?' I shout to the ceiling. I imagine my father telling me yes, but not to let it get in the way. I grab my notepad and frantically begin making notes. My hands are shaking.

Donald sips at his tea. The skin on his hands is wrinkled and brown. His fingernails are shaped and smooth. He silently scans the folder before him as I clasp and unclasp my hands. They feel sweaty. It seems wrong to sweat in a place like this with its soft furnishings, expensive china and people who talk softly. I have never been to this particular hotel before. I am not rich and, unless you are, there seems to be an invisible force field that prevents you from even considering crossing the threshold. Guests read newspapers or talk quietly over tea and tiny sandwiches. Move suddenly and people look.

I sip my tea and try not to slurp. Even the doorman looks superior. I gaze out of the window. Normal life continues outside but no sound leaks through. I can hear myself swallow. A flash of dark hair walks past and for a moment I think it is Nate. I want to jump up and look out of the window. Inside I am panicking. Sensing a shift in my posture Donald looks up and smiles. I smile back. He continues to read. As the clock ticks on the ornate mantelpiece, I think of Nate and wonder, still, where he is and what he is doing. I guess, for him, life moved on. Donald coughs.

'Girls and the City, eh?'

'That's what I'd like to call it.'

'And you think we have a market for this?' he asks, handing me the folder back.

'Yes, I do. Regional magazines rely predominantly on a female readership. This title will give them something more than gardening tips and photos of expensive houses. I want to encourage people under fifty to get the best out of Bath. I want to include interviews with up-and-coming artists, those who run charities, designers and business people – people who inspire others. I want to couple it with some great photography and artwork. There would be a weekly column with someone I know who runs an allotment. She makes some great chutneys and soups. Our fashion shoots will lead rather than follow and I want style pages of readers photographed on the street.' I take a deep breath.

'Good, good. I'll get my accountant to look at the figures and get back to you, but there shouldn't be a problem.'

'That's it?'

'That's it. Shall we have some more tea and shortbread?'

When I get outside I ring my mother.

'I think he said yes!'

'Ooooh. That's wonderful,' she squeals and then begins to talk to someone else. 'My daughter . . . she's going to be producing a magazine . . . oh yes, much better than that . . . I always knew she was the bright one . . . very bright as a baby . . . learned to potty train earlier than the other two.'

'Mum?'

'Sorry, love. I'm in the hairdresser's. What do you think of extensions?'

Girl Without a Date in Her Diary – Blog entry – December 1st

In the spirit of saving money I'm making home-made chutney for everyone this Christmas. In the spirit of being green I am also wrapping presents in newspaper. I will not, however, be making my own cards. It takes up too much time and everyone is doing it these days. I thought I might make some Mars bar vodka and take it around to all my friends. One of my New Year resolutions is to get out more. Now that I am cooking more (for the Grunt and Grub club, my reading group, my new friend Jo from dancing, and, much to Emma's horror, my family), I have also decided to have fresh herbs in my life. The boring bay leaf is still a bit of a mystery to me, but basil . . . now that is a wonderful thing. I might devote a whole issue of *Girls and the City* to it.

December 5th

Do rabbits like chutney?

The grass is crisp beneath our feet and frosted with white. Icicles hang like glass droplets from the branches of trees and white lights twinkle in the fading afternoon light.

I shiver and it travels through my entire body. Josie hugs me into her and rubs my arms. My bolero fake fur jacket is for show only. It wouldn't be so bad if I was wearing sensible shoes, but my stilettos have not been designed for practicality. I love them. I am taller than everyone else by miles, but I don't care. They can all look up.

We make our way into the church. It's even colder in here. Red and violet flowers with dark green foliage fill each corner. There are candles everywhere, flickering gently in the cold air. My steps echo on the stone floor and everyone turns. If I trip now I will cry. I slip in next to Josie and Ben and look around the packed pews. Perhaps he decided not to come. Perhaps he is back with Sophie.

Chloe emerges in the most amazing dress I have ever seen and I cry, along with every other female present.

At the reception we dine on roast beef cooked by a celebrity chef, followed by tiny champagne jellies moulded into the shape of Chloe's white Scottie dog, Tallulah. A tower of white chocolate cupcakes has replaced the traditional wedding cake and each guest is given one in a pretty pastel box to take away. Jason's chair is empty and I wonder if anyone should be worried. The speeches are funny, and despite my sporadic and often horrific appearances throughout, so was Tad's film.

I watch Chloe and Tad take to the dance floor. They look beautiful together, despite the fact that Tad looks like a younger Colonel Sanders from the Kentucky Fried Chicken ads. Josie and Ben follow. I wave and Josie gives me the thumbs-up. Chloe's auntie rushes over and offers her arm.

'If you can't beat 'em, join 'em.'

'I'd love to, Janice, but I need the ladies.'

Along with a handful of other female guests I huddle in front of the toilet mirror and reapply my lipstick. Chloe has promised an evening of our favourite records and a surprise appearance. We are all betting on Take That. Josie is convinced it's Tom Jones. I pucker up and straighten my back. No slouching tonight. I am walking tall and it's all good.

I walk back into the room. A woman passes me with a gun holster full of tequila slammer glasses. The dance floor is full. When he sees me he smiles. I smile back. He says something to Tad and pats him on the arm. Tad turns round to look. I am still smiling. The music fills my ears and I feel as if I am hovering ever so slightly above the ground. I wait for him to reach me.

'You look amazing. Dance with me.'

Jason takes my hand and I allow myself to be led on to the dance floor.

'Everything okay?' I ask. I can feel the pressure of his hand on my back.

'Yeah, some trouble with the car. I made it, though – just in time.'

'Just in time for what?'

'To sweep you off your feet.'

I laugh and he laughs with me.

He whispers something in my ear but I cannot hear him.

'Let's get a breath of fresh air,' he suggests, and I follow him out to the patio area. The trees are covered in fairy lights. Soon the sky will be full of fireworks.

'So, you going to forgive me?'

'For what?' I ask.

'For Sophie.'

'There's nothing to forgive.'

'Cool.' He looks confident and handsome. I remember seeing him for the first time and thinking the same.

I rub my arms because of the cold. A group huddle together smoking nearby. The music drifts out as people open the door to join them.

'Looking back she did me a favour,' I muse.

'What do you mean?' he asks. The confidence has gone.

'I mean that you weren't the One. I thought you were; but now I know.'

I kiss him lightly on the cheek.

'Take care, Jason.'

My heels click on the wooden floor. I take a glass of champagne from a passing tray and empty it. The dance floor is empty. I motion to Josie and Chloe. We take to the floor and shake our booties. God, I love weddings.

The cab driver talks and I let his words drift over me. I am looking forward to my bed. The hotel room was never used; well, not by me, anyway. My fantasies have changed and I was quite happy to come home. Back at the flat I make a cup of tea and take it to bed. My feet hurt from dancing but I sleep like a baby.

*

I resist the temptation to take up DateMate's offer of finding one hundred ideal mates according to my criteria. I click into my profile and think back to my first one. What did I put back then when my search for a date began? After every disastrous one my requirements were slightly amended and became more specific in the vain hope that it would weed out the less compatible and attract the one who would fit me perfectly.

> *My ideal mate: Six foot and over would be nice, dark hair, nice hands. Gentle but with a sharp sense of humour, intelligent, kind, generous . . . someone who cares, someone I can trust, someone I can look up to – literally; someone who will laugh when I am trying to be funny, but who will be there when I'm not; who will hold my hand when it gets scary and who lets it go when I want to do things my way. In short, I want a hero.*

It's describing Nate! How funny. Oh well, *c'est la vie*. It wasn't meant to be. I press delete and end my DateMate subscription.

The door buzzer goes. Aaah, my hero?

'Harry, is this your rubbish outside?' Martha Gennings asks.

'No,' I lie.

She knows I am lying. She has probably searched my rubbish bag for clues with her kitchen-utensil-grabbing thing and rubber gloves.

'Can I remind you that rubbish should not be put out before eight o'clock? It's now seven.'

'I'll tell the man upstairs.'

'I don't think he wears tights,' Martha replies.

'You'd be surprised.'

Martha snorts.

The door buzzer goes again.

'Yes?' I snap.

'Harry?'

I imagine this is the point where I faint. Instead, I lose the ability to speak.

'Harry?'

'Yes,' I squeak.

'It's Nate.'

I know who it bloody is. I have that voice imprinted in my mind. The picture that accompanies it is the one of him naked.

'Can I come in?'

'Not got your fireman pals with you tonight?' I ask. He laughs and I buzz him in.

He looks uncomfortable and gorgeous in equal measure.

'How are you?' he asks.

'Good.'

'I was just passing.'

'Uh huh?' I reply. I put my hands on my hips. I want to be angry with him, not relieved.

'I saw your sister earlier. Emma, is it?'

I nod, surprised.

'She told me that it might be worth me popping round.'

'Oh did she?' I am not moving an inch. He didn't ring. We slept together and I woke up to him kissing me softly on the lips. He said he would call, and he didn't.

'I had my phone stolen the day after we – twelve hours later I was in Ethiopia.'

'Mmmm,' I say, unconvinced.

'I've just got back. I couldn't remember your number.

I'm rubbish with things like that. It was on my phone.'

'You could have phoned *Life to Live*. They have my contact details.'

'I did.'

'You did?' I ask, surprised. 'And?'

'The first few days were just madness. We were existing on two hours' sleep a night and . . . well, it doesn't matter now, but when I came up for air, I managed to get through to the *Life to Live* office. After numerous broken connections, I finally got through to Ed. He told me in no uncertain terms that he was seeing you that night. I thought that maybe you were seeing him when we—'

I sigh. 'Ed is my friend. Nothing else.'

'That's what your sister said. Your mum was with her. She said that I should come round sooner rather than later. She suggested you might need rescuing.'

I smile.

He rummages around in a carrier bag. Flowers or chocolates? He pulls a Spiderman mask over his head.

'Does this help?' he says through the mouth hole.

When we are naked on the sofa he asks if he can take the mask off because he can't breathe.

'Does this mean you lose your super powers?'

'No. My powers are easily transferable. Like Spiderman, I am especially good with my hands.'

That night he sleeps soundly.

'I thought you had trouble sleeping?' I ask the next morning.

'I did. You must have a magic bed.'

'You'd best stay there, then.'

'You might regret saying that.'

'Something tells me I won't. As long as you keep doing that thing with the palm of your hand, anyway.'

Six months later . . .

Girl With a Date in Her Diary – Blog entry

I have two dates in my diary. One for the removal men to take my furniture to the flat Nate and I have just rented together. It has floorboards. We have also bought a large, impractical rug with big woollen loops. We can't Hoover it, but Mum says it just needs a bit more suction with a hand-held thing. She bought me one for Christmas. Nate likes it. He uses it to Hoover up the rabbit fur. Chloe and Tad, the white rabbits, are now living with us after they ate one of Tad's film reels.

The other date is Josie and Ben's wedding. I'm really looking forward to it. Talking of weddings, the September issue of *Girls and the City* will have a wedding supplement.

little
black
dress

Pick up a *little black dress* – it's a girl thing.

978 0 7553 4520 5

ANIMAL INSTINCTS
Nell Dixon
PBO £5.99

Clodagh Martin's celebrity sister Imogen couldn't have turned up at a worse time: Clodagh's beloved animal sanctuary is under threat. Facing ruin, can Clodagh figure out whether property magnate and bad-luck Jack Thatcher's interest is in her, or her assets?

Lose yourself in this gorgeous tale of romance, mystery and a foul-mouthed parrot!

SEE JANE SCORE
Rachel Gibson
PBO £5.99

Journalist Jane Alcott's big chance finally arrives when she lands a job reporting on ice-hockey team the Seattle Chinooks – and on their star player, Luc Martineau. Hot-shot Luc has no time for dirt-digging reporters, but he's about to discover there's more to Jane than meets the eye . . .

Cold ice meets red-hot tempers – grab ring-side seats for another brilliant romance from Rachel Gibson.

978 0 7553 4634 9

Pick up a *little black dress* – it's a girl thing.

978 0 7553 4801 5

TRASHED
Alison Gaylin
PBO £5.99

Take two suspicious, Tinseltown deaths and add them to the blood-stained stiletto of a beautiful actress who's just committed suicide . . . Journalist Simone Glass is finally on to the story of her life – but is she about to meet a terrifying deadline?

Hollywood meets homicide in Alison Gaylin's fabulous killer-thriller.

SUGAR AND SPICE
Jules Stanbridge
PBO £5.99

After the initial panic of losing her high-flying job, Maddy Brown launches Sugar and Spice, making delicious, mouth-wateringly irresistible cakes. Can she find the secret ingredient for the perfect chocolate cake – and the perfect man?

A rich, indulgent treat of a novel – love, life . . . and chocolate cake.

978 0 7553 4712 4